I0819895

Last of His Blood

Book 3 of the Empire of the Stars

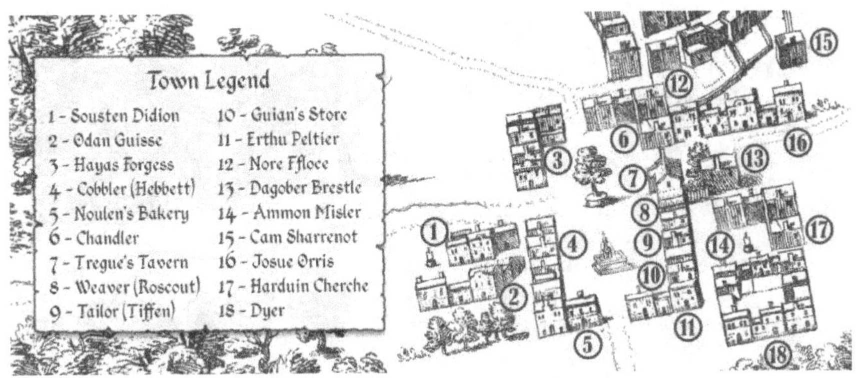

BY MELISSA J CAVE

The story, all names, characters, and incidents portrayed in this production are fictitious. No identification with actual persons (living or deceased), places, buildings, and products is intended or should be inferred.

Credits

- **Book Cover:** http://www.ebooklaunch.com/
- **Book Internal Formatting:** Melissa Cave
- **Map/Title Page Design:** Melissa Cave, with assets from mapeffects.co and map brushes from KM Alexander.
- **Chapter Headers:** Melissa Cave, using non-generative assets purchased from Etsy.com and out-of-print art from Old Book Illustrations.

Author's Note

Welcome to the *Empire of the Stars* series! The main story is already complete and will be published at six month intervals, so if you're worried about beginning a story that has no end: don't! It has already been written.

If you're new to fantasy, you will find a lot of unfamiliar names, titles, and even languages in these pages, but just let them wash over you. It's my job to make sure you remember the important ones, and if you need a reminder or are curious about pronunciation, there's a spoiler-safe glossary at the back of the book.

Last of His Blood is an adult fantasy with adult themes and sometimes dark subject matter. It will include graphic violence and explicit sex when the plot requires it. **Parents, please consider this book R-Rated. It is not intended for children.**

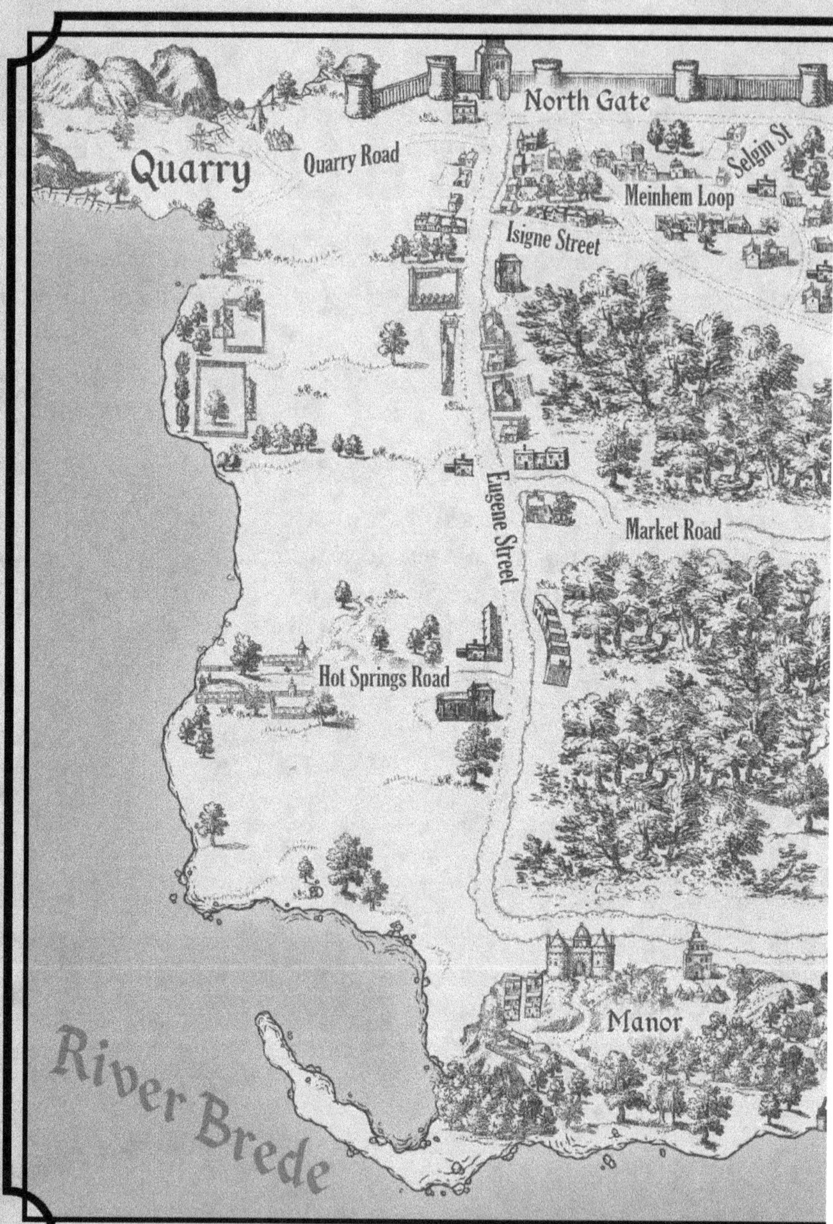
North Gate
Quarry
Quarry Road
Selgim St
Meinhem Loop
Isigne Street
Eugene Street
Market Road
Hot Springs Road
Manor
River Brede

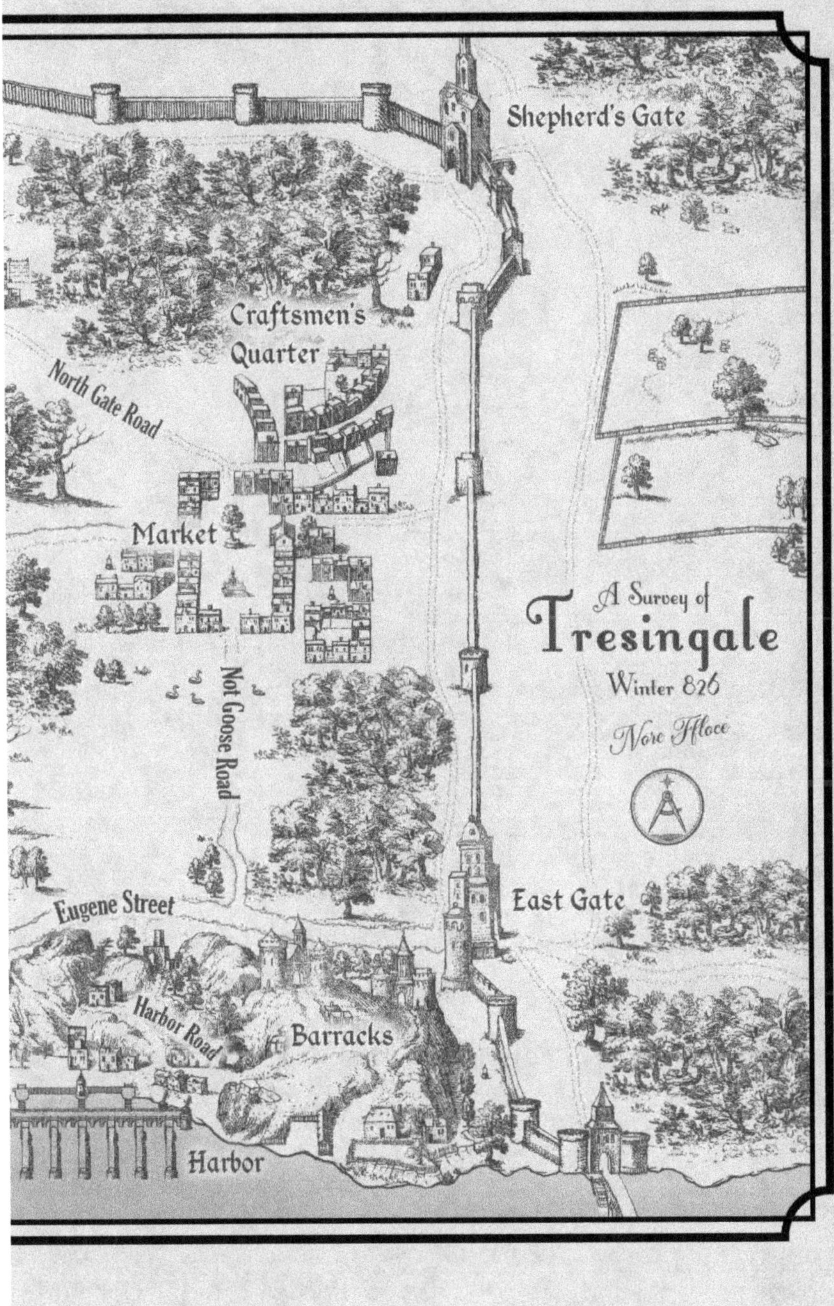

A Survey of
Tresingale
Winter 826
Nore Floce

Shepherd's Gate
Craftsmen's Quarter
North Gate Road
Market
Not Goose Road
Eugene Street
East Gate
Harbor Road
Barracks
Harbor

Previously, In the Empire of the Stars

"If I ever lay my hands on you with violence, may the stars in heaven strike me dead."

Their marriage began as a transaction. A royal bride given in grudging reward for an impossible war victory. And Remin Grimjaw, who has been hounded all his life by the Emperor's assassins, knows all too well that every gift from the Empire is salted with poison.

That's why he takes his new bride to the dangerous Andelin Valley, where even the monstrous devils that appear every night are safer for him than the capital. With his nights spent defending his fledgling city and his days laboring to raise its walls, Remin has no time for spoiled princesses.

Yet this princess is not so easily set aside. Born in exile, Ophele Agnephus knows nothing of the world outside her prison, and is far more timid than any princess should be. But she also proves to be clever, hardworking, and surprisingly devoted to Remin's dream: to make a garden of the Andelin Valley, a safe place for his people.

Remin likes that.

He loves that.

And as *Traitor Son* closes, his clever, timid bride finds her way past even Remin Grimjaw's defenses, to forge a marriage and a love strong enough to found a dynasty.

But what of the devils? What remains of his surviving villages? As the autumn leaves fall, the devils retreat to their winter dens, and Remin sends his knights on a dangerous quest to rescue whoever survived the deadly summer. Remin's journey will be even deadlier: to follow the devils back to the mountains, discover where they come from, and destroy them forever.

When he asked Ophele to learn more about the creatures, he never expected she would do the middle bit for him. With her love of patterns pointing the way, Remin departs, leaving her to rule Tresingale in his stead.

He has no idea he is also leaving her to face a reckoning with her past. From the disappearance of her guardians to the demands of a position she was never taught to fill, Ophele's many secrets are beginning to come to light, and the speck of stardust in her blood will not be a shield against their enemies.

Even as the surviving villagers begin to arrive in Tresingale and Remin returns with news of a terrible new devil, Ophele finally confesses the truth about a much older cataclysm: her mother was responsible for the catastrophe that shattered both their families, and those old echoes are stirring again in the distant capital.

As *Stardust Child* closes, a summons from the Emperor promises to drag them into those poisonous politics, where a cold war between the Emperor and his Empress has drawn the battle lines for decades. For in the capital, the seat of power is never where it seems, and even a Divine Emperor can be made to kneel.

With a perilous season in the capital on the horizon, Remin and Ophele have only the winter to prepare...**and someone in Tresingale is determined to make sure they never leave.**

Table of Contents

Chapter 1 – Segoile's Newest Rose

Lady Mionet Verr's debut into society was perfect.

At sixteen, she had still been Mionet Boscillard, the daughter of a rustic nobleman who had never seen a city, much less something as splendid as Segoile. But Grandmother Boscillard was a canny woman who had successfully launched three daughters into society, and so they arrived in the capital two months before the social season began, to give Mionet time to get the bumpkin out of her system.

By the end of the first month, she was navigating like a native.

The Wold was a labyrinth of markets, parks, and estates that composed the aristocrats' quarter of the city, with banners and lamps on every bridge and long rows of silver birches shading the promenades. From the many vantages over the river, she could see Starfall, distant and beautiful as a dream, its white walls and crystal-domed towers rising above the Emme.

No one was ever really prepared for Starfall.

They said Ospret Far-Eyes had raised his city from the bottom of the river, the place where his sacred celestial feet had first touched the earth of this world, the place where he had summoned and married Ambrosie Star-daughter. There his descendants had lived for over eight hundred years, along with the vast apparatus necessary for governing the Empire: servants, guards, and retainers whose loyalty had endured for generations.

There was the home of Emperor Bastin Agnephus and his Empress Esmene, who had sent an invitation to Mionet on silver-leaf paper, to welcome the next generation of debutantes.

The night of Mionet's debut glittered even in memory. The white coach drawn by four perfectly matched chestnut horses. Her new silk gown, the first gown she had ever worn that bared her shoulders, a vivid turquoise and copper that perfectly complemented her auburn hair and unblemished skin. Even at sixteen, Mionet had never been afraid to make herself noticed.

Under a sky of dusky violet, they drove across the north bridge and through the triple gates, their crushing spiked jaws glittering silver and fancifully formed. Even the sharp teeth of Starfall's gates were beautiful.

Beyond the gates were gardens and plazas, green lawns and temples, manmade pools overhung with ornamental trees and white star lilies perfuming the air. Through the carriage windows, she glimpsed the feet of the famous statue of Ospret Far-Eyes, sandaled and larger than the carriage. Crystal bells chimed with every breath of the breeze, adorning every door in the city.

House Boscillard was a powerful barony. For all Baron Boscillard's rustic sensibilities—and his questionable wife—there were few that could look down on them as they stood in the long line of girls awaiting presentation. For this event, admittance was restricted only to the girl and her parents, so Mionet silently repeated her grandmother's instructions to herself. *When they call you, pick up your train first. Lift your chin. As you walk to the Empress, imagine you are walking to your groom on your wedding day in the most beautiful gown you will ever wear, and that one girl you hate has to watch.*

Mionet's mother always objected to the last part, but it never failed to make Mionet lift her chin.

"Don't be nervous, lovely," her mother whispered now, though the common-born Lady Boscillard was far more nervous than anyone else.

"I'm not, mother," Mionet whispered back, gripping her lacy fan in both hands. She was not nervous. She wasn't the least bit afraid. She was *impatient.*

The presentation of debutantes took place in the Greater Court, the larger of the throne rooms where the Divinity sat on his high dais, watching the proceedings as if from a distant star. Mionet did feel a thrill of fear when she stepped through the doors. There was the Divinity, Beloved of the Stars, whose very presence sanctified the lands of the Empire. As the line of young women moved forward, he sipped wine and occasionally turned his head to murmur to his advisors, but he did take care to look as each maiden was called forth, to formally recognize their entrance into society.

"House Boscillard, presenting the Lady Mionet," called the herald, and Mionet picked up her train, lifted her chin, and fixed her eyes on the Empress, imagining that that bitch Onette was watching as she floated down the long violet Imperial aisle.

"Your Imperial Highness," she said when she reached the end of the wide carpet, bending into a curtsy so perfect, it might have been used for a diagram in a book on noble etiquette.

"Lady Mionet Boscillard," the Empress replied. "You may rise."

Mionet obeyed. The Empress was forty-four at the time, and maturity became her. Dressed in a silver gown spangled with diamonds and crystals and her long silver hair cascading down her back, she looked like a statue, or a being summoned from the stars. For a moment, Mionet forgot what she was supposed to say.

"I am honored to meet the Empress of Argence," she said, with a little internal jolt that she hoped did not show outside. She lifted her chin. "I am the newest Rose of Boscillard."

"I recall another Rose of that name, when I made my debut," the Empress replied, which meant she was pleased. "Have you an aunt?"

"Three, Your Majesty." Mionet met her eyes boldly. Roses of Segoile were not shy. They announced themselves. "My father's sisters are Clemenne, Seferie, and Tamenie."

For nearly three whole minutes they exchanged pleasantries, as much a test of Mionet's poise and wit as to give the Empress's secretary time to write her name down into the famous silver book. The Empress's middle-aged secretary wore white gloves, as if the book was too precious to be touched with bare hands.

Mionet was also conscious of the gaze of the Emperor, not twenty paces away, a shadow on the periphery of her vision. But her grandmother had warned her about that, too, and more than once.

Do not dare to look at the Emperor, unless he speaks to you directly, she said, deadly serious. *House Boscillard will never be powerful enough or foolish enough to step between the House of Agnephus and House Melun.*

It didn't *seem* like such a dangerous thing, but Grandmother Boscillard had sounded so terrible when she said it, terrible enough to impress even the brash Mionet. Mionet restricted her eyes to the ten square feet occupied by the Empress and her attendants, and the only time she looked in the Emperor's direction was when she and her parents paused to make their obeisance before his throne. She had the impression of thick silver hair, but she did not dare to meet the famous starry blue eyes.

Instead, she looked at his cloak, silver satin trimmed in ermine, cascading down the steps of the dais.

Even if she was only one girl among forty presented that year, the ball that night was a triumph. Mionet danced every dance. She made contacts among a dozen other noble girls—and more importantly, their mamas—and took her first heady sips of both champagne and the flattery of young men. Before the night was out, she had not one or two but *three* new suitors, though she would ultimately reject them all and wed Lord Athurin Verr before the next season.

It was a night of splendor and stardust, of music ringing to the high and glorious vaults of the Greater Court, touched by the otherworldly beauty of the House of the Emperor. The sort of night that comes once in a lifetime.

So Mionet could not for the life of her understand why a summons to court made the Duke and Duchess of Andelin behave as if the sky were falling in.

"...all right," the duke was murmuring, just loud enough for her sharp ears to catch it. On the front steps of the manor, he was clutching his small wife as if he thought someone might tear her away. "I promise. I'll write to Duchess Ereguil and see if she might like a season in the city next year. Perhaps we can stay at their estate, there's not much time to set up our own household, so it would save us the trouble..."

His voice was very different from his usual stiff, cold tones, and Mionet wondered whether she ought to silently excuse herself and the maids; this was not a moment for public consumption. But it was also likely she would hear some very interesting things if she stayed, and before she could decide, she heard the duchess speak, slightly muffled in His Grace's shirtfront.

"...time to plan a debut?" she asked anxiously. "Do we have to stay the whole season? Or could we just go and see what he wants and leave? I don't know if I can learn that fast."

"We'll prepare for both, but don't worry. The duchess is a Rose of Segoile herself, you know. Utterly terrifying, according to the old man. And I have been wanting you two to meet anyway, it won't be..."

As he spoke, he was nudging her toward the house, and for a moment, Mionet wondered if she might have been mistaken. The duke didn't seem bothered at all now; maybe it was only the shock of the summons, and worry for the duchess. But at the threshold of the house, His Grace glanced over his shoulder and shot her a look with such clear and piercing command, it effectively nailed her feet to the front steps.

There was time to think, while he was inside. She knew the history between the duke and the Emperor; every child in the Empire had heard it. Remin, the son of a House convicted and executed for grave insult to the sacred House of Agnephus. Innocent of any crime himself, he had still been tarred with the stigma of traitors, and Mionet could have listed half a dozen attempts on his life that were common knowledge. The Emperor expressed outrage every time, of course.

No doubt it would be dangerous for His Grace to go to Segoile. But it was hardly the first time; he had visited several times before and lived to tell the tale. And while fashionable society would be a nightmare for the timid duchess, it was not the end of the world. As His Grace noted, she would not go alone.

Mionet's lips curved. It was early, no doubt; maybe a little *too* early for her own scandal to have faded away completely. But perhaps it would work out as she hoped after all. She had begun to think the duke and duchess would hardly be moved from the valley by anything short of an imperial command.

It was some time before His Grace appeared again, his boots thudding down the stairs to the first floor. Mionet put on a carefully sober expression.

"Your Gra—" she began, but he cut her off.

"I don't know why Duchess Ereguil sent you," he said, looking down at her with eyes like black ice. "I am inclined to trust her judgment, for all that you are not the companion I would have chosen for my wife. I was going to wait, and give all of you a chance to get used to life here before I required your oaths. But we do not have that luxury. You will swear your life and your soul to my House now, or you will go out of this place tonight. I will provide passage to wherever you like. Choose."

Mionet hesitated. There was a very good reason Duchess Ereguil had sent her, but it did not align *at all* with Mionet's own plans. And this was not an oath to be made lightly; she had never sworn such an oath even to Lady Carolen, it was one thing to serve House Andelin but something else entirely to be *bound* to them. But life was a gamble and sometimes there was no choice but to roll the—

"I will swear it," she said as his black brows lowered ominously. Quickly, she gathered herself and knelt before him. "Your Grace. I, Mionet Verr, swear my fealty and homage to the House of Andelin, to His Grace Duke Remin and Her Grace the Duchess Ophele. I swear to guard your honor and your secrets in this life and the next, and to offer my skills and abilities unstinting in your service. If I should ever violate this oath, or fail in your trust, then may my life and soul be forfeit."

Stars above, may she not live to regret this.

"I accept your oath," the duke replied. "I swear to reward service with honor, duty with protection, and I will kill you myself if you betray us."

He paused, and seemed to find this insufficient. Mionet had a disorienting sense of darkness descending as he bent his head, those opaque black eyes looming above her, the broad face, the scarred cheek, and flashing teeth.

"That is not a threat," he explained. "That is an oath. If you betray us, I swear before the eternal stars that I will kill you with my own hands. It will be my sacred duty, the shackle placed on my soul, that I will find you wherever you go and slay you. I will not be foresworn. If I even *suspect* that you will betray us, then I may decide to kill you before you can. Do not give me reason to doubt you. Do you understand?"

"...yes." The word was faint, forced through suddenly numb lips. This was not Segoile, with its social posturing and theatrics. This was the Andelin Valley. And if Remin Grimjaw made an oath to kill her, it was because *he would do it*.

"Good. I will be out late tonight. Right now, I want you to go upstairs and sit with her, and no more foolish talk about how it will take a year to plan her debut or how difficult it will be to navigate society because she has four months to learn it and she knows *nothing*. She was taught *nothing*. Her father wants me dead and until now has never shown the least interest in whether she was alive. Understood?"

This was a lot to take in at once.

"I understand. Your Grace," Mionet added, grasping the courtesy like a lifeline. A month in the valley and a few tender scenes with his wife and she had forgotten that this was Remin Grimjaw, the butcher of Ellingen. Men, women, or children, he could, would, and had killed anyone who stood against him.

And she had just sworn an oath to bind herself to his House.

"Good. Then go and keep your oath," he said, and departed with the boiling air of a gathering storm, calling for Adelan as he went.

* * *

It didn't take long for Remin to gather his men.

Most of them were on their way to supper anyway, so it was a simple matter to direct them to the offices above the storehouse and have food brought up. As he waited for the last of them to arrive, Remin tried to calm the churning in his gut and assess the threat rationally. There was no danger *yet*. He knew that, but after so many years of war, sometimes it was difficult to convince his body.

Ophele was safe. She was at home under the watchful eyes of Leonin and Davi, who would die before they allowed harm to come to her. Remin congratulated himself for his foresight there; the thought of her hallows relieved his mind considerably. The devils had done him the dubious favor of scouring the valley of any other possible threat, and Juste had men searching the

Empire for any signs of forces mobilizing. They were safe. They were safe.

As they gathered, the summons from the Emperor passed from hand to hand, fine paper and many more words than necessary to say what the messenger had conveyed in a single sentence. The phrase *Emperor's beloved child* had appeared no less than five times.

"These are current as of last month," said Lord Edemir of Trecht without waiting to be asked, setting maps of the Empire and the capital on the table. He served as Remin's Court of Merchants and Exchequer, and knew exactly what Remin was planning to do.

In many ways, they had been preparing for this for years. Sir Jinmin of Oskerre appeared last, summoned from the North Gate where he commanded the night watch. The chair creaked beneath his weight as he took his seat at the long table.

Six men, his closest and most trusted knights. All of them had had opportunities to betray him over the years, and had steadfastly refused. Remin keenly felt the absence of Sir Huber Adaman, who would have asked the most uncomfortable questions, and Sir Miche of Harnost, who would have laughed Remin's fears down to a manageable size.

"This may be nothing," Remin began, trying to settle himself. "It may be just an inconvenience. It might be that we will go to Starfall, have our audience, and then come home. Or it might be an attempt to abduct or kill the Duchess of Andelin, the mother of my House, a child of the stars."

Viewing the Emperor's invitation as merely a threat to himself and his wife robbed it of its significance. She was a duchess, a princess, the mother of his heirs and his rightful partner in society and politics. An attack on her was not merely a crime. It was grounds for war.

"In either case, we have already been making preparations," he said, his mouth hardening. "Juste."

"Darri has been working on placing people into key positions," Sir Justenin said readily. His was the most dangerous and clandestine work in the capital. "Inside and outside Starfall, and within certain noble Houses. They are distributed in the structure we discussed, small units and individuals who are unknown to each other. We intended our decoys to be discovered early next year, but we will move that forward. The Emperor will never believe you are idle, my lord."

"Good. Before we arrive in the city, I want them to have secured routes in and out of Starfall," Remin said, looking at the map of the small island. Starfall was smaller than Tresingale, nine square miles, but far more secure. The city walls went right up to the river, and the Emme was wide and deep. It was a fortress.

"There are two bridges and four piers," Edemir said, tapping their locations on the map. "The piers are for deliveries. Servants in Starfall all wear livery and have to provide a badge to go in and out of the delivery entrances."

"I want eyes on all of them. Put guardsmen on the walls and workers on the docks, if we can." Remin studied the map, mentally listing priorities. He had long considered how he might break Starfall, if he had to, but it was a different prospect when he and Ophele might be inside it. "While we are there, nothing goes in or out without being observed."

Quills scratched as he spoke. Each of his men were accustomed to their own areas of authority, and it saved a great deal of discussion. It went without saying that this sort of clandestine, small-scale work was only possible while everyone in the capital was still being nice.

"Estimates of the forces inside Starfall, and estimates of the forces inside Segoile," Remin continued, examining the routes in and out of the city, the wide avenues that divided the estates of the Wold. The sprawling estates of the noble quarter of the city had changed since his parents' time. The nobility of Segoile had voted to convict and sent his whole family to the block, and only afterward realized that if one noble House could be extinguished overnight, so could another. Those estates now had high walls and many guards. "Make that Darri's second priority. He should be monitoring the numbers of every guard force in the city, and their movements."

"He has been working on that already, Your Grace," Juste replied, and Remin plucked up his own quill as he totted up Juste's numbers, rattled off from memory. Darri had not been idle in the capital.

"Bram, you will augment our forces." Remin jabbed the tip of his quill at his final figures. "I will send some of our men to the capital in ones and twos, but we dare not move any force of significance. You will have to acquire more. Move them into Waterside, no one will notice them there."

"Give me a few commanders for them," the former mercenary agreed. "I can't promise an army for you over the course of a winter, Rem, but maybe I'll go by Rendeva on my way to the capital, and see what I can find."

Rendeva always had a ready supply of mercenaries.

"Send word once you have them. Tounot, how is our messenger network?"

"Complete, from here to Segoile." Tounot had begun this work over the summer. His riders could cover the four hundred miles from the capital to Tresingale in four days. "I've begun a route from here to Ereguil, but we're still getting our horses into place and identifying transfer points. There are three duchies between us and them."

"Firkane, Pomeret, and Melun," said Remin, without glancing at the map. There were nine ducal Houses in the Empire, remnants of the old kingdoms that pre-existed Argence, and he knew every mile of their boundaries. "The Brede doesn't freeze over. We were planning to dock the ferries, but see what it would take to make them fit for winter travel. How long would it take to sail to Segoile?"

All of them looked at the map. Travel down the river would speed them considerably.

"Our ships aren't made for open sea," said Tounot slowly. "But we might go down the Pemburne. I'll look into it."

The matter of distance was paramount. If something happened in Segoile, it would take four days before anyone in Tresingale knew about it, and more than a month before an army could march there, never mind winter weather and possible opposition. At present, the forces Remin could place and maintain inside the capital would be his only forces to command. Ereguil had their own guard corps, and Remin knew the old man would back him to the hilt, but he did not like their chances, at present. They would have to work to level the field.

"Berebet already extended a hand to us," Tounot noted sourly. He and Justenin had disagreed strongly over the letter Duke Berebet had sent last autumn, offering to host Remin and Ophele for a social season, as if he had known already that they would come to the capital. "Firkane and Tries have been loyal to the House of Agnephus for decades. Pomeret and Sangevin are openly allied with Melun."

"Pomeret may be persuaded," said Edemir, lifting a finger. "There was a proposed marriage that fell through a few months back, and it was not the first broken promise. Melun may be taking their loyalty for granted. We can try to court them."

"It will be challenging," warned Juste. "All we can offer an ally is a great deal of money and even more enemies. We might sound out House Melun, but they will not look with favor on Her Grace as the Emperor's bastard. And the Crown Princess must be wary on two counts, unless we can persuade her that you will limit your vengeance to her father."

Remin could not truthfully offer any promises. Even after everything the Emperor had done, the thought of actually *killing* him was inconceivable; to destroy the House of Agnephus might revoke the blessing of the stars forever. That would mean the destruction of the Empire itself.

But if it came to war, Remin would end it as thoroughly as he had ended the war with Valleth. He would slay the Emperor, and if the Crown Princess seemed inclined to avenge her father, he would kill her, too. He would never allow his children to face the dangers he had known all his life.

"It doesn't hurt to listen," he said, and glanced at Edemir. "I will need you to go and do the listening."

"I know." Neither of them looked at Tounot, who would have been the obvious choice for this task before his father disinherited him. "Bendir can take my place. I have been bringing him along, just in case. We're lucky it's nearly winter, that will slow both the building and the buying."

The discussion of the political situation lasted longest. There were many pressure points to be exploited even within the duchies; if Remin could not have sincere allies, then he would blackmail, bully, and bribe. Edemir would go and set up a noble household in the capital, as loudly and luxuriously as possible, and let it be known that the Duke of Andelin would be arriving for the social season. It would be interesting to see who snapped at the bait.

"Take a few knights and squires," Remin added, scratching a few more marks to the balance of Edemir's forces. "Let them test themselves in the Court of War and tell them to win honor in my name. Let anyone who wants to know that I will be along directly, if they want to challenge the Supreme Sword."

"That ought to fetch some interesting people to the city." Tounot was making an effort to accept this gracefully. "There are some sturdy fellows in the peasant camps on the other side of the Brede. Maybe we ought to have Jinmin train up a few of them over the winter. Let their families into Tresingale in exchange for service."

"Do it, just keep them away from me," Remin agreed. It was a good notion, and he would have been allowing them into the valley next spring anyway. The time when he could personally vet every new resident was passing. "And Auber—"

"It seems I am of more use to you at peace than war," the former farmer observed mildly, and it made Remin's throat tighten. He had been so very close to that dream of peace.

"I count on you for it," he replied. "I need you to look after Tresingale for me. The planting, the building. The growing."

It was bitter, knowing he would not be here to see it. Instead, he must spend hours considering their enemies, from the threats outside the valley to the foes hidden within it. Assassins and traitors, just waiting their moment to strike. But there was always the chance that they might reveal themselves at this work, and Remin and his men spoke long into the night, memorizing and then burning their notes.

It was very cold when Remin and Juste rode back to the manor.

"I did not like to say it openly," Juste began as soon as they were alone. "But there are a few more considerations, my lord."

Remin had expected this, too. Juste always thought a great deal more than he said.

"Go on."

"The duchess. I will need to give her instruction some thought. I don't think it would be possible to turn her into a Rose of Segoile even if we had four years instead of four months."

"I don't want to," Remin said resentfully. This measure infuriated him more than any other. "I don't want that here. I don't want her to think that's what she should be."

"I am not sure it would be the right course in any case," Juste replied, with the thoughtful air of a sculptor confronting a likely bit of clay. "We must consider the matter from the Emperor's perspective."

Swinging right at the lane by the storehouse, Juste led the way toward the Benkki Desan *talimaru*. The baths were long closed for the night, but they needed time for this discussion, and Remin had to settle himself before he went home.

"In the first place, he will want to take your measure," said Juste, settling into his analysis. "He will wish to see how important she is to you. The Emperor will not be persuaded by songs."

"I am not sure we ought to try," Remin replied, doubtful. "I worried about this before. They will only try harder to harm her, if they think it will hurt me."

"It is a double-edged sword," Juste agreed. "There is no question, they will. But they will also pay a higher price if they dare to lay hands on a daughter of the House of Agnephus. My singers are going to tell the story of a secret princess, Daughter of the Stars, who redeemed the butcher of Ellingen with her love. I think there's a chorus to that effect."

"Oh, stars," said Remin, revolted. "Who writes these things?"

"I have a lad in Tries." Juste waved this aside. "It should tie her quite effectively to her father, as well. I judge it worth the risk, Your Grace. By the time we are done, anyone who dares to pluck a hair from her head will be hauled away as a heretic."

Juste's judgment was remarkably good in these matters. Remin eyed him for a moment, wondering that a man who had so little humanity himself seemed to understand it so well.

"Then do it," he said, sighing. "Try to take care that such songs do not arrive in my own hall, at least."

"If they do, it will not be for some time," Juste noted. "I think you will be a while in Segoile, Your Grace. Having tested her importance to you, the Emperor's second move will be to test the lady, and that will take time. He will try to discover whether she might be persuaded to act against you. And if she cannot, then he will likely attempt to take her from you."

"I know." Remin tried to ignore his sickness at the idea. He could at least be pleased that he had employed countermeasures against both possibilities. "But if it ever comes to it, and you must choose her or me, Juste, then choose her. I expect you to honor my wishes. I will tell the others the same."

"Then I will make sure it never comes to that." Juste exhaled, his breath puffing white. "And since we are discussing such delicate matters, there is one more. If I were the Emperor, and I could not kill you, and I could not deprive you of your wife, then my next step would be to deprive you of your progeny. You cannot get heirs if the duchess is fed certain herbs, or visited by certain healers. If I were bent on vengeance, and wanted to wipe out my enemies, then I would not be content with trimming away a few leaves of their family tree. I would rip out the whole thing, root and branch, and sow the ground with salt. Would you set her aside, if she were barren?"

"No," said Remin, after a long moment. He was shoveling a great many feelings into that dark pit inside him, and finding it difficult to lock them down.

"Then your blood will die with you, and I would call that victory," Juste said, and Remin knew he was right.

Juste did not point out that Remin could have avoided this by making an heir immediately. But Remin bitterly regretted his treatment of Ophele when they were first married. What had he been thinking? If only he had not been so suspicious of her, if he had not indulged the petty vengeance of putting the Emperor's daughter to hard labor, then she might almost be ready to deliver their first child.

It was not only the matter of his heir. A pregnancy would have been one of the best ways to protect Ophele herself. This was a self-inflicted wound, and even now, her body still had not resumed its natural functions. He had done that to her.

It might prove to be the costliest of all his mistakes.

"I will trust you to prevent that," Remin said, keeping his voice steady with an effort.

"Her food is already being tasted," Juste said, calm and reassuring. "I am yours, my lord, as always. I will do everything I can."

That was a fine note on which to end the night. Together, they deposited their horses in the stable and parted.

The golden warmth of the fire flickered in the solar despite the late hour, where Ophele and Lady Verr still sat together while

Leonin and Davi stood guard. Remin was greatly relieved to see that there was no sign of tears on his wife's face.

"Thank you," he said to Lady Verr and the guards, dismissing them, and as soon as the door shut, he went to Ophele, crouching to kiss her. "How much tea have you had, wife?"

"Three pots." She brushed his hair back from his forehead. "I didn't think you'd scold me just this once. Is everything...all right?"

"Yes." He didn't want her worrying. Genon said anxiety might make it more difficult for her to conceive. Rising, he transferred her from the chair into his lap, and felt better for it. "It's not so different from what we have already been planning," he said. "And it might amount to nothing at all. Juste said the Emperor might only wish to take our measure, now that he has gotten over the insult of having to give you to me."

"It's possible," she agreed, letting her head rest on his shoulder. They fit so comfortably together. Stars, why couldn't they just stay here? He hadn't thought to ask that question, about what would happen if they refused the Emperor's summons. Let the Emperor come here if he missed his beloved child so much. Would the Empire really march to war if they failed to appear, come spring?

There was so much to do. Juste would be coming early to discuss Ophele's education, which would require many people to remedy, and Remin resented that they must confide such personal matters when even *he* hadn't had time to process Ophele's revelations about her foster family. For *one day* he had imagined the teachers he would hire for her, the library he would build, the gowns she would have, as fine as the Empress in Starfall. He could not undo years of neglect and abuse, but he could make a comfortable nest for his little owl, and let her sate her every curiosity.

There was no point in dwelling on the things he could not have, or raging at the injustice of it all. But it seemed every time he had a little peace, room enough to begin to dream, something happened to dash all his hopes. He had wanted so much to make it all up to her.

His eyes fell on the papers on the table beside them, and what looked like the beginnings of a map. He recognized the names of the streets, written in Ophele's messy handwriting. She had been busy interrogating Lady Verr about the capital while he was gone.

Remin buried his face in her hair and tried to breathe.

They were safe. They were safe. They were safe.

He should not dwell on things that hadn't happened. He would move heaven and earth if he had to, to protect her. And he could not afford to let her see him distressed.

"Come," he said when he could trust himself to speak. "It is late, wife. It will be a busy day tomorrow."

And they still had to try for a child tonight.

* * *

Ophele awoke to the same sensations that had put her to sleep.

A warm mouth. Gentle hands. Dim light glowed softly behind her eyelids and a moan escaped her before she was properly conscious, swimming through layers of sleep to find that her nipples were aching with arousal, and between her legs was a deep, slow throbbing.

"Remin..." she mewed, disoriented as her eyes slitted open to see his dark head at her breast, his lips and tongue plucking skillfully at her nipple. His fingers stroked between her legs in a gentle rhythm that made her feel as if she were floating.

"I wondered how long it would be before I woke you." Remin's voice was deepest in the morning, rumbling and sleepy. "Do you want more?"

"Ahhh—yes..." Her body arched as two thick fingers slid inside to find her very wet, her body rippling eagerly. Remin drew a breath.

"I woke up wanting you," he murmured, shifting above her, the hard, thick length of him pushing eagerly between her thighs.

They moaned together as he slid into her, her body giving way in a heated, slippery stretch. He was so big, he had to angle her thighs upward to enter her fully, and even then it took slow and patient stroking before his hips finally pressed against hers. It felt as if he had filled her to her lungs.

"Is that—everything?" she gasped, and he laid his palm on her belly to feel himself there, drawing back and thrusting again.

"Yes." His black eyes filled with a hungry light, and she cried out as his hips ground heavily against her. "You're taking all of me, wife."

"Do we...have time?" she panted, clutching his shoulders as he surged into her. "You said—today would be, ahhhhh, busy..."

"There is nothing more important than this," he said firmly, and his hips rolled up and into her in that fluid, tireless rhythm that obliterated all possible thought.

She could still feel his ghostly, tingling presence inside her when they went to breakfast. Sir Justenin had brought a hamper of food up from the cookhouse and Ophele sat down at the table, feeling disheveled and unprepared for company. Remin had pounded her into a stupor and her brain was never really ready to grapple with the day before midmorning.

"My lady," said Justenin, revoltingly bright-eyed. "Forgive me for disturbing you so early. In light of yesterday's summons, I thought it best to begin straightaway."

"That's all right," she said, suddenly wide awake.

"I have already spoken to Lady Verr," he began, making Ophele offer a mental apology to the lady, who must have been awakened very early indeed. "If you are to learn the carriage and manners of a noblewoman of the Empire, then there is no one better to teach you. I propose that you spend your mornings with her, with additional assistance from Sir Leonin. He was raised in the capital and is considered an exemplary gentleman."

Ophele nodded, though her eyes shifted to her plate. Of course, Leonin and Davi must be told the truth as well; she had already skirted very near it with them. But it was one thing to bravely declare to Remin that she did not want to lie and another to actually face all the people she had deceived.

"By this time next week, no one will think anything of it, wife." Under the table, Remin's big foot nudged hers. "Endure it, and you'll see."

"Indeed," Justenin agreed. "You may be surprised at the general lack of surprise, my lady. I have already spoken to Tounot—"

Justenin had been very busy. Ophele nibbled at her toast as she listened to what would be the fourth or fifth major upheaval of her life this year. He proposed that she spend her mornings at the manor, learning etiquette, deportment, feminine courtesies, and a host of other social skills with Lady Verr. Sir Leonin and Sir Tounot would teach her other courtly arts. Master Didion could be invited to share his knowledge of the capital, which went back nearly forty years. Though he had indulged in frequent minor scandals, he was notoriously skilled at avoiding major ones.

Her afternoons would be spent in the office and filled with more practical lessons: mathematics, grammar, oratory, and all the other subjects she ought to have learned as a child. There was no way she could make up for all of them in four months, but Justenin explained which he thought were most crucial and Ophele nodded along, relieved to *finally* have a teacher. The only thing that bothered her was that it meant neglecting everything else.

"But there will be no time for Jacot's lessons," she said, looking at the schedule he had sketched out for her. "Or Elodie, or helping in the office, or with the devils—"

"The boy has learned enough to take his lessons with the rest of the pages," Remin replied. "How long have you been teaching him?"

"Four months." It was surprising to realize it had been so long.

"Juste, test him and let him move on if he's ready," he said firmly. "Nothing good will come of playing favorites among the pages and squires, wife. And how you manage your pagegirl is your business, so long as she isn't a nuisance."

She was foolishly pleased that Remin would consider even these small matters. Ophele poured him a fresh cup of tea.

"It is my hope that your work might supplement your lessons," Justenin continued. "If you would like to continue it."

"Oh, I would," she said fervently. "I have learned so much from helping Edemir."

"He was counting on you to assist in his absence," Justenin agreed. "Bendir will be taking over while he's away."

"While he's away?" she echoed, surprised.

"Edemir will handle some matters for us over the winter," Remin replied evenly, as if this could be anything but an ominous sign. Edemir could not be easily spared.

"I am sure...he will," she said, but her eyes moved from Justenin to Remin, watchful. Neither man showed any sign of worry, but Remin and his knights never did anything without reason.

Lady Verr herself was evidence of that, when she arrived a few minutes later. She betrayed no surprise as Justenin launched into the list of subjects Ophele must learn, his quill scribbling rapidly as they constructed a curriculum. The conversation was necessarily limited to the two of them; neither Remin nor Ophele was qualified to have an opinion, but Remin's face darkened as he listened to all of the things Ophele must learn to do, his black eyes resting on Lady Verr like two iron weights.

"To be clear," he said, when Justenin was done, "My objective is for Her Grace to learn what is necessary to endure a season in Segoile without scandal or undue anxiety. Nothing more. This is a coat of paint we will scrape off when we come home. I do not value the customs of the capital and do not wish to see them here."

It was one of the rudest things Ophele had ever heard him say. She bit her lip, looking anxiously at Lady Verr.

"I understand perfectly, Your Grace," the lady answered, with no sign of offense.

"Good." Remin set down his napkin. "Come and see me off, wife. I'll be sending Leonin and Davi up to you directly. Lady Verr, your aid is appreciated."

"You are very hard on her," Ophele said as soon as they were in the bedchamber, and Remin sat down to swap his house shoes for boots.

"I hope it is undeserved," he said bluntly. "I will beg pardon, if so. But until we can be sure, be wary of her. You have a good deal of sense; if something doesn't seem right, ask Leonin or ask me. Leonin has sisters, he should have some notion of what a noblewoman looks like. He will be supervising your morning lessons. If you aren't with me, your guards will be with you, from now on."

"All right," she said, troubled. "Remin—you aren't bothered that they will all know? I know I said I didn't want to lie, but I am supposed to be your duchess and I don't want them to think—"

"Of course, it bothers me." Catching her hands, he drew her to stand before him. "You *are* my duchess and my wife, and I don't want you to change. I would much rather have my duchess questioning my spending habits or dissecting devil quills with Juste. Yes, I heard about that," he added, as she let out a startled laugh. "Do you know how proud I would be to tell those fools in Segoile about it? But either they wouldn't care, or they would mock you for it."

"It will only be a coat of paint," she promised him, going into his arms. She felt him sigh as he held her. "I will learn it and then forget it as fast as I can."

"Don't be embarrassed that you don't know foolish things," he told her. "Be proud of the things you do know."

It pleased her so much to hear it. But it wasn't easy to go back to the solar and face Lady Verr, who was sitting at the table reading Justenin's curriculum. Whatever Remin might say, Ophele could not look at the lady without envy. It was as if Lady

Verr was conscious of even the angle of the morning sun through the windows and knew how to present herself to best advantage, the light sparking off the red highlights in her hair, so graceful, she looked like a portrait.

"Lady Verr." Ophele headed straight for the teapot. She felt the need to fortify herself. "I am sorry for His Grace's sharpness. I hope it did not hurt your feelings. He is unhappy at the thought of going to the capital. It is very...disruptive."

She had stood in the hallway for two whole minutes, composing this apology.

"I understand, my lady." Lady Verr set the papers down on the table, tapping them thoughtfully. "I am pleased to help, but I admit this is a rather extraordinary circumstance."

Ophele understood the underlying question.

"No one ever taught me," she said, fighting to keep her eyes from the floor. All she could think of was the scorn of the Aldeburke servants, Lisabe's mocking laughter, and worst of all, Lady Hurrell's gentle forgiveness for every humiliating mistake. "I have been trying to learn."

Lady Verr's eyebrows lifted.

"You had guardians in Aldeburke, did you not?" she said, her gray eyes sharpening. "We heard about them, caretakers of the secret princess. You had no tutors, no nurses?"

"No." Despite all her efforts, Ophele felt heat burn in her cheeks and hated it, wishing she could stop it.

"I see." Lady Verr looked once more at the list. "I had the usual education, myself," she went on in a lighter tone. "A nurse when I was a child, then a governess, and tutors for history and courtesies, as well as a dancing-master. My grandmother was a terrible tyrant about all of it. But do you know, once I entered society, I don't believe I used *half* of this."

"Really?" This sounded like the sort of thing Ophele should check on.

"Really," said Lady Verr firmly. "And you are the third woman in the Empire, the only people to whom you must defer are the Emperor, the Empress, and perhaps the Crown Princess. You are her elder and the Emperor legitimized you, so technically you do not owe her a curtsy, though it may be politic to offer one." She dipped her quill and scribbled a note. "That's the sort of trap one must take care to avoid. We will have to ask what message His Grace wishes to send."

Please leave us alone, Ophele thought, but did not say.

"That will be your first public appearance, then," Lady Verr went on. "If you are summoned to court by the Divinity, then you cannot accept other engagements until you have received his blessing. If you imagine exactly what will happen when you get there, and what you will do, then you will be less nervous."

"What will I do?" Ophele asked, intrigued.

"Mmm. Well..." Lady Verr smiled, mischievous. "I will tell you what my grandmother told me, when I first went to court. At the Greater Court, one waits to be announced before entering, so you will stand outside the double doors until the Emperor is ready to see you. When the herald calls your name, the first thing you do is pick up your skirt. Lift your chin. Then walk down the violet carpet of the Imperial aisle as if you were going to your bridegroom, *dripping* with jewels and wearing the most beautiful dress you have ever seen, and that one bitch you hate has to watch."

"Lady Verr!" Ophele exclaimed, scandalized.

"Now, you can*not* do that, no matter what shocking language you may hear," Lady Verr admonished, but her eyes were dancing. "Who are you thinking of?"

"I am not telling," Ophele replied, covering her mouth to hide a giggle. The thought of Lisabe watching as she walked into the Greater Court of Starfall on Remin's arm made her want to laugh and laugh.

"But you see how this exercise is useful," Lady Verr said, returning to business. "You will need a gown with a train to practice walking, my lady. And the first thing you will do when you reach the end of the Imperial aisle is to curtsy."

"I don't really know how to do that," Ophele admitted, and the lady nodded, as if she had expected as much.

"You will do it impeccably," said Lady Verr, rising from her chair with the clear expectation that Ophele should do likewise. "My grandmother made me do twenty every morning, the moment I got out of bed. Keep your back straight, and be careful not to crumple the fabric of your gown. I am about to be very vulgar and let you see my legs. Now, watch the position of my feet..."

* * *

As the day went on, it got easier to confess her ignorance. There were so many opportunities.

Lady Verr had a long list of questions and requirements by the time Leonin and Davi arrived, and though Ophele imagined Remin had already provided an explanation as to why their duchess had never learned to dance, she still felt compelled to face them and say it herself. They wanted to be her hallows. *They* must know the truth.

"I'd be pleased to learn with you, my lady," was all Davi said, and offered her a surprisingly graceful bow. "I don't mean to be a disgrace to you, neither."

"Either," corrected Leonin, with a sidelong glance. Ophele suspected that sometimes Davi's errors were deliberate. "And no one *here* should feel any disgrace. Such neglect is...unforgivable."

"It would be a scandal, if it were known," Lady Verr mused.

"It is not for us to determine whether to make it one," Leonin said oppressively. "If there is anything else that is unclear to you, Your Grace, I beg you will say so. You cannot be worse than this...person."

"His Segoile manners are so fine," drawled Davi. "He says *person,* but he means *pig farmer*. But that's all right, I'd rather be the pig farmer than the poor sod trying to teach him to dance, eh?"

"It sounds like a trying morning either way," Ophele replied, with some trepidation, and was surprised to see the flash of a smile from Leonin.

It might have been very difficult indeed, if it weren't for Davi. Ophele felt horribly conspicuous as Lady Verr and Leonin watched her first stumbling steps, and it was amazing that the instant she tried to *think* about making her body move in a particular way, it felt as if she had anvils strapped to her feet. But Davi was struggling just as much as she was.

"Stars and blazes," he said as he tripped over his own feet for the fourth time and caught himself on the table. "Buggering—that is, show me the blasted step again, Leonin. Never felt so left-footed in all my life."

"I can't imagine why, you manage your footwork well enough otherwise," said Leonin, who wasn't even breathing heavily. Ophele hated him for that, just a little bit. "One step at a time, and my lady, try not to think about it too much. I assure you, your feet cannot be reasoned with."

It seemed unfair. They were *her* feet and ought to do as they were told. But between curtsies, dancing, and the general rush to get where she was going, Ophele never really stopped stumbling all that day. It was a wrench, having to send Elodie away with the promise that she would summon her again the moment she could, and she barely caught Jacot as he was leaving the offices above the storehouse that afternoon, bolting out the door like he had devils on his heels.

"Oh, my lady," he said, drawing up short. "Beg pardon."

"You won't need lessons anymore?" she asked, disappointed. Jacot had come to Tresingale last year by swimming the Brede, and had dived into his studies with the same stubborn tenacity. It had been nice, having someone to teach.

"No, lady. Sir Justenin says I'm not far behind the other lads, now." Jacot scratched the back of his neck. "But thankee. Seems a while since that trick of nines."

"Yes," she agreed sadly, remembering their walks by the wall with Eugene and the water wagon. "But if you wanted to continue, I could—"

"No, m'lady," he said, so quickly her mouth shut with a snap. Jacot's eyes flicked toward the offices above them. "Shouldn't like to bother Sir Justenin, or yourself. You've got things to get along with."

"If you're sure," she said, and held out a hand. It probably wasn't done, but Jacot had helped her more than he knew. "Please take care of yourself, Jacot. And the other boys, I shall miss you all."

Jacot glanced at the looming Leonin and Davi before he took her hand.

"Well—I will," he said, his ears turning red. "Ain't like I won't be about, my lady. But you've been uncommon good to me. Uncommonly good. If you ever need a hand, you've got mine."

"Thank you," Ophele said, equally touched and awkward, and after another uncomfortable few moments he made his escape, leaving her curiously bereft.

Upstairs in the office, Sir Justenin had a stack of books waiting for her on her desk.

"All of these have the seal of the Tower, my lady," he said, pointing out the stamp on the cover of the top book. Tugging a chair over, he sat down on the other side of her desk and slipped on his spectacles. "They are part of the approved curriculum. I hardly expect anyone to ask you to solve equations at a banquet, but you should be familiar with these concepts. I believe the explanations in the text will be sufficient for your understanding, but I would rather you ask than persist in being wrong. And show your work."

"All right," she agreed eagerly, taking the book. She knew fractions and percentages, but this book used them in new ways, and it took less than an hour for her to complete the first three chapters, filled with joy at being quizzed. It was a lonely feeling when no one cared enough to even *ask* her to do algebra.

Sir Justenin was deep in conversation with Edemir's secretaries the next time she looked up, so Ophele went on to the next chapter with delight, her eyes skimming page after page of ideas that seemed so rational, so self-evident, it felt as if she must have always known them. She forgot all about showing her work. Her quill scrawled down answers as fast as she read the question, and she was halfway through chapter six when a shadow fell over her desk.

"I see you have finished the assignment," Justenin said dryly, taking her paper and skimming it. "You had no difficulty with the text?"

"No, I was just getting to graphs," she replied, her eyes shining. "I might have used those, mightn't I, for the devil problem? I could have expressed the data by region, or arranged it in sets. I didn't know there was such a thing. Why doesn't Sir Edemir use it for budgeting? He was so worried last month about where all the construction money was going, if we just categorized it—"

The ideas were fairly bursting in her brain, a dozen applications for the things she had just learned, but Justenin held up a hand.

"I am afraid that will have to wait, for the present," he said, with a hint of amusement. "You went further than I intended today. Have you encountered these topics before?"

"Oh, no, this was just what I was hoping for! In Aldeburke, there were only children's texts or books like *The Sacred Angles of the Stars,* and it took me ages to figure out how they were calculating their conjunctions..."

"I...see." Justenin gave her the same odd look Edemir often gave her when she was helping with accounts. "Then we will leave these for you to study on your own time, my lady. These books will carry you through trigonometry. You should consider them personal enrichment," he added severely. "I believe you can manage on your own, but if you have any difficulties, I will endeavor to assist you."

“I will. Thank you,” she added, resisting the urge to hug the books.

“It is nothing, my lady. Grammar and penmanship will be of more practical use to you now,” he went on. “You will be obliged to reply to a great deal of correspondence, and you must not give them any opportunity to find fault...”

This lesson went less well. It was not the rules that were the problem so much as the maddening number of exceptions. Diagramming a sentence was a satisfyingly methodical exercise, but Ophele felt surprised and betrayed that her own language was riddled with inconsistencies that Sir Justenin did not even attempt to defend.

“There is no definitive answer, my lady,” he said, when summoned to provide a *rule* about when to use a semicolon. “In this case, it is dependent on context.”

Her textbook certainly had opinions about the matter. Ophele was relieved when he called a halt to move on to the Court of Nobility. Surely government could not be as nonsensical as grammar.

Aldeburke had had the full course of the Imperial curriculum, so Ophele already knew the basic structure of the Five Courts and their bylaws. But she was surprised and disillusioned to have both her language and her government betray her in the space of an afternoon, and Rhetoric and Oratory was nothing short of a disaster.

“Your voice is pleasant, my lady,” Sir Justenin said as he produced this textbook. “Well-modulated and without accent, which will serve you well in the capital. But it is also exceedingly quiet. You must speak loudly enough to be heard. Please read this aloud. Look only at me.”

Oratory was one of the arts of the Empire. Ophele had heard Lady Hurrell rebuking Lisabe and Julot often for their speech, both for content and for expression. She had numerous examples of carefully cultivated voices before her every day: Lady Verr’s clear, bell-like tones, Sir Edemir’s pleasantly rounded vowels, even Remin's brisk and confident bass. A duchess would be expected to speak often and publicly.

Dread solidified in her stomach as she opened her mouth.

"The Lord and Lady Havellin had a h-happy..." He was looking right at her. Mild, patient Justenin, with his pale blue eyes and the scar bisecting his right eyebrow. She talked to him easily every day. But now, Ophele's tongue twisted and she halted as that hateful heat crawled up the back of her neck.

"A little louder, please, my lady," said Sir Justenin gently.

"The Lord and L-lady..." Ophele stopped, resisting the urge to hide behind her book. Drew a breath. Tried again. She hadn't read aloud since her mother died; there had been no one to read *to*. "The Lord and Lady Hav—Havellin..."

She plowed on, unable to meet his eyes, working down the list of tongue-twisters. The book explained that such exercises were meant to correct pronunciation and forced the speaker to slow down; things like *I saw a kitten eating chicken in the kitchen* could only be safely spoken one syllable at a time. But then one of the secretaries happened to glance in her direction and Ophele actually *felt* the beads of sweat burst along her hairline.

It was ridiculous. If she had been speaking to him at supper, it wouldn't have bothered her at all. There was no reason to be afraid, no one was doing a thing to her. But suddenly all she could think about was what if *all* of the secretaries turned to look at her, stuttering her way through the tongue-twisters like an imbecile, and a heavy weight thumped squarely onto her chest.

"That will suffice," Justenin interrupted. His eyes were thoughtful. "Let us discuss rhetoric."

The forms of argumentation were soothingly logical, and Ophele took a bitter pleasure in constructing her arguments and then refuting them, as she had done so often over supper with Edemir, Bram, and Justenin. She could construct arguments all day, so long as she didn't have to say them out loud.

Ophele was very quiet as Davi handed her onto Brambles' back that evening. It seemed an age had passed since she had been so afraid to confess her ignorance to Remin. Had it really only been a few days?

"You have consumed a great quantity of information today, my lady," said Justenin, who had elected to ride back to the manor with them. "Tomorrow we will see how much of it you can retain. If you find that it is too much, we will adjust accordingly."

"It's fine," she said automatically. Her head did feel strangely *full,* but she thought she still had the capacity for more grammar, perhaps with some nice linear equations for a reward afterward.

"If you insist on continuing to work, I would suggest oratory," he said blandly, as if these thoughts had been printed across her eyeballs. "I recall when I was a boy, the brothers would have us recite before the whole class."

The thought made her stomach drop, as if she had slipped on the stairs. Ophele nodded. He was right, of course. She would have to learn it. It was embarrassing, having lessons at her age, but hadn't Jacot said the same thing, that day by the wall? He had sat side-by-side with eight-year-old Valentin to learn long division. Ophele had been wishing for books and teachers for months, and now she had them. She would be grateful.

They rode up to the manor to find Remin coming out of the stables, huge and shaggy with his new black bear cloak over his shoulders and his sword strapped to his back. It made her feel better just to see him.

"I was hoping I'd catch you together," he said, moving to intercept Brambles. The big horse was steaming away toward the stable, eager for his supper. "I understand you've got reservations, wife, but if we're going to court, we'll need to talk about your hallows."

Stars and blazes.

She almost said Davi's oath out loud. And as Davi and Leonin turned toward her, Ophele tried to remember everything she had just learned about the construction of a persuasive argument.

Chapter 2 – A Trial of Steel

"Get up," said Remin, moving back a pace without shifting the ready angle of his sword. "Try again."

He took no satisfaction in watching Davi and Leonin wobble back to their feet, their panting breaths rasping through the visors of their helmets. Notionally, they had just secured an imaginary Ophele's retreat through the door behind them, but they had had to resort to absorbing his bruising, bludgeoning attack with their armor rather than fighting back. If he had wanted to kill them, he could have.

Wordlessly, the two men moved into position, Leonin in front and Davi slightly behind, where his greater reach could be used to best advantage.

"Are we guarding the door, each other, or another point, Your Grace?" asked Leonin, polite and breathless.

"Secure a route to a carriage," Remin replied, and pointed to the gate on the other side of the paddock. "There."

They barely had a chance to turn their heads and look at it before he attacked, chopping his sword toward Leonin's head. The other man swiftly pivoted to parry, the clash of steel ringing through the air. Leonin had been the one to suggest these exercises, scenarios a guardsman might reasonably expect to encounter, and Remin was the most ferocious antagonist available. They only had four months before they left for Segoile.

Though a lack of training was not their greatest concern. For now, and for the foreseeable future, Davi and Leonin were nothing but exceedingly devoted guardsmen.

Just thinking of last night's argument with Ophele was like a heaping of coals into his gut. Remin sucked in a breath and attacked again, pressing Davi and Leonin inexorably toward the paddock fence, constantly searching for a way to smash through the wall of their bodies to get to the imaginary Ophele on the other side. He had been planning to practice with them anyway, but he took a vindictive pleasure in it today.

Stars, did she think he *wanted* her to be bound forever to two other men? Did she think he enjoyed knowing that she spent a greater portion of her day with her guards than her husband? Had it not occurred to her, when she worried that they would know all her secrets, that Remin worried about the same thing? He had never thought he was a jealous man—though it was true, he had never before had an opportunity—but he could never like knowing that other men might know her better than he did. He hated that his wife must have such guardians. He was enduring it because he had no choice.

"Leonin, the gate," Davi puffed, muffled through his helmet, a split second before Remin lunged to intercept them. Knocking Leonin's sword aside, he smashed in with a shoulder charge, but the smaller man sidestepped just as Davi shoved forward, covering the gap between them. And they got the gate.

They were getting better. Neither of them would ever defeat Remin in a fight, but they weren't trying to unseat him as Supreme Sword. A good guardsman was a shield, an obstruction, and these two were learning to work very well together. In time, they would do some of these exercises with Ophele, and teach her how to simultaneously move with them and stay out of their way.

The three of them were already learning how to maneuver around each other, apparently.

It had been Leonin who explained their vision of Andelin's hallows the night before, once they had trooped into the solar for a more private conversation. A noble tradition, in which the hallow and the soul-sworn endeavored all their lives to deserve each other. Remin would have to think through the implications of such a scheme for his descendants, but he had to admit that this was normally the sort of thing he loved. A blend of ancient tradition balanced against the needs of the present, with high expectations and uncompromising judgments.

"That will be excellent, in the long term," Remin had told them, pulling up the new armchair he had gotten for his birthday. Even the buttery leather failed to soothe him. He was feeling blindsided and angry. "Explain how this will affect the short term. Beginning with March."

"I cannot argue with you, Your Grace," Leonin had replied coolly. "It is just as you said. When we go to Segoile, if the Emperor intends to harm Her Grace, then he will surely separate us from her, and we cannot protest if we are only guardsmen."

"Does this content you, Davi?" Remin turned to the other man, his lanky body folded up into his chair and visibly unhappy. Remin got the feeling that Davi was nearest to sharing his own opinion.

"'Course not." Davi glanced at Ophele apologetically. "Truthfully, I'd do whatever it takes to protect the lady first, and bugger the rest. For me, my lady, I already want to swear so I can do what you said. Protect you so you can live and do whatever you're going to do. I want to see what that is. You'd have my sincere oath."

"I know." Her glance took in both Leonin and Davi. "But I don't think it's right to take the oath just because it's dangerous if we don't."

"That is why you are taking it at *all,* wife," said Remin, with an edge.

"Then we shouldn't do it," she said stubbornly. The color was high in her face, but she was holding her ground. "It is the Emperor's fault we're forced to consider such a thing. To have to swear an oath that binds our souls for—"

"My first care is that you live long enough to contemplate the state of your soul," Remin interrupted hotly, and Ophele flushed.

"It's—blasphemous," she said, her voice high and excited. "I think. I don't know if the Temple would say it is, but this oath is sacred and I don't want to...to...insult it, because we took it for the wrong reasons."

She had never argued with him like this before. Remin bit his tongue.

"We know our souls are real," she went on, frightened but stubborn. "We saw our families' spirits at the Feast of the Departed. There is something after this life, and I don't know what it is, so I don't know what it will be to have both of you bound to me forever. What if we do it wrong, and I can never find you there, for all time? What if I can't find my mother? What if I can never find a heaven at all? And if I am—if I am really a child of the stars, wouldn't it be even worse if *I* did such a thing? Tied Leonin and Davi to me for my own convenience, or because I was scared, not because I am worthy of such companions?"

These were not questions Remin had ever considered. He could not argue the reality of souls; he had felt them through the clouds of sacred incense. His dark brows drew together.

"Others did not wait so long," he said slowly. It was a weak argument. His stomach knotted. "I read Juste's book, too. I'm sure there's something in what you say, but the reason hallows exist is to protect their masters in *this* life."

"I don't deserve them." She lifted her eyes to his, clear and golden and shining. "The only reason they would swear is because of you and my father."

He could not argue that. She would not need hallows if it were not for Remin Grimjaw. And he had promised he would not force her to take any oaths.

"It's your decision," he said, and rose, his face thunderous. At the door, he forced himself to stop and speak again. "We'll go to supper soon."

He needed to think. He needed to get a leash on the thing that was trying to thrash loose inside him. And all the next day, he had gone over and over the argument in his mind, as if some construct of logic would be sufficient to protect her.

He found no answers, but at least his exercise with Leonin and Davi had tired him enough to broach the subject rationally.

"I just want to keep you safe," he told Ophele in bed that night. The moon was nearly full, and its light cast diamond-patterned shadows through their wide windows, glowing on her fair skin. "Wife. I don't want to force you."

"I know," she said unhappily, closing her eyes as his fingers brushed her cheek. And that was *all* she said. Remin withdrew his hand.

"Then talk to Brother Oleare," he murmured. "Juste is no clergyman. Perhaps Brother Oleare can reassure you."

"I will."

They were both naked under the covers. He had made love to her again after supper, hoping to forget himself inside her, and hoping even more to beget a child. It would protect her, if she was visibly pregnant when they went to court. But the feel of her small, vulnerable body beside him was too much. Remin rolled onto his side.

"I love you," she whispered behind him.

"I love you," he replied, shutting his eyes.

It would have been so much easier if he had not.

* * *

Within the freshly painted walls of the tailor's shop in Tresingale, a polite war was underway.

On one side was Lady Verr, commanding with fierce and glittering gray eyes. Master Marin Tiffen, newly arrived from Belleme, led the opposing force, and somehow Ophele was the small, neutral nation between them that was about to be blown to bits.

"No, a double sleeve, inner and outer," said Lady Verr, peering over Master Tiffen's shoulder as he hunched at his worktable, making alterations to the current design. "That was the fashion when I was last in the capital, a very wide outer sleeve and an inner sleeve that buttons down the forearm. Or perhaps, if it was a tippet, we—"

"I don't hold with tippets," the tailor said loudly, squinting up at her.

There were many things with which Master Tiffen did not hold.

He was not at all what Ophele had expected of a tailor. Seated in his shop, which was still so new that everything smelled of plaster and sawdust, he moved with a strange, rolling gait from his design table to the high racks of cloth stored in the back, arguing with Lady Verr over brocade versus velvet. His gray hair sprang up in vigorous tufts everywhere but on the top of his head, and every time Lady Verr built up a really good head of steam, he developed a twitch in his left eye.

"—wider skirts, much wider," Lady Verr was saying. "I have heard they are still wearing fur this winter in Segoile, and you need wider skirts to bear the weight of fur—"

"You're going to weigh the lady down like an anchor with that much fabric." The tailor jabbed a finger in Ophele's direction. "And fur on top of it? Do you mean to have her guards ferry her about and stow her wherever she's needed for the day?"

"Please mind your tongue, sir," said Leonin evenly, while Davi cast his eyes up at the ceiling. There was a dangerous quivering in his sides.

"No, you needn't pleat the skirt, that would be far too heavy," Lady Verr replied with infinite patience. "The fabric will be tight to the waist and then widen, almost a bell shape. It would complement the sleeves."

"You're talking about a farthingale," Master Tiffen accused. He crossed his arms, left eye a-twitch. "I don't hold with farthingales."

"It is not for you to *hold* with anything," Lady Verr retorted. "We are employing your skills, not asking your opinion, Master Tiffen."

"Beg your pardon, my lady, but His Grace invited me here to make *sensible* clothes," Master Tiffen shot back. *"No nonsense,* he told me. *Don't copy the Empire, make something of our own,* he said. And the lady will need to be able to do more than putter up and down the hallway!"

As a spectator, all of this was high entertainment. Ophele hadn't understood more than half of what they were saying; she didn't know a farthingale from a farthing and *houppelande* made her think of the huge sheer netting bags Bhumi women wore to keep out the midges. It was fun to say, though. Houppelande.

"My lady?" Lady Verr prompted, and Ophele started. The two hostile powers were now staring at her.

"Well...I do like the silver fur with the blue brocade," she offered. She felt fairly safe in this opinion, but was prepared to capitulate at once if she met the least resistance.

"About the *fashion,* my lady," said Master Tiffen, as if it were a dirty word.

"Oh. I do need to get used to walking with a train and skirts and heels," she admitted. "I must be accustomed to them, when I go to the capital."

Lady Verr gave the tailor an *I told you so* look.

"But His Grace did say that we should all wear what we like." He had also sternly instructed Ophele to order enough gowns to fill her closet, or he would come down to the tailor's shop himself, and she would not like it if that happened. "But," she said in sudden inspiration, "Ought we not make both? Segoile clothes and the new style for the Andelin? What's a farthingale?"

"It is an underframe to support a wide skirt—" began Lady Verr, at the same time that Master Tiffen said,

"It's a bunch of reeds stuck up under your dress. If Lady Verr insists, I saw a likely bit of bog on the way here."

That did not sound comfortable.

"I want something...simpler, first," she admitted. "And *warm,* it has been so cold. Might we not begin with a Segoile dress and...simplify it?"

She indicated the sketch they had already begun, much altered and hotly disputed.

"Agreed," Master Tiffen said, sitting back at his worktable.

"You are dressing the daughter of the *Emperor,"* Lady Verr admonished. "Even if you insist on such plain lines, there ought to be embroidery, beads, silk, jewels—"

"I've all the silk and linen you want, embroider away," said Master Tiffen, sketching with a bit of charcoal.

Lady Verr's lip curled.

"I do want it to be...beautiful, too," Ophele said, oppressed by Master Tiffen's squinty left eye. "Not every dress must be jeweled, but I do want everyone to be...pleased. When they see their duchess, I mean."

And she wanted very much to be beautiful in Remin's eyes, but she wasn't about to say that.

"We can do better than stripping Segoile fashion for parts." Master Tiffen looked thoughtful. "Happens I've seen those double sleeves in Ispichov. Outers for warmth, and then they pin them back to work. Warm as toast, too."

"You've been to Ispichov?" Ophele asked, curiosity instantly winning over shyness.

"Yes, my lady. I was a sailor. There now," he said, sitting back with a refreshed expression. "See if this doesn't suit. And Lady Verr, I expect you can tack on some Segoile foolishness."

"Lower the neck," Lady Verr said with a glance. "And widen the skirt a little. The sleeves are cunning, I must say."

This amicable spirit only lasted until they got into the details of the bodice, and for the next twenty minutes they seemed to forget that anyone else was in the room and veered wildly from applauding their shared genius to Master Tiffen's resounding condemnation of the Empire, its aesthetics, its fashion, and the fools that offended the eyes of all rational people by wearing it. And while Lady Verr did not ever utter the words *peasant* or *clod* or *uncultured swine,* she could communicate a great deal with her eyebrows.

But the final design was that rare flight of inspiration that satisfied everyone. The dark blue brocade overdress was trimmed at the ends with the smoky silver fox fur and lined with satin to keep out the wind, warm and soft and utterly delightful to wear. The wide bells of the sleeves could be folded back and buttoned out of the way with large silver buttons, and these simple ornaments were echoed along the square neckline, where moonstones and sapphires glittered against a length of silver-white ribbon. It was truly lovely.

"I do believe these sleeves would be quite the rage, in Segoile," Lady Verr said thoughtfully. "They would be attaching bows and knots and all manner of cunning laces."

"I like the lacing on the back," Ophele said, admiring the twists of silver ribbon that would tighten the bodice to her torso, with the knot low enough that she could untie it herself. There was a certain helplessness that came with knowing she could not escape her gown if she wanted to. "Would that be the...the rage, too?"

"The lacings would be," Lady Verr agreed with a small smile, and after a few more minutes of mutual admiration, they set this design aside and began the next.

It was fun, at first. They put together a half-dozen ravishing costumes, as Lady Verr said, in green velvet and violet silk and a beautiful russet and gold that looked like someone had made silk from autumn leaves. But there was such a quantity of clothing to be ordered, nightclothes and morning dresses, robes to be worn to the bath, indoor gowns and gowns for audiences, and riding gowns that would not be crumpled or stretched by riding sidesaddle. Ophele's interest began to waver around the eighth dress and even Leonin was beginning to look glassy-eyed. Davi had long since lapsed into a coma.

And so, for the first time in her life, Ophele delegated.

"I think you both...know what I like," she said, rising from her stool in the corner. Other than examining her periodically to discuss her coloring or proportions, she wasn't of much use to them anyway. "I will leave you to it."

"Of course, my lady," said Lady Verr without lifting her eyes from Master Tiffen's rapidly moving charcoal. "If you would like, I will bring the designs to you for your approval tonight. Lady Carolen often entrusted such things to me."

"Yes, please," Ophele agreed, and escaped with Leonin and Davi.

The visit to Master Tiffen's shop had replaced her lessons with Lady Verr, and the sun was just beginning to slant over the roofs of the town as she stepped out into the brisk morning air. Though she quickly pulled up her hood and burrowed into her thin cloak, Ophele always felt the urge to linger when she came to the market. It was beginning to look like a *real* marketplace, a huge plaza three times the size of Granholme's, and two and a half sides were already lined with shops and houses.

The fountain at the center was nearly completed, too; the smashing sword and its scattering of stars now rolled in sculpted stone waves to four large statues of a farmer, a builder, a soldier, and a mother. All that stonework had been given to Remin by the masons on his birthday, though Master Misler confessed they'd had to employ actual sculptors for the statues.

For a little while, she indulged herself, walking down the line of shops to examine the shoes in the window of the cobbler's shop and smell the scents of beeswax and tallow wafting from the chandler's. Through the closed door of the weaver's shop, she could hear the clatter and bang of the loom. Mistress Roscout had bought the long-hoarded wool from Remin's sheep and once she was done with it, it would go to the dyer, and then she would sell it back to Remin at five times the price he had charged for the wool.

That thick, soft cloth was destined to become blankets, and Ophele would have all the sewing practice she wanted on their endless seams.

Remin was very pleased with this arrangement. At every stage, he was propping up the fledgling economy of his town, which was understandably wobbly in its first year. But while he counted every coin with his army, and didn't hesitate to point out shoddy work wherever he found it, he was unfailingly generous to everyone else.

Ophele hurried through her inspection and then headed back to the hitching post in front of the tavern where they had left their horses. The tavern was open and serving breakfast under the hospitable management of the Tregue family, and the warm and yeasty smell of beer and bread wafted through its open doors. Wen's cookhouse was now closed to everyone but Remin's army.

"How much it has changed," she said, looking around with satisfaction as she settled into her saddle. "I remember when this was all sticks and string."

"Seemed like the whole camp was made of that, in the beginning," Davi agreed, swinging atop his horse. "Remember, Leonin? We were still in tents this time last year."

"There will be more walls before the snow flies," Leonin said with the satisfaction of a prophet that has already seen his visions come to pass. And it was true. Even as they trotted up Goose Road to the outer edges of the market, the builders were bawling at each other and hauling heavy timber frames upright, to bring more of those visions into reality.

* * *

"Stop," said Leonin for at least the dozenth time. Tounot's fingers twanged on his lute and fell silent. "You missed a step, Davi, that's why you find yourself too far away to reach Her Grace. It is one two *three* four, one two *three* four, on the backfoot. Try again, if you please."

Davi did not have breath to apologize. Or snarl. Straightening painfully, he nodded and waited for Tounot to resume his infernal plucking. The tiny duchess offered her hand with an encouraging smile.

Davi Gosse's life had taken many strange turnings since that long-ago day in the fields outside Lomonde, but this was certainly one of the sharper curves in the road.

That was the day that changed his life.

Born on one of the small farms outside the city, his life had been placid as the slow-ripening grain until the year of the Vallethi invasion. It was not the first time that Valleth had ventured south of the Brede, but it was by far their most successful campaign, and by the time anyone thought to inform the farmers that the Vallethi army was headed their way, it was already too late to run. The Imperial Army, outmarched and outmaneuvered at every turn, had been exactly on the wrong side of the city, and so the farmers of Lomonde had hidden away their women and children and gone to confront the Eagle Knights with pitchforks.

It was autumn. The smoke of burning wheat blackened the sky and Davi had been so *angry* watching it, the destruction of the food that they had nourished from the soil, the grain that was to sustain them over the winter. But then he had heard the distant beat, beat, beat of those terrible war drums, and the approaching catastrophe of the Vallethi Eagle Knights, and he knew he would be lucky if he lived long enough to starve.

The air was rank with fear. When the Vallethi army appeared on the horizon, two or three men pissed themselves, an audible patter of liquid onto the earth. Davi was so numbed with terror, he wouldn't have been surprised to learn that he had done the same.

The drums rolled. The Vallethi infantry approached in two long lines, rattling in their scaled armor. Double time, *boom boom boom boom,* their strides lengthening as they lifted the curved blades of their bardiches, spotting their enemies. They were almost to the wheat.

Davi tasted dust.

Drums. Drums, like thunder. With ululating cries, the Vallethi swept into the wheat like scythes.

And fell over.

It was impossible. A joke, a prank, a miracle of some mischievous god, all those screaming men suddenly faceplanting into the wheat. Slack-jawed, the farmers of Lomonde watched as dozens, no, *hundreds* of blue-garbed Imperial soldiers sprang up with a roar of their own. Half of Valleth's soldiers were just tripping over their fallen brethren.

Someone behind Davi started laughing, high and hysterical.

The drums rolled again, but even that cacophony was lost under the earthshaking catastrophe of the Eagle Knights, the wood-framed wings mounted to their saddles buzzing with the charge. They had to circle around the wheat to avoid trampling their own infantry, and as they swung in a sweeping arc to the south, Davi had an eternity to contemplate all the errors of his life that had led him to this place.

The Imperial knights appeared from *nowhere.*

Davi would have sworn they burst from the earth. A sudden surge of horse and men that slammed into the side of the Vallethi army like a dagger, smashing into the Eagle Knights, through them, slicing straight into the meat of the army. Heavily armored knights with lance and sword that leveled the enemy like grass, more knights than Davi could count, and he and the other farmers watched, sinking slowly to their knees with tears streaming down their cheeks, and thanked the stars for their deliverance.

Even after it was over, he lingered. Davi had never been one to forget a favor, and he had spotted the man who had led the charge, easily the tallest fellow he had ever seen. It was only when he removed his helmet that Davi realized it was not a man at all. A boy. A prodigiously strong one, to be sure, but there was still a youthful softness in his face, and surely that smooth chin had never yet met a razor.

Later, he learned it was Remin. The son of the traitor Duke Benetot, fosterling of Duke Ereguil, technically not even a knight at all. But none of that mattered. Remin had saved Lomonde. He had saved the life of everyone Davi knew, everyone he loved. That night, when Davi went home to find his mother in the garden and one of his sisters standing nearby with a knife still clutched in her hand, he knew that somehow, he would have to pay that boy back. He would pay him back if it took his whole life.

Admittedly, he had not envisioned *this.*

"...two *three* four, one two *three...*" The duchess's lips counted as she stepped, more quick than graceful, her eyebrows pinched with concentration. This was their first actual dance, a combination of the steps they had been working to master for more than a week. Davi found he performed best if he pretended this was some bizarre form of sword practice.

"Turn, turn," said Leonin, whose remorseless repetition of the steps sometimes made Davi want to hit him. "Catch her hand, and bow..."

Pain stabbed into Davi's side, and his lips tightened.

"Oh, are you all right?" Ophele withdrew instantly, as if she had done something wrong.

"Fine, fine, my lady. Just moved wrong," he said, straightening. Remin had cracked him nearly in half the day before. "Beg pardon."

"We were doing so well," she said, a little breathless, and moved back into place opposite him. She was so earnest, it made Davi want to pat her head. "The music does help, doesn't it?"

"It is a high compliment to call this music, my lady," said Tounot, looking unhappily at his lute. He and Leonin had been charged with schooling the duchess in courtly graces. "My fingers have been more oft on a sword than a string, this last year."

"It will be winter soon, perhaps there will be more time for peaceful pursuits." Ophele produced this only a little awkwardly, her eyes flitting toward the floor. Having witnessed most of the duchess' training, Davi could say honestly that he preferred getting walloped with a sword. The aristocrats of the Empire were famed for their flowery speech, but until now he had never realized it was something they *learned.*

"There is a little art there, my lady," Tounot said, encouraging. "But remember to look up, and speak more loudly. It was difficult to hear."

She nodded, and then remembered one of their many other admonitions.

"I will," she said, with a visible effort to be louder. But her eyes still dropped to the floor.

She had asked them to correct her, in the privacy of the solar. But it still made Davi want to find and strangle whoever had made her so anxious, and just as bad, the fashionable society that was forcing her to painfully break these habits and adopt a whole new set of unnatural mannerisms. Davi didn't see what was wrong with her now. Some people were just shy.

"What you say is interesting, my lady," he told her, taking her hand to begin their dance again. "Are you planning what you say before you say it?"

"Yes. It sounds nice because there's alliteration," she replied, frowning down at their feet. "I always wondered why everyone says Sir Tounot is such a good speaker, and I think it's because he uses so many devices. Alliteration, simile—"

“And turn,” said Leonin, shooting a glance at Tounot, who looked surprised to find that he had been the subject of such study. “Please stand up straight, my lady, like a string is pulling upward through your spine.”

“—metaphor, consonance...” Ophele straightened, her arm extended as she and Davi paced off a circle with only their fingertips touching. “Only, you can’t use too much alliteration or it just sounds funny. I made a mental model of the perfect sound proportion, because too many close together lose their elegant effect.”

Sheer surprise made all of them burst out laughing, and she looked pleased.

“I thought of that last night,” she said, and then Davi had to lunge to catch her when she tripped over her own feet.

After a time, Tounot took a turn to dance with the lady, giving Davi a chance to nurse his ribs and observe. When Leonin corrected Ophele, he had to own that it was fair; she did slouch, she did look at the floor, and after a few corrections in a row she did start wringing her hands. But it was annoying to have to listen to everyone *pick* at her all day.

“You are too hard on her,” he told Leonin later that night, seated before the other man on one of the two chairs in their shared cottage. The two of them had moved up to the servants’ quarters in the manor, given how much time they spent with the duchess. “His Grace said that he didn’t want her anxious.”

“She will be a great deal more anxious if she does not learn these things before she goes to the capital,” Leonin replied, yanking on the strapping around Davi’s ribs. Davi grunted. “And she knows it. Did you really think she wouldn’t figure it out on her own?”

There was no denying this. His Grace was at great pains to conceal the true extent of the danger from her, but their lady was too intelligent to be deceived for long.

“All the same, you’re likely to make her worse instead of better,” said Davi. “Leave off, that’s good enough.”

Rising painfully, he reached for his shirt as Leonin took the vacated seat. They spent the early part of most nights patching each other up, and by now the routine was so ingrained, they hardly had to speak. Davi unwound the linen strapping over Leonin's shoulder, which had taken a hard hit from one of Remin Grimjaw's charges. It was a miracle nothing was broken.

"I'm wondering if we ought to say something," Davi went on, peeling away the heavy pad, which was soaked in some herbal concoction that smelled like grass and feet. "She's been practicing those stupid speeches every morning, but she can barely get out two words in front of Juste."

"That is not our role." That was Leonin at his Segoile prissiest. "She is a duchess, and we are not her hallows. And even if we were, Sir Justenin was given charge of her educa—*do* you need to yank at me like that?"

"Happens I do," said Davi balefully. "You like things to stay in their places when you stick 'em there, don't you?"

"If you want to win, you will get a great deal farther by playing the game than contesting the rules," Leonin replied shortly, and they lapsed into silence.

They had come to understand each other better over the last few months. They were very different men, but they were in agreement on the most important things: their loyalty to the Duke of Andelin, their conviction that the hallows of the Andelin would be one of the pillars of his House, and their determination that Ophele would live to be its foundation.

But this was something on which they could not agree.

"You're the one that said we ought to protect her dignity," Davi said, turning to soak a new padded bandage in the solution Genon Hengest had provided, which did a fair job of reducing pain and inflammation. "I don't see what's wrong with her as she is. One of the sweetest maids I've ever had the pleasure to know."

"That is part of the oath we will swear, not my own invention, and there are many ways that we must do so. Beginning with keeping the proper distance from her, for her sake," said Leonin patiently. "They will seize upon the least appearance of impropriety, in the capital. And what would His Grace think if he heard you say that?"

"His Grace would know it ain't like that," Davi retorted, provoked into poor grammar. "Stars and ancestors, I could almost be her father. Filthy minds they have—"

"Will you kindly *stop* inflicting your feelings on me?" Leonin said, glaring up at him with icy blue eyes, and Davi realized he was strapping the pad down on Leonin's injured shoulder with a bit more vigor than necessary. "I will be less than gentle with your ribs, come morning. We must think beyond ourselves. We will be the first hallows, but not the last. We will set the standard not just as guardsmen, but as men. In future generations..."

Leonin had spoken often of his vision for House Andelin's hallows, which in his mind seemed to be a sort of sect of warrior monks. When they had first met, Davi had thought him a typical capital lordling, rudderless and spoiled, but Leonin genuinely seemed not to care about possessions or comfort. His side of the cottage was as ascetic as a priest's cell.

"Our job is to protect Her Grace," Davi replied stubbornly. Leonin was a good talker; if Davi let him go, he'd talk until it seemed black was white and up was down. But Davi would not be shaken from their essential purpose.

"What do you think protection means?" Leonin gave him a sharp glance. "We will be *part* of her, Davi. Others will examine our relationship with Her Grace to model their own conduct. They will also examine our behavior during those times when we are not with her."

This was a shallowly buried reference to Davi's discreet visits to a redheaded prostitute named Arlet in the masons' camp, of whom Leonin strongly disapproved.

"The only person taking notes on my comings and goings is *you,*" Davi shot back. "That's my business. Ain't one word in the oath about not visiting whores."

"There is," Leonin said calmly. *"If thou art shamed, I will cover thy nakedness.* That is both literal and metaphorical. But only *think*. We are men proposing to guard another man's wife for the whole of her life. We can have no other bonds. No wives, no children, no loyalties to anyone but her. Can she trust us so far to be certain that if she were naked, we would think only to cover her?"

"Yes," Davi retorted, though he felt a sudden pang of fear for Arlet and her enormous bosom.

"I believe that is true. I would not stand beside you if it were not," Leonin replied. "But that may not be so for future hallows. What if your attachment to your...companion was to grow? What then, if she chose to test your loyalty to your lady? If we are to be trusted with a lady like Ophele, we must be above reproach. And what would she think, if she knew of your visits to the masons' camp?"

Davi would have liked to argue. But he was too honest to deny his first, instinctive response: that he very much hoped she would not.

"If your shoulder's not better tomorrow, you're going to see Gen," was all he said, and strode outside to rinse out the basin that held the stinking remains of the medicinal concoction.

There was a pump behind the cottages that brought up water from the river, and even working its handle made his side ache. Davi's breath puffed white in the still night air, and his eyes drifted up to the manor.

He had sworn to pay Remin back, no matter what it took.

He had been glad to do it. And he had never been much afraid to do it, not after that day on the fields outside Lomonde. Facing an army with a pitchfork, that was his standard for *real* fear. Now he had a sword and had learned how to use it. Tolerably well, in fact. He had not been afraid when he made his oath to Remin Grimjaw. He hadn't even been afraid when he asked to be the hallow for His Grace's lady. He had already given up his life.

It was stupid that this was harder. Was it really necessary? Was it a rule they ought to make, for the hallows yet to come? Because actually, he did know what Ophele would say, if asked; she would tell him to find a wife and have babies and be happy. She would be horrified at the thought of them making such a sacrifice.

He didn't know if he should. And even if he should, he didn't know if he *could*. Never bedding a woman for the rest of his life? He was a man. He had a man's urges. Yet was Leonin right? Could he truly swear that such a connection, given time, would not eventually divide his loyalties?

Maybe he should've thought harder about that, before he went about offering oaths.

* * *

In the very early morning, Ophele woke up.

She rarely slept through the night, unless Remin had exhausted her. Usually, she woke two or even three times, rising to re-stoke the fire or get a cup of water from the washstand. The brief foray into the cold made the warm bed feel so much nicer, and then she could crawl back into Remin's arms and drop straight into sleep.

But this time there was a drowsy sense that something was wrong, and she lay quite still, listening.

Beside her, Remin shivered.

The shudder ran from his shoulders all the way down to his toes, and in the dim light of the fire, she could see the frown on his face, the rapid, pulsing twitch of the muscle in his jaw. When she lifted a hand to him, her fingers brushed his chest and then she laid her palm flat in surprise. His heart was *racing*.

"Remin?" Was he having a nightmare? Tentatively, she patted him. "Remin?"

His shoulder twitched and he stiffened, his whole body going rigid as a board, and then his arms caught her and dragged her against him so hard, her bones creaked in his grip. Burying his face in her hair, he drew a long, deep breath.

"—mm-nnn?" He was crushing her face into his chest.

But maybe he was not awake at all. After a few moments, that crushing grip relaxed and the pounding of his heart began to slow. And then he was just sleeping, his face smoothing from those frowning lines, his breathing regular and deep.

"Did you sleep well?" she asked him the next morning over breakfast.

"Well enough," he said, eating with his customary focus. "How about you?"

"All right." Ophele watched him. Perhaps he just didn't remember. "I dreamed about dresses. They were all too big."

"You can always send them back if they are," he remarked, one black eye flicking toward her, glinting with amusement. There was a tall stack of dress designs on the table beside them to choose from, some of them Lady Verr's proposals, some of them Master Tiffen's, and no way of telling which was which. It was like a test that would inevitably end in disaster. "You needn't choose between them, wife. Just have them all."

"All of them are pretty," she conceded. It was not the worst problem to have. "You need new clothing too, husband. Don't you get cold?"

The sight of his smile warmed her to her toes.

"I have my new cloak."

"You're going to get sick if you don't dress warmer," she warned, though it lacked conviction. It had been so difficult to get him to smile, lately.

"You may dress me however you like, as long as I don't have to go see Tiffen myself. Magne has my measurements. I haven't the time to spare." And as if to prove this point, he inhaled the last of his breakfast and then rose to dress for the day, bellowing for his valet.

It was so good to have him home. Ophele listened contentedly as Remin filled the house with his shouting and thumping, the new timbers of the floor creaking under his weight. Magne's querulous tenor answered in the hallway, where he customarily lurked until breakfast was over. The two men were developing an awkward but somehow sweet relationship; Remin really did try to let Magne do his job, and Magne took a great deal of satisfaction in producing a young lord that looked *nice*.

"My lady?" Lady Verr appeared in the door a few moments later, a neatly choreographed morning dance that placed Ophele in the hallway just as Remin was exiting his dressing room.

"Your cloak only works if it's on," she reminded him, admiring the thick black fur.

"Your guards only work if they are with you," he returned. "I heard about you going to the stables by yourself yesterday. Don't do that again. Go nowhere alone."

"I won't," she promised, wondering who had tattled. It had been all of five minutes, going to fetch Brambles.

"Good. Edemir and Bram will be leaving midmorning, if you want to come and see them off."

Lady Verr dressed her accordingly in one of her warmest wool gowns, plain red enlivened by black and gold ribbons. Master Tiffen was working furiously on her first gown but had prioritized a new cloak, satin-lined, with mink supplied by the furrier that was black as pitch and warm as toast. From the wintry look of the sky, she would need it.

There had been a great deal to look at lately. Even as Lady Verr marshalled Emi and Peri, Ophele realized with a start that the maids no longer wore aprons when they attended her, a measure that made it much easier to relax in their presence. Had Lady Verr done that? Or had Remin said something? Ophele herself had not realized it was the aprons that reminded her so sharply of Leise and Nenot, her maids back in Aldeburke.

"Thank you," she said gratefully, as they turned her toward the mirror. Still plain as a sparrow, but a very well-dressed little bird.

Leonin and Davi also bore watching. The two of them had been somewhat battered lately, and when they appeared to escort her to the harbor, Davi took care in mounting his horse, when usually he swung up light as a cat. Leonin had barely been using his left arm for the last four days.

Training injuries? But they must have been training much harder than usual...

"Warm enough, my lady?" asked Davi when they were all aboard.

"Yes, thank you," she said, and they were off, trotting down Eugene Street to the tentatively named Quay Way. Tounot had called it that one day and it looked like it might stick.

It was very cold on the river. The wind whipping off the Brede was strong enough to push the hood off her head and the water was dark as iron, swirling and eddying against the docks. It was a small delegation that had come to say farewell; Remin was trying not to draw attention to the departures.

As such, it was only Remin, Justenin, and herself that stood on the furthest dock on the quay, with a single-masted caravel bobbing on either side. It was obvious to her why Edemir should leave, and where he was to go. He was the son of a count and doubtless had many valuable social connections in the capital. For him, at least, she did not think she needed to fear.

"Look after Bendir," Edemir told her when it was her turn to bid him farewell. "If you find any errors, don't be afraid to tell him. I am relying on you for the accounts in particular, Your Grace. And do try to restrain His Grace's spending. Mind the sens—"

"—and the sovs will mind themselves," she finished for him. Remin was a fundamentally frugal man except in very specific, very expensive circumstances. "Will we see you, when we come to the capital?"

Ophele did not see Justenin behind her, lifting his head with sudden interest.

"I—yes, my lady," said Edemir, surprised. "That is, I will hope so. I would enjoy showing you the city."

It might not be so bad, if Edemir and Duchess Ereguil and Lady Verr were all there. It was Sir Bram's errand that gave her more misgivings. He was clad in rough black traveling clothes that bore no badge or device to mark him as Remin's man, and he never troubled to hide the brands on the backs of his hands that marked him as a criminal. Remin had told her frankly that he had once been a mercenary.

"You will be careful?" She offered her hand and he bowed over it, touching his forehead to the back in the old gesture of fealty.

"I promise I will, my lady," he replied, long black hair sweeping over his scarred cheeks as he straightened. "I hope you will look after yourself, and His Grace. If the stars are good, then we will all be home again, this time next year."

"That's such a long time."

"Only when you are young," he said philosophically, and gave a warbling whistle to the sailors, stepping back as they raised the gangplank.

When those two boats set off, it was not on a straight course to the other side of the Brede. Sir Edemir's boat turned west, black sails billowing, sped by the current down the river in the direction of Segoile. But Sir Bram's boat turned laboriously east, its double banks of oars propelling it over the dark surface of the river. Why would he be going that way?

"Wife," said Remin, recalling her to the dock, and Ophele hurried over and let him warm her hands in his before they parted for the day.

Remin's prediction had been right. After a week, no one thought there was anything strange about her lessons, including Ophele herself. Her hours with Lady Verr were pleasant, if sometimes difficult; the manners and courtesies did not come naturally, and sometimes the glittering capital she described sounded impossibly alien. But Ophele devoured grammar, mathematics, and the rules and history of the Court of Nobility in huge gulps, gratified that at least that much was easy.

"Is there anything you find you have...difficulty remembering, my lady?" Justenin asked after one of their discussions. He had that odd look on his face again.

"No...?" she said, a little puzzled.

"What is the fourth codicil to Article Six, Section Twenty-Two of the Laws of Inheritance?"

"That's the one about minors who inherit leadership of their House needing a guardian until age seventeen," she said promptly. "The codicil says if the House doesn't appoint one, the Emperor will."

"What's the square root of 4,567?"

"Sixty-seven...point...five...seven...nine..." she said slowly as she worked out the decimals, perplexed but willing. This was like that strange quiz Remin had administered back in Aldeburke, the day they met.

"That is sufficient, thank you. How much do we pay for oats?"

"Sixteen copper sens per bag in the kitchen and eleven for the stables." They were not at all the same oats.

"Thank you, my lady," he said, and before she left that evening, he gave her a whole new set of mathematical texts and told her to go at them as fast as she liked.

Even at supper, the lessons continued. Most often, they dined at the cookhouse, and the high table had become very fine, with china and crystal and wine, for which Ophele was attempting to cultivate a palate. Sim and Jaose moved down the table to formally serve each course, though Wen himself was the only one allowed to bring Remin and Ophele their plates. Practice, to become accustomed to capital-style dining.

The night after Edemir and Bram's departure, Justenin took his place at her side and Leonin and Tounot sat across the table, a gathering of Remin's most skilled courtiers, with Lady Verr beside them to model her manners.

"Though I will not be so adept at transporting you to Segoile with my conversation," Justenin apologized as he took his seat.

"It's all right, I would rather go gradually than all at once," Ophele replied, poking at a leek with her spoon. She should have thought about it, to frame her words in a more flowery form, but it was the end of the day and it was hard with all of them expecting her to talk all the time.

"At least you will have familiar faces when you go to the capital," he said reassuringly. "You surmised very quickly where Edemir was going. Where do you suppose Bram might go?"

Ophele had already been considering this question. He had gone east up the river, and what lay to the east? On the south side of the Brede, it was the lands of the eastern empire, most of which were in the hands of the Emperor's strongest allies. It did not seem a promising place for Sir Bram.

On the other side of the river was the eastern range of the Berlawes, which bordered Rendeva, the mountainous land of metal and mercenaries. It could be that Sir Bram had gone there for the former, but this too seemed unlikely to Ophele; if Remin had wanted metal, Bram would not be the man he sent. No, a former mercenary could only have one errand in Rendeva. And Remin could only have one use for mercenaries.

But Ophele didn't think she should say that out loud. If Remin had wanted her to know it, he would have told her himself.

"I think, Rendeva," she said, meeting Justenin's eyes innocently. It was a truthful answer.

"There is no better steel to be found," he agreed. "But please remember to set down your utensils before you speak, my lady."

There were a thousand such rules, and though she could have rattled off the list of them from memory, it wasn't at all the same as *doing* it. Glumly, Ophele watched Lady Verr and Leonin going through the exquisite, soundless motions of their own meal, wondering if she could ever be so elegant.

It was an effective diversion. Ophele never noticed the gleam in Justenin's pale eyes, and the contemplative air of a man who had taken a new tool in hand.

Chapter 3 – The Flower of the Andelin

A coded message on a folded scrap of parchment, concealed in a post at the end of dock six in the harbor:

Manor too well-defended. Will attempt to separate target from guards.

* * *

Distantly, Remin was aware that he had acquired an audience.

It was one more detail to the mental picture he had of the practice yard and all its contents: the twenty small heads that had suddenly appeared in several rows around the fence, hoping to go unnoticed between the bushes and tall grass. No doubt the pageboys had somewhere else they were supposed to be, but the opportunity to see the Duke of Andelin at his training had tempted them from the path of righteousness.

Usually, Remin preferred private practice yards. There were many in the huge barracks, indoor and outdoor yards of varying sizes and configurations, with several for his personal use that had oversized equipment. If he worked his men hard—and with particular zeal for Davi and Leonin—Remin never spared himself.

The air was so cold it stung. In one of the larger practice yards, temporary barriers had been raised to mark off narrow corridors and chambers, mimicking the sort of treacherous ambush he might experience in the capital. Remin and his men performed their battlefield maneuvers religiously, which was why his enemies would never choose to meet him on that ground. Anyone who went with Remin to the capital must be prepared.

Having already taken his turn, Juste was seated on a nearby bench, nursing a bloody nose. He was not a Knight of the Brede merely because he could stomach the ugliest work of war. Alone, he had lasted nearly forty minutes before he was overwhelmed, using the narrow halls to devastating effect.

Remin had been at his own exercise for over an hour.

"Either stay down or get up and come at me," he snapped at the man at his feet, who was twitching like he hadn't decided whether he was really done or not. For the sake of realism, downed men remained where they had fallen, which made maneuvering that much trickier. Also for the sake of realism, Remin kicked any man that twitched in the head, to make sure he didn't get back up again.

This was not the mannered fencing of capital gentlemen. His soldiers were well-armored and fought like they meant it, kicking, punching, slashing. They used every part of their swords, from hilt to pommel to blade. The hilt of someone's sword crashed into the back of his helmet so hard, Remin's ears rang, and he swung around instantly, his armored fist crashing down. The man folded up like laundry.

If this had been real, Remin would have put his sword through him too, kicking his arm up to slam his blade into his armpit and through his heart. That was an additional layer of reality he was mentally imposing on this exercise, kicking and jabbing with the tip of his blade, scoring the kill. In a real fight, those jabs would have been backed with killing intent.

"Do you rehearse it in your mind, my lord?" Juste had asked him once, after that infamous melee in Segoile, when Remin had left over twenty champions sprawled in the dust of the exhibition field. "It looked as if you planned every move before you made it."

"I'm not really...thinking," Remin had replied, a little surprised by the question. He had never considered *how* he did what he did. "I just watch to see what they're going to do, and then I stop them."

Wasn't that what everyone did? If Remin could have described it, he would have just said that he was intensely *aware* of his enemies, where they were, the arrangement of their limbs, a sense of angles and weight and maybe even the shift of their balance upon the earth. He watched. He listened. He built a perfect mental image of the battle space and then moved himself through it in the blink of an eye, with lightning reflexes honed over almost twenty years of constant training.

In his mind, Remin was never defending. Not even now, as fresh opponents entered the yard. He had never defended anything in his life. He maneuvered his enemy into attacking him at a place and time of his choosing, and then he tore them apart.

"Go for his sword arm," said one of his opponents, as five of them circled him warily. Sometimes they tried this, playing for time, hoping to increase their numbers before they attacked together. Remin feinted a lunge at the speaker and then went the opposite way, smashing two swords aside in one sweep—when *would* they stop standing so close together?—and then took two men out at once by simply knocking their heads together.

Three men left. Two more on the way, judging by the noise at his back. Remin inhaled, deep breaths all the way from the bottom of his lungs, resting while he could. This room was getting crowded. As soon as the next two showed up, he charged, driving them into the other three in a rush and then making all five of them trip over the bodies of the men he had just knocked out.

Distantly, he heard the pages shouting and applauding.

Another wave of fighters. He could feel the slow motion of the sun overhead, sense the deepening awe of his audience. He had no idea how long he had been fighting. But eventually even his mighty arms began to tire, and Juste's voice called from the other end of the yard, strategizing with Tounot against him. More men, pushing him out of the narrow, defensible hallway and into the wider space at the end.

Hands grabbed for his arms. His legs. His feet. Remin kicked, driving an armored thigh into one man's chest so hard, he flew backward across the yard.

"Get his sword!" someone shouted behind him. Remin twisted, but more hands seized him, dragging at his hands. They were trying to take his sword from him and Remin reared up in instinctive rage, throwing off the weight of half a dozen men. In him was a banked fury that never wholly died, terror at the thought of failure, disgrace, a defeat that would be worse than death.

"Stars blast it, get his knees!" another man behind him gritted, and a heavy boot slammed into the backs of his knees. His legs buckled and a dozen men hurled themselves at him at once, toppling him backward with an almighty crash of armor.

White plumes puffed from the visors of a dozen men.

"Are you done, Your Grace?" one of the men on his arms panted.

"Please be done," said the man Remin had landed on, sounding rather smothered.

"We're done," Remin said, sitting up painfully. His whole body was one immense ache.

Even as he was dismissing his men, he could hear the cheers and excited conversation from the pages at the end of the yard. Normally, the boys would be beneath his notice; the attention of one's lord was not an honor lightly given. But now that it was clear that Tresingale was not going to be wiped out by devils, a few far-sighted lords had sent their sons to be trained by the Knights of the Brede. Remin's flock of pages was growing.

And he liked to know who was sworn to him, even if they were barely out of leading strings.

"Denin," he said, beckoning one of Edemir's boys. "Is there somewhere else you're supposed to be?"

"Master Trezan sent us to help with cleaning armor, Your Grace," Denin replied, a little fellow just going spotty with adolescence. He nodded to the men limping out of the practice yard. "Theirs is dirty."

"I doubt he meant the armor currently in use," Remin observed, amused. Cheeky little bastard. "When's your next lesson?"

"Midafternoon, Your Grace," said a blond boy, Gabrel or Gavrel. Suddenly, Remin was confronted with a sea of hopeful eyes.

"Go get your practice swords," he said indulgently, the last word almost drowned by the shouts of excitement as the boys stampeded off to obey.

"I suppose someone ought to inform the armorer where his workers have gone," said Tounot, as he and Juste approached together. Tounot had been supervising Remin's attackers. "Are we giving them a lesson, Rem?"

"Might as well see how the new ones measure up," Remin said, though all three of them knew it was as much a treat for them as the boys. They were already on their way back, tumbling all over each other and baying like hounds.

Remin put on a stern expression.

"All right, pair up, and don't let me see you big fellows picking on the little ones. Give me two lines."

The boys had sparred often enough to quickly pick partners and move into the yard, giving themselves room to swing their wooden practice swords. Juste, who did not like small children, went to the end of the yard with the older boys, and Tounot obligingly took the nine, ten, and eleven year-olds to let Remin have the little ones.

There were four of those now, boys so young they were still losing their milk teeth. Little Valentin, who was one of Edemir's pages and the pet of the barracks, offered a gap-toothed grin. Remin had always had a soft spot for the littlest lads.

Crouching down, he beckoned them over.

"Show me your grips," he said, beginning with Valentin and working his way down, adjusting small fingers on the hilts of their swords. "Don't squeeze, remember. Firm but not tight. Pretend it's part of your arm. You can't drop your arm, can you?"

"No, Your Grace," said Valentin and Niccoliot together, echoed faintly by the new boys. They looked to be brothers, brown-haired and freckled, with light blue eyes.

"That's right. That's a good grip," Remin said, patting the last boy's head. "What's your name?"

"Onsippe, my lord," the boy piped, puffing up his small chest.

"All right, Onsippe, you'll go against Niccoliot. Nicco, come here. Now, where are you *not* supposed to hit?"

"Not in the head," said Nicco, who was one of Huber's pages and had learned his lessons well. "And not in the balls."

"That's right," Remin said, repressing a smile. "Go on, show me your best form, don't just whack at each other."

There was much to correct in such small warriors, and Remin settled into the lesson, amused to hear Duke Ereguil's admonishments passing so easily from his own lips.

"Don't look at your hand, look at your target," he said, moving behind Onsippe to straighten the boy's sword arm. "Your hand will follow your eyes, and improve with practice. Try again."

After a while, Remin moved down the line to inspect the other boys, pausing to observe each pair. The nine and ten year-old boys showed significant improvement, and the eleven year-olds were beginning to be dangerous, moving fluidly through their forms.

"Easy now," Remin cautioned. "Remember to pull your strikes. I expect you to control your blade even if it is made of wood."

Some of the twelve and thirteen year-olds were nearly ready for steel. Moving down the rows, Remin marked out the best of them, pleased. His corrections to these wolf cubs were sharper and less kindly; they were nearly men, and should not expect softness. If it came to it, they might be expected to go and fight, and they would not thank him for coddling them.

"Good," he said as twelve-year-old Batistin disarmed his opponent, a lunging maneuver that drove his sword through the other boy's guard and slapped the sword down out of his hand. "Did you intend to disarm him?"

"Yes, Your Grace," said Batistin, straightening to look up at him with sharp green eyes.

"Why did it work?"

"I tried to knock it through his thumb," the boy replied, which was exactly what Remin wanted to hear. The thumb was the weakest point of any grip. A twelve-year-old tactician was going to make a dangerous adult. Remin clouted the boy's shoulder approvingly.

"Go show him how you did it," he said, and moved on.

He did not have leisure for a full lesson, but Remin gave them half an hour of his time, memorized the names and faces of the new boys, and paused to see how Jacot in particular was getting on. It was a pity the boy had such a late start. Auber had agreed to take him as a page and said he had both grit and aptitude, but it was hard for a boy of nearly fifteen to practice against boys two or three years his junior. He could have bested them easily with his reach and strength alone, but that would just mean he got walloped by boys his own age, whose technique was leagues beyond him.

Jacot was trying to do it right. He was so focused on his footwork and form, he never once looked at Remin, and it reminded him forcefully of Ophele, struggling to learn things that she should have been taught years ago.

And that gave him an idea.

"I am pleased with all of you," he told the boys when the short inspection was done, and he had gathered them all back together. "If things were different, there are some of you that I would bring to the Court of War, so you could test yourselves against the striplings of the capital. You would bring honor to my House, and your own. Work hard against the day when you can prove yourselves."

"Yes, Your Grace," the boys chorused.

"All of you have given me your oaths," Remin went on gravely. "You're young, but I will hold you to them. Even if you aren't very big or strong yet, what have you got?"

"Sharp eyes and sharp wits," they chanted together.

"I am going to ask you to use them," Remin said, looking from one face to the next to impress the order upon them. "We're teaching you to use a sword because the world is a dangerous place. There are new folk coming into the valley, and some of them might mean harm to our lady duchess."

A great deal of the fun died from their faces.

"You boys are all over town every day," Remin went on. "I want you to watch. If you see someone behaving strangely, or lingering where they ought not, then I want you to run and tell your master straightaway. You're never too young to keep your eyes open, are you?"

"No, my lord," they said together, and he was gratified to see a glint of ferocity in these wolf cubs.

"Good," he said. "I'll trust you to help me protect my lady. Go on, there's your tutor looking for you."

They would take his orders seriously. To boys training to be knights, it was very nearly a sacred charge; what else was a knight supposed to do *but* protect the fair lady? Twenty boys, aged from nearly-fifteen Jacot to seven-year-old Herebin, made an unlikely set of sentries. But he wouldn't have asked them if he didn't mean it.

That was one more measure against anyone that might come to his valley, seeking to do harm.

* * *

Ophele's week was off to a rocky start.

It was her own fault. In an excess of enthusiasm, she had asked Lady Verr, Leonin, and Tounot if there was anything she was doing that she ought not, thinking that they might naturally feel reticent to say so, as she was their duchess and Davi kept giving them death glares every time they told her to speak louder. But with the example of Lady Verr before her, Ophele couldn't help feeling that there were many areas for improvement.

So she had asked, and they had told her.

As a matter of fact, she got the impression they had been *bursting* to tell her.

They told her, and at her request, they *kept* telling her, a nonstop stream of corrections from the moment she left the bedchamber in the morning until the moment she returned to it at night. Stand up straight. Please don't look at the floor, or above my head, or at my nose. Don't fidget, don't slouch, don't hunch your shoulders, and above all: please speak louder, my lady.

"I *am,*" she said, loud and clear, when Leonin said he couldn't hear her for the dozenth time in less than an hour. She was sure he stood at the far end of the solar on purpose. It was the first time she had ever snapped at any of them, and Leonin barely had time to lift his eyebrows before she was apologizing. "I'm sorry. I am trying."

"You are, my lady," Leonin agreed, and she tried not to notice that he exchanged a glance with Lady Verr. "Habits are very difficult to break."

They were. It was hard, and draining, to have to think about how she was sitting and standing and moving every moment of every day, never mind the incredible amount of *talking* they expected her to do. In Aldeburke, she had sometimes gone for days at a time without ever once uttering a single word.

Ophele had never imagined she might wish that time back.

"Do I *have* to do this here?" Standing in the middle of the storehouse office that afternoon, she stopped in the middle of another wretched tongue-twister, scarlet to the ears and gripping her book in her hands. Reciting this nonsense in the middle of the busy office made her feel so dreadfully conspicuous, she wanted to jump out the window.

"Yes, my lady," said Justenin, without so much as the flicker of an eyelash. "The atmosphere of this office is the nearest you might come to the conditions of a social event in the capital. If you can speak confidently here, you will do well enough at a banquet."

"But we talk all the time at supper, and no one complains," she said plaintively. It was the nearest she had come to attempting to argue her way out of a lesson, but even the occasional curious glances of the nearby secretaries made her feel like she couldn't breathe.

"That is because we are taking great pains to attempt to hear you, Your Grace," Justenin replied. "They will not exert themselves, in Segoile. They will nod and smile, and then ignore you."

Ophele was silent.

"It's that bad?" she asked reluctantly.

"Yes, my lady." He met her eyes straight on. "It is."

Well, she could not argue once she understood why she was doing this. But it didn't make her feel less foolish when she was practicing alone in her bedchamber, looking at herself in the mirror as she read and seeing nothing but a squeaking little mouse.

"What under the stars are you doing, wife?" asked Remin from the door.

"Nothing," she said automatically, and then reconsidered. All the cats were well out of their bags now, and she thought for once she might tell him the truth about her troubles. “Oratory,” she confessed, showing him her book. He must have stopped by the baths on his way home; he was scrubbed and cleanshaven. “Justenin said I must practice.”

“Reciting?” he asked, holding out a hand for her book and skimming the page. “Oh, I remember these. Theophilus Thistler, the thistle sifter, in sifting a sieve of unsifted thistles, thrust three thousand...”

He said the whole thing in a single breath without stumbling once. Witchcraft.

“You know these?” she asked indignantly. Really, it felt almost unfair that he was a giant hero knight *and* he could do tongue twisters.

“Mmm-hmm. Most lordlings do them to practice their speaking, projecting and enunciating and so on. But for knights, we want to be heard loud and clear across a battlefield. It’s bad when soldiers mishear their orders,” he said, sitting down to take off his boots. “What’s the trouble, little owl?”

“I don’t know,” she said reluctantly. “Justenin says I need to practice being louder, but saying these things in front of someone else...”

“Tell me one.”

“Do drop in at the Dewdrop Inn...” The second he looked at her, she felt the heat flush her face. “...but d-don’t drop in during the dewdrop drought—”

Her voice wobbled, faded, and died, and Ophele bit her tongue, furious with herself. Why was this so hard? She had made a speech for Remin’s birthday in front of half the town, though admittedly there had been a quantity of honey mead to soften the edges. It was completely irrational. There was nothing to be afraid of, why couldn’t she *stop* it?

“Huber used to get nervous, when he had to talk in front of people,” Remin said, holding out a hand to draw her to him. “The old man told him to pretend everyone was naked.”

“No,” she said instantly.

"It's not what you want to picture when you're trying to talk a lot of soldiers into a charge," he conceded, as Ophele's imagination was briefly arrested by this image. "Come here and read them with me, slower. Which one is it?"

"This one." Ophele allowed him to pull her between his knees, his arm around her waist and his chin resting comfortably on her shoulder. "Do drop in at the Dewdrop Inn..."

It was better. Of course it was better, how could it not be? Remin's voice rolled forth strong and steady, measuring a careful pace as they went from one absurd phrase to the next.

"A little louder, wife," he said, with a squeeze. "Once upon a barren moor, there dwelt a bear and dwelt a boar..."

"Lesser leather never weathered wetter weather..."

That one was hard; she stumbled, and saw the flash of his teeth as he grinned and said it again, slowing the pace by half a beat.

"There was a young fisher named Fischer..."

It was like a game, trying to match him. Gradually, he turned her so she was facing him, and sometimes he paused to let her lead, alternating lines with her, funny rhyming lines, nonsensical ones, and a few limericks that were quite clever. His fingers slid lightly up her spine.

"Some shun sunshine..." His black eyes were very warm, and Ophele realized she was watching the motions of his mouth, forming those tricky syllables. Her eyes lifted to his as his head bent nearer, and his lips tickled hers. "Do you shun sunshine?"

Ophele lifted her hand to cover his teasing lips.

"Your Grace, I am *reciting,"* she said, exactly as Wen would have done, and Remin burst out laughing. But she did let him kiss her, a naughty smile curving her lips.

"Pretend you're reading with me, next time you recite for Juste," he said, tugging her onto his knee. "That's what Victorin did with Huber. They used to recite together as fast as they could go, to see who'd stumble first. It seemed to help."

"It makes me feel like everyone's going to turn and stare, when I'm reciting," she admitted. "It's a silly thing to be afraid of."

His arms squeezed her.

"Everyone's afraid of something."

"Even you?" she asked, a little plaintively.

"Of course." He turned her around to go to work on the laces of her gown. "I never much liked heights."

"But you're *tall.*"

"What, so you think I should be used to it?" he asked, pushing her backward over his knee, and set about doing the things that would make them very late for supper.

It wasn't the first time he had confessed to being afraid of something, and she knew it must be true, on an intellectual level. He was human, mortal, and fallible in all the ways a man might be fallible. But as a practical exercise, what could possibly scare him? Ophele had seen him unhappy, she had seen him angry, but her imagination could not conjure a Remin that experienced the sort of suffocating, red-faced fear she felt every time Justenin asked her to recite. It was an equation for which she lacked the necessary variables.

With the colder weather, her rides with Remin around the valley moved to the afternoons, and only if it was not too bitter. December brought their first dusting of snow and Ophele's first riding gown, a heavy satin-lined wool the color of moss with rusty silk and white lace as accents. Topaz studded her neckline, and the approval in Remin's eyes when she emerged from her dressing room was everything she had hoped.

"You like it?" she asked, revolving when he made a circling motion with his fingers. "It is in the new Andelin style."

"It's comfortable?" he asked, pleased. "It...fits you exceedingly well, wife."

His gaze was lingering on her neckline, where the curve of her breasts peeked between panels of modest lace. Lady Verr had explained that such artful concealment neatly straddled the line between good taste and appealing to one's husband.

"It's comfortable, and so warm. It's meant to be a riding gown," she hinted. Ophele was dying to get out of the manor for a few hours.

In Aldeburke, there was rarely more than two or three inches of snow on the ground at a time, so it was something, to see all the fields and forest buried under the white stuff, and deeply enough that only the tallest grass could be seen.

"When will we see a real blizzard?" she asked as they rode together toward the market, which looked positively picturesque with the snow coating the scrolling black iron of the lampposts. Her breath puffed white and her cheeks stung with cold, but in her new gown and mink cloak, she felt warm and graceful and maybe even a little bit pretty.

"Any day now," Remin replied, with a glance at the lowering gray sky. "Last year we were already buried by now, and we stayed that way 'til March. If we'd arrived a week or two earlier, I would've had to carry you to the cottage."

"I wish I could have seen it." She gave Brambles a little prod with her heels as the road widened, to draw abreast with Remin. "I suppose once it does, there won't be much wo—"

Underneath her, Brambles gave a sudden lurch as his hooves slipped, and just like that, the saddle vanished under her and Ophele was falling backward with an undignified squawk of surprise. The snow was not deep enough to provide any sort of cushion. She hit the cobblestones and her breath burst from her lungs in a gasp and she only vaguely heard the sudden clatter of surprised hooves and the thud as Remin dismounted.

"Ophele!"

"I'm all right," she said automatically, or tried to say, because she was winded and wasn't *entirely* sure whether this was true. She'd taken bad falls out of trees in Aldeburke and knocked the wind out of herself, so she knew this sickening, breathless feeling would pass. But Remin knew only that she had fallen, and skidded to the ground beside her, his big hands moving to her head. His face was absolutely white.

"Don't move," he said, yanking his gloves off. "Look at me, let me see your eyes. Did you hit your head?"

"Don't—think so," she gasped. Honestly, between her hair and hood, that had been fairly well cushioned. "I'm all right."

"Just...stay still," he instructed, and Ophele was shocked to see his hands were shaking as he inspected her, prodding gently at her head, her neck, and then down her sides. His black eyes were very wide. Obediently, she lay still. She needed to get her breath back anyway.

"I'm really, not hurt," she managed, as her lungs gradually resumed normal operations. "Remin, I'm fine. I think my dress, and my cloak, helped. And we weren't going that fast at all."

"I should have gotten you a proper sidesaddle." He sat down, scrubbing his hand over his jaw. His face was set in hard, forbidding lines, so rigid it seemed those sharp edges should crack. "Let me see you move your hands and feet, wife."

Obligingly, she moved them. She agreed there was no pain in her head or neck or anywhere else, and was allowed to sit up. There was a minor scare when Remin found blood on the back of her ear where one of her hairpins had jabbed her, but it didn't hurt and Ophele stood by herself while Remin went to fetch the horses, though he still insisted on carrying her upstairs when they got home, and ordered Sim off to fetch Genon at a run.

"I am fine," Ophele protested again as he laid her on the bed, as carefully as if she were made of glass. All this fuss was beginning to be embarrassing. "I promise."

"Let's just have Gen look at you, to make sure," he said, patting her hand as if *she* was the one who needed reassuring. Ophele's eyes narrowed as she watched him move about the bedchamber, fetching her water, removing her slippers, and stoking up the fire, all of which did not really need doing and especially did not need doing by *him*. Experimentally, she wiggled her toes. Might she be more hurt than she knew? Remin knew more of these things. Maybe it was something to fuss over, falling off a horse.

But no; she had taken enough knocks in her life to know whether she was really hurt or not, and as Remin himself noted, she did have a good deal of sense. Ophele watched as Remin paused at the washstand with his back to her, his big hands gripping the table there, his shoulders moving as he drew a long, deep breath.

"Remin," she said, and tried to inject a little uncertainty into her voice. "Is it really so bad, falling off a horse? I don't feel hurt, but..."

"No," he said immediately, and came over to take her hand. "It's not. It's probably just as you said, wife, we weren't going that fast..."

Ophele nodded, her eyes fixed on his face as she listened to him reassure her. It seemed she had discovered at least one possible variable, in the equation of Remin's fear.

* * *

"...and then, when he was five, it started to be a light yellowy-green," continued Mistress Tregue, lady of the Tresingale public house. Helpfully, she tilted back the head of her offspring so that Genon Hengest might have a better view of the boy's snotty nose.

"I see," he said politely.

Oh, for the days of a straightforward case of gangrene.

When a second herbalist had arrived in the valley, Genon had mostly been worried about some quack peddling a lot of trashy cure-alls, robbing Remin's folk blind and probably creating a wave of new patients for Genon himself. Herbs and tonics were serious business, and not meant to be handed out for every sneeze or fart.

And then, once it seemed Dagober Brestle wasn't going to kill anyone, Genon had worried that the valley's inhabitants might actually prefer the new man. Brestle looked like an herbalist straight out of a woodcutting, after all: a fortyish family man with a broad, kindly face and a woodsy air about him, and spectacles that Genon was *positive* he did not need.

Whereas Genon Hengest was a twisted old gargoyle with a crooked shoulder and half a face.

More than thirty years had passed since a dousing with boiling oil had left him half-bald and one-eyed, his flesh melted into pink-silver runnels and his left shoulder permanently crabbed. Genon knew how other people saw him. It was a sad truth that when a lot of folk saw a burned man, they assumed he must have done something to deserve it. A world where an innocent man could be burned so horribly was a terrible, frightening place.

But despite the catastrophe that had forever changed the course of his life, Genon knew he had been luckier than he deserved.

Lucky that he had found a healer in Ereguil with experience in burns, who preserved his life and the motion of his body. Lucky that Duke Ereguil had introduced him to Remin. Lucky that when the summons came to march to war, Genon hadn't been off another errand, though he had already packed his bags and saddled his horse. And it was only by the blessings of the stars that Remin was still alive after so many stabbings, shootings, and poisonings, including a crossbow bolt that had been smeared with some mysterious substance that began to rot his flesh *the moment it entered*. By the time they got Remin to Genon's tent, he'd had to cut away almost a pound of flesh above the young man's right hip.

To be sure, Genon was the one who had done the cutting and cauterizing, but Remin had survived something that would've killed any other man three times over.

You couldn't watch a man endure that and not admire him.

And so, like so many others, Genon had elected to stay with Remin when the war was over, knowing that he was not so much skilled in his healing as *incredibly* fortunate in his most famous patient. If Remin had ever called for another healer, Genon would have bowed his head and stepped aside.

He never had. And a surprising number of people were willing to have a gargoyle for a healer so long as that man also served His Grace, the Duke of Andelin.

"Do you find it's especially bad in certain places, or certain times of year?" he asked Mistress Tregue, who had had him in three times to inspect the boy's snot and was a bit of a hypochondriac besides. Genon suspected the trouble was an imbalance of air, specifically the amount of dust in it. Mistress Tregue was of the opinion that her middle son's nose was about to fall off.

It was the first time Genon had considered a referral to Brestle.

"He does sneeze a lot more after he's been to the woodpile," the mistress began, and the doors of the tavern burst open on a wild-eyed Sim, one of the footmen from the manor.

"Mr. Hengest, sir!" he gasped, sweating. "His Grace says you must come up to the house, the lady's had a fall off her horse and he said to fetch you double quick!"

"Did you see her yourself?" Genon asked, rising at once and gathering his things.

"Aye, His Grace was carrying her up the stairs."

"Any broken bones or blood you could see?"

"Well...no sir," Sim admitted.

"Was she speaking clearly?"

"Yes, sir."

"Good." This was not so much for his own benefit as to curb the valley's gossips, particularly the avid-eyed Mistress Tregue, who would've had the duchess on her deathbed by sundown and alarmed the whole town if Genon didn't squash it quick. "She's a sturdy lady, our duchess, for all her size. Mistress Tregue, excuse me. Lead the way, boy."

This was both reassuring and true. Genon repeated it to himself as he trotted after the boy to the manor, cursing himself for leaving his horse at the infirmary. Genon had known Ophele from the day she arrived in the valley and had seen her take a tumble or two with his own eyes, never mind the man's work she had done at the wall. Most people tended to put it down to her cleverness, to manage such hard work so well, but Genon knew how surprisingly tough she was. There weren't many women who could've lasted so long.

His first glimpse of Remin and Ophele only confirmed it. The lord was visibly shaken, but Ophele was propped up against her pillows with an air of patience that told Genon at a glance where the real trouble was.

"Well, well, my lady, let me have a look at you," he said briskly, straightening up and trying to catch his breath. That damned hill outside the manor and then a lot of stairs at the top of it, and Genon was not in his fifties anymore.

"Nothing hurts," the duchess said, turning her head at the pressure of Genon's fingers. She was dressed in a modest linen chemise that tied at the back, and slid out of bed so he could see her stand, touch her toes, and otherwise demonstrate that there wasn't a thing wrong with her.

"Nice, clear eyes," he said approvingly, making her follow his finger with them after she had done these minor calisthenics. And though it was awkward to be examining a lady, a duchess, and most importantly, Remin's wife, Genon tried not to let it show. Letting himself be embarrassed would only embarrass her, and she needed to trust her physician.

"It was a fall from a horse onto cobblestones," Remin said severely, watching through narrowed eyes as Genon inspected each vertebra.

"It never hurts to be careful," Genon agreed. "But I see no injury. A good night's rest and you'll be fit as ever tomorrow, my lady."

"Fit for...everything?" Remin sat down in the chair beside the bed, his big hand covering hers on the blanket. The back of his neck reddened.

"Aye, so long as there's no pain," Genon agreed, hiding his amusement.

"And it wouldn't do anything to...harm a baby, if there was one?" Ophele asked, blushing furiously. "Falling?"

"No," Genon asked, after an astonished moment. "My lady, do you suspect you are with child?"

"No. Well..." She glanced between them guiltily. Remin looked as if someone had hit him in the face with a brick. "I don't know. How would I...know?"

"It is harder to tell, as you still have not bled," Genon said slowly. "Have you been sick in the mornings? Sensitive to smells?"

"No." Her eyes widened. "Will I?"

"Those are the usual signs of pregnancy, though not everyone has them," Genon replied, and went to get a chair. He had a sudden, dreadful suspicion, and he wanted to be sitting down for this conversation.

"We cannot be completely sure until the babe begins to show," he said, blunt. "But absent the usual signs—no monthly bleeding, sickness, the obvious physical changes—then we can only assume you are not. My lady, forgive me, but...you do know how you *become* pregnant, don't you?"

"I...what Remin is...doing?" She dropped her eyes. "Not...specifically."

Merciful stars.

This possibility had never occurred to him. It was a tricky business, physicking a young lady when all of Genon's training and experience was with men in general and soldiers, specifically. But this was the most important duty of a lord and his wife, above all others: the getting of an heir to secure the succession. Everyone in the valley would breathe a sigh of relief once this all-important child was born, and ideally a spare afterward, just in case.

But given the many deficiencies in the duchess's education, it should not be surprising that the lady didn't know how it was...done.

"...ever told you?" Remin was asking, with a visible effort to pull himself back together. His Grace was having a chaotic day.

"No," she said, her fingers plucking at the blankets.

"I think it would be best if you discussed it together," Genon suggested. Really, it only added impetus to something he should've done long ago. "Forgive me," he said, puffing out a breath. "I suppose I ought to say now that this is not my area of expertise. If either of you have a fever, or stars forbid you break something, then I'm your man. But you need a proper healer, my lady, and a midwife too, sooner or later. I've delivered two babes in my life, and I don't fancy trialing a third one with the heir of House Andelin."

From the stricken looks on their faces, it was clear that this had not occurred to them, either.

"The sooner you start looking, the better," he said firmly. "And not just for your wife, Rem. This isn't a military camp anymore. You need real healers, as know how to treat women and children. I'm just a camp surgeon."

"I need someone I can *trust,*" Remin countered immediately, scowling, and Genon gave him a scarred, snarling smile. He knew very well that the Tower was still refusing any support to House Andelin, and their foolishness had been Genon's very great gain.

"I know you do," he replied gruffly. "I'll speak to Juste and Duke Ereguil, to see if we can find a midwife. And I'll look over their shoulders, if you like. Never too old to learn, and I can at least tell if they're like to kill you."

"Do that," said Remin, so flat that it made Genon wince. This was exactly what Remin would be afraid of. Though the Empire was one of the more enlightened places in the world regarding sex and childbearing, it was still a risky business, even without the chance of someone trying to sabotage it.

"I'll see if I can't make you some herbs and tonics, my lady, to tone you up and help regulate your cycles," Gen said reassuringly. "I'll see Wen gets them. Easiest to add them to your food each day, and they will do no harm to His Grace if he takes a bite."

"All right," Ophele agreed, glancing at Remin for approval.

"As long as no one but you and Wen handles them," Remin said, grim.

"I will make certain of it." Genon gave himself a shake. They both had faces like a gray winter day, and while they had reason to worry, it was no good going into this with fear. "I'm as eager as anyone else to meet the new little lord of the Andelin," he added heartily. "It's meant to be a blessed thing, the begetting of babes. There's naught to be ashamed or afraid of. I hope you'll talk about it together frankly, and then find joy in the begetting. If you've questions, I'll do my best to answer them."

The original reason for his visit had been entirely forgotten, and Genon was glad. There wasn't a thing wrong with Her Grace that a long talk with Rem wouldn't cure. Heaving himself to his feet, Gen bid them good afternoon, and promised to tell Juste that supper would need fetching.

"Thank you, Gen," said Remin, walking him down the stairs to show him out. His voice lowered. "About the...begetting. It's really all right?"

"So long as the lady is in no pain, then there's no reason to wait." Genon belted his herbman's jacket on at the door with a waft of spicy scent.

"I mean...it's usually three or four times a day," Remin admitted, with a worried glance at the ceiling. "Is that normal?"

"Ah. Well. Perhaps," said Genon, after a moment's internal consternation. It was fortunate that the duchess was a sturdy little thing. "I might...add some things to her diet. Make sure your lady feels comfortable to tell you if she's too tired or...sore, but so long as you both are enjoying it..."

He shrugged his functional shoulder and bit his tongue ferociously. They really did need a proper healer. But as a soldier and a man, his first impulse was to congratulate the young lord on his stamina. And maybe light some incense for the lady.

"Let her guide you as to how much is too much," he advised, and clapped his hat on his head. He kept the laugh buttoned in until he was well down the hill.

Blessed be the begetting, indeed.

* * *

"We brought back seven," said Justenin, extracting the remaining devil quills from their protective leather case. "We have used three for our own experiments, testing them with various implements, exposing them to cold, heat, water, fire..."

The stack of paper at his elbow detailed these experiments and their results, along with speculations from the Duchess of Andelin on their implications, carefully copied by a scribe. Juste had been tempted to furnish the scholars with the original, just to drive his point home, but that was a little unsubtle for his taste.

"Thank you," said Master Forgess. He did not reach to touch the quills with his bare hands. "We have heard rumors already. There were two children that actually saw the creature?"

"Glimpsed it, in the dark. They have been gently questioned," Juste added, flipping to the section of the document that detailed these eyewitness accounts. "But we are waiting for a fuller tale until they are settled. They are only children, and it upsets them to speak of such things."

"Of course," murmured Master Forgess, skimming the pages. The florid Master of the Library of Beasts had yet to learn patience or the management of his expressions; behind his spectacles, his eyes skimmed barely a full paragraph before they narrowed, and his lips tightened.

Juste smiled inside.

"You destroyed the other quills in your experiments?" Forgess grunted.

"Necessary sacrifices. You may do as you wish with these two," Juste added, sealing them in a small leather pouch. "But I will caution you not to handle them directly. Everyone who touches a quill with his bare skin has developed a rash afterward, which I am told is itchy and painful, and takes about a week to heal. And once a quill is embedded in flesh, it cannot be extracted. It did not react to dead flesh, but if it even lightly punctures the flesh of a living creature, it cannot be withdrawn. It...*burrows*. We are not sure whether it was poison or whether the quill reached something vital, but it killed the animal."

Juste had sacrificed a haunch of pork and an elderly goat in that experiment. The goat had taken four days to die.

"The devils are aptly named," Master Forgess grumbled, taking the pouch in gingerly fingers. "Her Grace wrote this? She assisted with these...experiments?"

"She did," Juste confirmed. Though she had not handled the goat. She was too soft-hearted for that work, and His Grace would be furious if she were exposed to any potential poison or contagion. "I have found her a subtle and thorough thinker."

Maybe it was petty, to keep jabbing at them. Forgess might be impatient and intemperate, but in time he would understand Juste's subtle rebuke, issued in the language of the Tower of Scholars: *this is the work of* my *student.*

They did not fully realize the opportunity they had missed, and Juste hugged the secret to himself with satisfaction. While he had never gone to the Tower, he had lived with many scholars and mystics after the slaughter of his family, and understood how they thought. Excellent teachers were much-admired and highly sought after, but what those masters prized beyond rubies was a gifted student. A student's fame reflected on their master, and this most promising pupil belonged to Juste.

He was going to have words with the Duke and Duchess Andelin about that subject tonight, as a matter of fact.

Most often, Their Graces dined in the cookhouse, but that evening Juste went to pick up their supper from Wen directly. The irascible cook was loading up the hamper, a massive wicker basket lined with wool and linen batting to keep the food warm on the trip to the manor.

"Give me a minute, give me a minute," Wen barked when Juste appeared, turning to stump down the single enormous counter in the long, narrow kitchen. "And don't take your eyes off that hamper while me back's turned. Gen's asked me to add a bit of this and that to Her Grace's diet. See that she eats her pudding."

"Genon told you that himself?" Juste asked sharply, as Wen produced a small, sealed crock from a locked cupboard.

"Aye, what d'ye take me for?" Wen snorted. "Handed me the herbs and syrup himself, enough for one pudding. No one else got within six feet of it."

"Be sure no one does," Juste replied. "There are many varieties of mischief."

"Not in this kitchen." Wen snorted, settling the crock in the center of the hamper. He did not like anyone in the valley to know it, but Wen was the son of a cook of some fame, and when disturbed, he had a tendency to *plate* things in attractive ways, which included the arrangement of crockery. "You're expecting someone to tamper with Her Grace's food?"

"It's a possibility. Inform me if there are any further adjustments to her diet," Juste said, hefting the basket, and departed. It was not a negligible burden.

Their Graces were occupied when he arrived at the manor. Sighing, Juste set the basket on the floor of the grand entry. Emi was scrubbing the evening mud from the stairs, Sim was bringing enough firewood to heat the house overnight, and the builders were wrapping up the day's work, sweeping away sawdust and plaster. So many people occupied with so many different tasks, and Juste's sharp eye noted all of them, alert to both shoddy work and new faces. He was the steward of Remin's house in all ways.

The work went well. The grand entry was well on its way to being grand, and the whole second floor had been framed out, with plasterers hard at work in the west wing of the second floor. Soon Juste, Miche, and Lady Verr would occupy their own suites there, the luxurious chambers of high-ranking members of the household. Juste had spent a few hours with Master Didion a few days ago, choosing his furnishings and selecting basic items for the delinquent Miche. By the new year, work would shift to the first floor.

Which meant they would have to find a new home for the Benkki Desan tree that currently occupied a sunny nook overlooking the courtyard. Turning that way, Juste found a pair of dark violet eyes peeping at him through the branches, framed with tiny white and purple flowers.

"Noble lord," said Madam Imari Sanai.

"Madam," Juste replied politely. "Well met. His Grace's gift flourishes in your care."

"It has come to a good spot," she agreed, in the liquid syllables of Benkki Desa. They had exchanged pleasantries several times before.

"It was a generous gift. I must thank you again, on his behalf." Juste inclined his head. "Though I still wonder why all of you chose to come to this spot, in all the world. Was it so great an opportunity?"

"The river here is wide and wild." Madam Sanai clipped away a branch.

"The greatest river in the Empire," Juste agreed, his eyes narrowing. "But all the great cities of Benkki Desa are built upon the river, are they not?"

"The Oboro-sati," she replied, nodding. "The river of all rivers, which flows straight from the sea to the great western ocean. Yet it is slow and sleepy, and I had never seen a river so wild. Would you not go and see such a wonder?"

"I have seen enough wonders in my life," Juste replied, interested enough to allow the evasion, and passed an agreeable time learning about her homeland, as her long fingers snipped buds from the tree, making room for others to grow. Benkki Desans called themselves the People of Twilight, for they were last born to the world, and moved through time in their own rhythm.

It was the sort of small talk that Ophele would have to learn before her departure to the capital, and Juste had to own it could be pleasant, though he was not a man that greatly enjoyed society. He nearly forgot his original purpose until the door to the solar opened upstairs.

"Please excuse me," he said, dipping his head again and snatching up the hamper.

He had been looking forward to this meeting.

The inspiration had burst upon him a few days before, a solution to the problem he had been turning over in his mind ever since Remin had come to him about Ophele's education. There was no such thing as a useless person. Juste's delight had always been in finding their *best* use, like slotting a perfect piece into the machine of the world. And all it had taken was a few words from Sousten Didion to make this solution strike him like a bolt of lightning.

"My lord, my lady," Juste said as he entered the solar. "Wen sends his compliments and hopes you will enjoy your meal. My lady, there is a pudding for you in particular."

"Thank you for fetching it." Remin rose, digging into the hamper to distribute its contents. It was not the place of a lord to serve food to his guests, but Juste was beginning to despair of ever making Remin a lord in the mode of the empire.

He would be content with shaping the lady instead.

"I have been considering Her Grace for much of the last week," he said when the meal was over and Ophele was serving tea. Her eyes lifted, instantly anxious, and Juste could imagine exactly what was going through her head: she would assume this was a test and she had failed it, and her greatest fear was failing Remin.

Justenin had learned the most potent lever that moved this lady.

"On all subjects," he clarified. "And I believe it is prudent that we accept now that absent many years of training, she is unlikely to ever become a Rose of Segoile."

The lamplight glowed on Ophele's face, illuminating the swift hurt in her eyes, though he only had an instant to glimpse it. The lady was very, very good at concealing herself. Juste observed it as it happened, a...shrinking, a withdrawal, a subtle alteration in her posture that made him feel as if she might disappear altogether the moment he took his eyes from her. And especially when she was seated beside the Duke of Andelin, who couldn't hide the enormous force of his presence if he tried.

Perfect.

"Explain," said His Grace, his mouth tightening in a hard line of displeasure.

"It is not merely a question of learning manners and conventions," said Juste. "A Rose of Segoile has *presence.* Some women naturally have that vitality, that commanding air, while others must learn it. In four months, Her Grace may learn graceful speech, and may even learn to offer it at an audible volume. But the confident bearing of a Rose of Segoile, much less the ready wit and sharp tongue of a lioness like Lady Verr—no. Not if we had ten years."

"Ready wit?" Remin echoed, his face darkening. "There are none that could match—"

"There is a difference between quick wit and intelligence, my lord," Justenin interrupted. It was time to put Ophele out of her misery. "My lady," he said, shifting his attention to her. "Has anyone assisted you with your lessons?"

She shook her head, mute and unhappy.

"And you had no instruction at Aldeburke at all?"

"No."

"Your Grace, you are very...*very* intelligent," Justenin informed her. "You may even be a genius. I don't think there is anything you could not learn, and more quickly than anyone else I have ever met or heard of. In a few months, in mathematics in particular, you will exceed my own abilities. You might have been wanting teachers all your life, but the masters of the Tower would tear out their beards if they knew there was such a student."

And in the silence that followed, it was obvious that she had no idea what that meant.

Remin did. The anger faded from his face and left only a mingling of pride and sorrow as he met Juste's eyes, because this was exactly the problem. Some opportunities, once lost, could never come again. If Ophele had been raised properly, she might have been a terror of society, perhaps capable of overturning it altogether if she wanted. But she was never going to be what she could have been.

"That's...good," she said, looking uncertainly between the two men. "But if I can learn anything, why can't I learn—"

"Something altogether different," Juste said firmly. "It would be convenient if you could be molded into a fashionable lady of society, but we would be foolish to waste time pursuing it at the expense of other talents. None of us have ever aspired to be creatures of the capital; why should we expect it of you? No. We will embrace it."

It was rare for Juste to speak with such fervor, but this prospect filled him with excitement.

"Let the Roses flaunt their thorns." He leaned forward, his pale eyes glinting. "You will conceal yours. What is it that Master Didion keeps calling you? The Flower of the Andelin."

He lingered over the words. Maybe this was how his own urge to create expressed itself, in the shaping of human beings into useful tools, and the duchess was exactly the sort of subtle weapon that appealed to his nature.

"But—I haven't any thorns," Ophele said, though the sudden blaze of color in her cheeks betrayed her excitement.

"You do," Juste said firmly. "You watch, you listen, you remember, and you think thoroughly about what you see. It will be more difficult for you in Segoile. There will be many distractions. But we are not going to teach you merely to engage in frivolous conversation. You will learn to direct conversation, gather useful information, and deflect attention away from yourself."

"You can do that," Remin said, looking down at her with approval. "Stars, wife, you do that to me all the time."

"Not so much anymore," she said apologetically.

"No," he agreed, his hand covering hers.

"It means you will need to learn to think more strategically, my lady," Juste continued. "Much of the work of the Roses of Segoile is in building alliances. Has Lady Verr begun to explain this art to you?"

"I don't...think so," she said slowly.

"She will begin tomorrow. That will be difficult for you," he acknowledged. "It takes a certain shamelessness, and many of the skills of society you lack. But we can use that, too. It is known that you are the Exile Princess. A secret princess. Segoile has no mercy for those that transgress its codes, but we will make it part of your mystique. They will come to you *because* of it."

"You mean you want to make a show of me," she replied, a little sadly. "And lower their expectations."

"Yes. We will see who comes, and you will listen to everything they have to say. You will encourage them to speak," he said pointedly. "Ask questions. Let them talk all they like."

"I can do that." She looked up at Remin. "That would help, wouldn't it?"

"I hope you will not be disappointed if you never have the chance," he told her. "I don't mean to linger in the city, if we can avoid it. But if we must, I like this course better. It would please me to cultivate our own breed of women in the valley."

"We are only telling the truth," Juste said, appreciating every nuance of this plan. It was also a slap in the face to the folk of the capital, but few would have the wit to see it. "You are the unworldly princess who has never seen a city. A lady who grew up a prisoner, and has never spoken to more than a dozen people in her life. That is what they really want to see. The lady with no thorns at all."

It was perfect. It matched every story they would be telling about her, the songs they would soon be singing, the narrative he was painstakingly building. The debut of the Duchess of Andelin would be a beautiful and subtle trap.

Justenin was eager to begin this work.

"Please, my lady," he concluded, with a small smile. "I beg you: look harmless."

* * *

There were a number of unsettling people in Tresingale. Until this morning, Mionet had never counted Sir Justenin among them.

He *looked* unassuming, seated at the rough table in the solar and quietly discussing some problem of geometry with Duchess Andelin. Blond, lean, and bespectacled, the only evidence of his violent trade was the scar that bisected his right eyebrow, seemingly contradicted by his soft, gentle voice.

But when he cast his pale eyes in Mionet's direction, it sent a shiver up her spine.

"Today I will be your pupil as well, my lady," he said, once the duchess had set her books aside. "We are adjusting Her Grace's education somewhat. I believe a more strategic approach will be beneficial."

"Is that so?" Mionet asked politely, though she did not expect any useful reply. Nothing beyond the barest essentials had been provided to her, though she had managed to deduce a great deal, between Duchess Andelin's shamefaced confession and her many nervous habits.

It was an incident with the maids that had really told Mionet everything she needed to know. A single moment months before when Peri had dropped a hairpin, reached quickly to catch it, and Duchess Andelin had...well, frankly, she had *cowered.* Fortunately, Peri had not noticed.

But Mionet had.

That was a weakness. That was a potent weapon, for a subtle woman. But it was best to minimize such incidents, at present; it was bad for the servants to know such a thing about their mistress, and Duchess Andelin would never be amenable to Mionet's overtures if she was constantly anxious and fearful. All it had taken was Mionet instructing the maids to look less like maids, and the duchess had relaxed as if by magic.

There was a great deal of information to be gleaned from that.

"...that's the sort of thing I would like to know," Sir Justenin was saying, bringing her back to the present with a jolt. Mionet had been listening with half an ear, absorbing information and making appropriate responses, calculating all the while. "A focus on the tactics of a Rose of Segoile. I expect you will be able to assist us most ably, Lady Verr."

"I am not entirely sure what you mean," she said, stalling.

"The business of the great ladies of society. Identifying key players, approaching them, and negotiating with them," he replied, with cool amusement. "I am told you were a formidable player of the game, my lady."

Were.

He knew. He absolutely knew.

Mionet had wondered, when she first arrived, whether Duke or Duchess Ereguil might have divulged her secrets. It had taken very little time to ascertain they had not, for Duke and Duchess Andelin were the most unsubtle creatures alive. But Sir Justenin knew, and was letting her *know* that he knew.

She lifted her chin.

"The first part will be difficult, from four hundred miles away," she observed. "It takes many years to learn who is who in society, and we have no *Gazette* or *Society Annual* here."

"But you know them."

"Of course."

"Then I would like you to tell Her Grace about them, in as great detail as possible," he instructed, which was so ludicrous that Mionet's jaw almost dropped.

"What good would that do, to hear stories of people she has never met? I beg your pardon, my lady," she added, turning to Duchess Andelin, who was listening with quiet interest. "I am perfectly willing, of course. But I get rather lost among the names myself sometimes, and I have met them."

"Her Grace will remember, I assure you." Sir Justenin gave a very small smile. "Please take care to discuss key figures daily. For now, it is the second and third steps of the process that must concern us."

Mionet's pleasant expression betrayed nothing. But inside, she was seething. This was the *last* thing she wanted to confide to Duchess Andelin, who was the target of exactly this process. Sir Justenin was making her confess it *and* explain in detail exactly how Mionet meant to do it.

"My, you put a rather cold cast upon it," she said, laughing lightly. "In Segoile, we would say that we were courting. Wooing friends is not so different from wooing a lover. You must discover the other party's interests and then share them together, to become better friends. There was one lady I knew, Lady Mailleur, who greatly enjoyed arranging flowers. When I sought her acquaintance, I invited her to a certain greenhouse I knew with many rare and beautiful flowers. It was quite a pleasant afternoon."

Pausing, Mionet looked at Sir Justenin apologetically, an intentional flourish of her beauty and innocent gray eyes.

"I am afraid it is no great strategy," she said, with a self-deprecating smile. "I imagine men find companions in much the same fashion."

Sir Justenin smiled back gently and uncorked the inkpot at his elbow.

"How did you discover Lady Mailleur's interest in gardening?" he asked, dipping his quill into the inkpot.

"We spoke about it at a banquet," she replied, watching uneasily as he began to write.

"Did she offer the information, or did you solicit it?" His spectacles flashed as he looked up at her.

"I believe...I confided several interests of my own first," she said.

"Often, if you give a little information, people will offer information in return," Sir Justenin explained to Duchess Andelin, and Mionet started. She had almost forgotten the lady was there. Duchess Andelin nodded solemnly and turned her large golden eyes back to Mionet.

It was a very uncomfortable conversation. Sir Justenin walked her through a dozen such courtships, taking notes all the way, and though Mionet was careful to discuss the most blameless of her relationships, it still felt like she was providing evidence that would be presented at her trial. And throughout the whole unsettling interview, Duchess Andelin was silently listening, thinking who knew what.

"I will leave you to your regular lessons. Her Grace must continue to learn a noblewoman's bearing," Sir Justenin said finally, gathering up his papers. "Please continue as you have been. It is important, as Lady Verr says, to know who is who in the city," he added for Duchess Andelin's benefit. "Lady Verr, I will ask you to be our *Society Annual* for the time being, if you please."

And then he departed, and Mionet drew a quiet breath to compose herself. Try as she might, she couldn't imagine what that could have been about.

"I am sorry for that," Duchess Andelin said, rising to put on the kettle. "I think I see what he means now, but I am sure that was very unpleasant. Like telling tales on your friends."

"Men always believe women are more conniving than we are," Mionet laughed, trying to recover. It would be good if Duchess Andelin framed it in those terms. "Sometimes I wonder if it is a test of heaven, to make us think we speak the same language."

"It was very interesting," the lady replied, frowning at her train as she attempted to sit. The first order of Tiffen's promised gowns had arrived, and today's gown was very much of the Segoile mode, apple-green and veined with golden embroidery that made the lady look like a jewel. It was also heavy, cumbersome, and too chilly to be worn out of doors, but those were secondary considerations. She would have been fit for the finest salon in the capital.

"Well, Segoile is quite a diverting place," Mionet replied, relaxing. "I know you are not pleased to be going, my lady, and I'm sure I was quite nervous, on my first visit. But it would be a shame if you let it spoil your visit entirely. There are so many wonderful things to see and delightful people to meet."

"Who should I meet first?" Duchess Andelin asked, and listened as Mionet told her about Countess Josune Desettier, originally of Noreven, a fascinating woman who had married Count Desettier. Mionet was rather proud of this acquaintance; it was nicely innocuous even if Sir Justenin should hear about it, and it had been the patient work of three solid years, earning an invitation to Countess Desettier's salon.

"Why would you choose to introduce her to me?" Duchess Andelin wanted to know.

"Well, because I have heard you on several occasions express an interest in magic, my lady," Mionet said, leaning forward confidentially. "The countess was a practitioner in her own country, though of course she cannot use it in the Empire. Have you heard of Noreveni magic?"

"No." Duchess Andelin looked perfectly thrilled. "I mean, I know they have magic, but nothing more about it. Madam Sanai has a little magic too, but she says there's only a wisp of it in the valley. I wonder why that is."

"And that is why I would introduce you to the countess," Mionet replied, smiling. "You see it is no deep design, my lady. In Segoile, it is often a matter of matching affinities and then enjoying the results. I believe you would enjoy each other's conversation, so I would make a match of you two. It is pleasant work, is it not?"

"It is, I like that. That's much the same way you described managing a conversation," said Duchess Andelin reflectively. "Arranging the proper participants and taking care to avoid any difficult subjects."

Threading this needle was tricky. Mionet already knew *exactly* to whom she would introduce the Duchess of Andelin; it was part of the elaborate dance of capital society, expanding one's influence by using one's contacts. There would be many people who wished to approach Princess Ophele, the Duchess of Andelin, and Mionet's gamble had given her entrée no one else could match.

The trick now was to parlay this priceless contact into more tangible favors, and ideally to do it so skillfully, Duchess Andelin was none the wiser. Or even better, enjoyed it.

All of which would have been tricky enough without His Grace thundering into the manor like a sporadic rockslide.

"Wife," he announced later that morning, ducking into the door of the solar. A *proper* gentleman knocked and announced himself before entering the women's area of a house, but Duke Andelin just burst in, leaving Mionet to terminate her story mid-word.

"Your Grace." She rose and curtsied in one motion, but she needn't have bothered. His eyes were all for his wife.

"Guian says he's got another shipment, and you can have first pick of it, if you go by the shop this afternoon," said Duke Andelin. His eyes narrowed as he looked around the solar. "Where are Leonin and Davi?"

"They haven't come yet." Duchess Andelin lifted her chin as he approached for an inspection, as if she might have sustained some injury over tea. "It's all right, Justenin left only a little while ago."

"I don't want you left alone," he replied, pinching her chin between his fingers. His gaze flicked to include Mionet in the admonition. "Next time, send one of the servants to fetch them right away. And lock the door in the meantime."

"Yes, Your Grace." Mionet's curtsy concealed her rolling eyes. The duke was always unreasonable where the lady's safety was concerned, but lately it had been escalating to ludicrous levels.

"But—they said they were going to see Genon," Duchess Andelin protested. "It's really all ri—"

"I told you that you are not to be left alone. *Ever,"* he said, glowering. "Lady Verr does not constitute a guard."

"I know," the duchess answered, so meekly it set Mionet's teeth on edge. "Genon came to see me before he went to see them, so I'm sure they'll be here soon. And he said that I'm perfectly well, I told you it was just a little headache."

"It does no harm to make sure."

"I've been sitting and resting all morning," she soothed. "Lady Verr was telling me about the salons in the capital, and look, Master Tiffen sent up another gown..."

"I like the color," he said grudgingly, and Mionet went to observe her embroidery basket to give them some privacy while he grumbled about Segoile nonsense and stole a kiss. A proper Segoile nobleman would have maintained a polite distance from his wife in company, and Mionet rather resented these repeated intrusions. That message could have been delivered by anyone, but lately he had been seizing the least excuse to come and look in on his wife.

At least their murmured conversation was informative. Mionet stilled as she heard excited murmurs about someone named Miche returning; surely that must be Sir Miche of Harnost, who had been dispatched to Aldeburke on some errand. There was not a woman in Segoile who hadn't heard of him: half cautionary tales, half torrid speculation, and the women he had *actually* bedded only told wilder stories. A number of ladies of Mionet's acquaintance had schemed to seek his favor, but she was not among them. Mionet Verr had no use for the notorious lovers of the capital.

"Don't let me find you so again," the duke admonished as he was leaving, with another impressive scowl. "Lock the door, I'll go turn up Leonin and Davi."

Such a *bully!* It was hardly necessary to take such a tone with Duchess Andelin; she wouldn't stick her nose out the window if the house was on fire, if she thought it would displease him. And though none of her pique showed in her expression, for once Mionet's temper got the better of her.

"My lady, please forgive me if I overstep," she said as she went to bar the door, resisting the urge to stick a chair under the knob. "But I was married for quite some time, and I must say, I found that if I allowed certain behaviors to persist in my husband, they only grew worse."

Duchess Andelin blinked.

"You mean Remin?"

"Yes." Mionet sat down and added an aggressive spoonful of sugar to her tea. "We are hardly likely to be attacked here in broad daylight, with servants and builders all over the house and the whole hilltop crawling with people devoted to His Grace."

"Oh, I know," the lady said unexpectedly, as if she were surprised that Mionet thought otherwise. "They're not for me. The guards, I mean."

"I—beg pardon?"

"I don't mind," Duchess Andelin said, and there was a curious look on her young face, unhappy and too wise. "This is what he needs right now."

Chapter 4 – A Cheerful Busybody

"It's the same shape as the one in the other book," Ophele said from her place in Remin's arms, leaning comfortably against his bare chest as they read together by candlelight. "It just looks so familiar..."

Her eyes gleamed in the soft light, shuttling back and forth over the page to absorb the rather graphic details. Remin had had doubts about delivering such a...frank text, particularly with the illustrations, but his first attempt at explaining procreation had not been a smashing success. Ophele had listened with rapt attention to the scriptures Brother Oleare had lent them, a rather romantic description of her lower abdomen as a garden with two large flowers that blossomed every month, and Remin himself the very large bee coming to fertilize them, and then ungratefully demanded anatomical diagrams.

"It wasn't *wrong,*" Remin remarked, examining them with her. "In a metaphorical sense."

"No, but I saw the chickens in the kitchen after Azelma was done with them," Ophele replied, with a scathing glance at her own flat belly. "I *knew* there wasn't a garden in there."

Even with all his worries, she still made him laugh. Remin laid his palm on the metaphorical garden, where, if the stars granted it, a child might have been planted.

"It's not a bad thought," he said, tracing the shapes of the relevant objects with his finger. It was an exaggerated *u* shape, the curve of her ovaries and womb, though even the anatomical diagrams still relied on Ospret Far-Eyes' sacred metaphors to explain their function. Every month, the fertile soil of her womb would till itself, so that the seed he planted within her would grow into a child. His lips brushed her temple. "You're not sore at all?"

"No." She granted him an absent kiss, her attention on the book. "I *know* I've seen this symbol before. Does it look familiar to you? Look, it's in the other book Brother Oleare gave us, too."

"Then isn't that where you saw it?" Remin asked reasonably, glancing at the two books and returning to his previous occupation, trailing a line of kisses down her jaw and over the smooth skin of her neck. Lately she had taken to dabbing on the perfume he liked at night, a warm and spicy invitation that was very hard to resist.

"I don't think so..." She nibbled her lower lip. Obligingly, he turned his head to help her, and saw the smile curve her soft mouth.

"You said you weren't tired," he reminded her, as his hand slid downward from her belly to the opening between her legs.

"Well, I'm not," she whispered back, setting the books aside, and then her eyes widened and she snatched one back up and slipped out of his arms, lithe as a cat.

"Ophele—"

"It's here," she said excitedly, pattering over to the washstand, cloaked in nothing but the clouds of her hair. "Look, Remin!"

"What is?"

"The tapestry," she said, pulling it away from the wall and turning it toward him. "Look, see the shape of the swans? Their heads curve outward in opposite directions, and their necks, and their bodies together, it's the exact shape as the one in Ospret's garden, and oh—look! It's all along the border too, and in the leaves..."

Tugging the sheet over his hips, Remin sat up and turned to the page with Ospret's garden, with that symbol meticulously illuminated in gold paint.

"It is," he said, looking from the page to the swans. He wasn't entirely sure what to think of it.

"It's a fertility tapestry," she said, awed. "That was our wedding gift..."

"Come back to bed before you take a chill," Remin said, raking a hand through his hair that made it stand up in black tufts. It was disconcerting to realize that the tapestry lovingly given by Duke and Duchess Ereguil effectively had *make babies make babies make babies* written all over it, but he couldn't repress a smile as Ophele returned to him, delighted with her discovery. As soon as she was near enough, his hand shot out to seize her and drag her back under the sheets, giggling and squirming away from him for the delight of being subdued.

Inevitably, this turned into play of another sort, and soon she was sighing beneath him, her body rising into his hands as he caressed her curves, squeezing the satisfying roundness of her hips.

"Remin," she breathed, her hands gliding along his sides, urging him over her.

"Wife," he whispered back, and sheathed himself inside her.

It was not the first or even second time that he had filled her tonight. He drove into her in long, deep surges, and she only entreated him to do it harder, her voice rising in gasping cries that roused him so unbearably, all he wanted to do was drown in her. Remin buried his face in her soft scented flesh, licking and kissing and biting and feeling nothing but her. Her silky body moving under him. Her silkier insides taking him, stroking his aching length.

It was all warm, and dark, and good.

"Ahhh..." The moans escaped him uncontrollably, every scratch, every thrust.

"Remin, oh, Remin..." Ophele's mouth captured his in a breathless, messy kiss, and his fingers tangled in her hair as his hips drew back and shoved hard, deep, straining his body into hers, striking together like flint and steel and flying sparks.

She gave a gasping, mewling cry and Remin drew back, but she caught him ferociously.

"No—no!" she gasped. "No, oh, do that again!"

Shifting above her, he did it again, pushing her thighs upward so the angle was even better, deeper, striking the places that he knew felt best to her. His arms shook as he braced himself above her and drove down, his deeper cries mingling with hers.

"Tell me," he gasped as her flesh seared him, because he wouldn't notice if someone clubbed him over the head right now. "If I hurt you, tell me..."

"I will, I—" Her body caught, arched, and gripped him in a sudden spasm, a slippery caress that blasted every possible thought from his mind. Remin sucked in a breath and came.

Understanding the mechanics of what he was doing didn't lessen his pleasure in the slightest. How she clutched him as he emptied inside her, drawing him deep, straining for his seed. It was what their bodies were made to do. And the new learning lingered in his mind afterward, as he lay beside her with one arm wrapped securely around her slender form, lazily replete.

"It is amazing," he murmured, bending his head to lay a kiss on her belly. "That you can make a babe in here. Perhaps by summer, you will be round with our child."

"You won't mind?" Ophele's head turned on the pillow to watch him as his lips trailed gently upward. "If I get...fat?"

"How could I mind?" But now that they had spoken of it, he knew that it worried her, the changes her body would endure when she conceived and carried their child. "You will be making our family for us," he said quietly, resting his palm over her belly as if he could already feel it curving. "I never really believed I would have one."

And inwardly he admitted that it aroused him, to think of her filled with his child, and her breasts swelling with milk. His lips tugged gently at her nipples.

"What if I can't," she whispered, her fingers combing his hair. "What if I never can?"

"I will not think of it." Remin turned his head to kiss both breasts, and then sighed and let his head rest between them. Because of course, he had been thinking of that. "I will not think of it for a long, long time. Nor should you. Promise me you will not."

"I promise," she whispered, and sealed the pact with a kiss.

"But Genon was right, we must look to our nursery now," he went on, turning to more pleasant topics. "It will take the better part of a year for Sousten to consider all possible configurations."

"I don't know what babies need," she said, in the slow tones of epiphany. "At all."

"That's why we will have a nurse," Remin replied comfortably. "One of my cousins had a swing in his playroom. My uncle had it hung from one of the rafters, I pestered my father about it for months afterward."

"I don't think we'll need one of those right away," she said, and giggled as he moved beside her, his teeth nipping her neck.

"The child will grow," he informed her.

"I want a rocking horse for him," she said, nestling against him. "Or her. I had one, it had a mane and tail made of real horsehair. I used to plait flowers into its mane with my...with my mother."

"You can speak of her to me, wife. It doesn't bother me." Remin willed this to be true. "What was your nursery like, do you remember?"

"It was a little garret off my mother's room, up these twisty stairs. I used to like rabbits, when I was little, and she even painted them on the walls..."

He tended to think most often of his sons, the role they would inherit, all the things he would teach them. But that night Remin drifted off to sleep with her voice conjuring a vision of his daughter. A tiny version of Ophele clutching a stuffed rabbit, her happy voice calling through the house. His little girl. Oh, what wouldn't he do for her...

He lasted all of two hours before the nightmare jolted him awake, and for a moment he lay rigid as a board, wondering if he might have screamed.

"Remin?" Ophele mumbled beside him, her fingers patting drowsily toward his face.

"Go...go back to sleep," he whispered, catching her hand and pressing it to his cheek. His heart was hammering so hard, he was surprised she couldn't hear it, and the afterimage of the nightmare burned behind his eyes.

For a long time, he lay still, focusing on the familiar shapes of the room in the dim light and trying to convince himself that dreams were just dreams. He had always dreamed often, but lately it was almost every night, and though he considered himself a rational man, it was hard *not* to see omens in the darkest hours of the morning.

What could he do?

Was he dreaming because there was something he'd missed? Some vulnerability, some obvious measure against the Emperor? In his mind, Remin ticked through each of his men and the orders they had been given, wondering if there was someone else he might send, some angle he had not yet considered.

He would have been less worried if he had just been planning to march his army to the capital.

After dreams like that one, he wondered if he shouldn't do exactly that.

This was not a problem he had anticipated, when he married Ophele. Back then, he had only been concerned for himself: *his* safety, *his* heirs, *his* line, the burden of ancestors that stood behind him, counting on him to survive for their sake. He feared death more than he feared anything else, but not for himself. Death meant the extinction of his whole family, forever. Ultimate victory for the Emperor. A complete and utter defeat that could never be undone.

But then he had come to love Ophele, and discovered whole new realms of terror.

He thought of Edemir. He thought of Bram. He thought of Juste, and the latest reports from Darri in Segoile. He thought of his army, filled with good men, loyal men. He thought of Leonin and Davi, more devoted than he had dared to hope.

When you have done all you can, go to sleep, Duke Ereguil used to tell him, in the early years of the war when Remin's insomnia had been staggering. It was good advice. The solutions to one's problems were rarely found at three in the morning.

And Remin thought of Miche, who would be back tomorrow, and always knew how to laugh Remin's fears down to manageable size. Nothing was going to happen to Ophele between now and then.

That was sufficient comfort to let him drift off, and at dawn he roused her again to reassure himself that she was really there, his lips moving over the rosy blotches on her neck and shoulders with a mixture of guilt and desire. It gave him a possessive thrill to set his mark on her.

"Again?" she asked fuzzily, and moaned as he pushed her thighs apart and inserted himself between them.

"As often as we can, as long as you want me," he said, and her slow smile was all the answer he needed.

Remin felt much better as they stood together on the quay to watch the ferry come in, with the cold air off the water slapping his face. Ophele was bundled up beside him in a heavy cloak and a pretty blue gown, with a scarf wound up to her ears.

"Is that him?" she asked excitedly, craning her neck as the ferry scudded over the river, and a tall man with bright golden hair came into view in the prow of the small ship, lifting a hand in greeting. "Oh, Miche! Miche! Welcome home!"

He was the first off the boat as soon as the gangplank was lowered, coming up the dock with his hands out to take theirs, bright and fearless, if a little scruffy.

"I was worried you might have closed down the ferry for the winter, I half killed the horses," he said, offering an extravagant bow over Ophele's hand and a hard squeeze of Remin's. "You both look well. I'm glad to see the place is still standing."

"It wasn't too long a journey, was it?" Ophele asked, her tawny eyes going over him anxiously. "You needn't have gone at all, really..."

"It was just as well that I did, as you will soon see. No trouble at all except for one bit of baggage," Miche said, with drawling good humor. "There she is. Now, you'll both have to keep your wits about you, for I've brought a lady home."

"A—you did?" Ophele's voice squeaked in surprise as she looked first at Miche, and then at Remin, watching with consternation as Miche went to retrieve his lady. "I didn't think he was ever...serious about ladies," she whispered as Miche helped the small woman down the gangplank. She was so well-wrapped in furs, it seemed she would have to feel her way down with her feet.

"It would be a first," Remin muttered, trying not to scowl. He would have welcomed anyone for Miche's sake, if she had come from anywhere but Aldeburke. A woman who had watched Ophele's abuse and done nothing would never have his favor.

But suddenly Ophele gave a cry and leaped forward, her hood flying back from her hair.

"Azelma?" she cried. "Azelma, you came! Whatever are you doing here, oh, how *wonderful!*"

At the end of the dock, the woman was pulling away her cloak and muffler to reveal the gray-haired cook from Aldeburke, holding out her arms to catch Ophele in a rapturous hug.

"My stars, Princess, look at you!" she exclaimed, pushing Ophele back long enough to admire her, and then the two women embraced again. Remin watched, the frown lines drawing deep in his face.

Of all possible people, Miche had elected to bring back the fucking *cook*.

"I ransacked that place," Miche was saying as he came to stand beside Remin. His beard was as golden and luxuriant as a lion's mane after weeks on the road, his hair caught back in a ponytail with a bit of twine. "Took two-thirds of the horses, wagons, carriages, you'll be ferrying it across the river for a week. Sorry I couldn't give you more warning."

"I don't care about the horses and carriages," Remin growled. "We spent a year investigating my servants, and now you put a stranger in my house? From *Aldeburke?*"

"She's not a stranger," Miche replied, without taking his eyes from the two women. "She's the only one Ophele wrote to from that place, Rem. The only one that protected her."

Perhaps that was so, Remin thought, biting his tongue on a snarling response. But that did not answer for Lady Rache Pavot, who had died young after a long illness, which spoke of nothing to him but poison.

* * *

Miche would have sworn he'd been gone two years rather than two months.

Seated atop a placid bay horse named Brambles, he and Remin kept pace with one of the carriages he had stolen from Aldeburke, an open-topped buggy that Adelan Cruce was managing capably. Miche could tell at a glance that Remin would've been happier seated inside, ideally with his body between Ophele and Azelma, as if the old lady might at any moment go for her throat.

Ophele looked decidedly better, dressed in a rich blue brocade with jewels on the bodice and fur on the sleeves, a style that he didn't recognize. Far more important than splendid clothing or the elegant coif of her hair, she looked *happy,* and quite a bit rounder in the cheek and chin than she'd been when he left.

Remin, however, was a bit worse, to Miche's experienced eye. Hollow in the eyes and very, very worried, though that only showed in the sharp cut of his jaw, clenched taut with tension.

After weeks in the saddle, Miche would have liked nothing so much as a bath and a stationary chair, but as the wagon trundled up the hillside from the harbor, he drew Brambles alongside Ophele.

"You've been busy in town, I see," he said, nodding in the direction of the market, which had been a large stone rectangle when he left.

"Oh, would you like to see?" Ophele lit up, looking between him and Azelma. "Unless you're too tired..."

"Not a bit, Your Highness. Why, it's quite built up, isn't it?" asked the old lady, craning her neck to look over the carriage horses toward town, where smoke was rising from many chimneys.

"I wouldn't mind," Miche drawled, before Remin could refuse.

"So many people have come since you've been away, the public house is open now and Master Tiffen arrived last week, he's the tailor, he made this dress, Azelma, isn't it lovely? And that's Master Peltier ahead, he's the potter, he has his sash from the Court of Artisans. Good morning, Master Peltier!" Ophele called, hailing this stoop-shouldered gentleman, whose donkey was hauling a wagonload of white Brede clay.

"Morning, my lady! Your Grace," he called back, doffing his cap. He had an impressive set of eyebrows.

She was shouting. She was *chatting*. Miche exchanged a startled glance with Azelma and sat back on Brambles, wondering if the world could contain any further wonders.

There were many, even in so short a time. After seven years of war camps, it was bizarre to see so many women about, but the market square was full of them, fetching water from the huge fountain, going in and out of their houses as they did their morning chores. And there were actual *children* too, a half dozen racing around and shrieking as they pelted each other with slush. The sun was melting the patchy remains of snow.

"...and we've a baker now, too, which is good or the Tregues would be run off their feet, feeding everyone," Ophele went on, pointing out one of the many signs that identified each establishment. The folk of Tresingale were skipping the village stage of development altogether; the main street might have been lifted straight out of Segoile, with Noreveni glass covering the display windows of Guian's General Goods and what must be the cobbler's shop.

"How fine it all looks," marveled Azelma. "I am glad of it, you know all we heard about the Andelin was about those terrible devil creatures. But I see His Grace has matters well in hand."

"Everyone worked hard this year," Remin said stiffly.

"He's not exaggerating, Mistress Bessin," Miche said, smiling. "Had me digging ditches all summer, I still dream of my shovel. How are the walls coming along, my lord?"

"Done," Remin said, brightening a little, and they caught a glimpse of them as they reached the east road, a line of white to the east, looming nearer as they headed toward the North Gate.

"The people from Meinhem are mostly there," Ophele explained. "Oh, and that's Amalie and her brother! Amalie! Don't you look well! They're from Nandre," she added with an eloquent flick of her eyes to Miche. Azelma would not understand what this meant, but Miche had been there during the planning to rescue what remained of Remin's villagers.

"Only the girl and her brother survived," Remin said, low. "Rollon took a dozen men to fetch them back. All dead, as far as we know. Huber went to Selgin and Isigne, but no sign of him yet."

"That's a long road," Miche replied, with a lift of his eyebrows and a mental note to come back to this subject later.

It was like that all the way to the manor, a mixture of joy and a sprinkling of sorrow as Ophele talked of everything that had happened while he was away and showed Azelma her new home. With the work on the walls completed, all those laborers had turned to other work, but there was one faithful beast who would labor no more.

"You named it Eugene Street?" Miche barked out a laugh, and had to restrain himself for reaching for Ophele's hand. There were tears in her eyes for her little donkey. "Well, I'm sorry it's a memorial, my lady, but I approve. A far nobler name than Harnost Highway, I say."

"It's for all the beasts that helped build Tresingale," Ophele explained, with a look at Remin that made even his grim face soften.

The manor was yet another marvel, looming on the hilltop and visible through the bare trees at a long distance. Though Miche had lingered long enough to see most of the walls rise, it was still amazing to draw up in a flagged courtyard, with those beastly wolf demon statues snarling from their pedestals on either side of the steps. The windows on the first floor were open to let in the chilly air, and Miche craned his neck to see the slate tiles going down on the roof, four stories above.

"You know when to turn up," Remin said, with his first hint of humor. "We just moved your things up to the manor last week. It'll be some weeks before the west wing's done, but Juste already ordered things for your chambers. I expect Sousten will be hunting you down as soon as he hears you're back."

"Good. I haven't had a chair with a cushion in ten years," Miche replied, though even as he dismounted, his eyes drifted automatically to the women visible in the doors of the house: two maids in dark, tidy dresses, and a third woman that could only be Lady Mionet Verr, elegantly upright with very straight, slender shoulders.

As if she sensed eyes upon her, she glanced back at him, and he could almost *see* the prickles. Miche turned away, laughing. Now *that* was a properly thorny Rose. But tempting as it was to tease, he didn't mean to make trouble for Rem and Ophele in their home, when it was so hard to get help in the first place. Miche handed Brambles off to a boy in footman's kit and strode forward as Juste appeared around the corner, taking off his spectacles and sliding them into a pocket.

"Juste," he said, clasping the other man's hand tightly. "Everyone's still alive, I hope? No sign of Edemir in town, and I expected him to turn up early and loud."

"Edemir is on his way to the capital," Juste replied, with a faint smile and a meaningful glance.

"You ought to help me settle in my cottage once this business is done," Miche agreed. "All these people are servants? We'll need to find room for a cook."

"We'll talk about that, too," Juste promised, and they parted to stand in the appropriate rows as all the servants lined up so Ophele could do her duty as lady of the house. She introduced Miche and Azelma to everyone from Adelan the butler to Samin the boot boy, who offered a jaunty bow and an appealing gap-toothed grin when Miche winked at him. Miche did not need an introduction to Leonin and Davi, who immediately moved to flank Ophele.

"They're my guards," she told Azelma, as the two men offered polite nods. "One day, they might be my hallows. I've so much to tell you. Sir Davi Gosse and Sir Leonin of Breuyir, this is Azelma Bessin, who was the cook in Aldeburke. I do hope you'll cook for us here, too, Azelma."

Oh, that did not sit well with Remin *at all*. Miche pretended not to notice the black glare directed his way.

The four new laundresses were settled in the third row of cottages, and Miche frankly would have been happier to miss this phase of development altogether. He had not missed his cottage in town, and he was amused to find himself positioned between Juste and Lady Verr, like a proper troublemaker. As soon as the servants were dismissed, he followed Juste and Remin into the manor to see the west wing, where his permanent chambers would be located. Hopefully soon.

"Just do it, you'll never hear the end of it otherwise," Remin advised as he sat down on a bench to swap his muddy boots for house shoes.

"I'm gone two months and they've already domesticated you." Miche shook his head sorrowfully.

"Sousten nags worse than the butler," Remin said dryly. "But it's not just him being fussy, I don't want mud up those stairs. The carpenters promised something less steep, but I had to catch Peri myself the other day or she'd've broken her neck, hauling a scrub bucket up there..."

It did Miche's heart good to hear Rem do the honors of his house, hazardous stairs and all. The west wing of the second floor was in the final phase of plastering, and he was deeply gratified to see it was larger and grander than any hall in Aldeburke. Once the plasterers and carpenters finished with the bas-relief and corbels and all the other whatsits, it would be one of the grandest homes in the Empire. The halls were so massive, they echoed as Remin led them down a wide corridor with tall double doors on either side, separated by graceful niches that made room for wide banks of windows.

"There are three suites here, and Juste already claimed that one," Remin explained, indicating a room facing the front of the house, overlooking the courtyard. "Lady Verr—that's Mionet Verr, née Boscillard, some connection of Duchess Ereguil's—is on the other side. Try not to outrage her, we need her for at least another six months."

"Wouldn't dream of it," Miche said promptly. "This will be mine?"

"Yes, though if you touch anything right now, Sousten will have a fit," Remin warned. "The plaster takes longer to dry in the winter, it's slowed things down a bit. But we can have a look inside, I think the plasterers finished the front room yesterday."

It certainly smelled like it. Pushing the doors open, Miche found himself in a wide and sunny suite of rooms, with a generous sitting area, a separate bed chamber, private bath, dressing room, and three small hearths, all of them with iron grates already in place. Bare though it was, Miche could see exactly where he would place his bed and how he would arrange his sitting room, the all-but-forgotten comforts of *actual* furniture, rather than camp stools.

"It will be a proper home, Rem," he said, flashing a smile at Remin and Juste. All three of them had lived in tents for most of the last decade.

"Do what you like with it, and don't worry about the cost," Remin agreed, obviously pleased to say it, and Juste shut the doors so their more serious conversation would not be overheard.

"The Hurrells were gone when I got there," Miche reported without preamble. "None of the servants could or would say where. Which is lucky for them, or I might be up before Duke Lein on murder charges. They were abusing her, Rem. I saw the fucking closet where they kept her."

Remin's face darkened, but neither he nor Juste showed the slightest surprise.

"She told me some of it," he said flatly. "Tell me the rest."

Miche had no scruples about doing exactly that. He was a cheerful busybody who interfered whenever he thought it best, and he knew that Ophele was not a woman who complained, even when she really should. But this was well beyond mere childhood hurts, and the disappearance of the Hurrells added a sinister layer to the affair. Over the next hour, he related every word of what Azelma had told him, as well as the things he had seen for himself, from that closet of a room to the sad little bolt holes all over the estate and—most infuriating—the fact that he had found caches of food in every single one. Well-fed people did not cache food away.

"She didn't tell me any of that," Remin said when he was done, scrubbing his palms over his face.

"I am surprised that *none* of the servants reported it," Juste said, frowning. "They cannot claim ignorance. All of them might be named blasphemers. Perhaps it would be best if they were..."

He trailed off thoughtfully, and then shifted his gaze to Remin.

"If you would like, my lord, I will handle this problem," he said. "I have already begun making inquiries. Did you think to take a list of names, Miche?'

"As it happens, I did," Miche replied, with no qualms at all about handing them over to Juste's questionable mercy. "I have all the household documents in my baggage. Though you needn't look for Leise or Nenot."

"You dealt with them yourself?" Juste asked, his scarred brow lifting.

"The law in such cases is clear," Miche replied, untroubled by his quiet execution of Ophele's nursemaids. "I would not presume to contest it."

"You presume when it suits you." Remin was not so easily placated. "You brought Lady Pavot's cook here, of all people. Did it never occur to you that Azelma might've been the one to send the lady to the stars?"

Miche blinked. His face hardened.

"No," he admitted. Trust Rem to think of that. "It did not. I thought we needed a cook for the house, and she's the only person Ophele trusted. And she did protect Ophele, at risk to herself. But more than that, you said it yourself. She is Lady Pavot's cook. All the way back to when she was in Segoile, and had the favor of the Emperor."

It was such a tangle of history. It had twisted all of their lives, but no one more than Remin and Juste, who still did not know why their families had been executed. For more than eighteen years, the details of the Conspiracy had been confined to the offices of the Emperor and the highest strata of nobility, sworn to silence with the direst of oaths. That was why it was *called* the Conspiracy.

"Perhaps she will know why it happened," said Juste finally. He had such a quiet presence, people often overlooked him, and even Remin's knights tended to forget that his family had been on the execution block right beside Remin's.

But Miche never did. Not once.

* * *

"Your Grace, if you like, you may use my cottage while we ready one for Mistress Bessin," said Lady Verr, neatly slicing to the heart of the problem. "It is too cold to be standing about outside."

"Oh, it wouldn't be too much trouble?" Ophele asked, relieved, and remembered her bearing even before Lady Verr's auburn eyebrow lifted. She had been very particular that Ophele's bearing should not only be noble, but *regal.* "That would be very kind, thank you. But only if it wouldn't trouble you."

"I insist," Lady Verr replied, and offered a smile to Azelma. "It's serendipitous, as they have just finished another row of cottages yesterday. I'll have the footmen bring your things over, and send Emi to make up a fresh bed."

"Thank you, m'lady," Azelma replied, with a curtsy. "Shouldn't like to trouble you myself. And it will be easier to make up fresh beds directly, Sir Miche brought so many trunks of bed linens..."

"He *didn't.*" Ophele forgot all about regal bearing. "He threatened to steal all the linens before he left, I thought he was joking!"

"Oh, I tell you no lies," Azelma replied, and regaled both ladies with the tale all the way to Lady Verr's cottage.

Ophele had secretly been dying to see it. She knew it was made of the same stuff as all the others, and had lived in one just like it for seven months, but she still half-expected to find a treasure trove of silk, satin, and jewels within, like one of the fantastical *xori* where the King of Noreven kept his wives.

But there wasn't so much as an embroidered sash to be seen when they ascended the steps, and the miniscule dressing table was even more bare than Ophele's, with everything except a single pair of slippers and a book packed away in trunks on either side of the hearth. Lady Verr could have walked out of her cottage forever at a moment's notice.

As Ophele was pulling the door shut, Davi's hand shot out to catch it.

"We won't follow you inside, my lady," said Leonin, quick and polite. "But pray keep some distance, or it will be our necks with His Grace."

"But it's Azelma," Ophele whispered back, and then realized that they could not know what that meant, and it would be no defense at all with Remin. She sighed. "I will."

"...the flue needs a little encouragement, if the fire is hot," Lady Verr was saying, as Ophele turned back to the two women. "But I have found it to be quite sufficient, despite the chill."

"Oh—I'm sure," Azelma said, though she looked a little dubious. "Dear me, such a place. Do you know, they would have had all of you in tents, from what they were saying back home."

"His Grace and I lived in a cottage like this, when I first arrived," Ophele said, a little proudly. "I did...I did write to you, about it."

"Oh, child," Azelma said sadly. "You know I never received a single one of your letters."

"If you will pardon me, I will see about having your cottage arranged," Lady Verr excused herself tactfully, allowing Azelma to breach etiquette once more and wrap her arms around Ophele.

"How I did worry, Your Highness," she said, and Ophele would've sworn there was a faint whiff of cinnamon and flour about the elderly lady, even so many miles from Aldeburke. "Tell me true now, you've kept well? His Grace looks a very...somber fellow."

"I have," Ophele promised, resting her chin on Azelma's shoulder. "It was hard, at first. There were the devils, I was so afraid of them, and we—well, we didn't get on very well at first. But most of the time he doesn't mean to be stiff like that, and he's so brave, and smart, and he doesn't like people to know how kind he is, but he tries to look after everyone in the valley..."

Ophele drew back earnestly as she was saying this, but shut her mouth with a snap as soon as she saw the twinkling in Azelma's eyes. Her face reddened. Oh, stars, and Davi and Leonin were right outside listening, too.

"I'm glad," Azelma replied, sitting in one of the two chairs and squeezing Ophele's hands. "It looks as if they've been feeding you better here, it shames me to say."

"I wouldn't dare look otherwise. I shall have to introduce you to Wen." Ophele stifled a giggle. "Wen of Tallford, he cooks for Remin in particular, he made something called a dacquoise for his birthday and it was as big as this table! Oh, I have so many things to tell you! But, Miche sent a message that the Hurrells were gone?"

"In August," Azelma confirmed, nodding. "Like thieves in the night, they were. Germain came down one night in the middle of clearing up from supper all in a tizzy, ordering maids and footmen upstairs to pack up, double quick. They never said where they were going, or if they'd ever be back, rot them."

Ophele could not think what this might mean, but surely it was nothing good.

"She's been waiting all these years for some chance," she said slowly, lowering her eyes to her fingers. "I don't suppose their exile was lifted because I reached my majority? Or they were sent somewhere else, perhaps, since I don't need a guardian anymore?"

"I couldn't say, Your Highness. Or Your Grace, I suppose I'd better get used to that sooner rather than later. I don't believe they even told the coachman where he was headed until they were at the gates of the estate. Oh, but bless all the bustle, I nearly forgot!" Azelma exclaimed, reaching for the valise at her feet, bulging nearly to bursting. "Now, I won't tell you that Lorene and I connived for spite, for I'd no notion that I'd ever lay eyes on you again, my lady. But I *did* see that Lady Hurrell didn't make off with all your mother's things. Here now!"

So saying, she produced a large handkerchief from the depths of the valise, and when it was unfolded on the table, there was a familiar pink opal pendant, a delicate set of champagne pearl earrings and matching necklace, and another set of tiger's eye and topaz strung on a fine gold chain.

"I'm sorry we couldn't fetch some of the finer pieces, child," Azelma apologized. "I thought they might come back if Lorene had scarpered with the rubies or the diamonds, and she was a bundle of nerves for weeks as it was. She's a good girl."

"No. Thank you." Ophele smiled, her throat was suddenly tight. She had never expected to see any of these things again. "Oh, Azelma, thank you. Lorene really did that for me?"

"Right out from under the lady's nose, as she was flinging all her things higgledy-piggledy into trunks."

That made her laugh, at least enough to keep from crying. She had to gather her courage just to touch the opal pendant; it had caused her a great deal of trouble, once. But she could remember the light sparking off that pendant at her mother's throat, and Rache Pavot's voice laughing as she said *there, there, my heart, only a moment and you shall have a proper look...*

There was so much to talk about. Had it really only been nine months since she left Aldeburke? It seemed incredible that so much had happened in so short a time, and Ophele forgot all about her manners and chattered away until Sim and Jaose appeared to say that Mistress Bessin's cottage was ready. Reluctantly, Ophele rose to help her to the little house on the back row of the servants' quarters, overlooking the river. But Azelma ought to have time to wash and rest a little, if she wanted to. It was a long journey from Aldeburke.

"I'll come back later this afternoon," she promised, pausing for one last embrace. "Oh, I *am* glad you've come."

Miche had brought back something even better than a library. He had brought back her friend.

And a cook. It had been a matter of concern, especially after the first dusting of snow; Ophele and Wen had discussed already how the manor was going to manage meals over the winter. Who was going to want to trek down to the cookhouse in a blizzard?

"She was your cook, m'lady?" Davi asked as he and Leonin fell into step behind her, winning a resigned sigh from Leonin. Davi never bothered to pretend he hadn't overheard every single word.

"Yes. For my mother, too. She was always...kind to me," Ophele said a little awkwardly, wondering if she could explain how hard it had been, and how much those quiet hours in the kitchen had meant to her. "So I would like to make sure she's quite comfortable. Does it get very cold in the cottages?"

"Not so long as the fire is there. But it would be better if you met her in the solar in future, my lady," said Leonin as he and Davi moved to either side of her, prepared to shield her from falling bricks and flying implements with their bodies, if necessary. "We will endeavor to give you privacy, but we cannot fail in our duty."

"I shouldn't like to trouble her with those stairs, and Azelma is my friend," Ophele replied firmly, scanning the building site for the artful orange curls of Sousten Didion. "She would never hurt me. If she wanted to, she might have done it a thousand times already."

"Please speak to His Grace about it," Leonin replied, equally firm. "We will be pleased to abide by your wishes."

He meant *your* in the plural sense. Leonin was tricky that way.

She found Master Didion by the shell of the library, which was currently connected to the rest of the house by the skeleton of a corridor. It would be a glorious structure, when it was done, with vaulted ceilings, miles of curving shelves, and sculptures and murals enough to employ dozens of artists and artisans.

"A Segoile-trained cook? Here?" Master Didion asked at once, seizing on the most exciting part of her question.

"Well, I know she joined my mother's household in the capital," Ophele said, wondering if cooks fell under the Court of Artisans and if there was a sash. And suddenly, looking at Master Didion, she really understood that her mother had been the Emperor's *mistress*. Not his wife. And Master Didion was old enough that he might have been there in Segoile, when all of it was happening.

Ophele suddenly felt as if she had flung open the doors of her wardrobe to publicly display her chemises.

"...*possibly* please me more!" Master Didion was saying. "I believe the masons have just finished, so it should be quite safe to offer you a tour, my lady, provided you allow me to solicit Mistress Bessin's opinion. Any cook put forward by the offices of the Emperor is assuredly of the highest quality, subtle and sublime. How I have longed for the cuisine of the capital!"

Master Didion enjoyed his alliteration. But it pleased her to think Azelma would be so respected for her own sake, and while Master Didion was effusive in his compliments when they met again later that afternoon, he was also quite serious about consulting her opinion.

"We shall have to smooth this path out," he noted, offering his arm to the elderly woman as they moved around the steep trail at the back of the manor. Azelma looked much refreshed after a wash and rest, and ready to set straight to work. "The servants' quarters are still under construction, please mind your head..."

Ophele had rarely visited the back of the house herself, and looked with some awe at the towering edifice, where three underground levels were excavated from the back of the hill. The kitchens, bakeries, butteries, and pantries would be on the level immediately below the main house, to help keep it heated and ensure food did not get cold in transit. Davi had to redirect her more than once as she twisted her head back to look up at the wide banks of windows overlooking the river, which would let some natural light into the lower house.

"It's big enough, isn't it?" Azelma observed as they stood in the huge empty kitchen, a vast cavern of brick and plaster and wooden beams forming a wide grid in the high ceiling. "You might fit a cow on one of those spits."

"His Grace will be feeding a great many people one day," Master Didion said, puffing at the prospect.

"He'll need a proper army to do it," Azelma agreed, and Ophele was pleased just to listen as Master Didion questioned her about the operation required. As duchess, she did not need to know such details, but oh, to think Azelma could be here, to help Remin set a table as fine as the Emperor's...

"...and we must of course consult Her Grace's preferences," Master Didion added courteously. He always remembered to ask at least once.

"Oh, I don't know," Ophele said with a start. "I don't know much about running kitchens. But I should like it to be...comfortable, please. Weren't you always saying those hard floors pained your back, Azelma? And poor Alcide and Clio always came out of the scullery looking as if they'd been boiled."

"That is a consideration," Master Didion agreed. "There are some comforts I might show you today, my lady. Mistress Bessin, this way, if you please, and mind the troughs of plaster..."

If the servants' quarters were not quite so fine as the rooms upstairs, they were at least going to be warm and comfortable. The plastering was not nearly so far advanced downstairs, but Ophele could see the frames of wide halls and generously sized rooms, with suites granted to higher-ranking servants like Adelan and the eventual housekeeper.

"And Mistress Bessin, though the cook's rooms are usually nearer the kitchen," Master Didion said, pleased with the arrangements. "Much of the décor from upstairs will be echoed down here, my lady, wooden floors and beams, and these long hallways will be perfect for the paintings we discussed."

"Remin said he wants the servants to be comfortable, and proud of their House," Ophele explained to Azelma, trying not to sound as if she were boasting. She failed utterly.

"I'm sure we all shall be, Your High—my lady," Azelma said, squeezing Ophele's wrist as she let herself be helped up the steps to the first floor, which were shallow and wide, to allow the safe transportation of heavy loads. They finished their tour just in time to see Remin, Miche, and Justenin at the front door, stomping back into boots that Samin had just finished cleaning.

"Oh, there you are, wife," said Remin, rising promptly for a visual inspection. "You were downstairs?"

"Yes, Master Didion was showing us the kitchen and the servants' quarters," she said, catching his arm impulsively. "Azelma knows all about how a proper kitchen is run, isn't it marvelous? She can tell us just how it ought to be set up."

"It will be good to have the benefit of her experience," he replied, and Ophele was too pleased to catch the acidity in his words. "I'll have Wen send supper up tonight, wife. We cannot ask Mistress Bessin to begin straightaway. And...Mistress Bessin," he said, turning his head to rest cool black eyes upon her. "Miche has told me of some of your kindnesses to my wife. You have my gratitude."

"I wish there had been more of them, my lord," Azelma replied, a slightly perplexing reply that made Ophele glance between them, wondering. Remin only squeezed her hand.

"I've some matters to discuss with Miche and Juste, wife. It may be a late night."

"It *will* be a late night," Miche said, with a wink for Ophele that made her smile. "Master Didion, a pleasure as always. Do something about those blasted steps, won't you?"

* * *

There were some discussions that could only be held with discretion. Dangerous conferences in closed rooms, held in whispers with guards at the doors. Sacred secrets that could only be confided over a campfire, beneath the light of stars.

Other conversations were best suited to the confines of an outdoor Benkki Desan bath, with Master Balad at a discreet distance, steam drifting into the cold air, and lanterns glowing, warm and golden.

And alcohol. Lots and lots of alcohol.

"...four hundred and ninety miles," Remin was saying heavily, and not for the first time. "It takes a month to get to Selgin, and that's with strong men and good horses. He might have five hundred people to bring back, what was I thinking?"

"You were thinking it was Huber." Miche jabbed Remin with his cup. "Fucking Huber."

"Fucking Huber," agreed Tounot, lifting his cup for a toast.

All of Remin's men had their strengths. Huber was the dark horse, metaphorically and literally: a worker of miracles, turning up when he was most needed and least expected. Tounot was the one for a song, when his heart wasn't broken. If Edemir had been there, he would've been the one sober enough to get everyone home, and slipping a few extra sovs into Master Balad's hand for his trouble. Juste would listen for hours, if a man wanted to talk.

And if Miche had been willing to own a skill, it was this: knowing when to get them drunk and let them complain.

"You didn' see the devils." Remin was on his way to being well and truly inebriated. "*We* didn' see 'em either. There's new devils, did you know?"

"One for sure," agreed Auber, floating on his back in the steaming water and naked as a jay. He lifted a finger, then considered it and raised another. "Maybe two."

"Is there really?" Miche asked, shocked.

"It could be more than two," said Juste without lifting his head. Miche had always found it strangely apt that the upright Juste was the first to keel over, when drunk; not unconscious, just boneless, as if whatever stiffened his spine was soluble in alcohol. "One of which has poisonous quills. Like a porcupine. It is quite fascinating, there was an experiment with a goat—"

"Thass the devil that destroyed Nandre," Remin said, as Juste trailed off into contemplative mumbling. And though the stars knew Remin had excuse to be a brooding sort of fellow, and Miche would've thought less of any man who wasn't bothered by the destruction of two villages *so far*, this wouldn't do at all.

"But you sent *Huber,*" he repeated. "'Member that day by the Herugel Pass, the day before we meant to march on the fort? He went for a piss in the morning and didn't come back, and we all thought a devil got him or he'd been captured or fell off the side of the mountain? And he came back that night with a hundred prisoners. The whole fucking enemy scout force."

"He made them tie themselves up," Remin said reminiscently. He was sprawled against the stone side of the bath with his huge arms outstretched, his big chest heaving with a sigh. Beside him were multiple trays filled with the sharp, heady spirit Benkki Desans brewed from some lethal white berry, sloshed into tiny wooden cups that were barely big enough for a good gulp. Miche had begun the night by challenging Tounot to see who could empty more of a tray.

Shit, Tounot.

Shaking his head to clear it, Miche fumbled about and hauled him out of the water by his hair. Tounot kept wanting to slide under.

"He's gonna build a village next to mine," Tounot slurred. "He said village 'cause fuck towns. Bottom part of the Talfel Plateau, he wants it for horses. Said he'd trade me horses for food."

"His horses have come," Juste reported, rousing. "Twenty of them. They were to come back in August, but one of the mares was late in foal and he would have no others. Another noble lineage, like that blasted bull—"

"Sometimes you don't *want* another," Tounot retorted. He was as adept as any nobleman at concealing his feelings, but the pain surfaced now, his voice ragged. "I have told her and told her, I don't *want* anyone else, and all she will say is that there's plenty of stars in the sky..."

"There are," Remin agreed, his eyes weaving upward until his head fell backward. "Lots."

"I wanted that one."

"We are not talking about horses," Miche realized. Reaching for one of the curving wooden jugs, he sloshed another measure of clear liquor into the cups and distributed them. "Drink it," he ordered Juste, who was gently contemplating the grain of the wood.

"Lady Bourdevane went to the capital," Auber explained as he took his own cup, lifting it in a sardonic toast. Mild Auber could drink them all under the table. "Thanks."

Ysmeine Bourdevane had been Tounot's intended, until the Emperor's machinations had severed them from each other. A true love match, for all that they had been betrothed since they were children, and now she was bound to the capital to seek another. No self-respecting family would allow a match to Sir Tounot of Tresingale; a man of no House, no lineage, with none of the protections of his kin and all of Remin's enemies.

It was the last gasp of all Tounot's hopes, which explained why he seemed inclined to let himself slip beneath the surface of the water and let nature take its course.

There was no consolation for the problem, and it would have been insulting to invent a silver lining. Miche frowned. Normally, he would have recommended solace between the thighs of another woman, as many as it took to numb the wound, but Tounot had kept himself for Ysmeine all these years, and Bram's rough prostitutes were not great consolers.

"She would sing for me," Tounot was saying. "You have never heard such a song—"

"Forget her," advised Juste, turning his head toward Tounot without actually lifting it. "There is no point in thinking of things you cannot have."

"No, you—you go *get* her," Remin argued. "If you love her, you go, you go find her and tell her. And bring her back. And tell her—you have to go *after* the things you want..."

It was a secret known only to the Knights of the Brede that Remin Grimjaw had no tolerance *at all* for spirits.

"He has to think what's best for her," Auber contradicted. "It's hard to ask a woman to come all the way here, an' live inna cottage with devils howling outside..."

"*My* wife did it," Remin said smugly. "And you should bring her, Tounot, anyone can come. She can be Ophele's friend."

"It isn' just that," Tounot said unhappily. "She'd be cut off from her family. Give up everything. Like me. I can' ask her to do that..."

There was a silence in which Miche eyed Tounot, whose face was a mask of tragedy.

"Drink," he decided, and dosed the other man thoroughly, then helped himself to another cup.

By the time Master Balad suggested they ought to seek their beds, Miche had a fair idea of everything that had happened while he was gone, which included many problems for which there was no solution. Nothing was likely to restore Tounot to his family or his sweetheart to his side, Auber had unwisely offered an opinion on his sister-in-laws' cooking that had gotten him barred from supper in *two* houses, Juste was a stodgy, miserable bastard, and Remin...

Weighed a *ton*.

"I have him, I have him," said Juste as they maneuvered their duke into the house on top of the hill, staggering under Remin's weight. "Close the door, quick."

"Don' s'pose there's a key for it." Miche squinted at the heavy brass plates. There were four of them.

"Never mind, there are guards outside. Help me get him up the steps."

"Boots off in the house," said Remin suddenly, rousing.

"I'll scrub the steps myself in the morning," Miche promised, though some deep, honest part of himself thought he would be more likely contemplating the bottom of a chamber pot. That Benkki Desan liquor was potent stuff. "C'mon, Your Grace, there's the stairs. Damn them."

If Remin had been entirely unconscious, their options would have been to winch him upstairs with a crane or let him sleep it off on the floor of the grand entry. But he was just conscious enough for Juste to pull and Miche to push him up the stairs, though there was a dangerous moment when his fingers slipped off the railing and he teetered backwards. If he'd gone over, all three of them might have broken their necks.

Grunting, Juste hauled him the rest of the way upward, then sat down hard on the landing and kept going straight over onto his back. His eyes closed.

"Juste?" Remin poked him, concerned. "Miche, whass wrong with Juste?"

"He is drunk," Miche explained, with an air of authority. The door at the far end of the landing was flung open, casting a long, flickering line of light into the hall.

"Who is there?" demanded a female voice, and even while wildly intoxicated, this had a bracing effect on Sir Miche of Harnost.

"Rem, leave 'im be," he said, reeling upright.

"Remin?" came Ophele's anxious voice, and her small shadow appeared in the door, dressed in a robe and slippers with her hair cascading loose around her. That meant the other one was Lady Something that started with V. Or B.

"He's all right," Miche said, making a massive effort to become instantly sober. "We had...a bit to drink."

"Lots," corrected Remin, painfully honest. "Wife?"

"Is that Justenin on the floor?" Ophele sounded fascinated.

"I will manage him, my lady," said Lady Something, and her tall, slender shadow drifted past Miche in a cloud of disapproval.

"My thanks, my lady," Miche managed, in indiscriminate gratitude to both women as Ophele darted forward to prop up Remin on his other side.

"Remin, are you really drunk?" she asked, and the tall man swept her up in an unsteady embrace and kissed her soundly.

"Wife, I am sooooooooo drunk..."

"Best if we just get him to bed, my lady," Miche said, giving Remin a pull to get him going. He was acquiring a certain dangerous bonelessness that meant he was minutes from passing out. Miche had no qualms about leaving Juste to the lady. Juste would cut off his own arm before he did anything inappropriate to a woman.

And Juste's mind was clearly on other things.

"I hate that bull," he was telling Lady Something as Miche and Ophele staggered off to the bedroom under the twenty-two stone Remin, who certainly *felt* like a bull. Ophele was bearing up under her share of the load, though from her occasional squeaks, Miche suspected the lord was not *entirely* unconscious.

"Remin," she hissed, and when they finally flopped him onto the mattress in the bedchamber, she went with him, sprawled over his chest with a length of shins and ankles showing that made Miche hastily cast his eyes to the ceiling.

"Wife," Remin said affectionately. "So pretty. Don' be scared, I'll never...let *anything...*"

His voice trailed off and terminated in a single stentorian snore.

"I know," she said softly as she escaped, eeling backward under his crushing arms. Her eyes went to Miche. "How much did he have?"

"You would actually be surprised how little," Miche told her, and shook himself. "Sorry to bring him back like this, my lady. I'll scrounge up a bucket, best to put it where he can find it, just in case. But he's more like to just sleep it off."

"All right," she said, glancing worriedly at the fallen giant.

"He told me...about the Emperor summoning you," Miche added, fumbling about for what he wanted to say. Dimly, he knew there was a great deal he wanted to tell her, and much that he should *not* say, but his tongue felt dangerously loose. "And—Juste is teaching you. Because you don't know."

"Oh. Yes," she said, with a blink of surprise, and her slim shoulders drew together in an embarrassed cringe. "I'm sorry. I...lied to all of you."

"There is nothing to forgive." Miche laid a hand on her head, bending to look into her eyes. There was a bitter taste in his mouth and the feel of acid in his throat. "My lady. You did nothing wrong, at all. It is—so many people failed you. I am sorry that you had to endure that, alone. If I had—if there is anything I can ever do, you have only to name it."

"You have done so much for us," she said, with a wry smile that included her drunken husband. "How could I ever thank you?"

"It's little enough," Miche said, with a final pat of her head, and then went to see a man about a bucket.

Chapter 5 – The Crimes of Lady Pavot

As penance for his overindulgence, Remin was up before dawn.

As soon as his eyes creaked open, he paused just long enough to make sure Ophele showed no sign of insult and then went to empty his belly and stick his head in a basin of cold water. This treatment was sufficient to get him more or less upright, and he went for a walk by the river with his ever-present shadows trailing behind, letting the frigid air slap him awake.

Recovery was a gradual process. There were a few dangerous moments when he saddled and climbed onto Lancer, lurching as the horse worked out his morning exuberance, and Remin still felt a little green when he dismounted by the kitchen at the back of the cookhouse. Heavy clouds lowered in the sky and smelled of snow to his nose, and welcome heat billowed out the kitchen door.

"Be a few minutes yet," barked Wen, without so much as a how-do-you-do. His huge hands moved unerring from skillet to saucepan on the immense stove, and he was red-faced and sweating, with a cloth tied around his bald head to avoid perspiring into breakfast.

"Eggs?" Remin asked queasily as the scents of bacon and tomatoes assaulted him. The icing on a tray of sweetbread looked particularly unappetizing.

"Aye, though from the looks of ye, ye'd do better with a bit of dry toast, Your Grace," said Wen, with a belly-slapping *haw haw haw*. His good mood directly correlated with the suffering of those around him. "Never mind, I've a cure for ye. Here."

"What's in it?" Remin asked doubtfully, eyeing the green-brown sludge.

"Ye'd not thank me if I told ye."

When Wen said this, it was best to believe him. Remin sipped first, then gulped, his face grim. He had always believed medicine had to be foul-tasting to be effective, in which case this concoction must resurrect the dead.

"You heard Miche came back yesterday?" he asked, setting the cup aside. He hadn't come to the kitchen just for breakfast.

"Aye, half the town heard, with that circus coming up from the harbor," Wen agreed, shooting Remin an amused glance. It had been a bit of a debacle, with all those carriages coming over the river. "Best watch those girls at the house, or you'll have trouble. The laundresses were noising about it when they came to fetch their supper. In *my* kitchen."

That was Wen's real objection. Not that the laundresses were coveting Miche already, but that he had been forced to listen to it.

"Miche wouldn't trouble them," Remin said dismissively.

"It's not about *him* troubling *them,"* Wen said, waving a ham-like hand. "But as ye please, Your Grace."

"He brought a lady back with him, as it happens," Remin said, segueing carefully into this dangerous subject. "The cook from Aldeburke."

"Did he now?" Wen began to inflate, like a toad swelling up to warn off enemies.

"Seventy if she's a day, and trained in Segoile," Remin said, with an edge to his own voice. He was willing to tolerate Wen's tantrums to a point. "You're always saying you need help in the kitchen."

"Seventy." Wen snorted and turned away, knife flashing as he sliced fresh bread into thick slabs. "Set in her ways and full of capital notions, I wager."

"Then you should understand each other perfectly," Remin retorted.

"And ye won't have her in your kitchen, even if she has her Segoile seal," Wen said shrewdly. "Do ye think I'll change me mind, Your Grace?"

"You could name your price." It was not the first time Remin had made this offer.

"And I've told ye, I'm not fit for a lord's household. This suits me," the cook said, gesturing at the long, narrow kitchen, with its stacks of tin pans and raw wooden shelves. "No one bothers me. And if they do, I yell at 'em 'til they go away again. Ye wanted to be a lord, Your Grace, well, ye got what ye wished for, and the blessings of the stars go with ye. I'll give her a bit of counter, if you want her away from ye. But it won't solve your troubles."

Well, he was just exploring options, Remin told himself as he gathered up the large breakfast hamper, along with a jug of Wen's cure for Juste and Miche. It was true that he had eaten Azelma's cooking in Aldeburke for a week, with no ill effect. But then, he had had one of his knights observing every step of the preparation, from the kitchen to the dining table.

And he was the Duke of Andelin. It was his right to have his food made however he liked by whoever he wanted and delivered in whatever way he preferred. But as Remin stepped outside to find snow falling, he was reminded again of the impracticality of the situation. And no, Wen was not likely to change his mind. He did not like people.

Resolutely, Remin shoved this problem away and swung up onto Lancer, pulling the heavy black hood of his cloak over his head. The snow was drifting down in huge, soft flakes like feathers. It looked like the first real blizzard of the season.

"It's snowing!" Ophele exclaimed as soon as he arrived back home, appearing at the top of the landing in a simple blue morning gown. "Are you feeling all right? I was worried last night."

"I saw it," Remin said dryly, shaking his cloak outside the front door before he stepped inside. "I'm well enough, I'm sorry I troubled you, wife. It looks like a blizzard. Have you seen Miche and Juste about?"

"Yes, they're both in the solar. Shall we have breakfast together?" she asked, brightening.

The prospect also pleased Remin. Usually, he and Ophele took breakfast alone, at first because Ophele was not ready to face a cookhouse full of people first thing in the morning, and then because they could hardly invite guests into their bedchamber. But it was pleasant to see Juste and Miche shuffling through the door of the solar and offering greetings to Ophele, even if they were still squinting and green.

Lady Verr was also there, but only because it would have been a gross insult to exclude her.

"I'll do that, my lord," said Juste, plucking the hamper from Remin's hand to set the table.

"Have you ever seen a blizzard, Lady Verr?" Ophele asked, watching the huge flakes falling through the windows with delight.

"Not a blizzard, Your Grace," Lady Verr replied. "We sometimes had snow on my father's estate, but rarely more than a flurry. Will there be so much more here?"

"A great deal more," said Juste, as Miche and Remin nodded their agreement. All three men were eating cautiously, making a trial of bread before attempting anything crazy, like bacon. "The clouds come up against the mountains and then linger. We will not fare too badly on this hilltop, but it will be up to the eaves of the cottages in town."

"A pity there weren't any sledges in Aldeburke, or I would have taken those, too," remarked Miche. "There's a few put by in the storehouse, but with so many folk in town, we're like to need more. Or maybe we ought to just dig out Eugene Street, for common travel."

"We'll need the market road and the barracks road cleared, too," Remin said. He was *not* calling it Goose Road. "It'll be heavy work."

"That's why the stars gave you soldiers," Miche said placidly.

It was pleasant, and homey, to be sitting safe and warm inside the house as the snow fell, listening to Miche tease Ophele and talking about other men shoveling snow. But however intoxicated he might have been the night before, Remin had not forgotten any part of their conversations, and he knew that many of his people were *not* tucked away, safe and warm by a fire.

"Some of the Third will stay here," he said. He had forgotten all about his iffy stomach and was heaping eggs, bacon, and fried tomatoes onto a thick slice of bread. "But the rest are going to Isigne and Selgin to see what has become of Huber and the folk of those villages."

"Who will go with them?" There was a warning glint in Juste's eyes.

"Not I," Remin said equably. He didn't miss the relief in Ophele's face. He still thought he was right to have gone to the Berlawes—who could say what might have happened if he had not—but he could not justify leaving now. Unless the new devils were entirely unlike any other devils seen in the valley to this point, the only risk to the men would be the weather. And his duty was to get an heir, above all else.

It was not exactly a hardship. Under the table, he nudged Ophele's slipper with his foot and saw a secret smile curve her lips, though she granted him only the slightest glance through her eyelashes before she went back to her stewed apples. She was teasing him.

"I'll do it, unless you've someone else in mind," Miche said, as if he hadn't already been on the road for two months. "I shall be your Master of Snow, Rem. I hardly know myself without a shovel in my hand."

"It would be good of you, thank you, Miche," Remin replied, and devoured the last of his breakfast in several large bites. "I'll come to the barracks myself later today. We'd already been planning to send someone after Huber. It'll be easier with sledges."

"I'll be about town this morning and then at the storehouse. My lady, I will come here for your lessons, if you prefer," Juste added for Ophele's benefit. "The storm smells like a bad one."

"Can he really smell it?" Ophele wanted to know as Remin steered her down the hall to their bedchamber after breakfast, leaving the clearing up to the servants. "The storm?"

"He is usually right," Remin admitted. "He grew up in the mountains, so his weather-sense is better than most."

And it was a convenient excuse to linger indoors. Though they both had important work, Remin was conscientious in his duties and shut the door of the bedchamber behind them, stooping to catch Ophele up and toss her over one shoulder, purely for the pleasure of hearing her squeal. One of her slippers fell off.

"Are you going to make amends for last night?" she inquired as he carried her across the room.

"Did I do something for which amends are required?" Remin deposited her on the bed with a puff of blankets and moved over her, his black eyes heating.

"Miche and I had to carry you to bed."

Remin thought that over and decided it was fair.

"Very well. I am sorry," he said, sliding her morning gown up over her thighs. She wore nothing underneath.

"And you kept pinching me," she said, in a voice suddenly gone breathy. Remin knelt by the side of the bed and sank his teeth into her silky thighs. He was already hardening.

"Then I shall have to beg pardon for that, too," he murmured, and she gasped at the first stroke of his fingers against her most sensitive flesh, her fingers tangling in his hair as his mouth closed on her nipple. If it was apologies she wanted, he was about to apologize until she begged him to stop.

* * *

Afterward, while they were lying together in bed and watching snowflakes swirl through the diamond panes of the windows, it was Remin who brought up Azelma.

"I spoke to Wen this morning," he said, one hand slowly stroking up and down her back. "If Azelma wants to help in the cookhouse, he'll allow it."

"Oh, thank you," she said, surprised and pleased that he had already gone to the trouble. And that Wen was actually going to let a woman in his kitchen. "She doesn't like to be idle. I don't think she had a holiday once in all those years, except when she was ill."

"Mmm." His sigh echoed through the room. Ophele had heard enough of his sighs to know it was not a happy one. "Wife," he began. "I don't want to upset you, but I don't believe this conversation will be improved by delay. Have you ever wondered how your mother died?"

"She...she was sick," Ophele replied, with a sudden sinking sensation in her belly. "She was tired all the time. And she said her head hurt."

"She was very young, to die of illness. It happens," Remin conceded, his arm tightening around her, pressing her to the warm solidity of his body. "I have seen it. There was a footman at Ereguil who used to have brainstorms, and he died when he was twenty-two. There was rotten water inside his head, the healer said."

"But you think it was something else," she said slowly. Turning over, she met his eyes. "Just tell me."

"I guess that she was only spared for your sake," he said quietly. "I think once you were old enough, the Emperor might have decided to have her killed. She likely knew something dangerous. I don't *know* anything, but...there are many poisons that mimic illness."

She said nothing. Maybe in some deep, dark part of herself, she had always suspected it. But she had been a child when her mother died, and her memories were few and hazy. It seemed to her that more than once, she remembered seeing her mother suddenly get up, her voice muffled, *it's all right, darling, play with Sir Bunkin,* which had been the name of her favorite stuffed rabbit. The fleeting vision of a handkerchief pressed to her mother's bleeding nose.

Might her father have ordered her mother's death?

There was no question that he could have. A man that would wipe out two Houses to the third generation, men, women, children, servants, would not scruple to kill even the mother of his child. But it made her feel sick.

"She used to get nosebleeds," she said, wondering why he was bringing this up now. "But I don't remember. I was six when she died."

"Poison is most often administered in food," he replied. There was a frozen moment, and then Ophele reared back as if he had slapped her.

"She *wouldn't,*" she said instantly. "No, you think Azelma would do such a thing? She never would, *never!*"

"She was your mother's cook." His eyes met hers, dark and knowing. "The only person that followed her from the capital to Aldeburke. Hired for her household by the Emperor."

"You—you think she came here to *hurt* me? Or you?" she asked in horror, shaking off his arm as she sat up. "Remin—she's my friend, she...no one else took care of me. I didn't tell you, but she even used to...sneak food to me."

"Oh, wife, I know. Miche told me," he said, so gently she felt like bursting into tears. "I'm sorry—"

"She didn't do it," Ophele interrupted, sliding out of bed and reaching for her chemise. She couldn't talk about this while she was naked, with the feel of his skin still tingling all over her.

"We can't be sure." He was so very *reasonable,* she felt a sudden surge of fury.

"You couldn't be sure of me, either," she said angrily, yanking her chemise over her head. "For months, even when I was trying so hard, and I never did anything but be my father's daughter."

"Ophele—" He sat up.

"No. Azelma is my *friend,*" she interrupted, with furious tears burning as she snatched up her morning gown. "She was my only friend my whole life, until I came here, and you're *insulting* her. Lady Verr!"

The bedroom door thudded shut. Remin did not come after her.

It completely spoiled the snow. It spoiled everything. Lady Verr and the maids were already in the solar, and only after she was in her dressing room did she hear Remin's heavy tread in the hallway, and his voice calling sharply for Magne.

"Master Tiffen sent a new practice gown, my lady," Lady Verr said in an encouraging sort of way, brandishing a glorious confection of a ballgown, deep violet satin and silk with embroidered feathers, gleaming and metallic.

"It's beautiful," Ophele said dutifully, though the train that fell from her shoulders and trailed six feet behind her felt as if she had Remin strapped to her back instead. Sitting silently, she allowed Lady Verr to make her up and dress her hair, the full regalia that she would wear to a Segoile ball, including the pearl jewelry Azelma had brought her. Lady Verr was so happy to have real jewels, she didn't even care that they didn't match the gown.

It made Ophele angry all over again to think that Azelma had risked so much, even stealing jewelry and bringing it all this way, just so Ophele could have a little bit of her mother.

How could Azelma do that, if she was the one who had killed her? Slowly, over *years,* with poison.

"House Pomeret?" Lady Verr said, when they were settled in the solar beside the roaring blaze of the fire, sewing in hand. Lady Verr had been conscientiously reviewing the key figures of each duchy of Segoile, beginning with Agnephus and Melun, though she cautioned that she had little personal experience with these most powerful families.

"Duke Wandrille Pomeret and Duchess Edelene," Ophele recited. "Forty-seven and thirty-nine years old, eight children. He is fat and likes his drink and she enjoys weaving and embroidery. She is pious and he likes to appear so, and they make many offerings to the Temple."

It was mean to say such things about people she had never met. And Ophele did not like knowing who had mistresses and whose first wife had died under suspicious circumstances and whose children bore a striking likeness to the head footman. It was all so...ugly.

"And?"

"And their oldest son is nineteen, and has made an offer for the Crown Princess." Ophele had not wanted to hear about the Emperor and Empress, but she was secretly wild with curiosity about her half-sister. What must it have been like, to grow up in Starfall, the object of so much attention and expectation? "But he is not expected to succeed."

"Or was not, when I left," Lady Verr qualified. "It is important to remember that such things can shift overnight. What are the names of high House Pomeret?"

This was easy, rote memorization, and Ophele hardly had to pay attention as she rattled off ages and names and hobbies, along with the names of key retainers and even some of the more interesting figures from the cadet branches, including one who had run away from home to join a troupe of actors.

Justenin had told her that the foundations of House Pomeret's power were cattle and piety: they had made their fortune on the inland plains of the Empire, then bullied their way into many other interests, particularly in the Temple. It was interesting to see how the scales of power weighed, and to learn how each of the Great Houses of the Empire had accumulated it. But today, it only reminded her that Remin had once made just such a dossier about *her,* and she wondered unhappily how much this exercise *really* revealed about those distant people.

"I know the gown is heavy, but please remember to sit up straight, my lady," Lady Verr reminded her, and Ophele adjusted herself again with a sigh. Silk and satin were all very well, but when the gown was sufficiently heavy she felt in danger of sliding right off her chair. "That was all correct; we will move on to House Firkane..."

Ophele had never been good at sustaining anger. But there were so many factors in its favor at the moment, from her gown to the gossip to the heavy blanket over her lap, upon which she was sewing an endless seam. The tight backstitches were meant to be as tiny and even as humanly possible, or else she would have to unpick them and do them again. It was excellent practice, and she was in *hell.*

She was so rarely angry, she didn't know what to *do* with it. She wanted to fling the blanket away and rip off the heavy, beautiful dress, she didn't want to be doing *any* of this. Learning nasty things about people she didn't know, with Davi and Leonin standing at the wall like statues, listening to every word as if this were *normal*. No one had ever asked if she wanted to do this. Any of it.

During her dance lesson, she was so singularly terrible at keeping the tempo, Leonin called a halt mid-lesson.

"My lady, are you well?" he asked.

"Yes."

"It's all right if you aren't," said Davi, bending down with a worried look in his eye.

"I am fine," she said, looking him dead in the face. There was a meaningful silence.

"Whether you are or you are not, my lady," said Lady Verr pleasantly, "this is an excellent time to practice appearing so."

It was noon before the Duchess of Andelin was finally permitted to do what she wanted to do, which was go outside and see Azelma. She excused herself and headed straight downstairs, forgetting all about the blizzard until she was out in it, with Leonin and Davi hurrying after her and objecting with every fiber of their beings.

"My lady, please let us go fetch her. You want to see Azelma, right?" Davi was loath to actually obstruct her. "I can bring her up to the solar—"

"She is seventy-two, she should not come out in a blizzard." But Ophele had had no notion what a blizzard would be like herself; she could barely see two feet in front of her, and she was wading through it up to her shins, dragging her train in her arms so it would not be completely ruined.

She had to talk to Azelma. But she didn't know what she was going to say. The two possibilities were irreconcilable: either Azelma had looked after both her and her mother all these years and was deserving of eternal gratitude and a comfortable retirement, or she had done something so awful that the only punishment could be death.

No. Ophele did not believe it. *Remin* might be suspicious, but he suspected everyone, all the time. She would not do that. It was a terrible way to live.

Deaf to Leonin and Davi's protests behind her, she waded over to Azelma's cottage and knocked on the door.

"Azelma?" she called. "It's me, I hope you're all right."

"Your Grace?" Azelma's voice was muffled from inside the cottage, and a second later the door cracked open and there was her face, wrinkled as a winter apple. "Bless you, child, what are you doing out there in the snow? Hurry and come in before the hot air goes out."

Ophele ducked inside and defiantly shut the door behind her.

"Are you warm enough in here? Did they bring you breakfast?" she asked as she slipped out of her cloak. She was half-frozen, colder than she had ever been in her life, and her fingers and toes burned unpleasantly as they thawed.

"Quite warm, as you see. Sit down, silly girl, what under the stars are you wearing?" Azelma scolded, bustling about the small space to put a few more logs on the fire and a blanket on Ophele's lap.

"It's a ballgown, I must practice wearing a train," Ophele explained, feeling foolish. She knew just how much work it must have taken, embroidering all the feathers on the bodice, and she might have ruined it in the cold and wet.

"I suppose you must, at that." Azelma's lips folded together and she rose and went to the hearth. "Let me put the kettle on. This is what you meant about your lessons?"

"Yes, they are all teaching me to dance, and oratory, and all about society. The Emperor sent a summons, you see..."

This was a sudden test of everything she had learned, from the management of her expression to the examination of the elderly woman sitting beside her. Because there was only one thing Ophele *really* wanted to say, a question that scalded the tip of her tongue, an impossible, impulsive, foolish outburst: *did you poison my mother?*

But what could Azelma say to that? Either way, she must deny it, and she would be hurt, terribly hurt, that Ophele could think such a thing for even an instant. Looking down at her hands, Ophele prattled on about all the things she was learning to hide her anger and confusion, attempting to employ the lessons in diversion Justenin had been teaching her.

"...but that's not why I came to see you," she said, accepting the teacup and spooning in a bit of sugar. "His Grace...His Grace went to see Wen in the kitchens this morning, to see if he would like your help. The manor kitchen won't be ready for a while yet. And of course, you needn't do anything at all," she added anxiously. "But if you like, then you can, that's all. If you want."

"No, my lady, I would be happy to be useful." Azelma patted her hand. "You know, I had no notion of coming here to run your kitchen. I will be pleased to bake, or help this Wen fellow, or pluck chickens if that's what's needful. Wen of Tallford, you said?"

"Yes. He shouts a lot," Ophele confessed. Guilt was overriding anger. "He—it's because he is protecting Remin's food, you see..."

"He must be a proper guard dog," Azelma said, and almost made her burst into tears on the spot.

"Oh, he is, I have heard him tear strips off people..."

It was only after the tea had actually passed her lips that she froze. For a single instant, she nearly spit it back out. And then she was appalled with herself, and angry with Remin for putting such a terrible thought in her head. Did she or did she not trust Azelma?

Deliberately, Ophele took another sip, letting the taste coat her tongue. It tasted like any other tea. She didn't know what she thought yet. She did not have a solution to Remin's problem. But she knew that Azelma would never *ever* have poisoned her mother.

"I am perfectly well, and Adelan is a thoughtful fellow, so don't mind about me," Azelma said when Ophele rose at last to leave. One of the logs had burned through in the fireplace, and Justenin would be returning soon for afternoon lessons.

"Well, you will tell me if you need anything," Ophele said, taking Azelma's hands and careful of her knuckles, which had always been knobbled and swollen from the hard work of the kitchen. "I do still want to visit you."

"You're a princess, and a duchess, for true now," Azelma said gently. "You can't be consorting with the cook."

"Remin...Remin said we can do what we like in his valley," Ophele replied, struck with a fresh wave of confusion, and submitted to being bundled up in her cloak and pushed out the door into the wrathful arms of Leonin and Davi.

"My lady, you will excuse me," Leonin said tightly, lifting her off the steps with the swirl of an additional cloak that covered her to her sodden slippers. Ophele did not have the nerve to protest as he carried her through the swirling snow toward the front of the manor, with Davi's stiff, angry back marching ahead.

* * *

Hard work had always been one of Remin's favorite refuges.

He was convinced it did him good to be just another man with a shovel, and it certainly did his men good to see him laboring beside them. In the excitement over the first real snow of the year, none of the men from the barracks protested when they were ordered off to the market with their shovels. Once that was clear, they moved out to the major roads, with many good-natured wagers over who would be done first.

"It is *not* called Goose Road," Remin said for the hundredth time, after Miche had ordered a second group of men up that way.

"Well, you'd better come up with another name soon, or that one's going to stick," Miche replied, sinking his spade into the snow. "Victorin Avenue?"

It was an unusually serious suggestion, and Remin's brows knit.

"No..."

"Clement Highway."

"No."

"Bon Street."

Both men paused in their shoveling. That one actually had a ring to it.

"Maybe," said Remin thoughtfully. "You know what *they* would have said."

"Mmm-hmm. Ludovin would've laughed himself sick, to be a namesake," said Miche, smiling crookedly.

"I thought about naming my sons after them," said Remin, resuming his shoveling. "When they come along. And I thought—maybe I would name the new bridge after Rasiphe."

"I like that," Miche agreed, tossing a shovelful of snow into the trees. "But if you ask me, I'd tell you to name your boys what they look like, Rem. If one strikes you as a Victorin, then fine, but that's a heavy weight to put on a boy, naming him for a dead hero."

That was a fair point; he hadn't thought of it like that. Remin was going to an awful lot of trouble to keep his children from knowing the burdens of their parents.

"But what do I know?" Miche added. "I haven't any youngsters of my own. That I know of."

"I think their mothers would have claimed you, if you did," Remin said dryly. A few of them had already tried. "I like Rasiphe for the bridge. And Bon did like to sing. You know Nore's planning to put a theater on that road one day. It would be a fine thing, to call it Bon Street."

"He would have liked that," Miche said appreciatively. "What about Clement?"

"Something at the Court of War. The training hall," Remin said, the idea coming to him as if it had been waiting for exactly the right moment.

"Clement Sparrowheart?" Miche laughed. That was one of the kinder names Clement had been called, and Miche himself had bestowed a few of them. Clement had wanted to be a knight, and Miche had done him the courtesy of believing him, and then doing his best to break him. "Promise me there will be a statue. The short knight, with spectacles and a stutter."

"Who trained harder than anyone else," Remin agreed, meeting Miche's glance with perfect understanding. If there was any example he wanted to set before his men, it was not himself. It was Clement in the stoneyards of Rospalme, in the rain, in the dark, in the sweating humidity of an Ereguil summer, working harder than anyone else just to be average. Sir Clement of Feuille, who they had found in the center of a small mountain of Vallethi dead.

"Some of the others will be more difficult," Miche said thoughtfully. "Unless you want to dedicate the Ludovin Saccey Memorial Brothel."

"I don't think so," Remin said, but he couldn't help a snort of laughter. Maybe they might name the theater itself for him. Ludovin, the accomplished mimic. Hanged as a spy.

The thought drove the smile off his face.

"We need to do something about these shovels," he said, after they had worked in silence for a time. "This is meant to take the place of morning exercises. I can't even break a sweat with this thing."

"And we're going to be all day about it, besides," Miche agreed, casting a glance down the lines of laboring men. "I'll see what I can do about it, as Master of Snow."

Shouldering his shovel, he about-faced and marched away, leaving Remin shaking his head. Miche's nonsense was exactly what he needed, and there was a great deal of satisfaction in imagining Tresingale's ever-evolving maps, where *Bon Street* would replace *Goose Road.*

But all too soon, Remin's mood soured, as all the other things he had been trying not to think about floated back to the surface.

He was *not* going to apologize.

Remin dug deep into the snow, wishing all his problems could be solved with a shovel. Along the lines on either side of him, dozens of other shovels were moving, the men jeering each other good-naturedly about who could fling their snow the furthest. The farther the better; winter would be long, and there would be much more snow to come.

But Ophele had never been *angry* with him before. The stars knew he had given her reason, and he understood why she would react that way. No one wanted to think a dear friend would betray them. Loyalty was a virtue, right up until it became a liability.

Was there another way he might have gone about it? A gentler way to say, *have you ever wondered whether your friend might have killed your mother?*

Well, it didn't really matter now. He had already said it.

And even if he could undo it, he wouldn't. He was not going to apologize if he didn't think he was wrong. Oh, Azelma might be innocent, and they would probably never know who or what had killed Ophele's mother. But he wasn't wrong to be cautious. He was still alive because he had been cautious, *exhaustingly* cautious, and he was going to do the same to protect Ophele whether she liked it or not.

Inwardly, he admitted he would do almost anything for her. But this fell on the wrong side of *almost*.

And didn't he have a right to be angry? Remembering what she had said that morning still stung. He did *not* like having his past mistakes flung in his face. Had he ever done that to Ophele? No. He had never once chastised her for her errors, even though they could have been spared considerable heartache if she had just *talked* to him.

Essential honesty forced Remin to admit that he *had* chastised her cruelly for things her father had done.

That was enough to dent his resolve, just a little. Remin finished his shoveling with a ferocious scowl, handily winning the competition for furthest-flung snow without ever realizing he was part of it.

Edemir's secretaries had been pleading for him to come and sign things with escalating desperation, so Remin spent a few hours sweating in the close quarters of the office, squeezed under a too-small desk. By the time he was done, he was glad to return to the yard behind the stables, where Leonin and Davi could help burn off the excess energy that was making him jumpy and irritable.

One look at Leonin's face warned him he was about to be more irritable.

"My lord," the knight began, raising his voice to be heard over the howling wind. "Before we begin, I think we must tell you..."

Remin listened expressionlessly as Leonin and Davi related what had happened that afternoon, or at least, related the details as far as they knew them, because the two men had been reluctant to actually force their way into Azelma's cottage.

"She is a duchess, Your Grace," Leonin concluded. He knew even better than Remin what courtesies this required, and Ophele was a Daughter of the Stars besides, and never to be lightly handled. "We wish to abide by your will, but we feel we must also respect her rank and wishes."

"We would've had to take hold of her to stop her," Davi added bluntly. "She was going where she wanted to go, my lord."

Both of them watched him warily, braced for an explosion. And while it was true that he was absolutely furious, Remin was not going to inflict it on them. They were in an awkward position, hoping to be Ophele's hallows while at the same time bound by oaths to honor him as their lord, and Remin had introduced this uncertainty himself, when he gave Ophele the choice of refusing her hallows. In truth, he had never expected his resolve to honor her wishes to be tested so severely.

"I see," was all he said, and drew his sword. All three men were in full armor, helmets and all, and he was suddenly, savagely glad. "You did right. I will speak to her. Please attempt to secure the gate."

None of them could even see the gate through the blizzard. It was late afternoon and the snow was falling so thickly that a man six feet away almost vanished. But they needed to practice in conditions of reduced visibility, too; they might just as easily be attacked in rain, in snow, in fog, at night. Remin exhaled a long white plume and then launched himself forward.

They might have been the only people in the world, moving through a deadly dance of shifting steel, muffled and obscured by the swirling snow. But Remin could not focus. His breath rasped in his ears inside his helmet, puffed hot and moist over his face, too hot. The anxious energy he had been trying to burn off all day was almost too much for him now. His strength was insufficient to his need, and still too much for Leonin and Davi as he battered at them.

Couldn't he have just a few months of peace? It was hard enough to keep Ophele safe without her fighting him about it, and come spring he would be forced to take her to the capital like a lamb to slaughter, his lamb, his fucking *heart* laid out on an altar for the bastard Emperor. As glad as he was to have Miche home, Remin would almost have traded his friend to get that old woman gone. Azelma Bessin, who had been just so perfectly placed beside Lady Pavot. And now was so perfectly placed to come near Ophele.

"Get up," he snarled at Leonin and Davi as he knocked them over. "Get up, get up, get *up*. Is this all you can do?"

He paused long enough to let them regain their feet and then savaged them again. They had to be better than this. None of them could afford to be weak, not for a single moment. Ophele had no idea how carefully she was being protected, how difficult it was to anticipate *everything,* how one single mistake could mean something happened that could never be undone. *He* knew. He was not wrong to be worried.

Remin forgot about the cold. He forgot about the snow. He forgot about everything but the two opponents before him, and the vicious brutality of the exercise. His sword sliced through the air in a massive, heavy arc, powerful enough to knock even Davi sprawling when it landed. Without armor, it could cut a man in half. His muscles burned and the frigid air seared his lungs as he breathed, but he didn't stop. He couldn't stop. It *never stopped,* no matter what he did.

"Your Grace! Your Grace! *My lord!*" Davi was shouting. Remin snapped back to himself to find Leonin and Davi were crowded up against the fence on the wrong side of the stable yard altogether, desperately defending. They had a great many new dents in their armor.

"My lord, forgive us," Leonin said, pulling off his helmet. His dark hair was plastered flat to his head with sweat and his nose was bleeding. "We failed to gain the gate. We will do better."

"No. You did well." Remin was ashamed of himself. A good lord did not vent his frustrations on his people, and Davi and Leonin would be no protection to Ophele if he broke them in training. "Go...thaw. You are welcome to join us for supper in the solar."

"My lord," they said courteously, and departed.

He did not feel better. His heart was still racing, his blood singing in his ears, and Remin took off his helmet in the snowy yard and let his head fall back, the soft flakes drifting onto his hot face and melting instantly. It was so quiet, he could hear the snow falling, the big flakes lightly patting down, one on top of the other.

It was very, very cold.

Remin made his way inside and stripped off his armor with numb, clumsy fingers, shivering so badly he had to clench his jaw to keep his teeth from chattering. In the steaming water of the bath, even his arms and thighs burned as they thawed, and he stretched out in the tub, covered his face with a hot towel, and waited for things to stop hurting.

The familiar evening noises echoed in the hallway outside and from the open door of the solar, an intimacy that normally would never be granted in the lord's portion of the house. There was Magne's querulous voice, consulting Lady Verr on what Ophele would wear to dinner, so that His Grace might be dressed to match. Juste's lower tones, bidding farewell as he went out into the blizzard to fetch food for them all. Miche's voice, cheerfully inviting himself to supper.

Ophele's soft voice moved up and down the hall as she went to dress for the meal, as she would in Segoile. In the capital, noblewomen might change clothes three or four times a day.

It wasn't only Ophele that he feared for. His men, his friends, the knights that he thought of as his brothers. His servants, who were proving to be good and faithful. His people. He had so much, now.

So much to lose.

* * *

Remin had not spoken a single word to her.

In the dark, he was only a few inches away, but it might as well have been miles. Lying on his side with his broad back to her, it felt like an insurmountable wall lay between them. As far as she could tell, when he had finally come to bed, he had laid down, closed his eyes, and gone instantly to sleep.

He hadn't even *looked* at her.

All through supper and the conversation that followed, she had been braced for him to bring up Azelma again, because she was positive she hadn't heard the last of *that*. She had been prepared for a scolding, knowing full well that Davi and Leonin would have told him what had happened; even if Leonin was as pleasant as ever, it was written all over Davi's face. And Ophele was guiltily aware that she had done the one thing that would anger Remin most: gone somewhere alone, and shut the door on her guards.

But he hadn't said anything. He had spoken very little through supper. Miche, Leonin, and Lady Verr bore the burden of the conversation, comparing various banquets of the capital. She hadn't noticed it before, but even with Leonin and Lady Verr's exquisite manners before her, Miche was every bit their equal.

"I think I will go to bed," she said, when she had picked at her food and could bear it no longer. It was still snowing outside.

"Good night, my lady," said Miche, glancing from her to Remin with a glint of sympathy. "The storm will blow over by morning, you'll see."

Davi, Leonin, and Justenin murmured farewells, but Remin only moved further down the table to fill everyone's cups with wine.

"Do not take it too much to heart, my lady," Lady Verr murmured as she removed the ribbons from Ophele's carefully curled hair. Remin hadn't even noticed them. "It is natural to have disagreements."

"Did you often argue with...Lord Verr?" Ophele asked, wondering again that the lady could look so untroubled at the mention of her dead husband.

"Yes," she said serenely. "But if you are right, you must not let him persuade you that you are not."

Ophele *did* think she was right. But it was very hard not to be shaken when she was sitting by the fire alone, trying to read her calculus book and absorbing nothing at all. It felt like hours passed before Remin finally appeared in the door, and when he did, he went straight to the bed, undressed, and slid under the covers without even saying *good night*.

Well, *fine*.

Blowing out the candles, Ophele pulled the covers up to her chin and pointedly turned her own back. She didn't want to talk to him, either.

It was *horrible* to be so suspicious of people. It was a terrible way to live. And even if Remin wouldn't trust Azelma himself, didn't he trust Ophele's judgment? Wasn't he always saying that she had a good deal of sense? Or did that only apply when she was sensible enough to agree with *him?*

As the fire crackled and the endless minutes ticked by, Ophele realized she was waiting for him to roll over and talk to her, to speak first, to be the first to apologize. Ever since her sun sickness, he had always been the first to reach out and ask what was wrong, what was she thinking, to coax her into confiding in him. Without even realizing it, she had been sure he would do that again.

Except...

She *had* said something terrible to him this morning. Even more terrible because it was true, and the truth hurt worse than any lie. In the beginning, Remin hadn't trusted her, and he had punished her unjustly, and she knew he still felt guilty about it. She had used that against him, even though he had apologized and tried to make up for it ever since.

What if he didn't forgive her?

What if things were never right between them again?

That thought was almost enough to make her turn and wake him and beg his pardon at once. But there was also a secret, sneaky part of herself, carefully nurtured by Lady Verr and Justenin, that knew there was another way. All she had to do was cry. If she cried and then gave him a nudge or two, Remin would wake up and ask what was wrong and give her anything she wanted.

But Ophele did not want to stoop to such tricks. She wanted him to agree with her because she was right, not because he wanted her to stop crying.

A few tears did escape as she lay there and thought about it. It wasn't just abstract principles of trust and judgment. She had hoped he would like Azelma. She had imagined them sitting together in the solar of an evening, and the look on Remin's face when Azelma teased him in the same tart way she had always done to Ophele. They were the two dearest people in the world to her, and she had been so pleased at the thought that Azelma would get to know Remin, and see how wonderful he was...

Neither she nor Remin had parents, after all.

It might have been hours or years, lying there in the dark with the glow of the fire dimming beyond the bed hangings. Sometimes its crackling seemed very far away and indistinct, and other times real and present. She dozed, and then came back to herself as Remin jerked beside her, letting out a single gasp.

"Remin?" she said before she could think the better of it, and was already reaching for him when he turned over and caught her. In spite of the cold, he was drenched with sweat. "Oh, Remin," she whispered, pushing his damp hair back from his forehead. "Was it a bad dream?"

He had been having them almost every night, but he refused to talk about them. And he didn't now, either, only held her tightly for a long time, drawing long, deep breaths with his face buried in her hair.

"You went to see Azelma alone," he said finally, low.

"Yes. I—"

"Don't do that again. Bring her up to the house if you want to see her. And don't eat or drink anything she gives you."

Even with his heart still racing under her cheek, this was too much. Ophele lifted her head.

"Remin," she began, exasperated. "I understand you're worried, but I *know* her. She is my fr—"

"Or I will send her away," he said. The words were quiet but implacable. "Don't push me on this."

The threat rendered her temporarily speechless.

"You wouldn't," she managed, a pitiful response when it was abundantly clear that he would. "That isn't *fair.*"

"Many things in this world are not."

"But—but...you can't *do* that!" she exclaimed, shoving at his chest until he let her up, gobsmacked by the *irrationality* of his position. Did he think they could live like this all their lives, never trusting anyone but the small circle of people that had passed some horrific psychological test of his devising? "We can't...live like that! I can't. If you would just—"

"Wife." Just that one word silenced her. "Did you know that Wen tastes all our food before he sends it up to the house?"

"No," she said, resigned.

"He was poisoned three times during the war, tasting my food. Not just from the Emperor, Valleth tried too. Wen always says he's too fat to poison. The dosages involved..." Remin trailed off. "But Bon died. He drank from a cup that was meant for me, pure luck. Gen stuffed charcoal down his throat and tried to make him sick it back up. It didn't work. He died badly."

She could not think of anything to say.

"Poison isn't like anything else," he went on quietly. "You can't see it. You can't fight it. Once you know it's there, it's already too late. And it hurts. Nothing hurts like poison."

The way he said that, so sharp and so brittle. Ophele gave up and flung her arms around his neck, squeezing as hard as she could, and felt his arms go around her so tight she couldn't breathe.

"But that won't happen," she told him, when he had held her for long enough. "Azelma wouldn't. Ever."

"You're willing to bet your life on that?"

"Yes."

"What about mine?"

She wanted to say yes, right away. Not an instant's hesitation. But what he had just told her shook her. Because if there was the slightest chance she was wrong...

"I don't know," she said finally, honestly. "But it's not fair to not even give her a chance. Does that mean you're just not going to let her cook for us, ever?"

But his silence told her that was exactly what that meant. It had never even crossed her mind that he might feel that way. Azelma had been the perfect solution to their problem, a capital-trained cook that suited even Lady Hurrell's picky palate, a cook who Ophele knew personally, who could be trusted never to hurt him. And Remin intended to turn her away without even a hearing? Without even *discussing* it?

"You never gave me a chance to defend myself, and I hated it," she burst out. "I know why you didn't trust me. I understand, Remin, I really do. My fa—the Emperor. But we never talked about it, and there was nothing I could do or say. And what will we do, if it's not her? Will Wen just cook for us forever? He's much older than we are."

She touched his cheek to make him look at her.

"I don't know," he said reluctantly. But that was a start.

"I would've told you I was sorry sooner," she said softly. "If we had talked. And that I had never spoken to the Emperor, not once, and that I wanted to help. I wanted to tell you that all along. Couldn't you listen to her? Please *try*, Remin."

"It does no harm to listen," he said, and laid his brow against hers with a sigh she felt through her own body. "I won't promise to change my mind. I meant to talk to her anyway. She was there with your mother, in the capital. She might know what happened. Or at least your mother's part. I won't blame you," he added, pressing a kiss to her forehead. "But I have to know. You don't have to listen, if you don't want to."

But he didn't say that the way he usually would. It wasn't a reassurance. And even in the dim light she saw the challenge in his dark eyes, a gauntlet thrown down. If she wanted to make such dangerous decisions, then she would have to listen, too. In a strange way, this would be the price she paid for allowing Azelma in striking distance of them both.

"No," she said, lifting her chin. "I want to hear it."

* * *

If Ophele had had her way, they would've gone straight to Azelma's cottage the next morning and talked about it at once. Like digging out a splinter. But though she and Remin had gotten over their disagreement—as evidenced by the fact that Remin had concluded the discussion by rolling on top of her and then into her, and did it again in the morning—he only shook his head when she proposed it.

"I have things I must see to," he said with a glance at the windows, where true to Miche's prediction, the storm had blown over, and the sun shone painfully bright on the hard crust of snow. "They need my help securing the last of the ferries, and they're hauling one up into dry dock, to see if it might be fitted for ocean travel."

"To go to Segoile?" she guessed. That would be much faster than going in a carriage.

"Yes, though I don't know if I want you on its maiden voyage," he said, covering her hand with his and trying to smile. It didn't reach his eyes. "And I don't want to have to cut this conversation short. Tonight will be soon enough. Invite her to supper, and let her know that I'll have questions after."

"All right."

His hand was hot. And he did not look very well, she thought, studying him over the rim of her teacup. His eyes were shadowed and red, and the downturn at the corners of his mouth didn't seem like his habitually grim expression.

"I am sorry I made you worry," she said suddenly. "I won't do it again. Even if it is Azelma. I will be careful."

"Thank you," he said, and it felt like things were back to normal again when he bent for a kiss after breakfast before he left, bellowing for Magne.

"I'll tell you what I know," Azelma said when Ophele went to visit her again, this time dressed appropriately for the snow and with Davi and Leonin standing just inside the door of the cottage, pretending they weren't there. "I suppose I shouldn't be surprised, that His Grace might want to know. But, child, there won't be much comfort to either of you in that business."

"I know my mother...did something," Ophele assured her, trying to sound brave. Inside, her heart was fluttering. "Lady Hurrell told me she did."

"She did," Azelma agreed, somber. "She was very ashamed of it, child. She never wanted you to know. But I believe she would have wanted His Grace to be told. He has the right, if anyone does."

Remin had promised that he would not blame Ophele, no matter what it was. But her fingers twisted together, and suddenly she wished she hadn't pushed this issue at all.

"Is it...very bad?" she asked softly. Azelma squeezed her hand.

"His whole family. Yes, that's as terrible as it gets. Your mother never meant for that to happen," Azelma added. "Though I doubt it will be much comfort. But it's naught to do with you, no matter what Lady Hurrell told you all those years. Just you keep telling yourself that."

"I will."

"And truth to tell, if I expected to be questioned, I wouldn't have expected something so gentle as a supper." Azelma gave her a pat. "As if *I* should come and sit at table with the likes of *them,* my stars. The Knights of the Brede!"

"That's what I said," Ophele said, summoning a ghost of a smile at the strangeness of the world, and sat down for a nice visit. It was even more astonishing that it was not strange at all to her now, and absolutely *bizarre* to think that in two hours' time, she was to go and stand before Sir Justenin of Tresingale, Knight of the Brede, and recite tongue twisters.

As promised, they sat together after supper that evening with steaming teacups and sugary plum cake. The furnishings Miche had acquired from Aldeburke had been brought up to fill the vast solar, with a seating area by the fire and a workspace at the far end of the room, making it feel warm and comfortable in a way Aldeburke never had. And best of all, he had retrieved her mother's old armchair, soft and warm and just Ophele's size, placed with honor beside Remin's larger chair. Even years later, the scent of her mother's sachet lingered.

Remin sat rigidly beside her in his chair, and Azelma faced them both, with her knobbled hands clasped in her lap and more unhappy than Ophele had ever seen her.

"I worked in the Emperor's kitchen," she began, heaving a gusty sigh. "When I was a girl, I came in as a baker's apprentice. My family owned a small bakery, you know, and it was a fine opportunity to come up. In time, I got my seal, and had charge of the Divinity's bread. He never complained."

Her mouth twisted ruefully.

"The downstairs, we always heard gossip, even the cooks. But that's all it is, gossip, for I never saw it with my own eyes, and most of the time I was abed while things were happening. Bakers rise terribly early. But we all knew the Emperor did not love his Empress, and took many others to his bed. I had it from the maids that sometimes the Empress even picked girls to send to him."

"To her *husband?"* Ophele asked, repulsed.

"Yes. They were long estranged by then, chi—Your Grace," Azelma corrected, with a quick glance at Remin. "Ten years at least, and still no babe. We heard about that often in the kitchen, they were always at poor Evrou, bless him, to add this or that to the Empress's meals, to try to encourage her to quicken. The first I heard of your mother was a call for melon sorbet from the Emperor's chambers. He never cared much for sweets. I didn't know until later who she was, or that she was in service to the

Empress. A new girl," Azelma added with a shake of her head. "The Empress takes debutantes into her service, if she likes the look of them; they are all presented to her, you know, Petals for the Roses. The Empress liked to have them trailing behind her about the palace."

"She might—the Empress might have sent my mother to the Emperor?" Ophele asked, a little faintly. Lady Verr had been acquainting her with some of the more palatable depravities of Segoile society, cautious of Remin's wrath, but the thought that *that* was how Ophele had been made was repugnant.

"Might be. Or it could be your mother caught the Emperor's eye on her own, and he sent for her. All I can say is that he did. Tea with honey in the morning," Azelma added, with a flicker of grief. "Fig roll, porridge with blackberries and cream. Apples in the afternoon, and..."

"...hazelnut cookies after supper," Ophele finished, with a grief that made her eyes burn.

"Yes," Azelma said softly. "We knew her preferences. And one day his steward came down to the kitchen to ask if anyone would like a temporary post as kitchen mistress. I said yes. I had my seal, but it's not the same as managing a whole kitchen. I hoped to have my own kitchen, one day. There is nothing like it, when everyone is humming along, and the smell of good food..."

"So you were not chosen," Remin interrupted. "You volunteered, without knowing where you would go or who you would serve."

"Yes, my lord," Azelma replied. What this might mean to Remin, Ophele could not guess; it sounded entirely innocent to her. "Later, I found out I was to serve the Emperor's mistress. He had given her a household of her own in Starfall, as a gift."

"Had he ever done that for his other mistresses?" Remin asked.

"Not that I heard, Your Grace, but that doesn't mean it didn't happen," Azelma replied, careful to distinguish gossip from fact. "The first time I laid eyes on her was in the entry of her manse, gathered with all the other servants when the Emperor brought her there. I've told you this before, my lady, but she was such a pretty girl, your mother. Golden hair and bright eyes, and a smile that made your heart glad. And not one ounce of meanness in her. She kept saying, *is it really for me?* And the Emperor smiled and said yes, to do with just as she pleased. As if a maid like that had any idea what to do with a manse in Starfall."

The girl without an ounce of meanness in her had still somehow seen Remin's family slaughtered down to his infant cousins.

"She really didn't mean any harm," Azelma said sadly, as if she could see this thought in Ophele's face. "If the Emperor was away, she was often up and down at night, and would come visit me as I was starting the day's bread. She talked about her home and her family. She missed them, and I think she was embarrassed to tell them what had happened, but...I believe she truly loved the Emperor. Maybe that was the trouble. She had been loved so well, she never thought anything bad could happen to her."

"Did she ever speak of the Emperor?" Remin asked.

"Yes, Your Grace." Azelma made a face. "He spoiled her. Gowns and jewels and twin kittens with blue eyes, she loved them dearly. And books. He would send books for her to read, and she said that they would discuss them together later. Riding, hawking, weeks at his country estates. He did...dote on her," she said, a little awkwardly. "She was very happy."

Until. No one said it.

"Then one day she came home and went straight to bed, and soon enough, there was a healer, and another healer, and late that night, there she was, coming down to my kitchen in her nightdress to tell me she was with child."

Instinctively, Ophele reached for Remin, and his icy hand closed over hers.

"I did not want to know that," Azelma admitted. "When I went to the Emperor's palace, my mother told me, *don't be mixing with the upper house,* and there I was, doing just that. And I can't say my mother was wrong," she said with a short laugh. "You mix with the upper house, and people start thinking you know things, and soon enough there's a man with hot pincers, wanting to have a talk."

She slanted a look at Remin.

"I don't think pincers will be necessary," he said, without the slightest alteration of expression. Ophele huffed, but Azelma just smiled.

"If I remembered the color of her nightrobe, I'd tell you that, too. But I listened, because she was a scared girl, and I liked her. And things happened fast, after that. They kept it secret, but your mother said the Divinity was over the moon, planning the nursery with her, already picking out names. She was sure he meant to acknowledge it. And you know, normally a girl in such a place would be off for a visit to the country, and that would be the last anyone heard of her."

"Bastards can't inherit," Remin said slowly, his black brows knotting. "It's in the Imperial Code. They can be acknowledged, and they can be granted property, but they can't inherit titles."

This was true. Ophele could have recited the relevant articles.

"Well, you would know better than I, Your Grace," Azelma spread her hands. "The last time I spoke to her in that kitchen, Lady Pavot talked about her family, her father and mother and brother, and did I think they would be dreadfully disappointed in her. She knew she had done wrong. But she thought...well. She said, *the Emperor needs an heir. It would be bad for the Empire if he didn't have one, wouldn't it?*"

There was a weighty silence. Even a cook would have known what that meant.

"But that would..." Ophele began faintly, after a rapid mental review of the Imperial Code. "The only way..."

"That would mean deposing the Empress," finished Remin.

"I don't know if she thought that far. I don't know what the Emperor might have promised her, or what plans they made,"

Azelma said, nodding. "But to me...that didn't sound like something she would have thought up on her own. Lady Pavot was never...scheming. That was part of her trouble, I don't believe she ever thought of him as the Emperor at all."

Azelma sighed and picked up her tea, but did not drink.

"And I know this next bit is what you most want to know, my lord, but there's little I can tell you. That was the year the Empress had her miscarriage, and all of Starfall was up in arms about it. The whole Empire, I guess. Everyone was afraid to stir a step while it was investigated, and there were some that said it was Lady Pavot that had caused it, that she had given the Empress poison. I will never believe it. But a carriage came for her, and she was gone for a while, at least a week. And when she came back, she was scared out of her wits. She gathered everyone together and said the household was to be closed. She thanked us, and said she had been happy, and wished us well. And I...well, if there was *ever* a time the lower house shouldn't mix with the upper, that was it, but those fool maids made me so blazing *mad*. They were all in the kitchen saying how the Divinity had had his fun, and that was that, and oh, my lady, it wasn't like that. I don't say that for *his* sake, but your mother wasn't..."

She exhaled sharply through her nostrils.

"Well, I went upstairs. And your mother was crying, of course. I talked to her a bit, but barring that night she told me she was with child, she did know how to keep a secret. She never told me what happened. She just cried and cried and kept saying, *he's letting me go, he said my family won't be hurt, so it's not that bad, is it?*"

"I didn't ask," Azelma confessed, with a guilty air. "I swear, Your Grace, I didn't want to know. You see a pregnant girl carrying the Emperor's bastard, you hear her say that...well, that's killing business, that is, and you don't need to know the Imperial Code to see it. When I left her, I said good-bye, and wished her the best, and I never meant to speak to her again. But everyone else *left*. One by one, over the next couple weeks, all of them scarpered, the maids and the footmen and the butler and even the boot boy. But you can ask anyone who was in the city back then, there wasn't a *whisper* of anything, before it happened."

"What happened?" Ophele's mouth was dry. Because she knew. Of course, she knew. Everyone knew how this story ended.

"I didn't choose to stay." The old woman looked down at her hands. "I just...didn't leave. Right up to the moment the carriage drew up in front of the manse, I was there, and it was loaded up, and wherever Lady Pavot was going, it wasn't home. She was shaking, she was so scared. So I thought, I'll just ride along for a bit. Just to the Starfall bridge, and then I'll hop down and that will be that. But I was there all the way into the city, and onto Crescent Street, and then we went past the Court of Rule, and then..."

"The Place of White Stones," Remin said quietly.

"Yes, Your Grace. We never actually got near it. The crowds were everywhere."

"What's...what's the Place of White Stones?" Ophele asked, looking between them.

"That's the place where they execute criminals, child," Azelma said gently. "We were caught up there for so long, even Lady Pavot roused enough to take notice. She asked the coachman what was the matter, and he went to check, and when he came back he told us they were executing House...that House." She glanced at Remin, her light blue eyes shining with unshed tears. "They had been executing them since dawn. Your Grace, I can stop if you want me to."

"No. Go on." His face was dead white.

"Yes. Well. Well, when she heard that, Lady Pavot gave a little scream and fainted dead away, but we were delayed so long, there was time for the coachman to run and fetch some smelling salts from an alchemist to bring her back around. We sat for hours before they finally started diverting traffic. She was...sick. We could hear it, every time the crowd cheered..."

Ophele covered her mouth with her hand, feeling as if she might be sick herself. She wanted Azelma to stop. She didn't want to hear anymore. No, she didn't want *Remin* to hear anymore. She wanted to cover his ears and tell Azelma to be quiet, but his face was so hard and cold and still, she didn't dare to move, and his eyes were like two open wounds.

"I could guess it had something to do with her." Azelma pulled a handkerchief from her pocket and blotted her eyes. "She kept saying, *but they promised they wouldn't, I said* I *did it, they said if I just signed*...she kept saying that, over and over again."

"Did she say what she did?" Ophele asked wretchedly.

"She confessed to poisoning the Empress." Azelma's hands knotted in her handkerchief. "Poison to keep her from conceiving, poison that would abort the Emperor's divine heir. She signed a confession that she had done it on the orders of Duke Benetot of...that House."

Ophele was frozen with horror.

"But—but she didn't," she whispered. "She didn't really—"

"No. I don't believe there was ever any such plot. Until the day she died, she said His Grace was innocent. And she was sorry for it," Azelma said quietly. "I know that doesn't help. Even when she began to get sick, she said it must be a curse from the stars, for what she had done. Mercy, child, I thought the same," she confessed, tears streaking her soft, seamed cheeks. "I will never forget that day. She was a good girl, but she was afraid, and she did a terrible, terrible thing. She was so afraid that you would pay for it, when she was gone."

The silence drifted down, soft and cold and complete, like a blanket of covering snow. Ophele's throat was so tight it hurt, as if all the words and thoughts and feelings were knotted and strangling her, and when Remin finally stirred and rose, she rose with him, terrified, horrified, and wanting more than anything else to somehow blot the last hour from his memory. But he caught her arms before she could wrap them around him, holding her gently away.

"Thank—thank you for telling me that," he said stiffly to Azelma. "I might ask you more questions later. I am—going out, for a little bit. Wife, I am not angry. You did nothing wrong. I am glad you were born. I will be back."

"Remin," she whispered, but she did not try to follow him. He did not even pause. He almost stumbled over Miche, who was hovering in the hallway right outside the door, and kept going, his heavy boots thudding toward the stairs.

"I'll go with him," Miche said quickly, and his face blurred in her vision as Ophele's tears overflowed, and she covered her face with her hands and sobbed wretchedly.

"Oh, child," said Azelma, just as she must have done all those years ago with Ophele's mother, and pulled her beside the fire to let her cry.

Chapter 6 – The Place of White Stones

It had not taken long for Remin to learn the details of his parents' executions.

Three months. He had not even turned nine.

They were traitors. The shock and terror of the Conspiracy followed him all the way to Ereguil, the last survivor of his House, a walking warning of the Emperor's wrath. Duke Ereguil had saved his life with some desperate gambit, but the logic of the people was that if the punishment was so terrible, surely the crime must have been unspeakable. Even in Ereguil, people looked at Remin askance, and common-born children called him a traitor to his face.

He felt guilty for years for visiting that shame on Duke and Duchess Ereguil. Though the Duke always swore that Remin's parents were innocent, for the longest time, Remin had been sure it was a lie, and the only reason the old man said it was because of some promise he had made to Remin's mother.

His father had died first. He learned that barely a month after it happened. Benetot of ________ had gone to the block in rags that scarcely covered his huge body, an unnamed prisoner whose House had already been blotted from the history books. It took six men to drag him to the block and hold him down.

"Stars above, protect my son," was all he said when they read the charges, and then they made him kneel, and put his head down on the block, and cut it off.

His mother had fought. Freezing in a ragged shift that was too cold for February, with her long hair shaved off, she had wept and struggled, refusing to lay down her head. Some of the Ereguil children had laughed at that, and called her a coward, but Remin had always wondered if she just hadn't wanted to put her face in her husband's blood.

Red blood showed very dark on the Place of White Stones, where rightful judgment could be witnessed by all, and then scrubbed white and clean after justice had been carried out. And after his mother had come Remin's grandparents, and then his uncles, and it had taken seven blows to sever his Uncle Soucine's head, after which they paused to sharpen the axe.

The executions went on for weeks, as all of the guilty were captured and brought to the capital. All of his father's House, down to the furthest cousins. All of his mother's House Roye, to the third generation. All the servants of both Houses, saving those who had fled. The oldest was Remin's great-grandmother Batilde, who was ninety-three and had to be helped up the steps to the block. His cousin Paole was the youngest to be beheaded; at twelve, he was tall enough to pass for sixteen.

All the other children and babies were strangled in prison.

Remin did not want to know these things. Others had flung this unwelcome knowledge in his face over the years, sometimes drunk and sometimes sober, sometimes viciously, and sometimes on the sands of the Court of War, hoping to unbalance him. When he was seventeen and went to Segoile, Remin had sought out the details himself, so at least he would know what was rumor and what was true, or malicious lie.

He had heard all of this before. He knew how all of them had died. That was a very old wound.

The cold air sank sharp teeth into him and Remin realized he was outside, but he hardly knew where he was going or why, only that he couldn't stay where he was. His long legs carried him down the lane beside the house, the white snow illuminating the dark enough for him to find his way, and the path to the stable had been shoveled only that afternoon.

His chest hurt. His hands shook as he clenched them into fists, striding faster and faster, and when he pushed open the doors of the stable, he didn't know why he was there. If he was running, he could not escape the thing that was chasing him.

There was no safe place. Ever.

* * *

Miche found him there a few minutes later, standing in the wide straw-strewn aisle between horse stalls, with his arms wrapped tightly around himself.

"Rem," Miche said, pushing the door shut. "A little late to go out riding."

"You were listening."

"Of course. Saves me the trouble of asking you and Ophele to repeat it later." Miche moved forward, but not too close. Even with the warmth of the horses, it was still cold enough in the stable that their breaths curled up white.

"I just needed to think." Remin's voice hitched. "I knew she had something to do with it. I knew—it doesn't change anything. They're all dead, and nothing will ever bring them back, and she...*betrayed* them."

"Whatever her mother did, Ophele is innocent," Miche said quietly.

"I know. I know, I don't blame her. I love her. I just don't...I don't know," Remin said, and sank down on a nearby bale of hay, scrubbing a hand over his face. "I know how it works. I can guess how it happened. She was young, alone, I'm sure they threatened her. They used her to kill my father, my mother, *everyone*, and I still don't know *why*."

Miche sat down beside him. Listening.

"If I don't know why, it could happen again," Remin whispered. His arms wrapped around his middle, his black eyes fixed on the floor. "I keep...dreaming about it, ever since that messenger came. I dream about the Place of White Stones, and...sometimes it's my father and my mother, and sometimes it's you there, or Juste, or Ophele on the block, and they cut off all her hair, and she's crying for me but I can't get to her, or I have to watch, and sometimes *he's* there and he *makes* me see it, he *makes* me watch..."

Miche did not need to ask who *he* was. There was only one person in the world that put that raw horror in Remin's voice, and Miche was one of the few people that knew that Remin was afraid of the Emperor, that he feared that man with an almost religious terror. The Emperor had destroyed his world, and had been terrorizing him since he was eight years old.

"He won't do that. That won't happen," Miche said, gripping his shoulder hard. "Juste is already seeing to that. And she's the Emperor's daughter, he can't—"

"Who says she is?" Remin yanked away, suddenly furious. "Can we *prove* that? What's to stop him from declaring her an imposter the second we walk through the gate in Starfall? He could say I killed her and got some woman to replace her, and who's going to argue? What am I going to do, wave fucking papers at him?"

"Oh." That was all Miche could manage, stricken.

"He could." Remin caught his breath. "He could. The Court of Nobility wouldn't stop him; they didn't stop him when he wiped out *two noble Houses*. The Temple wouldn't, not if he claims she's not an Agnephus. They might even have her flogged for blasphemy. He could have her killed, or imprisoned, or even if it's not now, it could be my children, he could take everyone away from me again, to the—the P-Place of White...and...and the crowd, and I can't...I *can't...*"

He was shaking all over, gasping, and Miche rose and went to him.

"Why can't he *leave me alone?*" Remin asked, his voice cracking, and even as Miche reached for him, he broke, in terrible, racking sobs. His shoulders heaved as he bent, letting Miche hold him even as Miche staggered under the weight and held on, arms squeezing as hard as he could, pounding the back of one huge, shaking shoulder with his fist.

"We'll think of something," he promised, forcing the words through his tight throat. "I swear it, Rem, I swear it. That will not happen. We'll talk to Juste..."

Remin wasn't listening. Not yet. His hot face pressed into Miche's shoulder just as he had done on a night many years before, the night when he had slipped away for his first kiss and come home with his first kill, and the blood of his sweetheart on his hands. And now, as then, there was no remedy. There was nothing Miche could say. Nothing he could do but hold on tight, and curse the Emperor in his heart.

But it wasn't long before this storm passed, and it wasn't because of anything Miche did. Remin just stopped, straightened, and sucked it in, shoving it all back down as he had done so many times before.

Gently, he shrugged off Miche's hands and stepped back.

"Sorry," he said, averting his eyes. "Sorry. I'll be back. I'm just going to...dunk my head."

Miche nodded. When Remin finally reappeared sometime later, his wet hair was freezing in spikes, and his eyes were very red.

"I had this put by," Miche said, producing a bottle of wine and patting the hay bale. Actually, he'd run off to Davi's cottage to steal it, but he had figured it might take Remin a bit to compose himself. "Drink. Don't stop until I count to five."

Remin did not smile. But he drank obediently for five slow seconds, and then sighed and handed the bottle back. His hands had stopped shaking.

"We won't let that happen," Miche repeated. "It's good that you thought of it. Edemir's there right now, and Juste is sending his singers out all over the Empire. If it comes to that, Bram will have his mercenaries in the Place of White Stones. The river's not far from there, and we'll have boats waiting. We'll have people in the prison. We'll get Brother Oleare to attest the authenticity of Ophele's birth records. Find some folk at Aldeburke to witness that Ophele is who we say she is. It's a good thing I didn't run them all off after all, I guess."

"Azelma?" Remin asked thickly, letting his head fall back against the stable door behind him. Brambles stuck his nose through the bars and chewed gently on his hair.

"Yes," said Miche, deadpan. "That was my plan all along."

Remin slanted a look at him.

"I never give you the credit you deserve."

"No one does," Miche sighed. He had a taste of the wine himself, decided it wasn't bad, and had a little more. One bottle wasn't enough to get either of them drunk, but it was enough to soften the edges, and possibly keep them from freezing to death. "You can't punish Ophele for what her mother did."

"I know. I won't."

"She would have been young," Miche offered, more quietly. "Lady Pavot was young when all this happened, the same age Ophele is now. And you can bet they threatened her family, and her baby."

"I know." The lines in Remin's face hardened. And there was not much more to say, after that.

"You had to go outside tonight," Miche said loudly as they were leaving, over the howling of the wind. It was actual work to haul the stable door shut.

"It's not that cold," Remin scoffed, though he did hurry his steps up the road, and soon they were skidding over the icy mud as they came to the corner of the house. Miche was glad to deposit him at the front door and then hurry back to his own cottage in the cold.

The conversation he had overheard had rocked him as badly as it had Remin.

Alone in the dark, his smile faded. His hands moved through the familiar routine: taking off his snowy boots, lighting candles, building a fire, sunk in gloom. He had been too late, again. Always, it seemed he was one step behind: too little, too late, arriving long after the worst of the damage had been done. One failure after another.

But then, he had accepted long ago that Miche of Harnost was a worthless man.

The cottage was small enough to warm up quickly with a fire in the hearth, and he was just pulling off his cloak when there was a soft rapping on his door.

"Sir knight?" asked a feminine voice.

Miche paused. Perhaps he should not answer that.

"Pardon me for disturbing you..." The voice went on after a moment, soft and breathy, beginning to be cold. But the woman out there would not have chilled yet, no; the other cottages were only steps away and her body would be a marvel of soft warmth, and so hot inside...

And Miche was so cold.

He hesitated, and opened the door.

"You have the advantage of me," he said with automatic charm, smiling down at a cute little brunette with cute little freckles on her cute little nose. The light of the fire glowed on her face, and he could see the small gap between her front teeth as she smiled. "You are one of the laundresses, aren't you? You're not required to work after supper."

"Oh, I want to," she said, opening her eyes wide. "I am Masilie. I was just collecting the washing for tomorrow, if you have any. Do you? Have any clothes you would like...removed?"

He had sworn to himself that he wasn't going to do this. This was Rem's home, the home he had worked so hard to build, and it took a long time to bring servants to the valley. But the rawness of the night was thick in his throat and when she stepped closer, her cloak parted to reveal the curves of pale breasts and a heat in her eyes that promised the sweetest oblivion. There was nothing like the touch of a woman to wipe everything else away.

"You should not be out so late," Miche said, wavering.

"I hope you will forgive me for disturbing you." Her fingers plucked at his shirt, then his belt. "I heard you had been long away, sir knight, and perhaps you would like someone to ease you..."

All by itself, his hand lifted to curve around her neck, his fingers slipping into her curly hair, his thumb gliding along the ridge of her jaw. He could feel her little gasp against his palm, her lips parting. He knew just how it would feel if that mouth was wrapped around him.

"You want to help me?" he whispered, bending his head so his lips tantalized hers without ever touching. It made her yearn after him, swaying toward him, even rising on her toes as he lifted his head just out of reach. His mouth curved, cruelly beguiling.

"Yes, sir knight," she breathed, and he stepped backward to pull her into his cottage, his eyes filled with a hot, hard light. He was angry with her for tempting him, and angry with himself for yielding. But soon enough he wouldn't have to think of anything at all.

As his door closed, the one in the next cottage cracked open, and in the flickering light was the slender silhouette of Lady Mionet Verr, who had heard those soft sounds of seduction.

* * *

When Remin opened the door of his bedchamber, Ophele was waiting.

"Remin..." She rose from her chair, but did not approach, her fingers moving through their familiar anxious dance. But for a long moment, he just let her fill his eyes. She looked so beautiful by firelight. Her fine skin, those large, expressive eyes, the gentle curves of her face. She had changed for the night into a pretty chemise and matching robe, red velvet lined in fur and trimmed in lace, and it made her look so...

In two strides he swept her up and found her every bit as warm and soft as she looked, and Remin buried his face in her and held on, reassuring himself that she was really there.

"I'm sorry. I'm so sorry," she whispered, wrapping her arms tightly around his neck. "Oh, Remin, that was so dreadful, I'm so, so sorry..."

"It's not your fault," he said huskily, and drew his chair up to the fire to sit with her. It felt better just to be there, with her in his lap, especially when she reached for a blanket to pull over them both and then nestled into him like some small, portable warming device.

"She always told me, there are some things you can't ever take back," Ophele murmured. "That I should be careful what I said. I know it doesn't matter, it doesn't fix anything. But she was always sorry."

It didn't matter. Regret would not bring his family back. But Remin thought about it.

"I am glad...she was sorry," he said, low. He didn't want to hear it. He didn't want to speak of her, ever again. He wished Ophele was *anyone* else's child. He sighed. "You can tell Azelma that I might want to talk to her again. And so will Juste. It will probably not be a comfortable conversation."

Remin let his head rest against hers, feeling a little sorry for the elderly cook. She did seem like a nice woman, and he was grateful that she had been there for Ophele, all those years. But it was not enough to win his trust.

"His family was there, too, weren't they?" Ophele asked quietly.

"Yes. His father and both his sisters."

The fire crackled in the quiet.

"Do you want me to read to you?" she asked at length, and when he nodded, she went to fetch one of the books Miche had brought back from Aldeburke, a story about the wood-folk of Illus. Ophele had been reading it to him whenever there was time, with the air of introducing him to a dear friend. It was good speaking practice for her to read aloud, and he could prop his chin on her shoulder, close his eyes, and empty his mind.

He never knew whether it was the wine or the conversation with Miche or Ophele herself, curled up against him all night long. But that night, if he dreamed, he did not remember it.

In the morning, it was snowing again.

"I have never seen so much snow," Ophele said, awed as she looked out the windows of the solar. Remin trailed behind her, scrubbing his eyes. He really had not wanted to get out of bed.

"The roads will need shoveling again," said Juste, setting breakfast on the table. His nose and ears were red with cold. Miche wandered in a few minutes later, his long blond hair loose on his shoulders, looking like a maned Noreveni lion as he yawned with all his teeth.

"We're going to need bigger shovels," he said, pulling Ophele's chair out for her like a gentleman and then repeating the courtesy for Lady Verr. "Sim and Jaose had to clear the walkways around the house three times yesterday."

"Let me know if you need help," Remin said, poking at his eggs with a fork rather than eating them. They looked singularly unappetizing this morning.

It was the first blizzard of the winter and he was already tired of snow. Pulling his cloak up over his shoulders, Remin kissed Ophele good-bye and went out into the cold, where Jaose was sweeping off the portico at the front of the house and Sim was clearing the path to the stable with a resigned expression. At least the snow had tapered off a little; when Remin drew Lancer up at the top of the hill, he could see all of Tresingale spread below him under a blanket of white, with smoke rising from many chimneys.

He did not like to think of Huber and his men trudging through that, along with who knew how many refugees. Miche would be leaving shortly with several hundred men to go and search for them, equipped with sledges, snowshoes, and heavy clothing, and enough spares to outfit all of Huber's men and half of Isigne besides. But travel in winter was dangerous. It was easy to get lost with half the landmarks buried in snow, and sometimes the Andelin blizzards were so fierce, a man could get lost between his house and his stable.

He would have to have a word with the folk in the cottages about that, just in case.

But his first stop of the morning was Genon's infirmary, which had been filling up over the past few days with patients suffering both frostbite and flu, especially the night guardsmen, who were not taking their winter clothing seriously.

"Layers. *Layers,*" Genon enunciated as he examined the purple nose of a grimacing soldier. "Don't take His Grace as your model, I beg, and think you've done enough to acquire a fur cloak. Ospret himself said that we have a little fire in us all, but it only helps if you bank the flames. Your Grace," he said, rolling one yellow eye toward Remin. "We were just talking about you."

"And without proper reverence," Remin agreed, though his glare lacked conviction. "That's what I was coming to check, Gen. Any casualties?"

"A few fingers and toes, but Tounot and Jinmin say so far everyone's accounted for," Genon replied, moving both Remin and himself nearer to the iron stove pumping out heat in the center of the room. The infirmary was a long, low stone building with small windows set high off the ground, sufficient to admit light and fresh air but protecting from the worst of the cold. "A lot of coughs and sniffles today, too. Brestle said he's seeing the same."

"The valley fever," Remin said balefully. It troubled his army every winter, enough that he sometimes wondered if there was some foulness inherent to snowy air. "Is there a...tonic to prevent it? Or something?"

"No," Genon replied, with a flicker of amusement. With a wife to worry about, Remin had become a sudden convert to the virtues of tonics. "Good food, good exercise, and keep out of the wet. And that goes for Her Grace, too, my lord. It's not good for her to sit by a fire all winter any more than yourself."

Ophele had already expressed this opinion several times.

"I'll ask Tounot to have another word with the men," Remin promised. Really, they should all know better; *how* long had everyone been in this valley? But every year it was the same thing, as if clinging to autumn cloaks would keep the winter from coming. "Is Brother Oleare about?"

"Aye, back in the shrine," said Genon, gesturing to the closet recently added to the back of the infirmary. A grand temple had been planned for the town, but without an actual cleric, no one had given much thought to what they would do while it was under construction.

It was a small room, but it had its own small stove, and Brother Oleare rose to offer Remin the second of two chairs with a bow.

"I hope you are well, Your Grace," he said in his quavering old man's voice as he sat back down, settling his luxuriant white beard. He had gotten a little meat on his bones over the last month under Genon's care, and Ophele said the brother had been very helpful with the refugees from Meinhem.

"I am," Remin replied, producing the books he had borrowed from under the safety of his cloak. "Thank you for these. Her Grace had many questions."

And objections.

"I will be pleased to answer them, as best I may," Brother Oleare replied.

"That's what I wanted to talk to you about." Remin braced himself. "There was no cleric in Aldeburke. She would like some regular instruction. From the beginning."

“The lady had *no* instruction?” The brother’s scanty eyebrows went up. It was quite shocking, especially for a daughter of the House of Agnephus; very nearly blasphemous all by itself.

“No.”

“There...there are many these days who do not revere the stars,” Brother Oleare said, with a visible effort to hide his dismay. “I will offer my humble best, Your Grace.”

“I will be with you when you do,” Remin replied. It was partly to see that the cleric didn’t fill Ophele’s head with a lot of nonsense, and partly to make sure that Ophele didn’t shock the old man too badly with her questions. But in the spirit of full disclosure... “The people of this valley deserve a properly pious lord. I have never had a close relationship with the Temple.”

That was an understatement. For most of his life, representatives of the Temple had actively shunned him. Remin’s frown deepened as he met Brother Oleare’s dark gaze, daring him to offer some excuse, or worse yet, some polite evasion to avoid the subject entirely. He would have respected the Temple more if they had had the courage to just excommunicate him. It was cowardly to tell him he was a child of heaven and then deny him support at every turn.

“I will aspire to bring you both closer to the stars, Your Grace,” said Brother Oleare, which was a distinction Remin greatly appreciated.

Most of his other work was concentrated in the vicinity of the North Gate, speaking to the men on guard, observing the progress of construction on the gatehouse—temporarily suspended by snow—and reviewing Master Guisse’s plans for additional reinforcements to the wall, to ensure that no new devils were likely to come bursting through it, come spring. He lent his own hands to shoveling again, to keep the men from complaining about it, and when he could no longer feel his fingers, he went to visit Auber, who kept his cottage among the farmers of the still-nameless north road.

"We're all doing well enough. I'll put on a kettle," Auber added as Remin sneezed. "It's good that we had so much forest to clear over the summer and fall; there's enough firewood to last the winter and then some. I've had some of the boys hauling it nearer to the cottages, and we've been taking it in turns to fetch food from the stores for the day's cooking. That is a bit of a hassle, Rem. If the soldiers weren't digging us out twice a day, I don't know how we'd manage it."

"We've had some carpenters making sledges," Remin mused. It was a fair complaint; a mile was a long way to walk in a blizzard, and that was just one way. "They could make a few more. And Miche brought back more than two dozen horses from Aldeburke, we could spare a few to pull them."

"Some of those horses might have seen him hanged for a horse thief," Auber replied with a flicker of humor. "I don't have Huber's eye, but there's some good blood there, unless I'm much mistaken."

"Be careful with the blooded ones, then." It was a good thought. They were working to improve the quality of their livestock in general, and in time, Remin meant for Andelin horses, cattle, and sheep to be the envy of the Empire. There was good grazing in the valley.

Auber updated him on the activities of the farmers while Remin warmed his hands around a hot toddy, and then they went to look in on the neighbors themselves. Dimly, Remin remembered his father making similar unannounced visits to his smallfolk; he had always said there was nothing like looking with his own eyes.

Though now that he was trying it himself, Remin wondered if his father had really lingered. Most of them looked so nervous to find the Duke of Andelin on their doorsteps, it seemed only merciful to refuse the offer of tea.

"There are a half-dozen widows living in these cottages," Auber explained as they crunched through the snow, breaking a path from the cottage doors to the road. "I've had some of the older boys looking in on them to make sure they've enough firewood and have help for heavy work, like hauling water. Another well nearby wouldn't have gone amiss, but we were in a hurry, building the cottages..."

So saying, he knocked on the next door, and gave courteous greetings to the young woman who answered, with two little ones clinging to her skirts.

"No, sir knight, we are quite well, thank you," she said, opening the door a little wider to offer Remin a curtsy. "Your Grace."

"Madam." Remin tried not to frown, but the two children instantly hid behind her anyway, and the smaller one started to cry.

They received a warmer reception at the next house. A boy of seven or so cracked the door open, looked upward, and flung it wide with a shout.

"Auber!" He catapulted at Auber, who caught him handily enough that Remin suspected it was not the first time. "Did you come here to see mama again? Mama!"

"No, no, His Grace is here," Auber said quickly as Remin eyed him. It seemed Auber's doom to be betrayed by children. "Careful, Vinzetin, you know you're not well yet. I thought you were meant to be helping the boys next door."

"We were gonna, but then Mistress Chenet said—" the boy began, but Remin would never find out what Mistress Chenet had said, because a thin but very pretty woman appeared behind the boy, with the look of a fresh scrub about her face.

"Sir knight," she said, looking up at Auber, then spotted Remin and flushed, dropping a curtsy and pressing the boy into a bow. "Good afternoon, Your Grace. Vinzetin, this is the duke, you must mind your manners."

"Good afternoon," said Remin, immensely interested, and glad to sit by another fire. Auber and the woman exchanged only the most banal possible conversation, enlivened by colorful interjections from the boy, and it lasted exactly the duration of a teacup. But Remin watched the interaction with amusement, nonetheless. There was a remarkable amount of blushing and stuttering going on.

"We had better continue, if we wish to check on everyone else, Your Grace," Auber said in desperation, and Remin allowed himself to be shepherded back into the cold, pausing to offer a farewell to Vinzetin's mother. Both Auber and the lady had been too flustered for an introduction, and Remin had wanted to see how long it would take for one of them to realize it.

"They were very pleasant," he observed as soon as they were safely back on the road, and the door to the cottage shut behind them. "The boy seemed to know you well."

"She does not have a husband," Auber said, answering a question Remin had not asked.

"I'm sure that's her business," Remin replied equably.

"His father was a passing Eagle knight." Auber gave the hood of his cloak a yank, as if he wanted to be sure it was concealing his face. "But I'm only a farmer's son myself, it isn't as if I have noble blood to disgrace."

"I don't know if it should matter if you did," Remin said slowly, as it dawned on him that Auber was asking his permission. And that it *would* matter a great deal to the rest of the Empire: the woman was bastard-born, judging by her ice-blonde hair and blue eyes, with an ice-blond bastard of her own. Hardly a fit wife for a knight. "Court her if you like her, Auber. I will only bless your happiness."

It was the truth. And Remin's spirits rose as he thought of gossiping about it with Ophele, as well as discussing the knottier question of whether he *should* care about the lineage of his knights. Society was a ladder. Auber would be choosing to place himself and his offspring on a lower rung. But there were probably a good number of arguments either way and thinking about it made him feel tired and fuzzy, and it really was hard work, trudging through deep snow all day.

"Your hands are like ice," Ophele said when he dragged himself home that evening. "Peri, could you call Magne up to run a bath for His Grace, please? And put out something warm to wear?"

"There is a blizzard outside," Remin reminded her a little sourly as he thawed himself by the fire. She was exactly where he wanted her, inside and warm, but it was hard not to feel a bit resentful.

"Were you outside in it all day?"

"Shoveling snow." His jaw tightened as heat lanced his fingertips. He glanced over his shoulder. "Lady Verr, Leonin, Davi, you are invited to supper. Juste will be back with it in about an hour."

He could hardly send them down to the cookhouse for their meal in the middle of an endless blizzard, but Remin did not feel like sharing a noisy, crowded table that night. Davi and Leonin had volunteered to help with the chores around the manor since Sim and one of the stableboys had fallen ill, and Remin tried to pay attention as Miche and Juste obliquely discussed further interviews with Azelma. Ophele was vibrating between several poles of anxiety, with the additional burden of another dispute between Lady Verr and Master Tiffen to mediate.

He wasn't sure whether that was the cause of the worried glances she kept sending his way, and he hoped she would just tell him what the problem was instead of making him guess. Remin picked at his supper and wished everyone would go away.

"Are you all right?" Ophele asked him in their bedchamber later.

"Yes," he said, giving himself a shake. He had been all but dozing in his chair. "Do you need help with the Imperial Code again?"

"No, I'm all right. I am a little tired," she said, taking his hand. "Would you lie down with me?"

There was nothing in this world he would have liked more.

"Make sure you're staying warm," he said as she pulled the blankets over them both and nestled at his side. "Remember what Juste said about Sim? You shouldn't take sickness lightly. Gen says there's a fever in town, too. Don't go near the cottages, I don't want you breathing sick air."

"I won't," she promised, and the last thing he felt before he fell asleep was her deliciously cool hand on his forehead.

* * *

"It's just a cough," a rasping Remin assured her the next morning, as he sat in his chair to pull on his boots.

"You were just telling me last night not to take sickness lightly," Ophele protested. "It doesn't count if it's you? Can't it wait until you feel better?"

"No. It looks like the storm's clearing off and Miche is leaving tomorrow. There's a lot to do."

"And *you* have to do it?" she asked anxiously, reaching once more for his forehead. People were always doing that in books, and his forehead was very hot and even beaded with a few drops of sweat, so obviously there was a fever, but what was she supposed to do about it?

"Yes." Standing, he stooped automatically to kiss her, and then thought the better of it. "Don't worry, wife. During the war, everyone came down sick with it, both us and Valleth. We used to stand in the snow and cough at each other. Some years I think it was Genon and his tonics that won the battle."

"All right," she said dubiously.

"I'll be inside most of the day, anyway," he added, and Ophele's eyebrows drew together in her own version of a ferocious scowl as she watched him go out the front door, carrying a muffler and mitts in his bare hands.

She did not have much experience of sickness. Ophele couldn't remember the last time she had been sick herself, and the folk of Aldeburke had hardly needed her to nurse them. At most there had been Azelma, who used to ask for tea and dry toast when she was feeling poorly, and made soup and porridge for others.

"Miche?" Ophele had donned her cloak and muffler and boots and headed directly for his cottage, hoping he had not yet left for the day. "Are you there?"

"A moment," she heard from inside, muffled through the thick door, and after the promised moment, Miche appeared in a loose shirt and breeches. "My lady?"

"Remin is sick," she said, too worried for preamble.

"Is he?"

"He was coughing." Ordinarily, Ophele would have hesitated to interfere in what was strictly Remin's business as the Duke of Andelin, but she and Miche had conspired in secret to take care of Remin before. "And he said there's sickness about..."

"We'd have to tie him up to keep him home," Miche replied, with an air of experience. "You might not have noticed yet, my lady, but His Grace can be remarkably pigheaded."

"But is there something I should do? I don't know much about sickness," she confessed. "There are books about such things, aren't there?"

"I should certainly hope so, when I went to the trouble of hauling an entire library here," Miche laughed, and laid an affectionate hand on her head. "Genon always prescribes tea with honey for a cough. I'll keep an eye on Rem today, and have Juste bring up some honey with supper. How's that?"

"Thank you," she said gratefully. She meant to go through the books herself, all the same. Perhaps Genon would have some to lend. "You will take care of yourself, too, won't you? When are you leaving tomorrow?"

"First light, my lady. Don't worry about me, I'm never one to suffer in silence," he assured her, and quickly lifted his hand from her head as the door opened in the next cottage. "Lady Verr."

"Sir knight," Lady Verr replied coolly. "You are in dishabille."

"Frequently," he agreed, turning his attention back to Ophele. "I'll keep an eye on him today. After I'm decently habilled, eh?"

He directed a cheeky grin at Lady Verr, bowed, and shut his door.

"It is inappropriate for a gentleman to appear before a lady in his shirt," Lady Verr explained to Ophele, with a rather frosty look at the door. "I beg your pardon for overhearing, but did you say His Grace is ill?"

"Yes, a cough, just like Sim," Ophele fretted, falling into step beside the taller lady as they moved back toward the house.

"Tea with honey will help, as will thyme and peppermint," Lady Verr said unexpectedly. "Though sometimes it is better to let them cough. It depends on the sort of cough it is."

"Oh yes, Duchess Ereguil said that you had some knowledge of healing," Ophele remembered. "There are different sorts of cough?"

"Yes, my lady." Lady Verr looked rather sorry for bringing it up, but explained the phlegm-y particulars on the way back to the solar, and then shifted the discussion to the House of Berebet, notoriously phlegmatic themselves. But Ophele was pondering her own duties, and as important as it was to learn about these faraway people—and to learn to dance for them, too, when Leonin and Davi appeared some hours later—she thought there were people nearer at hand to whom she was responsible. The Duchess of Andelin should know what to do, if her people were sick.

Davi and Leonin did not agree.

"My lady, I don't think His Grace will like it," Davi protested as she stepped out into the bitter cold. "This is dangerous cold. People lose fingers in weather like this."

"I have gloves," Ophele said stubbornly, though the first slice of wind made her eyes water. She had gloves, and a scarf, and was wearing so many layers she could scarcely move, but she had never imagined it could *be* so cold.

She would not be out in it long. With a clear day, the builders had descended on the hilltop in swarms and trampled paths in the wide field between the main house and the great husk of the library. Without them, the snow would have been up to her waist.

Inside the huge structure, there were a number of skeletal fireplaces that the men were constantly stoking, so the carpenters' hands would be warm enough to work. It was something, to see the entire library of Aldeburke crated up all around them. Ophele was still discovering whole categories of objects that Miche had stolen; only yesterday someone had cracked open a crate to find an avalanche of toys, and she had very nearly cried when Master Didion presented her with the long-lost Sir Bunkin, her stuffed rabbit, dressed in cloth armor and ready to defend his lady.

The toys were easier to organize than the thousands of books. Ophele was sure there were books on healing, herbs, anatomy, and similar subjects *somewhere,* but the crates were taller than she was.

"You can help me look," she told Leonin, when he again ventured the opinion that Remin would not like her to be out in the cold. It was tempting to remark that Remin was out in the cold *with* a cold, but she would not criticize her husband before others. "Books on medicine and illness."

They only managed to find one before Ophele was forced to concede that she liked her fingers and wanted to keep them. And Remin had been out in this all day yesterday and for who knew how long today! Her eyes narrowed when he came home that night, nearly bloodless with cold.

"J-just let me warm up a b-bit," he said through chattering teeth, trying to sound reassuring as he went to shiver violently by the fire.

"In a hot bath," she ordered, appalled, pressing a cup of hot tea into his hands. "Drink this. Oh, Remin, you look *dreadful.*"

"It's not that bad," he said thickly, trying to smile. "Don't worry, wife."

This seemed an outrageous lie. But again, Ophele hesitated, doubting herself. She had been reading *Harmony of Elements,* a healer's guide to common ailments, but how was she to know whether Remin had taken in bad air or bad water? Was there such a thing as bad fire? He certainly *felt* hot enough; even though he was shivering, his skin was hot and dry, and after a few token noises about kicking her out of the bath chamber, he just leaned forward and let her scrub his back with his elbows over his knees and his head hanging. He didn't even have the energy to argue.

That was a bad sign. Was it too much fire, burning him out? The book said an imbalance of the four elements—fire, water, earth, and air—was the cause of illness, and it felt as if all the fire in the world was blazing under his skin.

"I don't think you ought to come to supper," she said, watching him grimace his way through a second cup of tea. "Wouldn't you like to go to bed? I'll make you some toast later, if you're hungry."

"All right," he agreed, which was downright alarming. She had never *once* known him to miss a meal. He was asleep almost the moment his head touched the pillow, and Ophele covered him in furs and blankets and built up the fire.

"His Grace will not be joining us," she said as she came into the solar and shut the door, so as not to disturb him. Justenin was setting the table for supper. "Miche, you are well enough yourself, I hope? And the men that will go with you?"

"Not even a tickle in my throat," Miche promised, without his customary levity. "Though that was what we were about today, making sure the men who will march are well. We planned to bring tonics and medicine anyway, in case there are ill or wounded with Huber. It's no trouble to take a little more."

Like Remin, he was trying not to worry her, but Ophele understood this was another one of those dreadful choices that she was glad she did not have to make. It would be *awful* if Miche and his men were to get sick in the wilderness in the middle of winter; if another storm came, they really might all die, hundreds of them. But Huber and his men and dozens, maybe hundreds of villagers might be out there, sick and hurt and needing help. Would they not go to rescue them because Miche and his men *might* get sick?

No. They had to go.

"Is there anything else you need?" she asked, allowing Leonin to seat her.

"No, we've everything but the horses and men loaded up, my lady. And that reminds me, Auber sends his thanks for the use of your horses," he added. "They have been a great help. I expect His Grace meant to talk to you about that."

"You were the one that brought them here," she replied tartly. At first, she had been very upset when she realized exactly how thoroughly Miche had plundered Aldeburke; she never dreamed he might interpret the phrase *Lady Pavot's belongings* so liberally. If the Hurrells ever came back, the lady's vengeance would be terrible. But it was true that those horses were badly needed in Tresingale; they had only been able to spare her elderly little Eugene for hauling water, after all. And these horses would ensure the comfort of her people, and if they went to fetch Huber, perhaps save lives.

"There were some stunners," Davi agreed, setting heartily to his meal. "I saw a fair bit of horseflesh when I was growing up, and a couple you brought back must be fit for a king's stable. Did you see that big dun fellow with the white blaze? He looks as if he would go all day and still have the fire to kick you in the face."

"An evil eye," Miche agreed. "But I've never minded a horse with a temper—"

"That's—that's Regal," Ophele said faintly. "You took Regal? That's Julot's hunter, he cost fifty gold sovereigns, no one is allowed to touch him. You said...you said you only brought back carthorses."

"Oh, did I?" Miche asked innocently. "I never had much of an eye for horses. So he's a good one, is he?"

Ohhhhh, she just *bet* he had an eye for horses. Ophele had known most of Aldeburke's horses well; she had spent a fair amount of time hiding in the hayloft, after all, and had made friends with the gentler ones. It hadn't occurred to her to wonder about Miche's other acquisitions until now. Bad enough that he had stolen all the linens. Literally all of them, Azelma said he even stripped the sheets off the beds.

"There isn't a gold one, is there?" she asked in sudden anxiety. The golden Gevalle was the finest horse in the stable, a mare with large, soft eyes, of noble lineage and nobler temper, admired by all, and was *Lady Hurrell's riding horse.*

"You know, I believe there was," Miche replied, and she had to resist the urge to bury her face in her hands and moan. "Gentle as a kitten. You have many fine horses, my lady."

He met her gaze with affectionate insolence and a jerk of his chin, daring her to deny it.

"A Gevalle mare," she told Davi, looking away in confusion. It...it was true, everything in Aldeburke was hers, on paper, and though she had always been told she owed it to the Hurrells for what her mother had done, in the end, they hadn't even wanted it, had they? "They always said she had a very fine gait..."

Lady Hurrell had named the mare *Innuendo*. The name suited the lady better than the horse, in Ophele's opinion; she had never liked it. And sometimes she had slipped into the paddocks to pet the gentler horses, and that golden mare had looked like a butterfly going over the grass. Even at a gallop, she had moved like a...

"Dancer," she said, meeting Miche's challenging gaze with a sudden burst of defiance. "Her name is Dancer."

* * *

"No. You are not going," Ophele said the next morning, shutting the bedroom door in the face of an unhappy Magne and moving to block it with her body. For the second time in two days, she was putting her foot down.

"It's not as bad as it sounds," Remin rasped, and she certainly hoped not. He looked as if he had been dead a week before someone dug him up, and his voice had dropped an entire croaking octave.

"I don't care," she said obstinately, though her heart was thumping as she backed into the door, preparing to physically resist him. She had never defied him like this before, and he knew so much more about...*everything,* she couldn't help second-guessing herself. "Remin, just sit down, I can tell Davi or Leonin to go, or I could go get Ju—"

"Ophele, move," he said tiredly, and his black brows lowered as she moved in front of the doorknob. "I am not playing with you."

"Neither am I. Remin, *no!*" she cried, pushing at his hands. "Tell me what's so important that you have to go! You're going to get even sicker, and I don't—*no!*"

He was gentle, but he dragged her out of the way with one hand and gave her a push into the room behind them, opening the door to find Magne still on the other side, popeyed with terror.

"Magne, go get my—wife, what are you *doing?*" Remin demanded, looking down in astonishment as he found himself dragging Ophele behind him. Her arms were wrapped tight around his middle, and she was digging in her heels.

"I am going with you. Just like this. I swear to the stars, if you go outside, I will follow you *all day*. Magne, *don't you dare move.*"

Her cheeks were blazing with fury and embarrassment. Ophele didn't need Lady Verr to tell her that proper lords and ladies did not wrestle before the servants, and she had never dreamed that Remin could be so...so...*wildly unreasonable.* Poor Magne vibrated with the undecided terror of a rabbit between the conflicting orders of Remin Grimjaw and the Star Lady, and hugging Remin was like clutching an oven.

"Let go of me this instant." Remin was getting angry too. He was breathing hard, and his face was flushed red, and she almost flinched as he straightened up and *glared*. "I will *not*—"

But his breath caught, and he exploded into a fit of coughing so violent, Ophele had to shift from holding him back to holding him up. And while he was helpless, she darted a glare of such venomous ferocity at Magne that he sidled out of the doorway to hide around the corner.

"You know you wouldn't let me stir out of bed if I had just done that," she said when Remin was done, heaving himself upright with his eyes streaming. It was an effort to keep her voice from wobbling. She wanted to win this argument with the power of logic, but she was so worried that she could feel tears starting in her eyes. "Remin, *please*. Just tell me what to do and I'll do it. But you are too ill to go out, you know you are."

"Fine," he said hoarsely, and did not resist as she shepherded him back to bed. "A bit more sleep and then I'll be better."

"I'm sure you will," she agreed, pulling back the blankets.

"It's just a cough," he muttered, falling between the covers. His eyes were already closing. "During the war, we used to stand in the snow and cough at each other..."

"Yes, I know," she soothed, brushing his shaggy hair back off his forehead and letting her hand rest there. Hot. So hot. "You were all very brave."

He barely stirred as she pulled off his boots and wrestled him out of his breeches, to make sure he didn't go wandering. And while she had his clothes, she also confiscated his key to his dressing room, tucking it into her pocket. Pulling on her morning gown, she slipped into the hall and locked the door behind her. It wouldn't keep him in—there was another key on the mantle, if he wanted out—but she would take no chance of someone coming upon him while he was so ill, and trying to do him harm.

"Magne," she said softly, beckoning him over. "I'm sorry you heard us quarreling. His Grace is ill. You are well, I hope?"

"Yes, my lady." He looked terrified to be otherwise.

"Your throat doesn't hurt? You haven't been coughing?"

"No, my lady."

"You must tell me if you do," she said. "And Adelan. Like Sim did, remember? Do you know if Sim is still feeling poorly?"

This was not so much to gather information about Sim as to come at the problem of Magne from another direction. Sometimes he needed circular handling. Once she got the old man wagging his head over Sim, who was also in bed and coughing loud enough to disturb the whole servants' quarter, then Ophele managed to get Magne to own that why, yes, there was a little tickle in his throat.

"But I haven't coughed," he assured her.

"I am glad," she said grimly. She was beginning to be alarmed. Especially when she went into the solar to find Justenin setting the table for breakfast with nose and cheeks red with cold, and sunken, red-rimmed eyes.

"His Grace is ill," she told him as she sat down, observing the warning indications in his lean face. "Magne may also be coming down with it. The valley fever?"

"It seems likely," Justenin said, with a distinctly nasal note. "It often comes with a change in the weather. It is miserable, but rarely fatal. His Grace is still abed?"

"Yes. And if you are unwell, I hope you will go there, too," she replied, with a flat golden stare that, had she known it, born an uncanny resemblance to Remin's basilisk glare. "Someone else will fetch supper, if necessary. I should not like people in my household to insist on going out in the cold when they're sick, and it cannot be good for them."

The corner of his mouth quirked upward.

"It does sound a foolish thing to do," he agreed, and sat down, rubbing his head. "Then I will beg your pardon for the insolence of asking you to serve your own food, my lady, and mine as well."

"Because you're a vector of plague?" Ophele had never forgotten Wen's picturesque phrase.

"That is what Genon calls it," Justenin agreed as she opened up the crocks to find porridge, stewed peaches, and the familiar eggs and sausages. "It seems some illness can be transmitted by touch, or sharing the same air. Genon is always reminding everyone to wash their hands, and cover their noses and mouth, so as not to share the bad air. Pardon me," he added, and demonstrated by turning his head to cough once into a handkerchief. "If there were any other beds available, my lady, I would caution you against sharing one with His Grace. The fever is particularly hard on those who have not had it before."

"I will cover my face," Ophele promised as Lady Verr entered, took one look at Justenin, and sat down at the far end of the table.

It was an unsettling morning. After breakfast, Emi appeared with the news that Peri was also ill, and had not come because she feared to pass it on to her mistress.

"I hope she will stay in bed until she is better," Ophele replied. "And you, too, Emi. If you feel the slightest bit sick, then stay home. The house will not fall apart if the dusting is not done for a day. And perhaps...perhaps you will be needed to help, if Peri and Sim and Magne are all sick."

"I will, of course, my lady," answered Emi, opening her blue eyes wide. "Do you think it will come to that?"

"I don't know," Ophele replied honestly, looking at Lady Verr as the nearest thing to an expert at hand. But Lady Verr shook her head.

"I would help if I could, Your Grace, but my knowledge of healing does not extend far in this direction, I am afraid," she said regretfully. "There are many types of ailments. I know only the simplest herbs for sickness."

She did not protest when Ophele suspended lessons for the morning and instructed them to dress her to go out of doors. How fortunate that Master Tiffen had come, with his woolens and velvets, and especially the marvelous underclothes that Lady Verr said were a scandal and worse, hideous. But they were so very warm: a close-fitting woolen undertunic and trousers that went over her underclothes, and then her chemise, and then layers of combed wool and velvet, with fur lining the high neck and sleeves of her gown. All of it fitted together without a single wrinkle when Lady Verr was done, and once Ophele had on her cloak, muffler, gloves, and new fur-lined boots, she felt prepared to face any weather.

Remin was coughing in his sleep when she looked in on him, and Ophele paused to look at his sweating face, worried. Genon must come and see him. It seemed impossible that a fever could fell Remin Grimjaw where poison, war, hunger, and assassins had all failed, but he had not been sleeping well, and he had been out in the cold...

She should have insisted yesterday that he stay in bed. Ophele pressed her lips together and went to set the crock of porridge by the fire, where he could find it if he woke, then locked him in the room.

"You needn't come out yourself," she told Lady Verr as she wound her muffler about her neck, over her face, and around her head, leaving only a slit for her eyes. "I would not like you to take a chill."

"Of course I must go," said Lady Verr, who was repeating the same operation. "I am not meant to only be your companion, my lady. I am your secretary, your counselor, and whatever else you need me to be."

It was breathtakingly cold outside. It was a mercy that there was no sign of clouds on the horizon, but Ophele thought with renewed anxiety of Miche and his men, already miles away from the shelter of Tresingale. She and Lady Verr slipped and slid over the icy mud and paused first at Azelma's cottage, so Ophele could repeat Sir Justenin's instructions to cover her face and wash her hands through the door, and Azelma could assure her that she felt perfectly fine.

"You needn't fret, child, I will not die for lack of society," she said tartly. "And what are you doing out in this weather? Get inside by a fire."

The interview with Adelan—also through the door of his cottage—was disheartening. He himself was feverish, and had checked in on all the servants to find that Jaose had started coughing, and so had one of the laundresses. Sim, Peri, and one of the stable boys rounded out the tally. None of them felt so poorly that they could not fend for themselves, but Adelan apologized that most of the chores would go undone. The other stable boy was isolating himself in the tack room of the stable, which had an iron stove for the sake of the leather, and hoped he would be spared to take care of the horses.

Ophele was beginning to feel a bit overwhelmed.

"Oh, no, not you too," she said, despairing, as Davi cracked open the door of the cottage he shared with Leonin, to reveal one shadowy eye. "Both of you?"

"Leonin is worse," Davi said, and his voice didn't sound too bad. "What are you doing out by yourself, my lady? Saving your presence, Lady Verr."

"Everyone else is sick," Ophele said, with a thrill of real fear. "I want to go see Genon and fetch medicine. And I must know who else is sick in town, and at the barracks, to make sure they are all looked after."

What if the cooks got sick? What if people became too ill to fetch water for themselves, or food, when it was so cold? What if it snowed again, and everyone was too sick to clear the roads? How would they get food then? And firewood, the pageboys and the peasant boys had been doing much of the hauling from the huge piles seasoning about the town, but who would do it if they fell ill?

"I have to go," she said, more to herself than Davi or Lady Verr. Her mouth set in a firm line. "Davi, are you very sick? Tell me the truth."

"I am not," he said, meeting her eyes squarely. "No fever, my lady, only a scratchy throat."

"Please dress as warmly as you can," she said, already planning ahead. If he became too sick to go out, then she would get Auber, or Tounot, or Jinmin. "We will be in the stable, it's warmer there."

He didn't argue. Leonin would have, on the grounds of propriety and because Remin was likely to be very, very angry if he learned she had been gallivanting about town while there was a plague on, but Davi was practical to his bones.

"Perhaps everyone should get food once a day, and heat it over their own fires," she said as she and Lady Verr shoved open the heavy barn door together, and hauled it shut again. "Soup and bread will do; we cannot afford for the cookhouse to get sick. Or Wen," she added, her heart contracting with sudden fear. What would they do, if he did?

"We ought to see what herb stores Mr. Hengest has, my lady," said Lady Verr. "It is tempting to give medicine to everyone at the first sniffle, but you would be surprised how quickly it goes."

Ophele exhaled, a white cloud rolling upward.

"I wonder if ink will freeze in this weather," she said.

The stable door opened behind them, and there was Davi, lanky and reassuring, wrapped up as thoroughly as Ophele herself and steady as a stone.

"Genon first, hey?" he asked, looking between the two women. And as they were gathering their horses and tack, Ophele found a parting piece of insolence from Miche in the second to the last stall: a certain golden Gevalle mare with gentle eyes, who stuck her nose over the door of her stall as if she had just been waiting for Ophele to find her.

Chapter 7 – The Council of the Well

A coded message on a folded scrap of parchment, concealed in the hollow of a tree:

Do it this afternoon. Servants down to one maid, guard corps reduced and ill. Snowdrifts will cover an approach from the east. Southeast window will be open.

* * *

Mionet had not signed up for this.

To be a lady of Segoile was not at all the same as being a rustic noblewoman like her mother, and still less like the Duchess of Andelin. If Mionet's maids had been ill, she would never have known it. She could barely have matched a name to a face. That was the whole point of uniforms and caps, after all; to make the maids look like each other.

There were some terribly fashionable households that matched their servants the way they matched their carriage horses: footmen of like height, or Lady Hamel with her bevy of redheads, who looked so well in azure livery. Countess Vimont had begun the fashion with a retinue of willowy blondes, though cynical folk said it was only to divert her husband from her own bed.

Mionet would never have gone downstairs to look in on the servants herself, much less inquired after the nearby peasants. But neither she nor Davi tried to dissuade Duchess Andelin. In Tresingale, if His Grace was ill, the responsibility for the town rested on the shoulders of his eighteen-year-old wife.

"We must find out who is ill, first," Duchess Andelin was saying as they made their precarious way down the hill to Eugene Street. "Does it always come on so suddenly? It seemed almost overnight."

"No, not so's I recall," Davi said, grim and ungrammatical. He had yielded to Mionet's hints and finally acquired a proper eyepatch from somewhere, but no one would ever mistake him for a gentleman. "Usually, folk started getting sick over a week or so, and everyone would be sick for a week, and then it'd trickle off and everyone was well again by January. Sometimes it carried off the wounded, but I've never heard of a healthy man dying of it. Gen makes a tonic that knocks out the worst of it. If you ask him nice, it might knock out the sick fellow in the meantime."

Duchess Andelin gave him a sharp glance, but there was no doubt of his meaning. His Grace had been obviously getting sick for days, and Mionet couldn't imagine how he had been persuaded to stay abed unless he was physically unable to get out of it.

"Tastes like death, though," Davi added as they approached the storehouse and granaries. Nearer the river, steam rose from the bathhouses, where the constantly piped hot water kept them nearly as warm as summer, and billowed from the stacks of the laundry. But it seemed to Mionet that there were fewer people abroad, even with the cold, and she sat up straight in her saddle, observing with sharp gray eyes.

They deposited their horses in the town's stable, a few doors down from the infirmary, and Duchess Andelin admonished the stable boys to cover their faces and wash their hands, though it was probably too late. The one on the left was already coughing.

Welcome warmth blasted from the doors of the infirmary as they stepped inside, followed by a snarling salutation.

"Shut the damned door and stay back from the beds," ordered Genon Hengest, turning at the noise of the door. He was one man whose appearance was improved by the linen swathed round his head, covering up some of his more gruesome scars. Mionet had sympathy for a man so afflicted, but he was hardly a proper healer for the Duchess of Andelin. In Segoile, he would never have been let in the door.

"We will." Duchess Andelin lifted a hand to her scarf automatically and then thought the better of it. "I hope you are well, Genon."

"My lady? What in blazes are you doing here?" he demanded, with a jerking bow.

"I—that is..." The duchess hesitated, noting the men filling all the beds of the infirmary, covering their mouths to avoid coughing at their duchess. "Might I have a word? Outside?"

They stepped outside so she could confess in private that His Grace was ill, as were a number of others up at the manor.

"You might have just sent a messenger for that," Mr. Hengest said, frowning. "One of my boys is brewing up a vat of tonic, I'll have some jugs of it for you directly. Juste is sick, too?"

"Yes, and Adelan, and Leonin, Sim, Peri..."

"Leonin's in a bad way," Davi added, with an apologetic glance at the lady. "I was coming to fetch you myself."

"And that's the other reason I came," Duchess Andelin added anxiously. "There is only you and Mr. Brestle, and the pair of you can't be everywhere at once. We must know who is sick, and who is badly so. Have either of you seen Tounot or Sir Jinmin?"

"I saw Jinmin this morning, and he was fine," said Sir Auber, appearing from behind them. "It seems we've had the same idea, my lady. The sickness has hit fast and hard, I don't believe I've seen above a dozen people about today. And we've women and children to think of, and some older folk as well."

"I've been feeding Brother Oleare through the window," Mr. Hengest agreed wryly. "Man's a rail, one good cough would crack him in half. Years past, we broke up the camps into sections, quarantined each bit apart from the other bit."

"We sort of have that," Duchess Andelin said thoughtfully. "There are the cottages by the North Gate, the craftsmen's quarter, the market square, the manor, the cookhouse, the barracks...His Grace said there were about three thousand people in Tresingale."

"Yes, my lady. About half of them in the barracks."

"Then we shall survey the other half, while Genon goes up to the manor," she decided. "It is not so many with four of us..."

Of course, this set up an uproar on many fronts, from the cold to the fact that the duchess certainly would *not* go anywhere alone, and the lady actually stamped her small foot.

"I will stop and go somewhere to warm up, if I am cold," she said, glaring up at them. "This is not the time to fuss over such things, is it? When so many people are sick, and might need help? And you are His Grace's knights, not my nurses. I *shall* go, but I guess Davi must go with me. Lady Verr, do you mind dreadfully going to the craftsmen's quarter?"

Actually, Mionet did mind. If she had wanted to faff about dosing sick people, she might have stayed home in her father's cow hole. She had not come to the Andelin Valley to play nurse to a lot of crude laborers, much less catch some terrible *disease* from them. But to refuse was unmistakably to lose the duchess's good opinion, perhaps forever, and Mionet had come too far to stop now.

"Not at all, Your Grace," she said stoutly, trying to sound as if she were not already half-frozen.

It was astonishing, how quickly they cobbled together a strategy, and Sir Auber departed to pluck some helpers from the cottages and then headed to the barracks to acquaint Sirs Tounot and Jinmin with their plan.

It was endless, dreary, and depressing work. Dutifully, Mionet slogged through the muddy snow up to the cluster of buildings where the craftsmen were keeping themselves, a hodgepodge of whitewashed cottages and workshops for carpenters, blacksmiths, glassmakers, and the like.

"Hello," she said to whatever grimy peasant opened the door. "I am Lady Verr, and we are seeing whether anyone in the house is sick..."

And their names? Are they too ill to get out of bed? Have you any medicine? There were a half-dozen questions that Duchess Andelin had quickly listed to be asked at each house, and then she repeated Mr. Hengest's warnings about handwashing and keeping one's face covered. Slogging back to Brambles, she plucked ink, quill, and parchment from under the saddlebags, warmed by the horse's body, and wrote down the names of the house's occupants and whether they were sick or well.

At least she might stick her hands under Bramble's saddle blanket to warm them occasionally. The horse was the only thing keeping the ink from freezing and bursting its glass pot.

"Master Sharrenot," she repeated at one workshop, a carpenter's, judging by all the lathes. "Are you ill, sir?"

"It's not so bad," he croaked, though his eyes were blazing with fever.

"Are you here by yourself?"

"Aye," he said, squinting at her. He was an ill-favored, bandy-legged old man who would not thank her for interfering, but Mionet drew herself up, yielding to an impulse she was certain she would regret.

"Please go wrap yourself and lie down," she said briskly. "You should be honored, that your duchess sent me to look in on you. I assure you, I did not come all the way from the capital to tend a carpenter's sniffles. Have you no more firewood?"

"Aye. Boy didn't come this morning." It was a testament to how poorly the man was feeling that he didn't even argue. He just sank down into the little nest of blankets and furs at the back of the shop, hacking with a dry churning that did not sound good at *all.*

Gritting her teeth, Mionet stripped off her glove and pressed a bare hand to his balding head.

Hot as an oven, and dry as the Noreveni desert. Dry fevers were more dangerous than wet ones, and she paused to warm up a mug of ale over a small blaze. Her very specialized store of herblore recommended some basic treatments, but she was not a healer of this sort. As a matter of fact, she had done everything she could to forget the things she knew, and rather resented having to exhume them from the crypts of her memory.

Outside, she plunged her bare hand into a snowbank until it stung, wiping away whatever bad water she might have taken in from touching the master, and then went to scribble down his name, with a note that Mr. Hengest ought to look in on him. Soon.

The next house. The next. After an hour, she returned to the tavern to warm herself, the official base of operations, and endured the searing stab of thawing fingers and toes. Master Tregue, so thoroughly wrapped that only his eyes were showing, was keeping mulled wine and tea hot for the surveyors. Mionet drank, thawed, and then went back out again, hardly able to believe that she was doing this.

It was not the work of a lady. She should be huddled by a fire somewhere with a hot brick at her feet, and maids tending her, with nothing heavier than needlework to occupy her hands. None of these people had sworn any oaths of loyalty to Mionet Verr. She owed them nothing. These were just names scribbled on a bit of paper, sick faces in the doorways, hoarse voices broken by explosive coughs, answering her questions.

But this was what was required to stand at the side of Princess Ophele, Duchess of Andelin.

"Can I help y—is that you, Lady Verr?" said one young man, blessedly healthy, and she dimly recognized the voice.

"Aubin?" she said, surprised. She had never wondered where Sousten Didion's draftsmen lived.

"Yes, my la—"

"Aubin, I told you I must have *quiet!"* Another voice interrupted, shouting from some interior room. "You are letting in the chill! My head is splitting and the wretched mice are scampering in the thatch again, bring the broom and bash at them when you come back! The *ass end of civilization!"*

"Is that Sousten?" Mionet asked, appalled. "Is he fevered?"

"Much less than you'd think, my lady." Aubin stepped outside and shut the door. "How may I serve?"

Part of the reason for their survey was to find healthy and steady folk to look after their neighbors, so Mionet invited him to the meeting to be held in the tavern later that afternoon, which Sir Tounot had irreverently called the Council of the Well.

It was a sparsely attended council considering the population of the valley, but by the time she got there, Mionet was too cold to care. Taking a tin mug of mulled wine from the tavern keeper, she went to defrost beside Duchess Andelin, who had removed her gloves and was painfully warming pale hands.

"And Re-remin w-was out in th-this f-for *days,"* the duchess said through chattering teeth. "Oh, it is t-terrible, thawing. I w-was s-so excited for s-snow and now I never want t-to s-see it again. Davi, go and get s-something hot to drink. I am perfectly f-fine, but *you* are not well."

It was true. Mionet could see at a glance that Davi's cheeks were hectic with fever, and he was shivering more violently than the lady. As she accepted a chair from Sir Tounot, Mionet felt as if she had strayed into some bizarre dream. This could not really be happening to her, sitting in this scruffy tavern with these strange people, listening to them work out how they would divide up the town, and who would deliver firewood to each house every morning, and a hundred other details that a noblewoman of Segoile should never even have to contemplate.

There was Wen, bald and enormously fat, glowering as he declared there would be *two* meals a day, thank ye very much, he'd fed armies on the march under a hail of arrows and wasn't about to lower himself to *toast*. Each area of town was assigned to several healthy representatives, and the duchess—who had been sitting at a table and scribbling furiously—produced a list of names for each, along with indications of who was well and who was ill, in a truly terrifying feat of memorization.

"Please do not quarrel," she said when the argument over Mr. Brestle and Mr. Hengest's services began to grow heated. She had not had much to say otherwise; she was mostly listening. "Why don't we also keep a list of who is most seriously ill, and who might take it particularly hard? Like poor Master Sharrenot. I should like extra attention for him, it cannot be good to leave him alone all night, can it?"

"That is called triage, my lady," Mr. Hengest said approvingly, and a great deal of fire died out of the discussion.

But Mionet's eyes caught the anxious movement of Duchess Andelin's hands, frightened by interjecting herself into an argument, and she had to bite her tongue to keep from admonishing her. By now it was automatic to say, *please keep your hands still, my lady*. Such fidgeting was disgraceful in a grown woman, a barometer of anxiety and ripe for caricature in the salons of Segoile. Because *that* was what was most important, of course.

For a moment, the disconnect between her two worlds was so jarring, Mionet had to look away to compose herself.

"Very well," the duchess said when the conversation began to wind down, looking up through the slit of her muffler with large tawny eyes. And somehow, they were all listening to her, this slip of a girl who *yesterday* had to be reminded to speak up. "I will be here tomorrow at noon to take your reports and update our lists, and mind, if you cannot come yourself, please send someone in your stead. His Grace always says everyone's job is no one's job. If you cannot do something, please find someone to do it for you."

She sounded impressively steady as she bade them all farewell, but as Mr. Hengest approached to talk about those ill at the manor, the lady looked very small and pale. There had been no time for this discussion before the meeting. Reluctantly, Mionet moved away from the fire to stand beside her, offering a gloved hand. By the stars, she was *earning* the lady's good opinion.

"There's no need to worry," Mr. Hengest said reassuringly. "I looked in on all of them. His Grace is the worst, but he'll bounce back quickly so long as he stays still and *rests*. His fever is very high. Juste is with him, but I expect he'll have to take to his own bed tomorrow. It is a cruel sickness this year, I will not lie to you."

"But—they will be all right?" Duchess Andelin whispered, her fingers tightening on Mionet's.

"Aye, my lady. Sleep, tonic, and porridge, that's all. My only fear is that Rem will try to be out and about too soon, and as long as he's coughing, he must be indoors. That goes for everyone. Your man Adelan also seemed inclined to leave his bed. You'll have to make them mind."

"I will," she promised, her face resolute.

"And both of you look after yourselves," he added, looking at both women to impress his seriousness upon them. "It bears repeating. Dress warmly, wash your hands often, and cover your face, especially when you're tending the sick. Stop and warm up if you're cold, don't just endure it. I'll tell you true, lady, I don't know how you'd fare if you caught this sickness. My experience is with soldiers. I am worried for the little ones, and our older folk."

And with this ominous remark, they adjourned, and Mionet wearily allowed Davi to boost her onto Brambles. It had been such an endless, weary day, she barely felt the cold, and if someone had offered her transport to Segoile, she would have been tempted to fall at their feet weeping.

But she did not let that thought show even in her eyes. She was here, she had just endured one of the longest days of her life, and she was going to make a bosom friend of Princess Ophele, Duchess of Andelin, *if it killed them both.*

"You don't have to come out again tomorrow, Lady Verr," said Duchess Andelin when they had finally returned to the manor. With most of the builders and all of the servants sick, the manor was cold, dark, and silent, their breaths puffing white even inside.

"Nonsense," said Mionet, trying to sound cheerful. The day had been grueling, but it was not a total loss. She had waited a long time to take this next step forward, to gauge the moment properly, and she thought the time was right. "My place is at your side, my lady. And I hope you will call me Mionet."

And then she sneezed.

* * *

It was colder upstairs than it was outside.

"Justenin! What are you doing here?!" Ophele cried, appalled when she climbed the stairs and found Remin's faithful knight outside the door of the bedchamber, clutching his sword and shivering violently. "Oh, you look dreadful! Davi, help me—"

"I am q-quite all r-right, my lady," Justenin said through his teeth, but allowed himself to be steered toward the solar. His face was bloodless.

"I'll make up a fire," said Davi, trying to sound as if he wasn't just as miserable. "Takes more'n this to freeze the Coldest Knight, eh?"

"Here, sit down," Ophele ordered, bundling Juste up in her own pink lap blanket. There was the trouble: the window overlooking the balcony had been left open, with a bitter breeze whistling through and *icicles* dangling off the sill. "Oh, how could they! Who was working outside today? Sousten would have their backsides, if he weren't so sick—"

Fruitlessly, she yanked at the window, thinking of all Davi's worst curses. It had frozen in place, so it must have been open for some time. Why would anyone open it in the first place?

"Here, let me, my lady," said Davi, reaching over her head to slam the window shut. And then he paused, eye narrowing as he peered out into the swirling snow. "Why don't you look in on His Grace?" he suggested, turning the lock on the window. "I'll thaw Juste and then fetch supper directly."

"Warm yourself up before you go," Ophele warned.

She did not see the look the two men exchanged behind her, or the flick of Davi's fingers against a broken lock.

It was warmer in the bedchamber, at least. The fire was still roaring, and there was a basin of water and a chair on Remin's side of the bed. Genon had told her repeatedly to let Remin sleep, but even as she tiptoed nearer, the huge figure in the bed stirred.

"Wife?"

"Yes," she said at once, hastening over and pulling her scarf back up over her nose and mouth. "I just got home. Oh, dear, you look wretched, Remin."

"Hands are cold." He turned his face away as she touched him, his brow knotting. His eyes were slits, and the darkness burned with fever. "Are you...well, wife?"

"Yes. I don't get sick," she assured him. "And we're looking after everyone, and Tounot and Auber and Jinmin have been marvelous, and Genon has made medicine for you, you'll have more with supper."

"Mmm." His fingers wrapped around hers. "Good."

"Would you like some porridge?" Lightly, she brushed his face with her other hand, hoping the cool would do him good. His fever really was frightening.

"No..." he sighed, and then he was asleep again, his hand gripping hers, and she was so shamefully tempted to try to shake him awake.

Ophele had thought of dozens of questions on the ride home. There was so much she wanted to ask, so many things she didn't know, and her ignorance was hollowing her belly like a rotten tree. Things she knew she did not know, and worse, the things she didn't *know* she didn't know, invisible hazards she couldn't avoid because she didn't know they were there.

Remin would know what to do. He was so strong and so sure of everything, and without him she felt as if the very roof over her head had been torn away.

And she wanted to tell him about Dancer, and how they had surveyed the town, and how Auber had apparently become the mayor of the North Gate Cottages while no one was looking, because he knew every single person who lived there. Including his sweetheart Isilde, who had an adorable little boy, and that was such a delicious bit of gossip that she had actually squealed out loud as soon as she was safely down the lane, to Davi's amusement. But wouldn't it be lovely if they got married and had babies?

She would tell Remin about it when he was better. Rinsing the cloth beside the bed, she laid it on his forehead, washed her hands, and then sat by the fire with her writing things, basking in the heat like a cat.

She had made huge lists that afternoon, but Tounot and Auber had taken them, so Ophele put the kettle on and set about reproducing them, trying to remember every single word that had been spoken in the tavern. Her memory for things she heard was not as good as for things she read, but she thought she had most of it, and she lost herself in the work until she heard a tapping on the door.

"My lady." Davi's muffled voice sounded perfectly miserable. "Supper's on the table. Mind that lock on the window and make sure the guards check it tonight. We'll have a word about it with Master Didion."

"We certainly will," Ophele said grimly, wiping her hands on her writing apron and rising.

Three more unhappy people waited in the solar for their supper, standing far apart in the chilly room as if to avoid breathing one another's air. Juste, shivering in her pink blanket; Lady Verr—or Mionet—with an expression of resignation, and to Ophele's surprise and displeasure, Adelan the butler, still bundled up against the frigid walk from the cottages.

Hands on her hips, Ophele stood in the doorway and glared.

"All of you ought to be in bed," she said distinctly. "I will bring food to everyone. I will not hear it!" she added as everyone sought to object at once. She was getting a little tired of this. "I am perfectly healthy, and I dare just one of you to sniff at me right now."

None of them did.

"Then Tounot shall bring up our meals tomorrow, and I will divide them up and bring them to you," she informed them, determined to crush all resistance immediately. "Genon sent up several jugs of medicine, and he said all of you should rest and stay in bed, so that is what you shall do, or I will give you the medicine with sleeping elixir in it. And he said no one with a cough should be going outside, at all."

This was for Adelan in particular, who was old, but Ophele felt a pang of fear for Magne and Azelma, who were even older. And there was the new head laundress, Naisenne, who was gray and had wrinkles and must surely be at least forty.

"And Genon said everyone who is ill should not be left alone overnight. I am here, if any of you feel terribly ill," she said, looking sternly at all of them. She felt a little foolish, to be telling people so much older than herself what to do, but when Remin woke up, she wanted to be able to say all was well. "I shall never forgive you if you do not, and something dreadful happens."

"It is not as dangerous as that, my lady," replied Justenin hoarsely. "But we will obey, so long as you promise you will not venture out alone, no matter what. Let Emi manage the dishes, and Tounot will take them back to the kitchen tomorrow. Stay with His Grace and keep the door locked. Do not open it unless you know the person on the other side."

"Oh. I will," she promised, blinking at the crocks and trenchers, another problem that she had not anticipated. Ever since she had come to the manor, all her dishes and cups had taken themselves away as if by magic.

This was why she needed to think. Once she had distributed supper and many small beakers of medicine, she went back to work, making a separate list for the operations of the manor. It was strange and unsettling for the house to be so quiet, and more than once she started at some imagined sound outside the door. But the only visitor that night was faithful Emi, tapping at the door a little after sunset.

"Everyone's eaten and had their medicine, Your Grace," she reported, without opening the door. "I've done as you said and kept my face covered and washed my hands every time I touch Peri. So long as I'm well, there's no reason I can't help."

"That is very good of you. Please leave the dishes on the bench in the entry hall," Ophele said gratefully. "If you're still well in the morning, come up to my dressing room and we'll see what we might manage."

Was it normal for an illness to fell so many people so fast? Was it the change in the weather, as Justenin had said? She didn't know. But everyone kept saying how smart she was, so surely if she thought very carefully, she could work through this problem, too.

But Remin immediately gave lie to the idea. When he started awake a few hours later, his eyes were bright and dazed and Ophele had to help him to the privy, dismayed how unsteady he was on his feet. She got a few bites of porridge into him, along with another dose of Genon's medicine, but he hardly seemed to know what he was about, and every time he tried to say more than a few words, he lost his breath and started coughing in huge, violent spasms.

"Don't, don't," she said, alarmed. "It's all right, don't talk. Let's get you back to bed."

His eyes were dull, and she caught his hand as he sank between the covers. Genon had said much that alarmed her, but the worst had been his cautions about delirium.

"Remin, you do know me, don't you?" she asked, looking anxiously into his eyes.

"'Course," he rasped. "Wife."

"What's eight plus eight?"

"Sixteen. Stop fretting," he mumbled, and drifted to sleep again.

Feeling lonely but reassured, she went back to work, and then put herself to bed in the furthest corner of the mattress. She had gone over her lists a dozen times. She had thought so carefully, walking through the map of Tresingale in her mind, picturing every house, every occupant, every feverish face. She had even planned her morning for maximum efficiency, down to the location of her boots.

Ophele closed her eyes, and dreamed of missing lists.

* * *

Her excellent plans only lasted as far as the stables.

"Frechard?" she called the next morning, turning in a slow circle and wondering uneasily if the stable boy might have died in the night. Was it just too early? For a moment she waited, shifting on her feet, and then gave herself a shake. She knew where the saddles were. Picking one that looked approximately like the one she had used the day before and went to confront Dancer. For a long moment, horse and lady considered each other.

Horses were so *big*.

"Like a hand, lady?" A gravelly bull's voice spoke behind her as Ophele was teetering on a bale of hay, attempting to swing the heavy saddle up onto Dancer's back, and she almost threw herself off the bale with the saddle.

"Oh! Oh, Sir Jinmin," she said, turning and trying to recover. "I don't know where Frechard went..."

"The stableboy?" The massive knight lumbered forward, holding out a hand to take the saddle from her. "Tounot said you'd be up at the house."

"Oh, I was helping Emi..."

She knew Sir Jinmin the least of all Remin's knights, but she was so relieved to have someone to talk to, she found herself chattering away as he saddled her horse, asking him to explain exactly how to do it. Dancer was sweet and willing to be led, but she had not liked having a saddle flung about her sides.

"I will be your escort today, if you don't mind, lady," Sir Jinmin said, holding out a huge hand to boost her onto Dancer's back. "Hope it's all right."

"No, of course. I hope you're still well?"

"Fit as you like, lady."

He did have a way of letting the conversation drop like a stone, but after weeks with Lady Verr, Ophele was learning to persevere.

"Are they well enough in the barracks? Oh, and the pages, I hope they're not too ill? Some of them are so little..."

No one had mentioned the pageboys yesterday, and she reproached herself as she listened to Jinmin's report. Fortunately, none of them had taken the sickness too hard. They were all sturdy boys, active and well-fed, and she saw some of them darting here and there as they moved about town, looking in on the office, the cookhouse, and the Benkki Desans. Madam Sanai and Master Balad were both down with it. They accepted Genon's medicine with thanks, but they had a number of practices of their own, and Ophele almost had to be dragged away when Huvara appeared with long rolls of fine linen, saying something about a steam shroud.

Things were already slipping askew elsewhere. The pageboys had delivered food that morning, but it froze solid on quite a few doorsteps. Tounot was finally succumbing to the illness, and Genon could only spare her a few moments between his most fragile patients, of whom there were more than expected. Neither he nor Brestle had slept.

"But it's not as if there's a war on," Genon said, as if this were reassuring. "We've seen worse, my lady."

No doubt they had, but how long could they go without sleeping? Ophele watched him anxiously, and it colored her reaction when she arrived in the marketplace to find a wagon laden with firewood trundling past the fountain in the town square, a full six hours later than it should have been. She didn't hesitate to hurry over to it, appalled.

"There are sick people in these houses!" she exclaimed, looking up at the many chimneys around them, only a few of which were smoking. "Have they not had fires all morning?"

"Warn't no firewood by the stables, lady," said the nearest man, anonymous under many layers of clothing. "Had to get it from the cottages."

"But you're not meant to get it from there, there's a woodpile down the alley behind the smiths' forges!" She was beginning to be actually angry. "Do you mean you took all the firewood from the cottages? You can't just take it from wherever you find it!"

"I said it was all right, lady," said another anonymous man, appearing around the side of the wagon. "We only took half of what we found, no need to fuss."

Actually, there *was* need to fuss. They had planned out yesterday exactly where all the firewood would go so everyone would have what they needed and the cottages were much colder than the houses in town, much less insulated, and so burned wood much more rapidly. But they were all looking down at her together, tall men with gruff voices, anonymous in their woolens, and probably so much wiser than she...

"There—there is," she managed. It came out wavering and uncertain, and she stiffened. She was right, she knew she was right. "They need much more firewood, they—"

"Can't hear you, lady?"

"You're talking to Her Grace," Jinmin said suddenly behind her, flat and menacing. "That you, Auffray? Take off your hood and show your manners. P'raps you and I ought to have a chat."

"After they have fetched back the firewood, please, Sir Jinmin." Ophele raised her voice, her fingers clenching her skirts. "They burn firewood faster. In the cottages. Once you've unloaded, go and get half the woodpile from behind the smiths' and take it back. To the cottages, I mean. And don't do this again."

With Jinmin glowering behind her, they could do nothing but bow and murmur apologies, and she bit her tongue and waited through their belated courtesies, glad that her face was covered. It was easy to speak, wasn't it, so long as no one was speaking back.

"I'll thump 'em later," Jinmin growled behind her. "Lazy sods, didn't want to go all that way in the cold, is all."

"Genon said the people with the fever can't afford to take a chill," she said. Normally, she would err on the side of forgiveness, and it was her own fault if she felt afraid or embarrassed. But she would not allow the least risk to the sick, if she could stop it. "Please speak with them about it."

But that wasn't even the worst affront of the afternoon. Master Forgess was one of the last to offer his report at the tavern, pugnacious and glaring out of the slit of his large, woolly scarf.

"They're well enough to be complaining, Your Grace," he said of the people in his charge, which was so honest it made her smile. There were a few people at the manor in that condition. "Master Cherche is the worst off..."

But he was not smiling. Indeed, he seemed to grow angrier with every second he looked at her, reeling off the names of the ill so rapidly that she had a hard time imprinting them on her memory. He and his journeymen very nearly abased themselves every time they encountered her about town, but Master Forgess never really seemed to *mean* it. Even as he was donning his cloak and gloves, he kept glancing at her, as if he were chewing his tongue to keep from speaking his mind.

The explosion occurred just after she exited the tavern, as Sir Jinmin caught her boot to boost her into the saddle.

"Your Grace!" She heard the shout from behind her, sudden and furious. "In the name of every scholarly star, *learn to write!*"

Jinmin released her so abruptly she staggered, righted her by the scruff of her neck like a kitten, and then swung around and went for Master Forgess. The scholar stood his ground as if he was willing to die like a man, so long as he had his say first.

"Your ideas were *good!*" he exclaimed, his gloved hands held out before him in imprecation to the heavens. "But no one's going to read them if they look like they were scribbled by a ten-year-old! Your position may insulate you from criticism, but it is a *profligate waste!* Respect your own scholarship enough to learn to express it properly!"

The words echoed off the icy stone of the market square and then hung there, dissipating in white clouds.

"I don't know how," Ophele said into the silence.

"Then—then permit me to teach you. Please." Belatedly, he offered a deep bow and held it. *"Please.* Your Grace."

"I will. When this is over, I will," she promised, feeling a giddy rush of excitement. Oh, Remin wouldn't like it, he never forgave anyone who was rude to her, but she so wanted to learn properly. And hadn't he said she could study whatever she liked?

"I'll send my boy up to the manor with materials and arrange a meeting at your convenience, Your Grace," Master Forgess said, straightening. "When this is over."

But it was not over yet.

Late that night, Master Cam Sharrenot died. And he was not the last.

* * *

The day began hopefully. In the early hours of the morning, Remin's fever had finally broken in a drenching sweat, and Ophele sponged his cool limbs and watched as he sank into a sleep that seemed somehow deeper and...*healthier* than his previous leaden unconsciousness, or the drugged stupor from Genon's medicine. Ophele woke to Emi's knock on the door, and Remin sat up a moment later, groggy and complaining about his stubble.

"Does your head still hurt?" she asked, inexpressibly relieved to see most of the fever-fog had cleared from his eyes. He managed to sit to the table for breakfast, but was still only picking at his porridge.

"It's not bad," he rasped. His coughing had been so violent, it seemed even his powerful chest must fly apart, and she was sure it must have left his throat absolutely raw. Ophele added a little more honey to his tea. "You're still well, wife?"

"Yes. I told you, I don't get sick." But it was lonely, sitting down without their customary kiss and embrace. Both of them kept reaching for each other before they remembered. "We're looking after everyone, I promise. You will be pleased to hear it, once you're well. Genon said for now that you should just sleep as much as you can."

"You're not giving me much choice," he grumbled, with an ironic salute of his teacup to indicate he knew exactly what was in it. And though saying even that many words at a stretch made him cough again, still, he was *better*.

She found that Leonin was similarly improved, no longer feverish and energetic enough to protest staying in his cottage. She had to be very stern with him, but with Genon's admonishments in her ears, Ophele shut the door in his face and marched off to the stable with Auber trailing behind her, looking entertained. Somehow, it felt as if this must be a turning point for them all, as if Remin's recovery must drag everyone else along. How could they help but follow the mighty Duke of Andelin?

"I am sorry, my lady." As soon as she arrived at the infirmary, Genon drew Ophele off to one side and sat her down. "We knew from the beginning that this illness would be dangerous for older people. People lose their water as they age. They go up like tinder with a fever like this, and Master Sharrenot..."

This did not make sense. Ophele sat, stupefied.

"I...b-but was there nothing we could do?" she managed, stuttering in shock. "We kept sponging Remin with cold water when his fever was bad, could we not—there's *snow,* if his fever was so high, and make him drink water if he's so dry, I don't—"

Ophele bit her tongue. Jinmin, Auber, and Genon were all looking at her with pity as her voice broke and squeaked and she clenched her hands together in her lap. She could not cry in front of them. She was their duchess, taking Remin's place, she must be as strong for them as he would be.

"It doesn't work like that, my lady," Genon said, full of apology. "I am sorry. He was a good man."

"No. No, of course...you would know." Ophele swallowed a sob. Breathed, and stood. "I will not take your time. We will speak of the rest this afternoon. Please keep...doing your best."

Then she went outside and cried.

How could she not? Master Sharrenot was hardly her dearest friend, but she had *known* him. He was one of the craftsmen of the town, bringing Remin's great dream to life, and she had seen the work of his gnarled old hands all over Tresingale. She had watched him at the work of sawing and sanding, the effortless grace of decades of practice. He had made the chair for Remin's birthday, and Remin had liked it so much, he had asked for three more.

But he would never finish them now.

Was there something else they could have done? What if they had taken him to the infirmary straight away? Mionet had *said* he was very sick, but still he had stayed in his workshop a full day before they finally risked moving him in the cold.

It could not happen again. She had to think, to protect the others. She had to...

But as they rode past the cottages by the North Gate, she saw them carrying a small figure out into the cold, wrapped in blankets with its face covered. One of the children from Meinhem had died.

Before noon, two more refugees had followed.

"Please look in on all of them," she said to Genon through numb lips. As promised, they were meeting in the tavern to take reports, and the numbers of seriously ill were overwhelming. "I suppose, if they are still so thin, it would go worse for them, wouldn't it? Even if they are young?"

"Yes. I should have...told you." For the first time, Genon was awkward. "People die, my lady."

The same look was in all their eyes. Compassion. Pity. Because these men understood death so well, they did not need to be told. Death might come sudden or slow, but it would come. And as the reports went on, Ophele sat by the fire and felt the knowledge of death sink into her like a toxin, absorbed irrevocably into flesh and bone, part of her forever.

What if *Genon* died?

How long had it been since he slept? What would happen if he took ill? He was not a young man, and Master Brestle was run just as ragged. Two herbmen for three thousand people, with a half dozen journeymen to support them. Why hadn't they sent for more healers sooner? Never mind the Tower, if they were going to be so petty and vicious as to refuse aid, weren't there any other temples nearby? Lords who might be persuaded to lend them for gold? *No one?*

The machinery of her mind felt jammed. People were talking around her, but she didn't hear them. She was lost in a strange, shocking new world, a world where death wasn't a thing that happened to other people far away, but was happening here and now to people she *knew*. She was following the new paths of these terrible thoughts, and realizing that she *should* have contemplated these dreadful things. She should have asked herself, *what is the worst thing that could happen?* She had seen those starved children from Meinhem. One month of good food would not have repaired the damage to those wasted little bodies.

Oh, stars, how many more of them might die? What were the stars of healing? What could be done, they were already sick, what could Genon do that was not already being done?

"Have we more healers coming?" she asked abruptly, turning to Clovin, one of Edemir's secretaries. "Have any been found yet?"

"We have sent out inquiries, my lady," he said. "It takes time to investigate them."

"Only His Grace's healer and mine need investigation," she said. "Send out more. What's the largest town in Firkane? What about Sir Edemir's family? We can't afford to wait. Pay any price."

She saw all of them blink, exchanging glances. This might seem like she was exceeding her current emergency mandate, but Ophele did not think she was.

She turned to Genon.

"What happens if you get sick? You are over sixty yourself. Can your journeymen take your place? Is there ever more than one plague per winter? And Sir Huber...His Grace said there were four hundred and fifty people between Isigne and Selgin. Four hundred and fifty men, women, and children who might be starved and sick and weak from the cold, and they might come any time now in the middle of a plague. Mightn't they?"

She saw the shock of it strike them all. That was it. That was the worst thing that could happen.

"I will send someone," Clovin said into the silence. "I will send a messenger. The nearest academy of healing is in Lusse, in Firkane. It could be they will lend us a few healers for a sixmonth, or a year."

"Yes, do," she agreed. Temporary help was better than none. "If the people from Isigne and Selgin arrive," she said, looking from Auber to Genon, "then what will happen? From the beginning. They will send a signal..."

"We'll just hope the weather is clear enough to see it." Auber sat down at the table beside her, and the secretaries brought out more paper. "But it might not be. We had a couple blizzards a month most winters, as far as I remember."

"And a few smaller storms in between," Jinmin agreed, his chair giving a creaking protest as he sat. "Might not have much warning."

"Then we will send someone to warn them, as soon as they are sighted," Ophele said, nodding. "To tell them there is sickness, and to keep their faces covered. But what if there are sick and injured with them?"

"They can't be put in the infirmary," Genon said immediately. "They'll only get the fever there. We'll need a separate building. The cookhouse?"

"There should be enough room for everyone there, if we take out the tables," Auber agreed. "I'll get some of the lads to do that now, it's not as if we're all sitting to supper anyway..."

All afternoon, they were planning for this possibility. Including Huber and his men, there might be five hundred people entering the town, an increase of more than twenty percent of their population. It would be a strain on every resource, food, medicine, firewood, and though there were ample raw materials, the trouble, under conditions of plague, was distribution. How to get the food from the kitchen to the people. How to prepare enough food in the first place, when they daren't let anyone touch it if they showed the least sign of sickness.

Was there a *word* for this sort of limitation? If only she knew more! It was her devil maps all over again, trying to invent a solution when other, better methods already existed, if only she knew them. Why didn't she know them? Why had she been spending weeks learning how to curtsy instead of how to take care of her people?

"You must both take care of yourselves, too," she said severely as they were wrapping up. "Mr. Henghest. Mr. Brestle. Have either of you slept? What will happen to us, if you collapse?"

"We will, my lady," Genon promised, and outside the tavern, everyone bowed and parted in the pale twilight.

At least she saw no more small corpses being carted out of the cottages on the way to the cookhouse. But when this was over, she would have to go to them and apologize and beg pardon before the stars that she had not taken care of them better.

"Try not to take too much on yourself, my lady," said Auber as he dismounted by the cookhouse. "It's like Genon said. Sometimes people die, no matter what we do."

"I know," she said, mutinous.

"My lady. No matter what you do, people will die." Auber took her hand, arresting her. He was as well-wrapped as everyone else against the cold, his eyes looking directly into hers. "You've done more than most, coming to help. But you need to set your mind to it now, that there will be some folk that die tonight, and tomorrow, and maybe we could've saved them and maybe we couldn't. We won't know until it's too late. Because that's how the world is."

He was right. She knew he was right; Remin had told her the same sort of thing before, more than once. But Ophele couldn't accept it. This wasn't like a war, or an accident at the wall, or devils coming to tear people apart. Sickness was treatable, preventable, wasn't it? If they had only seen it coming, and prepared better, or thought harder, this wouldn't have happened.

Back at the manor, she and Emi divided up supper and went back once more into the cold, setting out small crocks of stew, medicine, and bread on the steps of each cottage. Frechard was back at the stable, with no good reason for his absence, but Ophele could not care enough to shake the truth out of him.

"Azelma, here's your supper," she called, knocking at the door. Smoke rolled up from the chimney, steady and reassuring.

"Thank you, my lady," Azelma said from within, but even through the solid door, Ophele could tell that her voice was thick. She froze, one hand gripping the door handle.

"You're—you're not sick, are you?" she asked, the words falling in leaden syllables.

"Just a touch of fever." The old lady tried to sound reassuring, but they both knew what it meant. "You don't need to worry. I've plenty of tea and am quite comfortable."

"I'll send for Genon tomorrow," she managed, trying to think past the sudden surge of fear and anger. "You will be all right tonight, won't you? You won't be too cold, and can manage your fire yourself?"

"Of course I can, child, don't be a goose," Azelma replied, and even opened the door so Ophele might glimpse her face, pink but still fierce. "Now go on, you ought not linger in the chill either."

She would be all right tonight. Surely Azelma could hold on to see Genon tomorrow, she could not have come all this way to die, like poor Master Sharrenot. But Ophele finished bringing food to the rest of the cottages in a numb, helpless horror, struggling to think of something, *anything,* that had not already been thought of.

"I can look in on everyone once more before bed, Your Grace," Emi promised. "Isn't Mr. Adelan already getting better? I'm sure there's naught to fear."

"Thank you, Emi. Make sure you dress warmly." Ophele tried to smile. It was true, Adelan did seem better, though Magne's voice had been hoarse and querulous with fever. The valet was a small man going dry with age, just as Master Sharrenot had been.

Who else would die tonight? How many more would die before the sickness ran its course?

Inside, a hot and choking lump swelled in her throat and Ophele covered her mouth with her hand to stifle a sob. People died. She knew that. But she was supposed to protect them somehow, only she didn't know how, and how was she ever going to tell Remin what had happened?

The high, grand halls were cold and still, and filled with the soft sound of weeping.

* * *

For a long time, Remin knew nothing.

His sleep was long and deep, like falling into a pit. He dreamed. Sometimes of Ophele, often of the war, sometimes of long-ago summer days. Sometimes it was the same dreams that had haunted him ever since the Emperor's messenger had arrived, horrible visions of the Place of White Stones. He woke up calling for Ophele, terrified when she did not come, but he was so hot, it was never long before he fell asleep again.

He dreamed of that, too, the day in the Brede when Ophele had had her sun sickness. Maybe this was how she had felt, broiling as she labored under the merciless summer sun. Maybe this was how Bon had felt as his guts writhed inside him until he died. There were many awful things that he might have seen in his fever-dreams, but the one that left tears on his cheeks was the fleeting vision of his boyhood in Ereguil, with Victorin shoving him awake and Miche's voice drawling from the door...

"My lord," said a voice. Sometimes it was Juste. Sometimes it was Genon. Most often it was Ophele. They gave him sweet tea and foul-tasting medicines. There was cool water and Ophele's soft hand touching his face, the scent of her skin, and Remin was tired of being sick, he wanted *up*, but he just couldn't seem to stay awake...

And then one afternoon, he sat up in bed with a watery winter sun shining through the windows and looked around.

For the first time in days, it didn't feel as if his head was going to fall off and shatter on the floor.

Squinting, he found his bedchamber in the usual configuration and a fire crackling in the wide hearth. The house was utterly silent. Though he was not often home in the middle of the day, Remin knew that the manor *should* be a hive of activity, with builders, carpenters, and plasterers busy on every floor, servants moving up and down the stairs, and Ophele in the solar, cramming knowledge into her head as fast as she could.

Ah, but Ophele had said that everyone was sick.

The memories came back to him in stages as he rose and tottered off to the bath chamber, and he felt almost human again after a bath and a shave. And since he was unsupervised, he dug through his wardrobe to pull out his oldest and rattiest clothes, which he had carefully concealed from Magne. To be sure, his appearance had improved considerably with the attention of a valet, but formal clothing always made him feel faintly harassed, as if he must account for every lost button.

Where was Ophele?

Remin felt like a bear lumbering through the chilly house, a headache thumping behind his eyes. He had told her she should stay home, he didn't want her out in the cold, breathing sick air. She was so small, what would happen if she got sick herself?

In the bedchamber, he found stacks of papers on the table by the fire, maps of the town that looked almost like the plan of some campaign. Someone must have taught this to Ophele; he recognized the movement of supplies at a glance, and the division of the town into quarters. What on earth had she been doing while he was ill?

"Ophele?" he called, and heard only the echoes of his own outburst of coughing.

He found more clues in the solar. All the food and medicine in the house was being distributed there, with many small earthenware crocks and beakers lined up at one end of the long table. But Ophele herself was nowhere to be found, and neither was anyone else. Even these small exertions laid a film of sick, slippery sweat over his skin, but Remin wrapped himself warmly with a thick muffler around his throat and went outside.

He wasn't going to do anything drastic, like fetching Lancer and riding into town to demand a report. Yet. But as he stepped out into the cold and looked through the naked trees to the town below, with smoke rising from the many chimneys, he had the infuriating sense that important things had been happening without him, and his hands had been forcibly removed from the reins.

"Juste?" He knocked on the door of Juste's cottage, squinting against the brightness of the sun on the snow. It looked like almost every chimney in the servants' quarters was working away, belching forth woodsmoke. "Juste, are you there?"

If Juste answered, it was too quiet to hear. Remin jerked one shoulder impatiently and pushed the door open, shutting it before the heat could escape. Juste was asleep in his bed, his angular cheeks hectic with fever. Remin paused to make sure he didn't look like dying and then went to build up the fire.

Whether it was a tent or cottage or apartment in Segoile, all of Juste's spaces always ended up looking the same: comfortably disarranged, with stacks of books on every available surface and half-burned candles squeezed between them. Juste had been carting the same shabby chair from place to place for the last seven years, much-battered, patched, and repaired, and Remin pulled it up to the hearth and laid a few logs in the grate, feeding the coals with some kindling.

"You should be abed, my lord," croaked Juste, and Remin looked back to see his eyes were slits of awareness, dull with sickness.

"I came to see that you're not like to die in yours." And to find out what was going on. Remin dusted off his hands and dragged the chair beside Juste's narrow cot. "You look wretched, Juste."

"Still better than you," Juste replied in a reedy whisper. "You made us worry for a little while, my lord."

"It would take more than a fever to finish me off. Do you know what's been happening?" Remin managed to deliver this without coughing and then quit while he was ahead. There was a basin of water on the floor beside Juste's bed, and he soaked and then replaced the cloth on Juste's forehead, feeling the heat baking from the man.

"I spoke with Her Grace last night," Juste whispered. "Auber and Jinmin have been guarding her. But you ought not be alone either, my lord. Someone was in the house. One of the windows in the solar was left open, and Davi saw a print in the snow on the balcony."

"No guards are assigned there," Remin said slowly, his brows lowering.

"There are now." Juste covered his mouth, coughing. "I thought someone would try for you, my lord. I didn't realize they'd gotten so close."

"I'll have a care," Remin promised, flicking open his cloak to reveal the mailcoat underneath. "How many guards down?"

"Six. But we will have a full complement tonight."

"Good. I don't suppose we managed to track who—" This time, Remin coughed. "—ever it was?"

"No, my lord. Dol said the footprints joined the paths to the library, and disappeared."

"East rather than west," Remin muttered. But that was all; there was nothing more to glean from that information, and no further action he could take. Yes, he could order Ophele home now, lock the doors, and harden the manor into a fortress, but all that would accomplish was informing the traitor or traitors that they had been detected.

And then they would lie low. And wait.

Because sooner or later, he would have to come out again.

"I'll speak to the guards," he snarled. The thought that someone had been so close, maybe even *inside the solar* when Ophele arrived home last night, made him want to break things. "Tell me the rest."

"Genon has been spared so far," Juste whispered. "Most of the town has it. Her Grace said two-thirds. They've set up quarantines."

"And why does she know all that?" Remin asked flatly.

"Who was going to stop her? I heard her telling off Leonin this morning, when he tried to follow her." A smile twitched at Juste's mouth. "She shouted."

"Ophele shouted?" Remin's mind briefly boggled, until he remembered her glaring up at him as she blocked the bedroom door. That whole confrontation was rather fuzzy in his memory, but he was almost sure it had happened.

"Leonin had it badly. Water," Juste said, gesturing to the cup on the table above his head, and sipped slowly as he conveyed the remaining details he knew. It wasn't much. He had heard Ophele and Emi moving through the cottages twice a day distributing food, and Emi came on her own to knock on doors and make sure everyone had fires and was taking their medicine. Genon had visited several times and told Juste as much as he thought it was good for him to know.

"I see," Remin said when he was done. He rose and added another log to the fire. "Go back to sleep, Juste. Get better."

"You—do the same." Juste was struggling to keep his eyes open. "Rem...she'll be back soon. Just wait. Genon says...trust her..."

There was no one this side of the Brede that could stop him from going wherever he wanted, but Remin paused, scowling down at the sick man. Even halfway conscious, Juste made a compelling argument.

Rewrapping the muffler around his face, he went outside again. He was roasting under the many layers of clothing and fur, but it was better than taking a chill as he moved from one cottage to the next.

"I'm sorry, my lord," Leonin said the moment he opened the door. "I know I should be with Her Grace, but she...strongly opposed the idea of my accompanying her."

"What did she say?"

Leonin shifted.

"She said if I came outside, she would take off her cloak and sit in the snow until I went back in," he said stiffly, and Remin could very easily imagine Ophele issuing this threat, no doubt with a stomp of her small foot.

"Well, I wouldn't want to risk that," Remin replied, torn between anger and pride. "Thank you, Leonin."

He could not be easy in his mind until he had checked on everyone else, amused by the horror of his servants as they realized their lord was at the door. What Juste had said was true. Almost all of them were sick, in various levels of croaking, feverish discomfort, but someone answered every door except one.

Hell.

"Lady Verr," he repeated, knocking again. Her cottage was between Miche's and the maids', and was the only one where smoke was not rising from the chimney. For a moment, he hesitated, glowering, but he was not about to leave the lady's corpse to be discovered by Ophele, the manners of Segoile be damned. "Lady Verr. I'm coming in."

Well, she wasn't dead. Like Juste, she was burrowed into a nest of furs pulled up to her chin, her auburn hair loose around her head, but she stirred when poked, and then her eyes flew open.

"Your Grace," she gasped, and went at once into a fit of coughing.

"Your fire's out," Remin said accusingly, and handed her a cup of water. "And I couldn't find that dratted Emi. Never mind, just lie there, I'll be gone in a minute."

"A gentleman...in a lady's chambers..." she tried to say between coughs, and Remin shot her a black glance as he squatted by the hearth.

"This is a cottage on the edge of civilization," he noted, cracking kindling apart in his hands. "Allowances must be made."

"Emi has been looking in often," the lady managed, with a painful effort. Remin couldn't help a twinge of sympathy; he knew exactly how much those coughs hurt. "She is still well. You needn't trouble yourself, my lord."

"That's a relief. That she is well," Remin added, though both of them knew exactly what he had meant. "But you didn't answer, so I had to check. The sickness is bad this year. We can't afford to worry about etiquette."

"You have made that very clear," she said, with a glint of feverish gray eyes. "There is a reason for it, you know. Manners, graces..."

"I am aware of that." Remin pulled down his scarf and puffed on the coals of the fire, grimacing. This was the part that made him feel most like coughing.

"It's what puts everyone in their place...and comfortable together..." The words slurred together. Remin eyed her warily, hoping he wasn't going to have to actually *look* at her.

"I know what manners are," he said.

"They are the reason I can politely misunderstand what you said about Emi, for example, my lord."

"You mean, they're the reason you have to smile when I insult you to your face," Remin retorted, and then pulled up his scarf to muffle a cough.

"That is a privilege...of rank..." Lady Verr turned her face away, coughing right back.

That would be an amusing farce, two sick people sparring about rank and etiquette until one of them expired. Remin swallowed, buttoning in another cough, and swiped at the sickly sweat on his forehead with his sleeve.

"Are you badly fevered?" he asked, once he was certain his chest wouldn't instantly explode.

"Yes," she said hoarsely. "But I need nothing else, Your Grace. Please take care of yourself. Her Grace was very worried for you."

The lady had spine, Remin admitted grudgingly as he made his way back to the house. There was no question that he was not well yet himself, and Juste's admonitions were still ringing in his ears. It would be foolish and dangerous to go charging off into town when he had only to wait a few hours, and Ophele would return. But he *hated* it. Had anyone died? How bad was the sickness this year? The last thing he wanted in this world was to leave her to manage this by herself. What could Genon be thinking, involving her in it?

Locking the doors of his chamber behind him, he had another wash to get rid of the sick sweat and then stoked the fire in the bedchamber and sat down, eying the jug of Genon's tonic. He did not want to sleep anymore. He wanted *out*. If he was being fair, he knew he could trust Genon, Auber, and Jinmin to keep things in hand, and the stars only knew what Ophele might have been doing; she was always a wild card in the operations of the valley.

Wrapping himself in a blanket, Remin glared at his medicine, gulped it down, and then sat back and plotted what he would do the instant he was well.

And then he fell asleep. He woke with a crick in his neck as the lock rattled in the door, and Ophele appeared in the shadows, wrapped so that only her golden eyes showed through the slit in her scarf. She was sniffling.

"Wife," he said, sitting up and trying to focus. "What's happened?"

"Oh. Oh, you're awake?" she said, and quickly wiped her eyes, as if she thought he might not notice. "I'll get supper, there's chicken with dumplings tonight—"

"That can wait. Come here, tell me what's wrong," he ordered, with something like his usual strength and only a little tickle in his throat.

For a moment, she hesitated, and then her shoulders sagged.

"Master Sharrenot is dead," she whispered, and looked up at him, more tears welling. "I'm sorry. And Berren Sekrost, Mathie Campagne, and Gustere Neloe. He was six. From Meinhem. I saw them bring him out, I'm sorry. I didn't think of them, but I should have. Genon says the fever is too much for them when they're still so weak and I even made a list of people that needed extra care, but I never thought—"

"Slow down. Come sit down," Remin admonished, his jaw tightening as he *refused* to cough. Rising, he gestured her to her chair and set a kettle over the fire. "Tell me from the beginning, wife. I'm well enough to listen."

He wanted to know anyway. And though normally he would have pulled her into his lap and consoled her at once, today he sat down in his own chair across the table, listening as she explained everything that had happened and everything she had done. Today, she was not just his wife. She was Squire Rollon, returned from Ferrede and struggling to explain why twenty people had died there. She was Sir Ortaire, who hadn't noticed the small, fatal hill outside his camp, just high enough for a wolf demon to spring inside and tear a dozen men to pieces.

Today, he was taking a report from her, just as he would have done from any of his young commanders.

"And now Azelma is sick too," she said miserably, fresh tears soaking into her scarf. "She's not...*dry* the way Genon said Master Sharrenot was, but she's so old, and what if she's come all this way for me and she dies? I keep trying to think what we can do, and Genon says more people are going to die tonight, and I don't know what to do, I can't think of *anything—*"

"Sometimes people die." Wearily, he wondered what sort of hellish garden he was really building for her. It was so hard to focus, he had to admit that perhaps his own fever was not *completely* gone. "What are you doing to help them tonight?"

"There are people watching the Meinhem refugees now," she said, her fingers knotting together. "Auber is managing them. There are four people who will be checking on the sickest overnight, making sure they have fire and medicine and cooling them if they get too hot or are coughing too terribly. That is one trouble, how can we tell if someone is too hot until they're wandering in their wits? You never did, but Genon said your fever was so high, and there must be a way..."

"If Genon doesn't know it, you can't be expected to invent it," Remin pointed out reasonably, and waved at her to continue.

That was all he did, over tea and eventually supper. He listened. The chicken and dumplings might as well have been wet straw, but he forced them down, absorbing every word as she described everything they had done, every problem she had tried to anticipate, every measure she had taken. Setting her clever mind against the world and frustrated that it would not conform to even the most carefully laid plans.

And though there were a few errors and areas where she had been excessively cautious, as Remin listened, he realized with a swell of pride and amazement that she had done *well.*

She still had much to learn. No doubt Jinmin and Auber had saved her from a few mistakes. But this...this was what she was *supposed* to do. She was his duchess. Not only his wife, and one day the mother of his children. She was his other half, bound to him for eternity, his partner in all things.

"If you thought Master Sharrenot needed watching, then you ought to have ordered someone to watch him," he said, and lifted a hand as he stifled a cough, scowling. She lacked self-confidence, and this was a good opportunity for his clever wife to learn a lesson. "Did you truly think he needed it, at the time? Hindsight doesn't count."

"Well...Lady Verr thought he was dangerously ill," she said, picking at a bit of chicken. Her delicate eyebrows knotted together. "I thought of having Aubin watch him that night, but..."

"Why didn't you?"

"Well, I was afraid he wouldn't get enough sleep, himself. He was already getting up once in the middle of the night to look in on a dozen cottages, and looking after Master Didion besides. And Genon says if people don't sleep, then they haven't the fire to fight off illness."

"What would happen if Aubin got sick?" Remin asked, and listened patiently as she talked it through.

How many times had Duke Ereguil walked him through exactly this exercise? Remin was twelve when he became a squire, and began learning the business of leading men. Ophele had not had any lessons at all. All she had was her sharp, methodical mind and her determination to do her best, and this was a far more bitter test than he would ever have wished for her. But that was *his* fault. He had never planned for what would happen if he fell ill.

"Those are called second- and third-order effects," he explained, with some appreciation for the irony. "I think Juste confiscated my books on such things, I'll have him look them up. You need to consider those, too, when you're making decisions. Not just the immediate, obvious impacts, but the ones that will follow down the line. If Genon didn't think it would help, and you might have risked Aubin falling sick by spreading him too thin, would you change what you did?"

"No," she said after a long moment, and looked up at him. "But...Master Sharrenot..."

"Died," Remin answered quietly. "People die. He was a good man. I'm sorry for it, for I will miss him."

"That's what Genon and Auber kept saying," she said, with a flash of frustration. "People die, just like that. But there must be *something,* why isn't there—"

"Come here." He held out his arms with a mingling of relief and pity as she came at once, settling into his lap to cry. It did no good to tell her there was nothing she could have done. She would always feel this burden. He knew.

"I'm sorry," she sniffed as he wrapped his arms around her, wishing she could pull off her scarf. He missed her face. "I guess I should get used to it, after the devils and everything..."

"Maybe we are all too used to it," Remin said soothingly, and then wondered if it was true. He had experienced so much death, it had lost its power to shock and horrify him, unless that death was hers. "I don't know if it's a good thing," he added reflectively. "Juste always says to learn what you can, and send their spirits to the stars. You can't take all that weight on yourself."

"Hurry up and get better," she whispered. "I am always wondering what you would do."

"I'm sorry I wasn't there." He rested his forehead against hers and found her blessedly cool. "I would never have chosen this test for you, little owl. But do you know, I think the stars were very good, when they gave you to me for my duchess."

Chapter 8 – Solstice Night

"Your Grace. My lady," said Brother Oleare, offering a bow before he folded his long body into a chair. "I have kept the solstice night for you."

They sat at opposite ends of the solar in the midmorning light, Remin having commandeered the space to accept reports while his cough stubbornly persisted. With a fire blazing in the enormous fireplace, it was so warm, robes and lap blankets were hardly needed. But Brother Oleare had so far avoided the illness, so he was wrapped all the way up to his eyebrows.

"You have my thanks," replied Remin, who had been wondering uneasily if his failure to observe such religious rites might not be the cause of the plague. "Under the circumstances, I would not have tried to gather everyone together, but it is hard for us to go under the stars during winter even when there is no sickness."

"I have been considering that, my lord," the cleric agreed. "And with respect to the lady's fears for the Meinhem dead, as well."

"We wanted to do something for them before this, and for all those people in Nandre, too," Ophele agreed unhappily. She was the other reason Remin had summoned Brother Oleare; with nineteen dead of the sickness so far, and eight of them from Meinhem, she was taking it hard, and asking the most unanswerable questions. "We were going to wait until everyone came back, and pray for them all at once, but Sir Huber still hasn't returned..."

It was a familiar problem. During the war, it had always been a struggle to balance rites for the dead, allowing the living to grieve, and the demands of the war. Constant funerals were terrible for morale.

"Ah, I have a thought, in this circumstance." Brother Oleare shifted forward at the edge of his chair, his bony knees poking through his robe. "Some of the solstice rites may inform us. Now, I have kept them, as I said. I burned the incense, and contemplated the void between the stars. The spirits of your dead will not linger. But there is a prayer called the *segarde*—do you know it?"

"No," said Remin, on behalf of them both. He did not know the names of prayers.

"It is a simple litany done with the burning of cleansing blue incense, which I have in good supply," Brother Oleare explained. "I would suggest waiting until the sickness has passed, so that the vigil will not be too taxing for weakened people. But it will do them good to breathe the clean air, and even if your people cannot congregate under the sky, for one night they might lift their prayers together for all their sorrows and troubles, and find comfort in sharing their intentions with the stars."

Remin and Ophele exchanged glances.

"I would like that," she offered hesitantly.

"Do that," Remin agreed. "We can provide hands to help you distribute incense. Genon believes we're almost through the worst of the illness, if only because almost everyone's had it. But once we have a fine day, I want a proper funeral. There are many who have not had rites."

"Yes, Your Grace." Brother Oleare bowed his head. "I have heard of what happened in Meinhem and Nandre."

"It is not just the deaths from this autumn." Remin met his eyes, unsmiling. "We have not had the aid of a holy man since the war. Two hundred and forty-three have died. They died from devils, and in the accidents of building. And there are my villagers, who sickened and starved, and never once had the prayers of the Temple."

"Remin," Ophele whispered. Remin himself hadn't realized how angry he was.

"I will write their names, and burn them with incense, so the stars might know them better. People might be forgiven for losing faith, in such trials." Brother Oleare lifted his head to peer at them more closely, as if he wondered whether that might be the case now. "I beg your indulgence. You asked for instruction; hear me now. The stars govern our ways from birth to death, but they do not intercede among the living. They shone on the struggles of your people, when they called out in their suffering. Bet Agasse attended upon your men who died in arms, defending others. Nuyin and Ayan are the twin stars of healing, and are moved by compassion for those who suffer. No one who walks beneath the stars walks alone."

"Then what need have we of clerics?" Remin asked, unimpressed.

"For the living," Brother Oleare replied, sighing. He stroked his long beard. "And there, we failed you. I will not offend you with excuses, Your Grace. Nor can I speak on behalf of the Temple. But I am sorry your people were forsaken. I can only promise that they were never forsaken by the stars."

"I will give you the names of our dead."

"Does that mean, that's where they went?" Ophele asked, glancing between the two men. "If Remin's men died bravely, Bet Agasse would take them in?"

"Yes, my lady," the cleric replied. "Bet Agasse opens his gates to the steadfast. Perhaps you have heard that someone was born under a particular star?"

Remin took a furtive sip of tea while they talked, fighting back a cough. Genon had strongly recommended that he should not venture outside until he had gone twenty-four hours without coughing, and Remin had made it all the way to supper yesterday before he got into a spirited discussion with Leonin about various schools of swordsmanship, which had set them both off.

Remin was trying not to have strong opinions today.

Ophele was having enough strong opinions for both of them, as she sought consolation in her own way. Remin's rather fatalistic attitude toward death had not been much comfort, and he had hoped that Brother Oleare would have something wiser to offer. But though Remin was not very pious, it was still shocking to hear Ophele questioning the man with no reverence whatever for the cult of the stars, employing every tool of logic and argument that Juste had taught her.

"But the second volume of *The Will Immanent* implies there is such a thing as destiny," she was saying, wielding the deadliest weapon in her arsenal. Her tawny eyes bent mercilessly on the old man. "In the third chapter, discussing the pathways of the dark..."

Remin pretended not to see the look of astonished betrayal from Brother Oleare. *He* would not have wanted to be on the receiving end of Ophele's interrogation. Maybe the holy man could consider it a form of atonement for the Temple's neglect.

"I will bring some of my own books next time, young la—my lady," Brother Oleare said when time was up. The old man was huffing, his thick scarf puffing around his face, and perhaps that was fair; one wouldn't look at Ophele and expect a rhetorical mauling.

"Oh, yes, please," Ophele agreed, blissfully unaware of his pique, and trying not to laugh made Remin cough instead.

He didn't get to go outside that day, either.

But over the next few days, as the pernicious illness worked its way through Tresingale, it certainly didn't seem to *him* that the stars could have any particular plan. Azelma endured a frightening, feverish night and then rallied; Naisenne, the new head laundress, died of the fever, and she wasn't much more than fifty. What sense did it make, for a woman to come all this way and then die before she could even unpack? Remin had her body carried away to lie in frozen state with the other victims of the plague, feeling angry and guilty and tired. He did not understand the logic of the world.

In practical terms, that left him with three remaining laundresses, young women who did not seem reliable, in his admittedly limited experience. But he supposed they could not all be like Emi and Peri: sturdy, dependable girls of whom he heartily approved.

"Maybe this is what it's like to be old," he grumbled to Ophele as he took his seat in the solar for another day of attempting not to cough. "Sitting in a room watching other people go in and out all day."

"Until I met you, I thought that's what lords did," she whispered back, taking her seat at the table beside him and putting on her company face. She took copious notes throughout his interviews and was swiftly learning what details were worth writing down, gaining a general grasp of the business of the valley. Perhaps some lords would have restricted their wives to household affairs, but Remin had learned this lesson. If he was ever injured or ill again, he would not leave Ophele scrambling to catch up.

The next man came in on a blast of cold air, like a Hara Vosi storm-herald. Pulling his scarf off his head, he knelt.

"Your Grace, I am Laide Torimel, I was sent with Sir Miche," he said, lifting his head. Under all that winter gear Remin recognized him, a young soldier of around twenty and just this side of frostbitten. "He sent me back. We found Sir Huber and his men about a week's ride from Tresingale. They had many on foot. Sir Miche asked to send Mr. Hengest at once, if he can be spared, and as many sledges and supplies as you can."

"Sir Osinot, go and make them ready," Remin ordered one of the guards by the door, and beckoned for the messenger to rise. "Stand by the fire, man. How many still live?"

"Two hundred, Your Grace, mostly from Selgin. Everyone's cold and we have some sick and injured. Sir Huber..."

Remin felt his stomach sink clear through his boots.

"It was a wolf demon, Your Grace," Laide said heavily. "Late in the season, it was, and it got his arm. We thought we'd surgeoned it proper, but a fever set in. Sir Miche sent him ahead on one of the sledges, so he may not be far behind me, if the stars are good to us."

"Take Genon and go meet him. Now." His body chose that exact moment to betray him; Remin was furious as a fit of coughing abruptly wrenched him over, a short but wracking spasm. He had to take a sip of tea before he could speak again, and he pulled himself up straight, his hands gripping his armrests until the wood creaked in his grip. "Two hundred? Marching from Isigne? I'll send a party of men with sledges and supplies behind you. Keep lanterns lit, and send up smoke when you make camp."

"I will, Your Grace." Laide wrapped himself back up with gratifying energy. "He was hanging on, you know everyone always says there's iron in Sir Huber—"

"I know. Go. Bless you," Remin added, and though he knew the stars were uncaring, and offered neither comfort nor aid, the prayer came to him anyway. "Bet Agasse, witness the courage of one born in your light..."

"And Ise Arun, bring him home," Ophele finished for him. She was learning the names of all the stars.

Maybe that was the last refuge of a helpless man, Remin thought, despising his own weakness, the tightness lingering in his chest. When a man did not have the strength to move mountains himself, he could do nothing but appeal to heaven.

* * *

The survivors of Isigne and Selgin blew into Tresingale on the wings of another blizzard.

When the messenger came, Ophele did not even attempt to talk Remin into staying home. There was a certain wetness in the frosty air, a scent that tingled on her nose that made her think of snow as they rode down to the cookhouse from the manor, alerted by an errand boy that the survivors were approaching the North Gate. All her preparations stood them in good stead. The people were sent straight to the cookhouse, where everything was ready and waiting for them.

Mistress Amise Conbour was there, as were Mionet and Madam Sanai, and there were even a few women of Meinhem who had escaped the sickness and were eager to help. Behind them were Genon's journeymen, and two of Auber's older nephews to fetch and carry. Everyone was scrubbed and well-wrapped in the hopes that they would not pass on the sickness to these already-weakened people.

Anyone who had coughed within the last twenty-four hours was forbidden to enter the cookhouse, and Remin had met this requirement through sheer brute stubbornness. Since his fit before Miche's messenger, he had not allowed a single cough to escape, even if it meant he had to stop and hold his breath mid-sentence.

"This is mostly what we did for the folk from Meinhem, too," Ophele told him quietly as the survivors came in, directed to long rows of cots by the women. "Amise has a nice way with them, and she and the other women get them seated and fed so the healers can look them over. And if Genon says it's all right, then Madam Sanai will take them for a bath. I really think it helps, it warms them right through."

"It is well thought, wife," Remin agreed, taking her arm to keep them both out of the way. Leonin was with them, guarding them from this multitude of strangers, but Davi was still confined to his bed.

"I just wish we could do something ourselves," she murmured, watching helplessly as they limped in, or were carried. Huber's men were almost indistinguishable from the refugees: ragged, starving, and injured. More than half of Remin's villagers had been killed by devils.

"Let them get settled first, and then we can go speak to them," Remin promised, though she could see the frustration in his dark eyes. "It's enough for them to see us here and watching, for now."

Like the stars. Ophele stifled a sigh. *She* did not find it especially comforting, especially when Miche himself arrived a few minutes later, bringing up the rear to make sure no one was left behind.

"How's Huber?" he asked instantly, shaking the snow off his shoulders.

"He'll live," Remin replied. This news had come up to the manor at sunrise. "His arm is gone."

"He can wrangle horses with one," Miche said, but there was no lightness in his gaze as he turned to Ophele and bowed. "My lady. I've brought back as many as I could, but this is Huber's work. There's a trail of dead from here to Isigne and as deep as the snow was, it's a miracle he came back at all. They saw their last devil two weeks ago, Rem."

"Why not?" Remin said bitterly. Every other assumption had already been upended, why not this one? "Why wouldn't they linger late if they arrived early? Devils can survive in the cold in the mountains, can't they?"

"They can survive in the *dark,*" Ophele replied, the thought striking her all at once. "Was there early snow to the west?"

"I'll ask," Miche promised, pushing his head back with an enormous yawn. He looked a proper barbarian with his golden beard and long hair, but his face was very lean, his tawny eyes shadowed and grim as he watched the activity before them. The first few rows of people had found their cots, and Genon's journeymen were among them, peeling back boots and taking off gloves to reveal ill-healed wounds and purple-black flesh.

For a moment, Ophele thought she was going to be sick.

"What—what," she tried to say, covering her mouth with her hand. "That man—Remin, his feet—"

"That's frostbite, wife," Remin answered, turning her away from it. "Don't let them see you upset. That foot will have to come off, I expect. It happens when the flesh freezes, and then it goes foul and begins to rot."

She had heard of frostbite; adventurers in books got it, especially on their noses. But the books of the Aldeburke library did not have pictures of such things, and once again, her imagination was not equal to reality.

Miche went on with his report as she tried to collect herself, both men neatly covering for her until she could turn back and face this latest horrible thing. She was finding it hard to accept that there was something worse than the emaciated children of Meinhem.

"...about forty miles away," Miche was saying, accepting a mug of savory beef tea from one of Wen's kitchen boys. "Sledges worked a treat, we might see about breeding up some of those dogs they use in Navatsvi for winter travel. We took turns walking on the way back. I tell you, we take our shovels for granted in Tresingale..."

His humor was black, black as their feet, Ophele thought, and was horrified at herself. But Miche was telling the same type of jokes, and worse, and even his smile seemed to show biting teeth. Remin listened, but his gaze was on the healers moving from one person to the next, checking extremities for frostbite and examining emaciated bodies. Those who needed to see Genon or Mr. Brestle immediately had a red ribbon tied to their cots, while those who needed extra watching got a green one. Those who had been examined and cleared got white ribbons.

There were not many white ribbons.

"Let one of the journeymen have a look at you," Remin said when Miche was done, clasping his hand. "I'm glad you didn't take the sickness with you. I was worried."

"We had enough trouble already, without bringing more with us." The two men squeezed hands, and Miche slanted a look at Ophele, one corner of his mouth tugging up in a rueful smile. "You weren't sick a day, were you? I believe I'll accept Master Balad's invitation to the baths. I'll report for supper later, my lord."

It might have been worse. That wasn't much comfort, but Ophele looked at the men who had gone with Miche, lining up for their own inspections by the fire. They might have taken the sickness with them. They might never have come home at all. At least, at *least* they had come back.

"Let's go and speak to them, wife," Remin said, taking her arm and glancing over her head to signal Leonin to precede them. Most of the refugees hardly looked capable of picking up a weapon, let alone using it, but he wasn't taking any chances.

What could they possibly say to these people? She was glad that Remin went first, moving to the nearest cot.

"I'm Remin, Duke of Andelin," he said to the man seated there, and squatted down and deliberately shifted his gaze to the child in the man's lap. "Who is this?"

"H-her name is Ylinor, my lord," said the man, looking from Remin to Ophele to Leonin with clear nervousness. He didn't look like an old man, but his face was so thin and drawn, it was hard to guess his actual age.

"Ylinor," Remin said, holding out his huge, gloved hand to the child, palm up. "My name is Remin. How many summers do you have?"

Children were almost always afraid of Remin. Ophele had seen a dozen of them burst into tears at the sight of him, and all the warning signs were there: the round eyes, the quivering lower lip, but he still kept trying. Ophele hastily crouched down next to him, making herself ludicrously small in comparison.

"No, let me guess," she said, assuming a pose of exaggerated thoughtfulness. "Have you...three summers, Ylinor?"

Mionet's head would have exploded, to see the Duchess of Andelin crouched down and making faces for a little peasant girl, but by the time she got up to five summers, with escalating drama and suspense at each new guess, the little girl had forgotten all about the looming Duke of Andelin and was giggling as she offered Ophele her hand. The tiny fingers were so *cold.*

"What good manners," Ophele complimented, trying to mimic the way Amise and Lisset spoke to children. "Would you like to shake His Grace's hand? He is very pleased to meet you."

"Yes, my lady," piped Ylinor, turning to offer her hand to Remin, who was doing his best to look pleased and unthreatening.

All of that made it much easier to speak to Ylinor's father, by comparison. Or at least, it was easier for Ophele. It only took a minute to see there was something amiss with the man.

"It was v-very hard, Your G-Grace," he said, blinking. He had introduced himself as Siyoun Arpelle, a fisherman from idyllic little Isigne. "There were so many d-devils, it was barely May when we s-saw the f-first..."

What was wrong with him? Ophele tried not to stare. He wasn't stuttering because he was cold; his teeth weren't chattering at all. Every few words he ducked his head and blinked hard, and then his eyes opened wide and he clutched Ylinor to him, his arms around her as if he thought someone might snatch her away.

"S-so many d-devils," he repeated, his eyes enormous. "So many d-devils, Your G-Grace. I don't know..."

"There were a lot this year," Remin agreed, angling his head to make the man look at him. "But you got here, didn't you? You brought your girl all this way, just as you ought. Did you see the walls when you came through the gate? Those walls are twenty feet high."

"I-I saw. Yes. Yes, Your G-Grace." The man blinked. Gulped. Ducked.

"Nothing will harm you now. I'm very glad you've come," Remin said firmly, and Ophele started as she felt his foot nudge hers.

"Yes. Yes, we have baths waiting for you, if you like," she said, checking his cot for the white ribbon. "You can take Ylinor with you, so both of you will be clean and warm, and there will be new clothes for you. Would you like that?"

"I'd l-like that. She's been so cold. Ylinor," he repeated. "I promised, I p-promised my wife I'd protect her, I did, but she's been c-cold and hungry—"

"Then you must certainly take her to the baths. Bilaki," Ophele said, waving over the nearby Benkki Desan woman. "Bilaki will take you to get warm. You did so well, to bring Ylinor all this way. You're safe now, don't worry about a thing."

That was what Amise had told the people from Meinhem, over and over again, repeating it as many times as it took to make them believe it. Ophele stepped back to let Bilaki gently usher him toward the doors, where a sledge and thick furs were waiting to bundle him up for the short trip.

"He's in shock," Remin explained under his breath. "Let's see about putting a green ribbon on his cot. Such folk are unpredictable, they need watching. Were the ribbons your idea?"

"Yes," said Ophele, too unhappy to be pleased with this small cleverness.

There was just no end of horrible things to learn, was there? Her heart was wrung with pity for that poor man and what he must have endured, and his little girl, and Ophele repeated his name to herself as she followed Remin to the next cot, wishing she had paper and ink. Siyoun Arpelle, a fisherman. Ylinor, his daughter.

It was *something* she could do, even if it was only remembering their names. So many names. She saw Brother Oleare moving between the cots, listening, blessing, his head bowed as he prayed with them and over them. Ophele had feared the devils, and she had been fascinated by them, but she was learning to hate them as she moved with Remin from one cot to the next, witnessing the miseries the creatures had caused. They were not like a wolf or a bear at all. Wolves and bears did not seek people out to hurt them and destroy their homes and tear their babies to pieces.

Before each new family, Remin bent down so he wouldn't tower over everyone, and if there was a child, he crouched to greet them too, determined to win them over, trying to gentle his face. And then he listened. He listened to their losses, and the names of their dead, and then he told them he was glad they had come. He told them they were safe, and that he was sorry for what they had suffered.

"You will have it back," he said to another small family, who spoke brokenly of the home they had left behind. "It may take some years, but if the day comes when you want to go home, I'll see that you do. Until then, you're safe and welcome here."

How did he know exactly what to say? He was normally stiff and abrupt, and as the suffering mounted and they listened to awful story after awful story, Ophele lost her own words completely. It was just too horrible. She couldn't listen to them and not cry, and if she started crying, who knew when she would stop. Twenty-three people had died of the valley fever, and Azelma had nearly died, and Remin had been so sick, and she hadn't even figured out how to deal with that and now here was this fresh tragedy, orders of magnitude worse than anything that had come before.

But...no. This wasn't a fresh tragedy, she thought, looking at all these starved people, their faces so gaunt as to show all their teeth. This had been happening for months. While she was cowering under blankets in her cottage, devils had been smashing down their doors. While Remin and his men had been bringing in the harvest, these people had been starving, trapped on the other side of ten thousand devils. While she was marveling at her first blizzard, they were walking through it on frozen feet. And leaving a trail of dead from here to Isigne, according to Miche.

The thought was overwhelming. It made her angry and ashamed and so sad and she didn't know what to do with these feelings.

"How do you always know what to say to them?" she asked Remin as they walked out of the cookhouse. Snow was falling thickly outside, and the first groups of bathers were coming back, scrubbed pink and warm and well-wrapped for the short journey back to their cots.

"I've said it all before." Remin swung up onto Lancer's back and extended a hand to lift her before him in the saddle. "More times than I can count."

"During the war?"

For a while, she thought he might not answer. There were many things he didn't like to talk about. Lancer moved beneath them, his satiny black hide covered in a thick wool blanket, and Remin was warm behind her as he wrapped his cloak about them both.

"I never knew what to say, when my men came back," he said finally, and she looked up to find his face was remote. "After a battle. I was the one that sent them. And they came back hurt, or didn't come back at all, and I didn't know what to tell them. They didn't want to hear, *I'm sorry*. Why had I sent them, if I was going to be sorry about it? So I told them they did well, and they were safe, and to get better. And I told them when the war was over, we would have a good place, where they would never want for anything again."

"Siyoun Arpelle is a fisherman," she remembered, looking toward the river. "That first man. The stuttering one. There are a lot of fish in the Brede, I bet."

Lancer's hooves clopped onto the cobblestones of Eugene Street. The snow drifted, soft and silent.

"Then we'll build boats," said Remin.

* * *

Thirty miles north of the caverns system of the Aven Bede, there was a trail that Remin's men called the goat track.

High, narrow, and precarious, it vanished a dozen times on the way up the mountain, so cold and windy that it seemed only the wooliest creature could survive. In some places, the gaps between rocks were so narrow, a man had to crawl to get through, and the summit of the mountain was almost always a blinding storm, capped with snow year-round.

If Valleth knew of it, they almost certainly had dismissed it as a strategic vulnerability. Only a madman would attempt it.

But one September night, Remin Grimjaw did exactly that.

The fourth year of the war was a low point. He and his army had smashed into the Berlawes like the sea against the Cliffs of Marren, and Valleth had been defending their mountain fortresses for nearly a year. Remin was never defeated, but that year saw a string of increasingly bloody victories at Marcke and Lunbren, culminating in the horror of Sanghin.

For Juste, that was the winter of Iverlach, the starving place, which he took and held through seven months of siege. When Remin broke through the following spring, Juste was so starved, he had to be carried out.

Everything depended on breaking this line in the mountains. Valleth hardly needed to build walls in the Berlawes, much less defend them; the sheer granite of the mountains was impassable, and Remin had had scouts out for months, searching for the slightest weakness. The goat track was the key to the impervious gates of Valleth. Once he broke the doors down, he would roll up the other mountain forts like a carpet.

To that end, Tounot was marching north with a substantial force to Kernne, though unless Remin got over the goat track in time, all he was going to be able to do when he got there was yell insults at the men in the gate tower. And fifteen miles south, Victorin and his much smaller group of men were moving into position to intercept any Vallethi reinforcements.

He just had to hold them off long enough for Remin and Tounot to take the fort.

"You could lose everyone." Huber had come to Remin's tent the night before all these pieces were to move into place, gaunt and grim and hollow-eyed. "You don't even know if you can get over the mountain."

"If we don't take these mountains, we don't take the valley," Remin had replied, rummaging through the gear that would take him up and over the mountain. "You had a chance to propose an alternative an hour ago. Do you have one now?"

"At least give Victorin more men," Huber argued. "Give him a *chance*. That's not a small force to the south, if they push him out onto the flat—"

"Every extra man I give him is another man who might be spotted by a Vallethi scout. Victorin just needs to hold out long enough." Remin sent a black look over one shoulder. "He's not arguing, so why are you?"

"Of course he's not going to argue, he'll do whatever he thinks you need him to do," Huber snapped. "That's why you picked him, you bloody bastard."

Four years into the war, no one questioned whether twenty-one-year-old Remin could lead an army. He was a prodigy that had broken the Brede, the general who could not be defeated, a knight out of legend, with a string of victories even the Emperor could not contest. After twelve years of assassins, even Valleth's pain-mages could not stop him. With Juste's singers building his legend in both Valleth and the Empire, even his friends had begun to regard him as something not quite human.

Except for Huber.

"I chose him because he can do what I need him to do," Remin said flatly. Outside, he was ice. Closing himself off was the only way he knew how to cope. But inside, it felt as if his guts were boiling in oil. "If you don't have anything useful to say, then leave. I have things to do."

"You said...hold out *long enough,*" Huber repeated slowly. "You don't think he's coming back."

Remin was trying very, very hard not to think of this.

"Once I let Tounot in, we'll go back for him," he said, though his hands shook as they picked through the piles of rope, woolens, furs, and the other things scattered on his cot. He had forgotten what he needed to pack.

"Don't lie," Huber whispered. "You're sending him to die. You know he's going to die, he's our *friend,* Duke Ereguil's *son.* How can you...*do* that?"

What had Huber wanted to hear? Would it have made any difference if Remin had acknowledged it? Of *course* Victorin was his friend, Victorin was Remin's *brother* in every way but blood, and had been since both boys were five years old. But what was he supposed to do? They were caught between the hammer of Valleth and the anvil of the Emperor, and Remin knew the Imperial Code. A defeated general could still be charged with treason.

He could not lose. Not once. Not ever.

Everyone expected miracles from him. No matter what they faced, everyone turned to Remin, sure that he would find a way, that he would lead them to another smashing victory. Well, this was all he had. This was the only way he knew how to do it. Victories were bought with blood. His blood, and the blood of the men that marched with him, and sometimes with the blood of a brother.

"Should I send someone else?" Remin asked coldly. "Will that make it better, if it's someone else's friend? Someone else's son?"

There could be no answer to that. Huber's mouth shut, but the look in his eyes seared Remin's heart, like watching something die before him, a light forever extinguished. A fracture that could never be mended.

Remin's hands stopped.

"If I do this, we'll win," he said. It was as close to a plea as he could get.

"Never for nothing, right?" Huber's voice was hard.

That was what Remin had said, after the killing field of Sanghin. *Many have died,* he had told his men. *But I will never ask you to die for nothing.*

In the end, Victorin had gone. And before he left, Clement had volunteered to go with him, to buy a little more time, though Clement had known it was a death sentence. Both of them knew. When Victorin came to say good-bye, he had tried to smile and laugh, and he had promised to see Remin on the far side of the mountain. But Remin had known that he would never see his best friend again.

Had Huber been right?

Remin didn't know. He would never know. *Someone* had to intercept the Vallethi reinforcements and hold them back long enough for Remin to get into the fort and take down the men on the gate. And if that someone was *not* Victorin—Victorin, a lancer whose fame nearly rivaled Remin's own—then perhaps the Eagle Knights would have ridden right over them.

If victory could justify any measure...well, Remin had taken the fort. And he had rolled up the Vallethi line like a carpet.

And Huber had never forgiven him.

"I'm sorry," Remin whispered. In the stillness of the small room behind the infirmary in Tresingale, Huber lay on a cot, too vulnerable to be placed in the common ward. Remin hadn't hesitated to kick Brother Oleare out of his shrine.

The fever had all but melted the flesh from Huber's bones. There was a bronze cast to his brown hair in most light, a glittering remnant of some Noreveni ancestor, but it was dull now, soaked with sweat. Even under the heaped blankets and furs, Remin could see the place where his left arm was not, his shield arm torn away by a wolf demon. It had been gangrenous when he was brought in, and there were still red streaks crawling up over his bare shoulder from the amputated limb. He was insensible, with great beads of sweat rolled down his face, but Genon was sure he would live.

Maybe it was cowardly to come and apologize when he couldn't respond.

"Miche brought them all back," Remin said into the quiet, covering Huber's remaining hand with his own. "A hundred and seventy-four people. You brought back a hundred and seventy-four people in winter. I was afraid you wouldn't make it, but everyone else was so sure..."

Gen said that even if someone was unconscious, they could hear. Their eyes moved beneath their eyelids, their hands might twitch, proof that they lived and felt and were trying to come back. Gen said to call them back, to let them hear the voices they knew, to give them the will to fight.

"They're in the cookhouse now, and we're looking after them," he went on, trying to think of good things to say. "They'll have homes, and work, even if they have to learn a new trade. Ophele has some scheme to teach them to weave, they can do that even...even if they've lost their feet..."

He was clinging to these plans like a lifeline. There had been plenty of things to distract him from the reality of what he had done to his people over the last year, and though it was cowardly, he was secretly relieved that the people of Meinhem had arrived while he was gone. By the time he came back, they were already settled and healing and he had never had to see the full extent of their agony.

But now, he had no choice but to face it, and he didn't know if he could bear it.

"You saved so many people," he told Huber. "I can never...thank you. I can't repay you. I can't..."

But for once, the usual promises would not come. *I am sorry. You're safe now. I will make you whole again.* He did not have that power. No power would undo what had been done. No apology would ever make it right.

Huber's hand twitched under his, and Remin looked up to find Huber was awake, his chest rising and falling in long, slow breaths.

"Rem," he whispered. His lips were blistered with cold. "Rollon?"

"Dead," Remin managed. Rollon. Huber's page. Huber's squire. Huber's *son*. "He brought back two children. They are all that is left of Nandre. He saved them, there was a devil hunting them. He...led it away."

Huber's throat worked.

"Go away, Rem," he whispered, and turned his face away, his shoulders shaking as he wept.

* * *

In the waning days of the year, the people of Tresingale kept the solstice night.

Ophele's solar actually felt crowded with the whole household gathered, sitting in a semicircle about the hearth. She had planned the event with customary care, to ensure everyone who wanted chairs would have them, and a full tea service sat on the sideboard, gently steaming. It would be a long night.

It was something, to see everyone together at once. Mionet was elegant in a dark gray gown, seated with Justenin and Miche on either side of her, the men freshly shaved and dressed in somber finery. Leonin and Davi took their usual places behind Ophele, while Azelma and Magne had seats by the fire, in deference to their age. Crowded nearby were the maids and stableboys, footmen and laundresses, and seven-year-old Samin sat on the floor by the woodbox, doomed by his youth to stoking the fire. Over twenty people, the first members of the Duke of Andelin's household.

If it were possible, Ophele would have invited everyone in town.

They had been through so much. In her mind's eye was the memory of Genon by the fire in the tavern, that day he had fallen asleep sitting up and everyone else tiptoed out the door so he might nap a little longer. There was the eternal vision of Adelan in only his drawers, crouched beside Magne and frustrated out of his wits as he tried to coax the simple man to take his medicine. Auber, good and solid as the earth, weeping with his sweetheart when Genon finally assured them that her son would live. For a dreadful day, there had been serious doubt.

All of them would be watching. Right now, Genon would be standing outside the infirmary, watching for the smoke to rise from the chimney of the manor house, signaling the start of prayers. In the North Gate cottages, Amise and Elodie would be looking out their window. From one of the upper windows of the barracks, Tounot would see it, and call all the rest of the soldiers there to the litany.

Next year, they would be together and hold solstice night properly.

"I believe everything is in order, my lord," said Brother Oleare, turning from the table where he had laid out an assortment of incense, the sacred powders that were the nearest thing to magic the Empire possessed. In an assortment of hues and scents, they drew the all-seeing eyes of the stars, and he took up a handful of red powder to call their attention.

"Go ahead," said Remin. He had been very quiet, the last few days.

"Your Grace." Brother Oleare bowed and then sprinkled the red powder on the leaping flames.

It puffed and sparked, to Samin's obvious delight, and then red smoke rolled up, scarlet as an anemone. All of Tresingale would see that smoke in the moonlight, and it was a signal to begin their own vigils, the simple *segarde* that Brother Oleare had taught them all.

He was dressed in the robes of a mystic, with a rope belt that signified an ascetic order, in the pale blue of an incense scribe. By daylight, he was a thin old man with a quavering voice, but there was a curious power in his face as he stood before the fire, his dark eyes shining. The red incense burned sharp and spicy.

"My lord and lady," the holy man said. "Though we would prefer to stand bare before the stars, and look upon them with our mortal eyes, we may have faith that *they* see *us*. Stone walls do not blind the eyes of heaven. Clouds do not obscure their sight. They are the celestial divine that observes all, understands all, and knows the truth of our ways. Beyond the clouds, the sky is dark and infinite, and you may be sure those stars are shining."

So saying, he turned to wash his hands in the basin on the table, dried them carefully, and then took a handful of pale blue powder.

"This is the air of cleansing and healing. Breathe it slowly, but deep," he said, sprinkling it over the fire. It smelled like...juniper, small blue berries, sharp-scented and clean. "The *segarde* is a litany of reflection. There is a reason it is performed at the end of the year, so that we may come before the divine celestial presence and seek the judgment of the stars."

Light smoke rose from the burning incense, silver-blue and vaporous, coiling upward in tendrils. Brother Oleare bowed his head.

"Ur Se, first among the stars, know my mind. Ur Se, first among the stars, witness the work of my hands. Ur Se, first among the stars, weigh the worth of my heart."

That was the prayer. He repeated it once more, and then Remin joined him, his deep voice clear and steady. His right hand reached for Ophele, and his left for Miche, his dark head bowed as he repeated the words. *Know my mind. Witness the work of my hands. Weigh the worth of my heart.*

It was a prayer meant for a winter night, when the cold dark lingered and granted time for reflection. Ophele had never kept a solstice night. She had never even heard of it. But she liked hearing everyone's voices murmuring together, speaking the names of the stars, and seeing their hands joined.

Brother Oleare gave them new stars. He knew all their names. He knew their place in the heavens and he knew their governance. His voice went on, calling the attention of each star in turn, asking them to stand in judgment of the year's work. And though at first Ophele was just interested in this new thing, and trying to memorize the new stars, as the litany went on, she began to wonder.

Remin's stars were easy. Bet Agasse and Memech: she loved them both, the defender and the nurturer. But what stars governed *her?* What would they think of the work of her hands? The worth of her heart?

If there was a star that appreciated *effort,* maybe that one would look upon her kindly. If Ophele could say one thing of her year, it was this: she had tried. She thought of that day all those months ago, when she had come to Tresingale, afraid of everything and resolved to help, without the least idea how.

She had worked hard. She would never forget those days beneath the wall, the hot sting of blisters as she hauled bucket after bucket of water. The weary miles she had walked with Eugene the donkey at her side, day after day. Honestly, that time was hazy in her memory, an endless, grueling toil by day and nights filled with the terror of the devils.

Culminating in the haziest day of all, the day she had fallen from sun sickness, and awakened to find Remin sitting on the floor beside her bed, his face drawn with worry and fear, promising that things would be different.

He had meant it.

Looking back, she wondered if there hadn't been signs of his true heart even before that day. Clumsy efforts to ask what she needed. They had missed each other, and misunderstood each other, and though she would never forget his cold suspicion, at least she understood it.

And how many mistakes she had made. How often she had failed. If Remin hadn't taken care of her, *she* hadn't taken care of herself, at all. Ophele knew whose fault it was that she was not yet with child. She and Remin had come together often enough to make a hundred children. How could Remin be expected to know something was wrong with her body if *she* didn't? She had been ignorant, and cowardly, and if Remin had ignored her...well, she did not like to think she was so helpless that she needed a keeper.

But then, maybe all of that was part of the turning of the stars. Because Remin had learned to ask, over and over again, and she had learned that he was a man that gave with both hands.

Her hand squeezed his, and Remin glanced down at her.

"Reshim, star of learning..." he said, and she said it with him, her voice joining his. How she loved him. She wished she could say so now, but maybe something of it showed in her face, because his black eyes softened and his fingers squeezed hers.

Was it the work of the year to earn his love? Or would it be the work of a lifetime to deserve it?

She had tried. But even the valuable things she had done had been undermined by her fear: the maps to the devil's dens, and all her work on the devils themselves, when she had been so afraid of being wrong that she had almost missed the chance to prove she was right. So often, she had been afraid to tell him the truth, and again and again he had proved that he would listen, if she could only find the courage to speak.

Really, Azelma had had the right of it from the beginning. *Be brave, and don't tell lies.*

"Solstice night is the longest night of the year." Brother Oleare paused the litany to let them all sip a little, their mouths dry from the prayer. "On a winter's night, the sky is often clearest, and the devoted will have long hours to view the heavens. Yet it is not only the stars that we must contemplate. Between them stretches the void."

He drew a breath.

"The celestial divine makes all things. All things have a purpose under the stars. The darkness *is*. And on solstice night, we may find we are lost. Often, to reflect is to regret. All of you gathered here have suffered. You have struggled. Sometimes together, sometimes alone, sometimes only in the secrecy of your hearts. You may feel yourself small in the sight of the stars."

His voice was so kind. Ophele had struggled in her heart. For months. She had struggled with her own self-doubt, her knowledge that she was not what Remin needed her to be. Her weakness, her ignorance, the *smallness* of her life, compared to the heroes that surrounded her.

"The dark is inescapable," Brother Oleare said quietly. "Suffering and death are inevitable. But it may not always be evil, to look around and find you are lost in the dark. That is the moment you should stop and seek out the stars. It is a mercy of the dark to make the stars shine brighter, so we might choose our way anew."

Like the mercy of an imperfect world. Wasn't that the same thing? It was a cold comfort, to think that she had been given an imperfect world so she could become strong enough to survive it, as if the divine stars required that she pass through a crucible before she could find paradise. But maybe that was exactly what it was.

The prayers went on until midnight, and Brother Oleare reached for the last pouch of incense, a yellow powder with flecks of gold. It sent up another shower of sparks, crackling as it went, the signal that the vigil was at an end.

"Any other year, the litany would last until dawn," he explained. "But the stars know there are sick and injured here, and that it is good for people to offer their personal prayers in their own way."

"Thank you, Brother." Remin rose, offering a hand. "It was well done. And thank you all," he added, turning to look at the assembled household. "I don't know what the stars will make of our work or our hearts, but I could not have asked more from any of you. It has been...hard," he admitted. "But I will never forget what you have endured with us."

"Your Grace," they said. There were bows and curtsies, and a few murmured blessings as they moved their chairs out of the way. It was late; everyone was tired, and they did not linger. Bundling up against the cold, Justenin led them out with a lantern, and Miche had a sledge waiting to take Brother Oleare home.

That left Ophele and Remin alone by the fire, and Remin sank back down in his chair, holding out an arm to her.

"I liked those prayers," she said, coming obediently to stand before him. His arm went around her waist and he buried his face in her belly with a deep sigh. Something had been bothering him for days, and it wasn't so much that he was trying to hide it as that there were too many possibilities to guess which it might be. Gently, she ran her fingers through his hair. "Remin, what's wrong?"

He didn't answer. His arm only wrapped tighter. The fire sparked and crackled and she stroked him, her fingers sliding back and forth over his neck, over the powerful cords of his trapezius, bared by the loose opening of his shirt.

"The year's work," he said at last. "I don't know that I'd like the stars to look too closely at the work of my hands."

"Why do you think that?" she asked softly.

"Wife, we were just visiting the survivors from Isigne and Selgin again this morning."

"But there was nothing anyone could do," she reminded him. She had thought about it herself, again and again, unable to reconcile herself to the cruelty of the situation. "You tried, and Huber and Jinmin went, you said thirty men died and that was only a mile awa—"

"It's not just that." He lifted his head, and though he always seemed so strong, so sure, his eyes were filled with guilt and uncertainty she had never seen before.

"Tell me." She made room for herself in his lap. "I can listen."

"It's Huber. Huber was always the one that reminded me of the...cost. He knew all the names. And then the numbers, when it got to be too many names. And then, somehow, even the numbers were so big, we couldn't be sure..." He trailed off, his eyes flicking to meet hers with guilt and shame. "The numbers of the people who died. Juste always says it doesn't matter, it can't be changed, and if I were put back there, I would do the same things all over again. But I don't know. I don't know."

His arms wrapped around her, his chin resting on her head as he sighed.

"Sometimes I think I should have just left the Empire. If I'd just accepted that my family had lost, and gone somewhere else, maybe he would have left me alone." Ophele did not need to ask who *he* was. "But I thought...I thought it was right, to try to take it back. That's what you're supposed to do, isn't it? If someone takes something that's yours? And to do that, I had to be a knight, and I had to learn to fight anyway, or I would have died..."

"But so many got hurt, because of me. I can never repay the old man, you don't know how much he and Duchess Ereguil have suffered. And their people, they got hurt protecting me. Two tasters died. And I killed...Merrienne. I wonder sometimes if she really wanted to do it. I thought she liked me. When I gave her flowers, she put them in her hair."

"That's not your fault," Ophele whispered. It was all she could do to keep from screaming it.

"I know. I know," he said, glancing down at her. "And then there was the war with Valleth, and I know I didn't start it, but I chose to fight it. I went after them. I was good at it, and I could take back what was lost, and we were going to fight them anyway. And I didn't have anything to lose. But everyone else did."

His brows drew together as he looked into the fire, and it was so heavy, she could almost see the burden on his shoulders, feel the suffocating weight of it on her own chest.

"*They* had families. Lives. All those people that fought for me, all those people I killed, I sent them to fight, I sent them to die, and I killed them myself, and I did it for me. Because I didn't want to die. I wasn't going to run away. I was going to take it all back. I didn't care about protecting the Empire, they let my family die. It was...*convenient* that there was a war."

The fire crackled softly.

This was not something on which she felt qualified to comment. Ophele barely felt qualified to *listen*. His voice went on, wondering and uncertain, sometimes talking to her but most often talking to himself. Questioning his own motives. Wondering that he had benefited when so many others were dead. Doubting his own terrible calculus over the course of the war, by which he decided how many lives he was willing to lose.

"We had to fight," he murmured. "There would have been a war even without me. And maybe we would've lost. I don't...know. I don't know how many died. It was twenty thousand, in the Empire. I don't know how many Vallethi died. No one will ever know the number. But I know Ludovin is dead, and Clement and Bon and Rasiphe...and Victorin. And I thought I was right, but they're all dead and I'm alive and now Huber...his arm, *he* lost his arm, but *I* didn't, and I have you, and the valley, and I don't know...I don't know how that can be *right...*"

That was it. The story had not ended, but there was no more to tell. He looked at her as if she might have some answer, some wisdom, when the only thing she knew was that she knew nothing of such terrible matters.

"I don't...know," she began. She thought she could think about this for years, maybe her whole life, and never come to an answer that was *right*. "I think...I think if it's *numbers,* then you have to think about the lives you saved, too. Valleth invaded first, didn't they? And maybe if you weren't there, they wouldn't have been stopped at Lomonde."

"Juste said that too, once."

"Well, it's true. And Davi would be dead, and his family," she said, warming to the counterfactual. Numbers were where she felt most comfortable. "And if Lomonde fell, how many people would have died? Valleth had already destroyed three cities. How many people died there?"

She waited expectantly. This was not a rhetorical question. She wanted numbers.

"It was almost eight thousand in Hassen," Remin admitted. "Six thousand or so in Vielles, and I think three thousand in Bergue."

"Seventeen thousand..." Stars, that was so many people. She had seen the twenty-three who had died of the fever, covered with sheets and arranged with dignity in the shed behind the infirmary. Twenty-three people, and she had gone to see them over Genon and Auber's protests, and cried and said she was sorry, sorry, sorry. And many nights since, she had laid awake in the dark and wondered what she could have done to save them.

Remin had known exactly how many people died in the valley since the end of the war. Two hundred and forty-three. Plus the dead of Selgin and Isigne, that was four hundred and thirty-nine. That was so many, so many! There weren't enough tables in the whole cookhouse to lay out so many dead. And Valleth had *chosen* to do that, they had chosen to do forty *times* that. How *could* they? How could anyone choose to make war like that, against innocent people?

"I think the numbers are on your side, if that's what matters," she said, feeling hollow and furious. They deserved to have Remin come after them.

"But it isn't," he said. Almost as if he were prompting her, encouraging her to figure this out for herself. Or maybe even help him to understand it.

"No...or you wouldn't have sent Rollon to Nandre, I guess," she said slowly, remembering their earlier conversations. "Twelve men went, and only two children came back. But it was still right that they went, wasn't it?"

"I think so," he agreed. Rollon had volunteered to go. Remin had told her about it, and told her about knighting him before he left.

"I think...Miche is right." She chewed her lower lip. "He said people can choose what they do with their lives. You never forced anyone to follow you. Sometimes you can't stop them even if you want to," she added, nettled. She still couldn't imagine why anyone would choose to risk themselves for her, particularly over her own protests. "They all had their own reasons to fight, too. Davi wanted to fight for you, because you saved his family. Maybe a lot of them fought for you, and maybe others fought to defeat Valleth. I don't know if either is...wrong."

"Victorin knew I was sending him to die," Remin said quietly. "And Clement went with him so he wouldn't die alone."

Her throat tightened.

"I don't know," she repeated, reaching to touch his cheek, aching for the grief she saw in his eyes. How could something that cruel ever be *right?* "I guess...they loved you, and each other, and that's why they...went. That's why they followed you. Because *they* thought you were right."

"Miche said something like that, too." His arms tightened around her. "I have so much. I don't know if I deserve it. If I deserved...them."

This was something Ophele understood to her bones. She wrapped her arms around him.

"Then we have to earn them," she said. Because while Remin might doubt the work of his hands, it was the effort that showed the worth of his heart.

Chapter 9 – Small Blessings

***...SO** pleased that we shall meet! Do you know, I think it is exactly what Laud needs. Last year all he could talk about was how much he wanted peace and quiet, and if you ask me, it was the worst thing for him. Grumbling all day and up all hours of the night, as if he couldn't sleep for all the rest. I tell you, he has been a new man ever since we got Remin's letter asking us to host you for the season.*

This was putting the best possible face on a terrible and likely dangerous imposition. Ophele sat back to appreciate that bit of Duchess Ereguil's letter, marveling.

We sent people straightaway to begin readying our estate at Mimosa. It's a lovely place, named for trees imported from Ereguil, with flowers like pink silk floss. I must beg your pardon for a little bit of presumption; I am sure the Princess Ophele will have any number of tailors, jewelers, and shoemakers assaulting each other for the privilege of draping her, but as time is short, I judge it good to give them a little notice. By the time you arrive, half the bloodbath will be over.

That is to say, as I am sure you are concerned about very many things: my dear, you may show up on our doorstep in your morning gown and slippers, and we will be ready to receive you.

But there is yet winter before us, and you ought not let worry for the season to come spoil the one that is upon you. I shall hope for many more letters from you, sending me tidings of Tresingale, and do make them long ones! We were both so pleased to hear of your doings. You know how Remin is, his letters are like a report on the progress of the current Andelin campaign, and he never even mentioned the tourney at all. Laud read that page over three times at least. He is dreadfully proud of Remin, but of course they are men, and too bull-headed to ever just <u>*say*</u> *so to each other.*

Be assured, every morsel of gossip is devoured with relish, so be a dear and send us a feast.

Well, where to begin?

The days after solstice night had been filled with many solemn rituals, from the funerals for all those dead in the past year to the swearing of fealty to Remin and Ophele, performed with all due ceremony in the solar. Every morning for a week, the new arrivals to the valley dutifully made their way up to the manor to kneel before the Duke and Duchess of Andelin and swear their oaths: loyalty in exchange for protection, and trust given for trust.

Those oaths were painful. Ophele felt a hypocrite, accepting them right after she had watched the dead burn on pyres, people that she had *failed* to protect, and she knew Remin felt even worse. But there was also nowhere to go but forward, and that was the promise she and Remin made to each other, as the new water clock in the market square tolled the year 827: to try and do better.

But she certainly wasn't going to commit any of that to paper.

Ophele tapped her quill thoughtfully and dipped it into her inkpot, forming each letter with painstaking care. This was the first bit of news that she was willing to share: Master Forgess had kept his word, and the moment the town was declared free of the fever, his journeyman had come trotting up to the manor to make a formal request for an audience with the duchess.

"Why would you want to speak to him?" Remin wanted to know when she told him about it, his eyebrows mobilizing for a frown.

"I want to learn to write better," she said, with a frown of her own. She was still working through her grammar textbook, which only seemed to add weight to the necessity. "There's so much I don't know..."

"Juste isn't keeping you busy enough?"

"He is, but I want to learn from them both," she said firmly. "And I want to learn what everyone else has already thought of. I'm tired of trying to...to solve problems that other people have already solved. Do you know what I mean?"

This had happened with the devil maps and with the supply problems during the plague and too many other times to count, where Ophele had struggled with problems whose solutions already existed. She wanted to know them with a hunger that kept her awake at night, her mind ticking over, hungry and relentless. Remin considered her for a moment and then bent to kiss the top of her head, as if he could see exactly where the trouble was.

"Yes, I do," he replied, with some reluctance. "Tell me when you are going to meet him."

When the meeting was arranged, she dutifully told him, without the least idea that he meant to turn up for the audience and proceed to crush Master Forgess through the floorboards with the power of his glare.

Perhaps it was good that Ophele was incapable of holding a grudge. Remin was fully prepared to carry one for both of them.

Indeed, Master Forgess never knew how close he was to annihilation, for he arrived with a copy of her work on the devils that was so thoroughly corrected, it was almost impossible to read the original text.

"This is what you did wrong," he informed her, plopping it on the table. "Look, in the first paragraph—"

It was incredibly tactless. It hurt her feelings very much, to listen as he ripped apart a work she had poured her heart into. But the sight of Remin's darkening face made her bite her lip and suck in her hurt, if only to save the revered Master's neck. And after the first shock, she tried to listen and understand *why* she was wrong, finally bridging the gap between Edemir and Justenin's too-brief lessons and the demands of the Tower.

Then she lost herself a bit in all the excitement and started interrogating Master Forgess so enthusiastically, he tottered out of the manor a few hours later looking as if he had been bludgeoned repeatedly about the head.

Her life was so busy now. Saving the seventh day of the week, which Remin insisted should be kept for the stars, her days were filled with lessons from dawn until well after dark. In the mornings she spoke with Mionet, then learned to dance and essayed her first clumsy pluckings on Tounot's lute, and in the afternoons Justenin busily crammed all of his eclectic knowledge into her head. It wasn't just the basic mathematics, grammar, and oratory that she should already have learned; his was an eclectic course of study that included theology, philosophy, and lengthy discussions on the nature of mankind.

"Do you think people are basically good, or basically evil?" he asked her abruptly one day, between rhetoric and practicing facial expressions in a small mirror.

Ophele blinked.

"I haven't met enough people to guess," she said, pondering. "*The Will Immanent* says we are an experiment. Which people? All people, ever?"

"That would be a difficult thing to quantify," he agreed, looking amused. "But your answer tells me a good deal about you, my lady. As does your expression. Serenity, if you please. Pretend you are Madam Sanai, contemplating the water."

He was so tricky. Ophele eyed him as she returned to her mirror, reciting nonsense and trying to look peaceful about it. All of Remin's men were clever in their own ways, but Juste was by far the most subtle. Half the time, it seemed the real lesson was figuring out what the lesson was. But even as he taught her to observe and analyze the people around her, Ophele coolly turned around and applied the lesson to *him*. How did he know about Madam Sanai contemplating water?

It was only natural to apply her learning to the rest of the world. Even as the last of the fever faded, Remin had left some of the work of the town in her hands, particularly the day-to-day needs of Sir Huber's survivors. A cynical person might have thought Amise Conbour, who was becoming the unofficial headwoman of the North Gate, helped with this work to enhance her own status.

But even if that was so—and Ophele didn't think it was—she was so good at it, Ophele would never have dreamed of replacing her.

"We're generally short of blankets and spare clothing, m'lady," Amise reported during one of their regular meetings, squeezed into Ophele's spare hour at noon. Remin's smallfolk felt more comfortable saying such things to Amise when they would hardly say a word to their duchess, much less Princess Ophele Agnephus, Daughter of the Stars.

"I know we have bolts of linen and wool laid by in the storehouse," Ophele said thoughtfully. "I guess it is hard to ask them to make everything all by themselves at once, when they had to leave it all behind..."

Or to demand that the other common folk make it for them. Ophele did not think it was good to *order* people to be charitable. But Amise had a solution.

"Well, m'lady, in Engleberg, if a family had a fire or some such, we often got together to help them replace what they had lost," she suggested. "There was one poor family that lost everything, even one of their babies, and so the wives got together a few afternoons running to make what was needful, clothes and suchlike. If you've cloth to spare, I might see if there are some who'd like to help. Most of the folk from Isigne and Selgin can scarce rise from their beds."

"Yes, and we shall ask the ladies in town too, and the ladies at the baths, I shouldn't like to leave anyone out," Ophele said, gently but firmly. She was sensitive about excluding anyone. And then she hesitated and gathered her courage. "And I—do you think it would trouble anyone if I came, too? I am not very good at sewing yet, but I could help with blankets, and I would like to learn, but if anyone would not like it, please tell me directly. I know I am a duchess and the most important thing is to have the clothes and blankets made, so if you have any fear at all—"

"No, my lady." Amise looked embarrassed. "I daresay...it's not in the usual way, and as you are a Daughter of the Stars, everyone might worry...but I can see that things are different here. I think everyone will be...very pleased."

Ophele glowed. She wanted so much to learn to sew; it was a promise to herself, and to Remin's mother. But it was also an opportunity to get to know the other women of the valley.

"When ought we have it, do you think?" she asked eagerly. "We might have it here, if you like."

It was a challenge, moving a dozen or so women to a single location in the valley with four feet of snow on the ground, and even more difficult to make room in Ophele's busy schedule. But Justenin was unexpectedly supportive of the idea.

"You might learn a great deal from this," he said, when she told him she would need to miss their lessons for a few afternoons. "Whether highborn or low, people are people. I shall look forward to your observations."

"You might like to have tea and some sweetmeats on hand, my lady," Mionet suggested, once these plans had been made.

"Even if they are commoners, it is only courtesy to offer them proper hospitality, if you will host them in the house of their duke."

Mionet was very good at helping Ophele to do what she wanted while also making it clear that in Segoile, the roof of the Duke's house would fall in before such an event occurred beneath it. But Ophele didn't care. All her life she had been excluded from things, and she wanted nothing more than to sit and listen and learn all the things she didn't know. She would like to have friends, no matter what their birth. She had a home of her own, and she would be pleased and proud to invite them there.

That was when it occurred to her that she *had* invited them there. She had invited a lot of people, many of them strangers, and they were actually going to come, and she would have to talk to them, and they would all be looking at her and what if she stuttered, or couldn't talk, or blushed, or did something terrible?

"Invite as many as you like," Remin said, as she had known he would. Remin did not see why this was a matter for concern, so long as Davi and Leonin were there. "You can charge all the tea you want at Guian's, though best to leave Wen alone about any snacks. He's run off his feet, cooking for so many extra people."

"Maybe Azelma will help," Ophele said, a little faintly.

Oh, stars. Now there was a menu.

* * *

When this sewing circle nonsense was first proposed, Mionet had taken her concerns to Sir Justenin.

"It may be that His Grace has no objections to the duchess consorting with peasants, but I assure you, it would excite much comment in the capital," she warned. Nothing good could come of mixing classes. "I understand Her Grace wants to help—"

"The lady wants society," Sir Justenin replied, looking at her over the rim of his spectacles as he stood in the doorway of his cottage. He looked more like a secretary than a knight. "This is the best practice she will have, learning to manage in company, before we depart for the capital. I will depend on you to ensure it goes smoothly, my lady."

Of course he would.

It wasn't as if it would be a *challenge,* managing a lot of farmwives for an afternoon. Mionet had spoken with the peasants in her father's cow hole on multiple occasions. But this was precisely the trouble of mingling classes: the structure of society existed for a reason, so all the rules were laid out clearly and everyone knew their proper place before they even walked into the room. If such an event ever occurred in Segoile, it would be an exceedingly quiet affair, with the duchess and her ladies-in-waiting conferring amongst themselves while the farmwives sewed in industrious silence.

The whole reason Mionet had come to the valley was to *be* the lady's companion. Why should Duchess Andelin go seeking society among the common folk?

"Oh, mercy of the stars, the stairs!" Duchess Andelin squawked the morning of the sewing circle. The treacherous stairs were in the process of being replaced with something less steep and hazardous, which meant there were a number of sawhorses, nails, and similar objects to trip over and step on in the meantime. "Will they be all right, do you think? Coming up with their sewing boxes? Davi—"

"I'll land them at the top safely, my lady." Davi looked a reassuring bandit with his eyepatch. Mionet knew Leonin shared her misgivings as to the wisdom of this event, though no man would ever understand how merciless the Roses of Segoile could be over such transgressions.

Davi thought it was a splendid idea.

The duchess had been a bundle of nerves, vacillating between chattering anxiety and petrified silence, and had an unusual number of slips, spills, and breakages that made it a trying morning for everyone. Her current ensemble was the third of the day; the first had fallen victim to spilled tea and the second one to a tear that ripped out a large panel at the back of the skirt, and

Mionet couldn't imagine how she had managed it; there was nothing on which *to* tear it in the whole east wing. She was presently wearing one of Tiffen's plainer efforts, so she might not appear too fine for the farmwives, a pink velvet with cream and gold trimming. She would have been pretty if her eyes hadn't gotten rounder with every arriving guest.

"There is tea, if you would like," she said, just this side of audible, and accepted the curtsies of arriving women with a bob of her head. Her hands were pressed together before her, a moment away from wringing together.

Mionet had almost forgotten how shy she was, in the months since they had met. Duchess Andelin was talkative enough among people she knew, even if she had to be reminded to speak up. But as the solar slowly filled with people, she was soon standing alone in the crowd, with two red lines streaking her cheeks. Common women could not make social overtures to her. If the duchess wanted conversation with someone of lower rank, she had to initiate it.

Which was further evidence of Mionet's contention: all of this was a bad idea.

She was just moving to intervene when someone else beat her to it.

"My lady!" cried Elodie, bursting through the crowd and stopping before Duchess Andelin as sharply as if she had run into a wall. She curtsied, repeated the greeting, bounced on her tiptoes, and then flung her arms about the small woman's waist. "Are you well? Mama says I am old enough to come!"

Mionet had not missed this little wretch in the least.

"Elodie!" Duchess Andelin exclaimed at the impertinent embrace, brightening instantly. "I am so glad to see you, did you bring your sewing things? It has been so long! Have you grown?"

"Like a weed," Mistress Amise Conbour said, moving rapidly to peel the child off the duchess. "Elodie, you mustn't hug the lady unless you are invited, some ladies will think it very rude. Never do so again. Please forgive her, Your Grace."

"Not at all, I have missed my pagegirl," the duchess replied, straightening with a brighter face. "Have you been practicing your samplers, Elodie?"

"Yes, my lady, I even made a pair of trousers all by myself," Elodie boasted. "So I can help today."

"Perhaps you will teach me, then," Duchess Andelin said, a little wistfully. "Mistress Conbour, is this everyone?"

"I believe so, my lady," answered Mistress Conbour, scanning the room. There were nearly twenty women present, and Mionet could just imagine what might happen if all that attention was fixed on the duchess at once. "Would you—"

"Perhaps you might explain what we're about to everyone," Mionet suggested, with a sharp, glittering smile to impress upon her the excellence of this idea. "I have never attended a gathering like this myself."

"Of...course, my lady," she said, her eyebrows lifting. Mistress Conbour was a perfect specimen of a farmwife, a sturdy woman in her middle thirties, round and dimpled, with wheat brown hair caught on the back of her head in a coiled plait. "Your Grace, first we will mark out patterns, if you like."

"Yes, please," Duchess Andelin agreed, following Mistress Conbour to one of the nearby tables. All conversation ceased as the other women crowded around, far more attentive to the duchess than the patterning.

Mionet's sharp eye noted all these volunteers: a good number of the promised farmwives, as well as Mistress Roscout, the weaver, and Mistress Tregue from the tavern. It was interesting to see that Madam Sanai had not come, and had sent another of the Benkki Desan women in her place. Was she truly still recovering from the fever, or was there some disaffection between her and the duchess?

"We can begin cutting these out, if someone else would like to make the next pattern," Mistress Conbour suggested, stepping aside and taking up a pair of shears.

"I will," another woman replied, one of the hollow-cheeked refugees from Meinhem. "We make ours a little differently, if that's all right?"

"No, please. That–that is, please show us," said Duchess Andelin, and subsided with embarrassment.

It was interesting to see the regional variations in something so simple as children's clothing. It was even more interesting to feel the change in the air when Bilaki stepped forward to take her turn, tall and foreign in appearance, with her long, loose hair and mannish attire.

"In Benkki Desa, it is not so cold as here," she began, the words thickly accented. "Only in mountains. We make different shirts for little ones, they tie closed..."

"Perhaps it would be better to give children the sort of clothing they're used to," said Mistress Tregue, just this side of patronizing.

"Yes...you say so," Bilaki agreed, setting her chalk down and moving aside.

There had already been complaints around town about foreign women. The Benkki Desans occupied an awkward niche in the feminine hierarchy, and in the Empire, bathhouse attendants might be anything from skilled healers to beauticians to prostitutes. There had been much speculation as to where the Benkki Desans fell on that spectrum, as well as grumbling in certain quarters about workers of magic, profaning the blessing of the stars. There were some people in Tresingale who disdained the baths.

But as everyone took their seats to begin sewing, it became clear that Madam Sanai had not sent Bilaki out of disaffection. The woman's stitches were exquisite, so tiny and perfect that one could hardly be discerned from the next.

"Oh, can you show me how to do that, Bilaki?" Duchess Andelin asked, leaning over to watch as Bilaki willingly repeated a neat double backstitch, sturdy enough to endure the impatient tugs of children. "You must have practiced so much."

"Since I have five years, noble lady," Bilaki agreed. "In Benkki Desa, girls make sewing bags when they have five years."

"That is when girls in the Empire begin their samplers," Mistress Tregue remarked from a few chairs down. "I imagine you are not used to such plain work, Your Grace."

On the contrary, Mionet knew that when the duchess had time to sew, it was only on the humblest projects, endless blankets and samplers of her own. Duchess Andelin demurred.

"I haven't sewed much at all," she said truthfully. "That's why I was happy when Mistress Conbour suggested this. I do want to help with the blankets and clothes, but I was also hoping to watch and learn a little..."

She could hardly have said anything that would have pleased them more. And it would have worked a treat on the great ladies of the capital, too.

"Perhaps we might take it in turns, my lady," offered Mistress Roscout, scenting an opportunity. "Then you might have a chance to observe everyone."

It was not an entirely innocent suggestion; everyone was eager for their moment with the duchess. But it wasn't only for her benefit. Needlework was an essential part of life for all women, and everyone had their own small secrets, decorative stitches and family traditions passed from mother to daughter. Mionet was so absorbed, she was caught by surprise when Duchess Andelin turned her attention to her.

"Could you show us one?" she asked. "I like those little flowers you embroider, the ones with the hollow circle in the center of the petals?"

"Of course," Mionet replied. She had been working on a smock and wondering what peasant child was going to be so fortunate as to be clothed by a noblewoman of Segoile, and turned it over promptly to demonstrate on the single large pocket. "It's a little snip of the shears, first, and then looping stitches to pull it back and make a round opening..."

Heads leaned forward all around to watch as her needle flashed, making a raised border around the center of the flower, and then petals. In ten minutes, she had inscribed a small, cheerful buttercup on the pocket, with green leaves on either side.

"My mother used to call it *blessing the work,*" she said, turning it for the duchess's examination. "I believe every dress my mother made for me had some small bit of embroidery, even if she hid it where it wouldn't show."

"Oh, how lovely," breathed Duchess Andelin. "I wonder...does anyone know how to make an owl?"

There was a babble of volunteers, and Mionet willingly ceded the field.

It was a surprisingly pleasant afternoon. The stack of new clothing and blankets grew, and for a while everyone forgot the time until there was a knock on the door and Sir Miche stepped inside, looking as surprised to see them as they were to see him.

"I beg your pardon," he said, offering a swift bow and a charming smile. Every time she saw that smile, Mionet felt her hackles rise. "My lady. Ladies. I had forgotten the solar was to become a garden this afternoon. Ophele, I'm off to fetch supper and Mistress Bessin, is there anything you need from the office?"

"More paper and ink, please," she replied, oblivious to the pricked ears of the assembled women. "Stars, I had not realized it was so late, I suppose we ought to begin clearing up..."

"Sim and Jaose have horses and sledges ready in the courtyard," His dimpled smile set off a wave of feminine fluttering. "If there's anyone left when I get back with Azelma, I'll send them home."

"Thank you, Miche," Duchess Andelin replied, as if she had never heard a single one of Mionet's lectures on the importance of formal address. The women rose in a murmur of voices to begin gathering their things and bundling up for the journey home.

Mionet was sure that what they said now would not be half so interesting as what they said when they got there.

* * *

Someone was sewing bugs all over Remin's clothing.

They were small things, less than half the size of his fingernail, and they appeared in the oddest places: behind a button, tucked into his sleeve, and once even inside a pocket, a raised, bug-shaped object that he discovered by chance. It was not a mystery he had much leisure to solve, but he frowned as he examined the latest object, a blotchy little thing with huge round eyes. Was Magne doing it? Why?

Maybe it was a valet custom? Like signing a painting.

"How did it go today?" he asked as he and Ophele were getting ready for bed. By now she had held her sewing circle several times, and he knew she had barely been able to sleep the night before the first gathering.

"It was so nice. They showed me how to make a smock, and I finished my first one by myself today! I even sewed a flower on the pocket," she said happily. "And I like listening to them. I never knew so much was happening in town. Did you know that Master Peltier is courting Mistress Roscout?"

"Really?" The man was *ancient.*

"Yes, Mistress Tregue was teasing her about it, I thought it was sweet—oh, and Auber!" Her eyes opened wide as she turned to look at Remin. "He's been calling on Isilde, one of the ladies from Meinhem. Isn't that lovely?"

"Blast, I knew and I forgot to tell you." Remin was disappointed that she had beaten him to it. "I found out before the fever."

"I saw them together when Vinzetin was sick, Isilde was beside herself..." For a moment, her eyes darkened. She still was not entirely over the losses of the valley fever. "Will he ask her to marry him, do you think?"

"He asked if I would allow it. She's a commoner, and her boy...Vinzetin is a bastard," Remin replied, with a reassuring caress. "I told him to marry who he wants, but it will be difficult for both of them."

"That isn't *Vinzetin's* fault, or hers," Ophele said indignantly. She always turned fiery on the subject of the women who had suffered Valleth's ravages; Vinzetin was not the only fair-haired child among the survivors of Remin's villages.

"I don't think so either, but it's something they must consider," Remin answered, smiling to himself as Ophele waved this away to imagine their wedding instead, wondering whether they would stay in Tresingale forever and how it would be, when Vinzetin had a little brother or sister to look after.

Setting his robe over the footboard of the bed, he spotted yet another embroidered bug, this time inside the collar. Really, that was a little *too* intimate.

"Wife, remind me to talk to Magne tomorrow about my clothes," he said, disgruntled.

"What about?" Ophele was laying out her own robe and slippers for the morning, and examining the pretty embroidery on both with a pleased expression.

"He's been sewing bugs all over them," Remin said, bluntly and unwisely.

There was an indignant squeak.

"They aren't bugs, they're owls!"

"Of course they are." Remin instantly reevaluated everything he knew about the natural world. Obviously, it was an owl. A fat, bug-eyed, spotted owl with two-antennae-like objects sticking out of its head. As soon as he imagined Ophele sewing it, it was adorable. "I love it."

"You're just saying that."

"I'm not," he assured her, sliding into bed and pulling her beside him to examine the object together. "Look, eyes and wings."

"It's supposed to be a blessing," she sulked, picking at it with a fingernail. "It does look like a bug."

"Maybe if it had a beak," he said guiltily. "I'm sorry, wife. I do like it. Sew as many as you like, I'll wear any quantity."

"It would serve you right if I did," she replied, looking up at him with a reluctant smile. "What would you tell everyone, when they wondered why you suddenly had bugs all over your shirts?"

"I would tell them that this is a sacred owlbug, which my wife sewed for my protection," he answered solemnly, and made her burst into giggles.

"It's an owl," she said as he moved over her, pushing her legs apart. Her voice was suddenly breathy.

"It's an owl," he agreed huskily. The scent of her perfumed skin was making him giddy. With the valley fever and the somber reflections of solstice night behind them, he had been applying himself conscientiously to getting an heir, and the hours spent above her and in her were the most blissful of his life. If he still had dreams, they were easier to bear with the feel of her etched in his skin.

And her little blessings, stitched into his clothes.

He was aware of the small bump of another owlbug against his wrist when he met Tounot at the barracks a few days later, to prepare new quarters for Huber. Respecting Huber's wishes, Remin had stayed away from the infirmary, though Genon had had to amputate a further two inches of Huber's arm before he finally rallied. Now there was nothing to do but let him heal.

"It'll be better for him here," said Tounot, as he and Remin heaved a heavy bedframe into position in Huber's new bedchamber. "Gen says there's no risk of further infection, and lying in that closet all day isn't doing him any good. His color's poor. He needs sunlight."

"There will be plenty of it here," Remin replied, shoving the bed further under the window. The deep copper in Huber's skin and hair always seemed to gleam brighter when he'd had some sunshine, as if he needed a regular burnishing. "You might tell him about those horses Miche brought back. How's he been doing otherwise?"

Tounot shrugged, raking a distracted hand through his curly hair.

"Juste sits with him often," he said. "And Miche comes by to stir him up every day. But he won't talk to any of us, and he won't let us bring Nicco and Lege to see him. His pages need him, Rem. They're still grieving for Rollon, too."

"Then moving him here will be the best thing for all of them," Remin said firmly.

They did the best they could for him. The new rooms faced south to let the sunlight pour in, and Huber's treasures glittered on the deep windowsills: the stones he collected, books worn from his saddlebags, the strange carvings he had made beside so many lonely campfires.

His healing would not be swift. To be maimed in this way was almost a form of death, for a knight. Some men shrugged and got on with things; others brooded on the loss, and never got over it. If anything would call Huber back to himself, it would be his boys.

Remin had cause to think of Huber again a few days later, when he and his knights gathered in the council room of the barracks. There was one more village that needed rescuing.

"We need to fetch the people of Ferrede back to Tresingale," he began. "I won't risk leaving them to the devils when the snow begins to melt. Or when the devils start bursting out from under it," he added grimly. Ophele had voiced this unsettling possibility.

"They might need persuading, Your Grace," said Ortaire, who had gone to that village with Huber last summer. "We thought about bringing them back with us while we were there, but all of them refused."

"Tell them what happened in Nandre," said Auber, frowning. "If those houses couldn't keep the devils out, nothing in Ferrede will."

"I will tell them myself." Ortaire looked at Remin. "Let me go, my lord. They know me. It might mean something if I tell them that the thing that killed Rollon is coming. They...thought highly of him."

This was how it happened. Over and over, this spiral of self-sacrifice, from Rollon's guilt for the dead of Ferrede to Ortaire's grief for his friend Rollon. They wanted honor, and they wanted redemption, and so these good men kept saying, *I will go*. And over and over, Remin sent them, knowing they might come back maimed, or never come back at all.

Under the table, his fingers found the owlbug in his sleeve.

"Very well," he said. "You'll take a large force with you. Fortify your camps. We can't count on anything with the devils this year."

"You'll want to get the men practicing with snowshoes now," said Miche, Master of Snow. His face was unusually somber. "It's no joke, traveling with commonfolk in this weather. They're not used to marching. You'll do better to put them in sledges."

"There's time, I don't mean for you to leave straightaway," Remin agreed. "Provision well. We'll need to have more cottages built before they arrive."

"Nore Ffloce is going to have a fit," remarked Tounot, with some amusement. But that was only one of the secondary effects of this migration. Remin had never expected Tresingale to support so many over the winter. They needed food, firewood, medicine in the event there were sick or wounded, and all the infrastructure of fledgling Tresingale was already straining.

And every additional person was another person to evacuate, if the devils had any more surprises, come spring. If they came over or through the walls of Tresingale, then maybe the Brede would devour them all, in the end.

"Let me see the town map," Remin said, to groans of complaint. He ignored them. He had been outside town digging trenches right alongside them, sharpening pikes and other defensive objects, but it still didn't feel like *enough*. They had never had so many noncombatants to protect, and once the people of Ferrede arrived, he would have emptied the valley of every other man-thing, to use Ophele's words. When the devils re-emerged in a few months, all of them would be coming for Tresingale.

"I begin to be persuaded of Her Grace's arguments," Juste told him after the meeting, as they walked together toward the harbor. The road was steep and winding, too treacherous for horses in winter, and Remin wanted to evaluate the harbor for evacuation potential. "That mountaintop concerns me, my lord. It does not seem so great a leap to think that somehow the devils are coming from inside it, and perhaps it was only the size of the entrance that restrained them before."

"If there's one new devil, I don't see why there couldn't be more," Remin agreed. Flying devils, for all he knew; didn't they tell stories of such creatures in Daitia? He cared less about where they were coming from than where they might be headed. His jaw tightened as he looked at the distant walls. "Those walls don't look so sturdy now."

"We cannot prepare for every conceivable disast—"

It happened even as he said it, in the cruel irony of the universe. The guide rope yanked loose and Juste cursed as he twisted, grabbing for the nearest tree. It was already too late. He was falling.

"Juste!"

Swearing, Remin floundered after him, the crust of snow giving way beneath his weight. He had to drag himself forward from tree to tree and it felt as if there was all the time in the world to see Juste sliding ahead of him, twisting fruitlessly as he shot down the icy slope. His body spun sideways, and the trees rushed up.

There was a sickening *crunch.*

A moment of silence.

Then Juste yanked the muffler off his face and turned the air blue with profanity.

"Don't move!" Remin cursed as the snow broke under him again. Snowshoes. He would have given anything for snowshoes. At least Juste wasn't hurt too badly to swear. "Did you break something?"

"My shoulder," Juste said tightly, and as Remin waded toward him, he could see Juste's lips peeled back from his teeth.

"I distinctly recall telling those simpletons to mind how they secured the ropes. I will tie the lines to their boll—"

"Hold still," Remin replied, pulling out his belt knife to cut off Juste's shirt. It was so cold, the air had fangs, but it was too risky to try to move him without a clear idea of what was injured.

"It's dislocated," Juste said through his teeth.

Both of them had seen this injury often enough to identify it. His right shoulder was misshapen, his arm hanging loose from the joint, and Remin plunged his knife into the snow to make a rapid survey of the rest of him. He hardly needed to speak; Juste knew the routine as well as he did, a check of bones and joints to make sure nothing was broken before he dealt with the shoulder. Their eyes met, and Juste's lips pressed together.

"Do i—" The order ended in a howl as Remin took his hand, braced his back, and *yanked.*

Another *crunch.* Juste unleashed a second volley of insults, the cords of his neck standing out.

Remin was glad he couldn't understand more than a third of it.

"Sorry," he said, making a sling to bind Juste's arm to his chest. Juste had a very slow temper, but when he lost it, it was cataclysmic. "Looks like we'll have to check out the harbor another day."

"Not for some weeks, unless I am much mistaken." Juste's cold, flat voice promised a terrible vengeance, and he grunted in pain as Remin carefully hauled him over his shoulders. "My lord. This is unnecessary."

"I suppose you might still break the other arm, or just go straight into the Brede if you fall again," Remin retorted, using Juste's uninjured arm to settle him into place. "Quit whining."

This kind of thing had happened during the war, too. Sometimes Valleth hardly needed to be clever when there was sheer, stupid mischance to bungle a plan: a lamed horse, a broken wagon, a dislocated shoulder. They were silent as Remin trudged back up the hillside, testing every foothold before he committed his weight.

There was no need to speak. They were both doing the same thing.

Counting the weeks that remained until they left for the capital, and wondering if Remin would be able to count on Juste's sword.

* * *

Until recently, Ophele would have never dared to think it.

It was disrespectful. He was a national hero. A Knight of the Brede. A teacher, a scholar, a man of cool and rational judgment whose opinion she trusted absolutely. It was the last thing she had ever expected to see, and mentally she tiptoed around the idea, poking it to see what happened.

Sir Justenin was cranky.

"But they all just want to help," she protested. "I don't think everyone is...*plotting* every time they come to visit."

"They may not be, but you must consider that they are," he replied shortly. Sitting together at the table in the solar, his right arm was all but bound to his side. She had heard both Genon and Remin telling him it was not to come off for any reason whatever, and every time he looked the least bit tempted, Leonin and Davi stiffened to attention, as if they might swoop down on him like hawks.

It was very inconvenient that Justenin was right-handed.

"Did any of them ask you for anything?" His lips tightened as he scribbled laboriously with his left. Even from the other side of the table, she could see that his handwriting was worse than hers.

"No..." Ophele thought back to the most recent sewing circle. Justenin had quizzed her after each one, teaching her to manage and analyze the women who attended. It had been more or less the same group each time, a kindly assortment of the townswomen, and she had learned so much and enjoyed their conversation and each gathering had been so pleasant, and he was *ruining* it with his cold dissections.

"Did they speak of any particular troubles?"

"Yes. Their husbands, their children, Mistress Tregue says she can't keep her husband tidy either..." Ophele shut her mouth. She had been sworn to secrecy regarding the foibles of husbands.

"Anything else?"

"Mistress Roscout said she was having trouble with the dyer," she confessed, shifting unhappily in her chair. "Just that he was trying to winkle her out of every copper sen he could get..."

As soon as she said it, she remembered that Remin had bought the wool fabric for Ophele's blankets from Mistress Roscout, and they were due to renegotiate their contract for a further year in the near future.

"But I'm sure she was just talking," Ophele added quickly. "She's been very helpful, teaching everyone invisible stitches."

"I find that an apt metaphor. People may be helpful for a purpose, my lady," Juste said, and tossed his quill down in disgust. "This is useless."

"Perhaps you might like some tea," Ophele suggested. She still had some of Genon's pain medication that she sometimes slipped into Remin's tea, when he was welted from sword practice and crabby about it.

"No, thank you."

Ophele was beginning to suspect, based on certain patterns observed over time, that wounded men did not want to feel better. They just wanted to complain about being wounded.

"Or I could write for you, if you like. My handwriting is getting better," she offered a little desperately. She knew he wasn't angry with her, but it made her very uncomfortable to hear that edge in his voice.

"No, thank you," he repeated, and then sighed and bowed his head. "I beg your pardon, Your Grace. I am out of sorts. I have always said my left arm is largely decorative."

"Let me help then, please," she said, rising to put the kettle on anyway. She might like a little of Genon's medicine herself. "Are you writing down what I'm saying? I can do that much."

"It would be inappropriate for the Duchess of Andelin to be a secretary. But I will take a cup of tea," he said. "With a little of Genon's medicine in it. I assume you were planning to dose me."

"It must hurt a great deal," she said sympathetically. "Your shoulder. I never thought joints might just pop out of place."

"It does not often happen spontaneously," he replied. "If you wouldn't mind, perhaps Lady Verr will share her observations. Do not worry overmuch, my lady. This is a very...low-stakes game you are playing, at present."

"It is?" Ophele's eyes flicked the request to Davi, who nodded and slipped out the door to call for Mionet.

"Yes. The town is small and fairly uniform in its purpose. But you ceded a great deal of power to Amise Conbour when you allowed her to choose who to invite into your home. How do you know there is not anyone she chose to exclude? Or if she might have chosen certain individuals to attend with some purpose in mind?"

"I told her I didn't want anyone left out," Ophele said, her eyebrows drawing together.

"How would you know if she did?" Justenin asked ruthlessly. "That is not to say that she did, my lady. She *might* have. You must be careful not to allow others to control access to you. No matter who they may be," he added, with a pointed look at the doorway, where Mionet's voice was audible as she approached.

It was a warning. Ophele offered a distracted greeting and went to examine the kettle, which was not yet boiling. She did not like to think of these things, suspecting people she liked of selfish designs. All of it was enough to make *her* feel cranky, dull and headachy and her belly had been troubling her all day.

"We are discussing yesterday's gathering, Lady Verr," Justenin explained, and Ophele wondered what it meant that he was so polite when he was talking to Mionet. Maybe it was some sort of perverse compliment that he felt comfortable being grumpy at Ophele.

"I will be pleased to help." Mionet sat, smoothing her skirts. "Is there anything in particular?"

"No, we would like your observations in general," he replied.

"Did Amise really invite everyone who wanted to come, or did someone get left out?" Ophele burst out. This question bothered her extremely.

"Ah," Mionet said, her auburn brows lifting. "As far as I can tell, she did, my lady. That is a good question."

"I didn't think of it." Ophele thumped into her seat, wishing the kettle would boil faster. "Sir Justenin warned me about it. How would I know if she did?"

"It is something I would look for over time," Mionet replied. "There are...currents, in society. They are subtle, but if you watch, you will notice who often attends, and who often makes excuses. Who speaks, and who does *not* speak. And also, if there is anyone who is prevented from speaking, or excluded."

"Oh," Ophele said, blinking. Those were patterns. She hadn't thought to look for them here. The sewing circle had met four times so far, and she had thought each visit was very pleasant. "But I thought it was going so well," she said, dejected. "I don't remember anything bad happening, everyone was so nice and helpful, teaching each other..."

"They will always be kind to *you,* Your Grace," Mionet replied pointedly.

"Oh," Ophele said again.

"Have you noted any currents in particular?" Justenin asked.

"Nothing of great concern, I think," Mionet answered. "I was going to suggest that you invite women from Isigne and Selgin to the next gathering. It is not to be wondered that they have not come yet, when they are still recovering. And you see, it is not always a matter of unpleasant scheming," she consoled, noting Ophele's unhappy expression. "The women from Meinhem and Tresingale have been here longer, and are healthy, so of course they know each other and will invite each other along. It falls to you to ensure that these natural cliques do not become set in stone."

That did not sound so bad.

"Though I believe you may have trouble with the Benkki Desans, Sir Justenin," Mionet added.

"Why do you say so?" Justenin looked up from his papers.

"Bilaki is not greatly welcome," replied Mionet, as Ophele cast her memory over every single gathering, wondering how Mionet could know this. And the curious thing was, while Ophele could remember speaking to Bilaki at the first meeting...had she even attended the third?

"She *was* there, wasn't she?" Ophele asked aloud, almost to herself. "Last time. I'm certain I saw her..."

"She was there, my lady," Mionet confirmed, and Ophele flushed angrily.

"Would they—somehow did they not let her speak, or make her feel uncomfortable or unwelcome?" she asked, angry with herself that she hadn't noticed. She knew just how that felt and never wanted anyone else to experience it. And in her own house! "And—you said they don't like *any* of the Benkki Desans? Why?"

"They have not confided it to me directly, my lady," replied Mionet. "You know that Madam Sanai speaks often of Niravi, and the building of serenity. That is the Benkki Desan belief, but in the public bath, it is not always received well. There are some women who have come once and not returned."

And Ophele would not know this. She always had her baths alone.

"But it is not only that. It is also a question of manners, of dress," Mionet waved a hand. "Women will disagree over such things. The Benkki Desans carry staffs to defend themselves, they are unmarried..."

"And they have come to Tresingale to show their strange ways," Justenin agreed, and Ophele looked between them, honestly shocked. She had grown up with Lisabe's hand-medowns; it never occurred to her to look askance at anyone else's clothing. And why would it matter if they were not married, or knew how to fight with staffs? Wasn't there a good reason for it? Was it somehow blasphemous to the stars to contemplate the serenity of Niravi?

"I don't understand," she said, grappling with the irrational problem. "Madam Sanai and her ladies haven't hurt anyone, why..."

"You remember the book I lent you?" Justenin asked. "*The People as a Beast.*"

"Yes." She frowned. It had been a terribly cynical book. "About how one group of people reacts to another group of people, and how the collective can become a sort of animal in itself..."

"Tresingale has grown large enough to have groups," he said, nodding. "Now they are deciding what behavior is acceptable, and what culture will prevail. You may not like what they decide, if you do not take a hand."

"Well, the Benkki Desans are acceptable," she said, with a flash of her own rare temper. "How could anyone think otherwise? We invited them here."

"How would you enforce that?" asked Justenin.

"I—I would, next time, have Bilaki sit with me," she said defiantly. "Then they can't exclude her."

His gaze flicked to Mionet, a silent question.

"They may feel chastised if you are too pointed, my lady," she warned. "In your place, I would invite Madam Sanai to the next gathering, with the excuse that her recovery has prevented her attendance until now. Bilaki is young and her command of the language is still poor. Madam Sanai is more confident."

"I will. And I will...I suppose I shall have to bathe with everyone, from now on." Ophele rubbed her head. The prospect was not pleasant. She still could not bring herself to let Peri and Emi bathe her, and the bare thought of so many eyes on her scrawny body made her cringe inside.

Little mouse.

She should have noticed all this. Wasn't that the whole point of everything Justenin was teaching her? To observe, and analyze? And yet at the same time she wished Justenin and Mionet had never said a thing about it.

"You must tell me if you notice such a thing from now on," she told Mionet, adding a generous dollop of Genon's pain medicine to her tea. "I want everyone to feel welcome when they come here. And that's what His Grace wants, too."

"I will do my best, my lady," Mionet promised. But as Ophele poured a cup for Justenin, she saw the knowing flash in his pale blue eyes, as clear as if he had spoken the words aloud.

Mionet also might choose what she noticed, and what she reported. And what she did not.

Ugh.

Ugh.

* * *

Ophele was still turning the problem over as she sat with Remin later that night, reading aloud with less than her usual enthusiasm. Reading to Remin really seemed to help her to speak better, and though Remin was usually buried in stacks of paper in the evening, she had no doubt he was listening.

"You already read that paragraph, wife," he noted without looking up. His quill slashed over the page. "Is something wrong?"

"No. Not really," she said, and cracked almost instantly. "Only maybe some of the women aren't as nice as I thought."

Remin's eyes lifted to hers, instantly hardening.

"What did they do?"

"Nothing to me," she answered, and set her book down. "They wouldn't, would they? I'm the duchess."

"Ah."

"Justenin and Mionet were talking about it today," she said unhappily, and explained what they had said, resisting the urge to rub her abdomen. Had she eaten something bad? It felt as if someone had tied a knot in there and was yanking on it.

"I suppose it's a caution." His brows lowered. "I've never been especially good at such things, wife. I don't have patience for it. But I don't mind if people have their opinions, so long as they don't make trouble."

"Justenin says we ought to take care to be seen with Brother Oleare." Ophele felt a surge of relief as he bared his teeth. "I know! It makes me not want to, even though he's perfectly nice."

"Juste's instincts for such things are good," said Remin reluctantly. "I suppose there might be busybodies who worry we might convert to whatever it is they believe in Benkki Desa."

"Atar Ma, it's a sort of animism and it's lovely." Ophele's chin jutted belligerently. "They have poems about the Lady of the Moon. Why should anyone care what we think?"

"We are meant to be the example," Remin said, with a hint of humor, but Ophele did not find any of this funny.

"I shall set the example by speaking to whoever I like," she retorted, with such irritation that he looked at her in surprise. "You said we should welcome everyone, and my mother said that's what a proper lady does. So I will."

Even if she wasn't quite sure what that would look like yet.

But it came to her the next day, unplanned and unprompted, in a chance encounter that Mionet would certainly have protested if she had been there.

As the last sufferers of the fever recovered, work had resumed on the manor, and it was once again filled with carpenters, plasterers, and masons, plowing away at their various projects. Blown through the front door after a visit with Azelma, Ophele found a crew of masons building a fireplace in the shell of the office. It was not an insignificant structure, in a house this big; the hearths in the bedchamber and solar were taller than she was, and this one was nearly as tall as Remin.

Peeling off her gloves, Ophele slipped off her outdoor shoes, watching curiously.

"Why is there brick?" The question escaped her before she even realized she was speaking. Ophele flushed as the four men turned toward her, but decided to brazen it out. "Instead of making it all stone, I mean."

"Flat surface reflects heat better, Your Grace," said one of the bricklayers, splatting mortar on the edge of his trowel.

"Oh. It does look very well done," she replied, eying the straight lines of the bricks and wondering what on earth was possessing her. Maybe it was some spirit of defiance, or lingering resentment for the sudden, unwanted burden of social expectation. Leonin and Davi were staring. "It must have taken a great deal of practice to learn to set them so straight."

"Some, lady." The bricklayer was puzzled but willing. "Apprenticed when I was twelve."

"Oh, did you? I should like to hear about that," said Ophele, and then realized it was true. And why not? She was the duchess, no one could be rude to her or Remin would crush whatever was still wriggling after Leonin and Davi were through with them. "You take a rest at noon to eat, do you not? The four of you?"

"We...do, m'lady." The bricklayer's friends were looking at him with expressions that said *now see what you've done.*

"Then I would like to invite you to luncheon, the four of you. And you can tell me about building fireplaces, and becoming apprentices and journeymen," she said, trying not to sound nervous. "If you don't mind. It will be quite proper; my guards and lady-in-waiting shall be there. If you would like to come?"

"My lady," said Leonin, in a warning undertone, but Ophele ignored him.

"I...suppose," answered the bricklayer, with reluctant murmurs of agreement from his fellows. She didn't miss their consternation and wariness, commoners called to entertain a duchess, but Amise said men would forgive almost anything if you fed them something nice.

"Good. Shall we say tomorrow?" She forced a smile as prickling heat blazed up the back of her neck to her ears. "I will have s-something brought up from the kitchens. Please don't be troubled. I am only curious."

Turning away, she blew out a silent breath. Her heart was hammering. Even she had no idea where that had come from, and oh, stars, please don't let them all stare at once like that tomorrow. There was an anxious, tugging ache in her stomach at the thought that she might have made a very embarrassing mistake.

"My lady, I am not sure His Grace will approve," Leonin warned as she ascended the stairs.

"Then he can say so," she replied. It would be embarrassing if he did, but she did not think she had done anything *that* bad. And though she knew Leonin was only trying to protect her, she was a little annoyed as she climbed the stairs, until a sudden, half-remembered sensation made her pause midstride. Frowning, she tried to place it. She hadn't felt it in quite some time.

"Lady?" Davi asked behind her.

"I'm fine." Ophele sped up the steps, her eyes averted. Oh, no.

Even before she arrived in the Andelin Valley, this was not something she had experienced often. She had always been too anxious and ill-fed for any regularity. But as she hastened to the privy, she felt that twisting pain inside and could only hope she had noticed quickly enough, and that Emi and Peri had stocked things with their customary thoroughness.

Pulling up her skirt, she found red spots on her chemise.

Filthy girl.

Her shoulders cringed. She had been fourteen at her first bleeding, a deeply humiliating experience. She had come into the house crying that she was sick, and Leise and Nenot had shoved her into a tub and scrubbed her so vengefully, it was as if they thought she had made a mess on purpose. Lady Hurrell and Lisabe had taunted her for days, asking whether she needed to go and change her dress.

Twisting, Ophele reached futilely for the laces of her gown. She couldn't even undress herself, the knot was midway up her back, and there was no bellpull in this room. Was there anything on the back of her skirt? Oh, stars, what if there was, and Davi or Leonin had seen? Her face felt as if it were on fire.

"Davi?" She cracked open the door. "Would you call Emi, please?"

He would certainly guess. Both he and Leonin would guess, and Emi and Peri would know, they had to change her clothing and restock her things, and Mionet would know too, and so would the laundresses. And while everyone in the manor would understand that Ophele was an adult woman and would do what every other woman did, she hated that so many people knew such intimate things about her.

"My lady?" Emi's voice came a few minutes later, and Ophele opened the door just wide enough to admit her.

"I'm sorry," she said, her eyes fleeting away from the maid's. "I'm sorry. Could you...help me get my gown off?"

"Of course, Your Grace," Emi replied in her cheery way, moving behind Ophele to untie her laces. It wasn't hard to guess what was needed, between the open cupboards and the disarranged skirts. "Oh. I see. Well, it happens to the best of us, doesn't it?"

"Yes." Ophele looked anxiously over her shoulder. "It didn't hurt my gown, did it?"

"I don't think so..." Emi lifted the skirt, examining, and then pulled the gown over Ophele's head. "No, it looks fine. Would've been a shame, wouldn't it? I like this one."

"Yes," Ophele said again, dumbly grateful. She had to look down to hide the tears in her eyes as Emi went briskly back and forth, producing the necessary undergarments and sanitary linen, then fetching a new chemise. "I am sorry."

"Please don't mind, Your Grace. It's no trouble. Well, it *is*," Emi said, angling her head in a friendly way to meet Ophele's gaze. "Being a woman is a pack of trouble."

The gray sky lowering outside the windows suited her mood when Ophele emerged, to find Justenin waiting with a stack of papers and a cup of tea. A blizzard had been threatening all morning, but it did not seem an unpleasant prospect. It would be nice to curl up by the fire and sleep.

Unfortunately, that was not an option. Her brain felt infuriatingly foggy as she sat down for her interrogation, and the previous day's lessons felt very long ago and far away. The third time she couldn't remember something, Justenin frowned.

"Is there anything wrong, my lady?" he asked. Ophele did not forget things.

"No. Well, I have a little headache," she admitted, which was true. "I'm all right."

Justenin eyed her, as if he was reading her mind, and Ophele hastily looked down at her book.

Embarrassing. Embarrassing, uncomfortable, at times very painful, and though she would have liked to conceal it from Remin, even if she thought she could, she wouldn't. Over the course of the afternoon, it dawned on her that this was more than just an embarrassing inconvenience.

"Are you well, wife?" he asked as they retired to their bedchamber for the night. He lifted a hand, brushing gently at the pain line between her eyebrows with his thumb.

"Yes. Well. Yes." She stopped, drawing a breath. "I...it...it started, today." Her hands went to her abdomen, willing him not to make her say it. "So...it means I'm not pregnant now, but now I can..."

"What—it did? Today?" Remin stopped in his tracks, his eyes lighting up. "So you're well now? Really well."

"Well, it hurts," she said, a little sulkily, and then gave a shriek and burst into giggles as he snatched her off her feet and all but crushed her against him. "Remin!"

"Thank the stars, I am glad," he said, catching her chin to kiss her. "It hurts? I will find Genon's tonic, there's a bottle somewhere. I remember the book said it might, and that you might be tired, or have—"

"Yes, yes," she said quickly, before he could get into further details. Ophele did not mind such things in an academic sense, but it was deeply mortifying when applied to her person. "But Remin...it means I should be able to have your baby. For your House. House Andelin's heir."

"Our House. Our baby." He kissed her, striding across the room to deposit her in bed. "Lie still, I'll go find that tonic."

"You don't need to fuss," she said, as he hunted through the cupboards and drawers of the sideboard.

"I do. I didn't like to say anything, but I've been worried, all this time." Producing the small, stoppered jug, he brought it to her and knelt beside the bed, rubbing her head gently as she drank. "Not just because of the child. I've never forgiven myself that you were so thin. That I did something so terrible to your body. I am sorry."

"It was as much my fault as it is yours. Would you rub here?" She guided his big, warm hand to her belly, where a twisting ache made her grimace. "That feels better."

"It looks as if it hurts a lot," he observed, frowning. "Give me a minute to get settled, and I'll rub all you like."

"It's worse that I can't *think,*" she complained, as he went about setting out their robes and slippers for the morning. "I couldn't remember half my lessons with Justenin, I had to write them all down."

"Is that normal?"

"Mionet says some ladies get muddled." Ophele had been annoyed enough to ask, in a roundabout, metaphorical way. And soon enough Remin was curled up with her in a roundabout, literal way, making a comfortable pillow for her head as his hand gently rubbed exactly where it hurt.

"I'll have Wen send up something sweet from the kitchen tomorrow," he promised, his voice rumbling pleasantly. "I'm sorry it hurts, little owl, but I'm glad your body is doing what it ought. We are both finally well. It has been hard."

It had been. It had been very hard, in so many ways.

"Hazelnut cookies?" she asked, brightening.

"I don't see why not, when we gathered the hazelnuts ourselves," he replied, amused. "I'll bring up a cask of honey mead for supper, and Miche can make you a hot toddy, and you can lie abed all day if you like..."

With the fire crackling and her foggy head and the dull ache twisting through her body, the thought of lying in bed and watching the snow swirl outside the windows sounded lovely. But Ophele suddenly sat up.

"Oh, no, I can't," she remembered all at once, and turned to tell him about the surprising guests she had invited for luncheon.

Chapter 10 – The Duchess of Andelin's Salon

Year 799 of the Divine House of Agnephus

From earliest childhood, Empress Esmene Agnephus, née Melun, had heard one ringing and eternal admonishment.

For the glory of House Melun.

It explained everything. Commanded everything. Justified anything.

Melun was an ancient House, high in honor and tradition, even more ancient than the Divine House of Agnephus. Almost all the ducal Houses had preexisted the Empire; there had been people in Argence before the arrival of Ospret Far-Eyes, after all. Back then, they had been a cluster of many kingdoms, constantly fighting among themselves.

Technically, the only land to which the House of Agnephus had any claim was Starfall, the island that Ospret had raised from the bed of the River Emme. But even before this feat, his wisdom and vision were so great that seven kings had chosen to bow to him, and made war on those who refused.

House Melun had been one of the seven. When she was four, Esmene had learned the line of her ancestors, descent through the male line all the way back to Heveroult Melun, the earliest patriarch of the House. To this day, those names were invoked at the Feast of the Departed. The proof of a true scion of House Melun was the ability to reckon one's cousins to the fifth degree.

That was how she knew exactly when the sacred blood of the House of Agnephus had entered House Melun, and they had been husbanding this precious resource ever since. The Emperor's House had never been prolific, but every so often there was a princess or second son to spare. House Melun had fought clandestine wars to snap up these sacred scions for themselves.

And when Emperor Onsetin Agnephus had produced a single son named Bastin, House Melun already had three daughters of appropriate age, candidates to be his Empress.

"That will be your husband," Esmene's father told her when she was eight, on the day the five-year-old Crown Prince was presented to the Court of Nobility. "You will be the perfect Empress, Esmene."

It was not for her sake that he made that promise. Nor even his own, though Dardot Melun secured his own legacy within the House when she was betrothed to the Crown Prince, and became the patriarch of House Melun when he was scarcely more than forty.

It was a triumph all the way around. Esmene was born to be an Empress. There had been something intoxicating about the fact that even the Divine Emperor could not keep her out of Starfall, even if she had had to settle for the Palace of the Distant Star. She had married him, she had taken every prerogative and honor due the Empress, and she could look into the face of Emperor Bastin Agnephus and know that through him, she had achieved every dream of her House.

Well. Almost.

“I hope we might leave early tonight,” she murmured to her husband when they arrived at a state banquet for the merchant princes of Ispichov.

“We will do our duty,” Bastin replied, intentionally ambiguous, and moved away to speak to a merchant prince with gold and silver chains dangling from his pointed, barbarous ears. But tonight, Esmene followed. This was one area of their marriage where she had not yet been able to subjugate him.

“Radiance,” said the merchant prince, Eminent Malkhaz Kandelaki, one of the long-lived Lords Merchant in Ispichov. He bowed, smiling at Esmene with the glint of a diamond embedded in one sharp incisor. “Your Highness. Your beauty is blinding.”

Bastin threw her an irritated glance, but Esmene smiled, smiled, smiled. It was mortifying to be seen tagging after him, no matter how gracefully done. But tonight was the night he would come to her bed, and she meant to keep him there, even if it required the crude tool of wine.

Since that first agonizing night together, Bastin had been specific and adamant about the nights he would share her bed. They were scheduled weeks in advance, they were loveless, and they were never more often than was absolutely necessary.

And five years into their marriage, Esmene had yet to become pregnant.

At first, it hadn’t seemed a matter for concern. Esmene’s father sent a woman to educate her on the fundamentals, and the Emperor visited her palace once a month, regular as clockwork. There was no hurry. The great battle had already been won. They were married, and House Melun was notoriously fecund. A child would come, sure as starlight.

Even if it hurt. It was excruciatingly painful. It was humiliating. After their first year of marriage, her father summoned her to remind her that a child was necessary to cement their control of the Empire, and she had had to bite her tongue. How could she tell her father what it was like? Surely, *surely* this was not how it was supposed to be between a man and his wife.

Esmene heard enough gossip from her ladies-in-waiting to know that the act should be pleasurable. But every month, Bastin appeared, and performed his duty exactly as he had the first time.

He undressed, laid down in her bed, and told her to get on with it.

And there was no child.

She comforted herself with his compliance, at first. It was proof of her victory that she could compel the Divinity, Beloved of Stars, that she could drag him to her palace and put him in her bed. Sometimes that gave her a little vengeful pleasure, that even though his *spirit* refused her, she could command his body. She could *force* an orgasm from him. Those fleeting moments when he grunted under her and began to helplessly thrust were the nearest thing she felt to satisfaction.

But there was still no child.

After four years, she had begun to reconsider. Perhaps she had been short-sighted to alienate him so completely. Four years was a dangerously long time to go without a babe.

"You must come more often," she had told him when they were done, lying in bed with her thighs clamped together and tears in her eyes. Sex with him did not arouse her. Even oils were not enough to ease the way. "I cannot make you an heir if you only visit my bed once a month."

"I *must* do nothing," Bastin replied coldly, shrugging into his shirt. His chest was marked by her fingernails; Esmene had tried to rouse him, but except for a few grunts at the end, he had done nothing but stare at the ceiling. "I am fulfilling my obligations to you."

"Bastin." She rolled over and spoke softly. She had not said his name a dozen times in their entire marriage. "I want to fulfill my obligation to you. A child. I know we began poorly, but—"

"Is this another Melun Proposal?" he asked contemptuously. Bastin was not an ill-favored man, but in private, when he did not have to conceal his hate, his face twisted with loathing. "Do you think to confine me to your bed, as your father confined my father to his? You will find it more difficult, this time."

"No," she said, stumbling out of bed and catching his arm. She could feel the hot sting of blood between her legs and let him see it, used her pain as a weapon. "Can we not make it better for both of us? Bastin, it...hurts."

"Yes, it does." He shrugged her off and buckled his belt. "Good night."

Furious that she had humbled herself, she had gone again to her father. But this time, whatever levers he had been able to apply to Bastin four years ago had been removed.

"Do whatever you must," Duke Melun told her. She had gone to see him in the vast study at Ereseide, the estate named for House Melun's patron star and the seat of their power. "The Temple will not support us in this, not with that fool Dardinne as the Prior of Segoile. This is becoming a problem, Esmene. There are whispers that you are barren."

"Not that *he* is infertile?" she asked icily. Her beautiful face showed nothing, but inside, she was burning with fury. She wanted to scald her father's ears with the tale of what she was doing for the glory of House Melun, how she tortured herself with every sexual encounter, how she tore inside because she had never felt anything like desire during the act. How Bastin made her feel like some base prostitute. Or no, *worse,* as if *he* were a whore she had summoned, unwilling.

For one moment, the thought rose, bubble-like, that that was the truth.

But no, she was the Empress. Sworn and blessed under the stars, joined eternally to the Emperor and the only proper vessel for his seed. And they had come too far to stop now.

"They will never say the Divinity is infertile," said Dardot Melun. "It is blasphemous."

"Father. The Emperor has never been...willing," she admitted. "It must make it more difficult to conceive."

It seemed a very long time since she was a little girl, and her father had tucked a silver bellflower behind her ear and told her that she was *his* glory.

"Then you must make him willing," he answered pitilessly. "Win him, whatever it takes, for the glory of House Melun. One child, Esmene. That is all we need."

He had no idea what he was asking.

But Esmene gritted her teeth and tried.

"Bastin," she began, after their next agonizing assignation. "Please give me a moment. You cannot like this either. I confess, I did not consider your wishes as I ought. But surely it would be better if we could come to some terms. We will be married all our lives..."

He listened. It wasn't quite an apology, but Esmene had begun to build a very reasonable case for why they ought to mend things when he walked out of the room.

The next month, she had offered an actual apology.

The month after that, she cried.

She made efforts outside the bedroom, sweetening herself to him in every way. It was difficult. They lived in separate palaces; she could not offer the small, intimate attentions of a true wife. But every time he laid eyes on her, she made sure she was dazzling. Her voice was musical. Her compliments to him were elegant. Her gifts to him were expensive, exotic, and extravagant.

She was *courting* the wretched man.

He never refused the gifts. A new horse. A new sword. Luxurious teas and gems and stunning jeweled chains that would complement his starry blue eyes. She delivered them herself and endured the wits of the court, laughing that the Empress had fallen in love with her husband.

That love was not requited. Bastin looked at her, listened to her small, graceful speeches explaining the latest offering, and set it aside.

But if he rejected her utterly, he would have sent them back, wouldn't he?

The chain he wore to the Ispichov banquet was made of sapphires, but it was not one of the chains she had given him. A little after midnight, she extracted the Emperor from his throne and led him to her carriage.

He had consumed a fair amount of wine; Esmene made sure to keep his cup full. And at the doorway of her bedchamber, she beguiled him to kiss her for nearly a minute before he remembered who she was. Striding to the bed, he began to undress as he always did, refusing to look at her. It only made her more determined. He would have it over as soon as possible, and she was not going to let him win.

"Wine," she commanded, snapping her fingers for a maidservant. As it was poured, she brought forth other things, oils and candies and oysters in sauce that she had ordered prepared for their arrival. It had never been difficult to physically rouse him, but she wanted him to linger. She needed him to seed her. And she would have done almost anything to make it hurt less.

"This is not necessary," was all he said when she emerged from her dressing room in the scantiest of silks, so thin it left her nipples visible.

"I want to make it better for both of us," she whispered. Was there a hint of interest in his wine-fogged eyes? She poured him another glass and fed him candies, pretending desire as she roused him with oil. After four years, his body was nothing but an instrument of torture to her.

One child. One child of the male line of Agnephus, for the glory of House Melun. Her child would give her a hold on the Emperor that he could never escape. She would leash him like a dog. Esmene would never have to humble herself again.

Steeling herself, she impaled herself on him. She was utterly dry inside, but the oil at least made it easier to get him into her. Some months she barely had time to heal before she had to take him again. But it didn't matter. Once she had a child, let him be banished from her bedroom forever. If only she could get him to respond!

Braced above him, she began to move, her hips gliding. She feigned pleasure, hoping her noises would rouse him. The lights in her bedchamber were low, a warm glow of candlelight, and perhaps he was intoxicated enough to forget himself. She moved faster, panting and groaning as she attempted to stimulate him, and as she was working away above her motionless husband, Esmene looked up and chanced to see herself in the mirror on the other side of the room.

Dressed in those silks.

Her bare breasts bouncing. The vulgar motions of a whore, her lips blown out as she faked loud moans.

A sight instantly seared into her memory forever.

She froze. Her breath hitched.

And Empress Esmene of House Melun burst into tears.

"Go. Go," she sobbed, falling onto her side and curling up in bed with one hand pressed between her legs. And he *knew* it, that hateful bastard *knew* she was hurting herself even as she was pretending to enjoy it. Bastin rose obediently.

"Your efforts are most gratifying," he said, his starry blue eyes glittering with appreciation as he looked down at her. Even though she was mortified and in agony, she could see the hateful satisfaction in his face. "Good night."

There was no question who had appeared the prostitute this night.

It was a humiliation she would never forget, and never forgive.

But that was not even the worst of it.

It tickled the back of her mind in the weeks that followed, an unsettling sense of some crucial detail overlooked. His smile haunted her. Why had he seemed satisfied? When had he begun to smile? When had his loathing transmuted to include that smirk?

It must mean something.

And it had been strange, to choose the night of the Ispichov banquet as the night when they would be together. It was inconvenient. The banquet was hardly unexpected; it had been planned months in advance, and there was no reason why the Emperor should choose that night to do his duty. Why then?

"Vironet," Esmene called. Vironet was her Lady of the Bath, in charge of all matters relating to Esmene's health and person, and had documented every one of Esmene's monthly courses for the last four years. Her Lady of the Chamber documented the dates of Bastin's visits. For an Empress, everything, no matter how intimate, was a matter of state.

"Leave me," she said when these records were provided. She waited until she was alone in her bedchamber to open the thick books, a bedchamber from which every mirror had recently been removed. She already suspected what she would find.

As she matched up date after date, Esmene felt a heat rising to her head, a rage she had never felt before.

Not just with him, callous and manipulative, so determined to deny her that he would put her through unbearable torment for *four years*. Esmene was livid that she hadn't detected it sooner. She could remember that damned Celestial Sister explaining fertility, delivering Ospret's sacred revelations in the same way she might have chanted a *segarde*. Esmene had listened and nodded and never dreamed that the Emperor would *deny himself an heir* rather than submit.

It was unthinkable.

It was blasphemous.

It was the duty of the House of Agnephus to replace itself. That was the Covenant of Stars, and the reason the House of Agnephus lived in such luxury and splendor. They had always been few in number, producing a child or two per generation when most women could have a dozen. He was the *Emperor*. He *must* make an heir.

But every single one of his visits corresponded with her periods of lowest fertility.

From now on, she would have to endure the additional humiliation of *checking* to ensure he seeded her.

What could she do? Surely this deliberate, calculated refusal would not be permitted by the Temple. Marriage sanctioned the creation of children. It was the tree that sheltered those future babes. And it was a sacred duty of the Divine House of Agnephus to *endure*.

"Vironet!" she called again, thrusting aside the records. "Summon a cleric, and send a message to my father. Say—"

But there she stopped.

Say *what?*

Was she going to put the sexual behavior of the Emperor on trial before the Empire? There were decent odds that she would win; he could not deny the Empire its heir, and she was his wife. She was the only one with the right to bear his divine children.

But to put him on trial was to put herself on trial right beside him. And he would divulge *everything*. The blackmailed consummation. The pain. The gifts. The wine. The oils.

The scanty silk clothing.

Esmene scrambled to her feet and vomited in her chamber pot.

She could not blot that vision of herself from her mind. She would have paid any price to rip it out. She had been raised to be an Empress from the day Bastin was born. She had never known an ungraceful moment in her life. She had never known such humiliation. *Except with him.*

Slumping to the floor, she wiped her mouth, trembling.

Stars, would he do it? Would Bastin go that far?

Your efforts are most gratifying.

Her stomach heaved.

Her pain gratified him. Her humiliation would please him. Oh, how he must have relished all of it, how she had humbled herself and chased after him and abased her own dignity to please him. If she insisted on making this part of their lives public, he would make *all* of it public. She would suffer for it far worse than he. He would absolutely go that far.

For the first time, as she crouched on the cold tile floor with the taste of vomit sour in her mouth, Esmene felt a chill of the same implacable hatred she had seen in her husband's eyes for four miserable years.

Then she would go even farther.

* * *

Year 827 of the Divine House of Agnephus

It was fortunate that the Duchess of Andelin was wealthy enough to be regarded as eccentric.

Crouched between three burly masons by the hearth of the solar, she was a ludicrous little figure with her skirts dragging in the ashes as they explained the mechanics of a hearth. Behind her, the fourth mason sketched industriously at the table, a rough schematic of the fireplace venting system for the main house.

And she was wearing such an *elegant* dress!

It had taken so much negotiation before Tiffen struck upon a style that offended no one: soft, comfortable clothing made of the finest silk, velvet, satin, and combed wool, exquisitely tailored and often with some innovation of bodice or sleeves to set it apart from Segoile. If Mionet had been tied to a rack, she would have admitted that Tiffen was actually a quite capable tailor. In the capital, he might have been a designer of note, barring his refusal to hold with some more impractical innovations of women's dress.

The duchess's gown was one of those artistic compromises, a soft melon like a watery sunrise, with satin panels embroidered with mossy leaves, tiny rosebuds, and thistles. Frills of lace edged the neckline and lined the panels of the bodice, and Mionet could see a pink diamond brooch at the center of the neckline so clearly, it was always shocking to realize there wasn't one. She comforted herself with the careful pleating at the back of the lady's skirt, which cascaded into a train that was like the last rays of sunlight rippling on the Brede.

It was a gown that Mionet would have been proud to wear herself, if it had not suited Duchess Andelin so exactly. The colors, the cut, even the soft, feminine ruffles were scaled perfectly to the petite woman, complementing her youth and beauty while lending some of the dignity required of a duchess.

A spark burst from a log in the fireplace, landed on Duchess Andelin's skirt, and singed, unnoticed.

Mionet's eyes very nearly filled with tears.

"...different sort of stones for the inner hearth, as won't crack in the heat or cold," one of the masons was saying, tapping one of the ashy stones. "And that's the thing about mortar, too, you need a good mix to handle changes in temperature..."

The duchess listened with fascination as they explained how mortar was made, where they got the stones, and even how they made the bricks, with a charged debate over various kilns. Mionet exchanged a glance with Leonin, the only other person of sense in the entire estate.

"And it's only the four of you making all this," the duchess marveled as they huddled over a sketch of the flue system. "How many fireplaces will there be?"

"Well, we haven't added it up exactly, lady, but one for just about every room in the house. Though we won't be doing the kitchen," said the shortest mason, tapping that area of the diagram with a thick finger. "Needs special work, that."

"I suppose it would, they are a different shape, aren't they, and with all those iron things in them? The kitchen hearth in Aldeburke could fit three pig spits, or one whole cow." She bent over, examining the various diagrams. "Will all the hearths in the house be so big?"

"A fair size, even for the small rooms. Too bloody cold in the winter, beg pardon," the man added, bobbing an apology before Mionet could reprimand him. The duchess heard enough such low talk from Davi.

But it was inevitable, when the duchess invited low men into her solar. And when the bizarre luncheon had finally dragged to a close, she bid them farewell and sat down in her chair beside the fire, looking pleased.

"I was so worried, but they were very nice, weren't they?" she asked, and then a frown fleeted between her eyebrows. "Please excuse me."

She had had to excuse herself several times that day and begged off dance practice altogether, blushing and stammering and making poor excuses. It was a weakness she would have to work on. The lady was good at evading a subject with partial truths, but she was very, very poor at outright lies.

"Is she sick?" Davi asked, glancing at Mionet.

"Indisposed," she replied, in a tone that forbade further questions. A servant would have known better than to ask, but Davi was in an ambiguous position as an almost-hallow; something more than a mere servant or guard, and he had some right to inquire after the health of his ward. But it was not for Mionet to divulge.

All of these lines were so *ambiguous* in the Andelin Valley, the careful divisions between rank and role blurred as they would never be in Segoile. And it only got worse when the duchess returned.

"I wonder if I might invite—oh, Justenin." She brightened as he appeared in one door at the same time she was coming in the other. "It was such fun, talking to the masons, I would like to invite others as well. It only seems fair to include everyone, doesn't it?"

And Justenin, a common knight of no background at all, saw no problem with this whatsoever.

The duchess hosted luncheons several times a week thereafter, inviting all manner of strange people, from architects to plasterers to a selection of merchants from town. She invited Brother Oleare and Justenin to discuss the nature of man and made everyone else fall asleep. She invited the carpenters to discuss the decorative gables in the library. She hosted a fiery debate on breadmaking between Wen, Azelma, and Noulen, a baker who had just arrived and was getting an explosive introduction to Tresingale. And as the crown of this string of lunacy, she invited all the pages from the barracks one afternoon. Twenty-some boys between the ages of seven and thirteen, and one spotty, scowling fifteen-year-old.

It was chaos.

"Jacot!" Duchess Andelin exclaimed as the boys trooped into the solar, lined up by height as if for a parade. It had taken half an hour for all of them to be divested of muddy boots and winter clothing downstairs. "Oh, there are so many of you, and Valentin, look how tall you've grown! You must give me your names one at a time, please, and then we shall have luncheon."

She was nervous. Her fingers clutched tightly in her skirt as she went down the line to allow each boy to offer his courtesy, and some of the boys were hardly less awkward. But most were noble-born and set an example for the others, and there were a few that the duchess had apparently met before, who greeted her with delight. Soon, all of them were seated at the long table, with hot water crust pies filled with venison and game fowl to tempt even the picky palates of little boys, some of whom had to be seated on folded-up blankets to reach the table.

Mionet had objected when this was proposed. What had a duchess to do with a lot of dirty little boys? Really, she could barely articulate her objections. It just was not *done.* But the duchess had looked at her and said *why not,* and for this particular occasion, there had been surprising opposition not just from Duchess Andelin, but from Justenin, Miche, and even Duke Andelin himself.

"They need to know their duchess," His Grace had replied, when Mionet voiced her concerns. "Everyone in the valley must know her on sight. One day, these boys will be men, and they will have to defend her, if necessary."

"And they will need to know how to behave in the presence of a lady," drawled Sir Miche, with an amused glance at the duchess. "You never know how you might improve them."

It would be nice if the presence of ladies had worked some improving magic on *him*. Mionet had to bite her tongue to keep that thought to herself. Miche enjoyed great favor from the duke and duchess, but all three laundresses visited his cottage with scandalous frequency.

She had never anticipated this. She had known Tresingale was the back of beyond and would lack all amenities, grace, and refinement, but never dreamed that they would *choose* to reject every convention of the Empire. At least once a week someone burst out with some new heresy that left her open-mouthed with shock and struggling to produce a reason *why* they should observe even the most basic hierarchies.

Which was how Mionet came to be sitting between two pre-pubescent pageboys, eating venison pie and pointedly demonstrating the proper use of a napkin.

The conversation was stilted, at first, between the boys' close attention to their food and shyness before the duchess. But she soon coaxed the boys she knew into telling her about their training and adventures, and then confiding more disastrous secrets that made even Leonin cover his mouth to hide a smile.

"Not on the hill by the quay," Duchess Andelin protested, appalled, as the boys explained that shields made excellent sleds.

"Suicide hill!" said a blond boy enthusiastically.

"Sir Miche said, Sir Miche said that three pages are buried at the bottom, after they went sledding there last year and went straight in the Brede and froze all up," piped one little boy, his eyes round with horror at this dreadful tale.

"I don't know about that, but it *is* terribly steep," Duchess Andelin replied, reluctant to call the honorable Sir Miche of Harnost a liar.

"We built up a snow wall at the bottom," another boy reassured.

"And I hit the wall and went up and my hat and boots fell off!" exclaimed Valentin, around a mouthful of greens. "Denin said I flew twenty feet!"

"Did you really? I mean, you must be careful," Duchess Andelin corrected, though it was clear to Mionet that she would have liked to try it herself.

There could be no other word for this but *eccentric.* Especially after the meal, when the long table was pushed back against the wall and the boys formed a circle on the floor, with two boys taking up position in the center with wooden swords, to demonstrate their skill for their duchess.

"My lady," Mionet murmured, trying to signal polite disapproval as the Duchess of Andelin sat down on the floor between the smallest boys.

"It's all right, the floor isn't dusty," Duchess Andelin said, flashing a happy smile at Mionet. She had quite forgotten herself; she was as enthusiastic as any of the boys, clapping and cheering as each of them took their turns and asking questions about the maneuvers they were demonstrating.

The boys had taken her completely into their hearts. And even if it was bizarre, it seemed harmless until one of the boys disarmed his opponent with a smashing swipe that made Mionet's hands sting with sympathy, and the wooden sword whipped through the air directly at the duchess's head. As one, Leonin and Davi lunged to intercept it, too late.

Ophele caught it with one hand, inches from her nose.

"Wow," breathed a tow-headed boy, and the pages offered a scattering of applause.

"That was a good strike, wasn't it, to disarm him?" Duchess Andelin asked, looking at the boy who had disarmed his opponent. But Davi and Leonin were completely unappreciative.

"My lady, would you mind sitting back a bit?" Leonin bent to take her elbow. *"Please."*

"Oh, but—" she began, looking automatically to Davi for her ally. But he shook his head, his left eye narrowed, and offered his hand to help her to her feet. She sighed. "Very well. I can't see so well from back here. Batistin, how did you do that, that thing with your hand?"

"I saw His Grace do it, isn't it great?" The boy boasted. "You strike hard, for this part of the sword..."

This was why.

Even as the duchess sat down a safe distance away, Mionet instantly realized that this was a living example of a reason for many of the manners of nobility—no, the *caution* of nobility. The Duchess of Andelin could not afford to risk the least harm. There was small chance that being struck with a wooden sword would do any lasting damage, but stranger things had happened. Princess Ophele Agnephus, beloved child of the Emperor, Daughter of the Stars, had a duty to protect her own sacred blood, to perpetuate it, and to join it to His Grace's in the creation of his heir.

Blissfully unaware of these considerations, Duchess Andelin cheered and applauded, congratulating the boys on their skill in the final demonstrations. There was only a little trouble in her face when they finally bid farewell, and the boys trooped back out the door to be bundled off to the barracks.

"Jacot didn't look well," she said, once the door was safely closed, her brows puckered with concern. "Has he been ill, do you know?"

"No, my lady, but we don't see much of the pages," replied Davi, dragging the heavy table back into place with cheerful disregard for the existence of servants. "I'm sure he'll be fine."

"He swam the Brede to come here," she said reminiscently. "His Grace wasn't letting anyone in, but Jacot swam across the river, and Miche threatened to throw him back in. It was so good to see them all again, I swear Valentin is three inches ta—"

"You ought to be more cautious of yourself, my lady," Mionet interrupted, with careful moderation. It was not for her to chastise a duchess. "You might have been hurt if that sword had struck you."

"That can never happen again," Leonin said immediately, as she had known he would. "We ought to have anticipated that. You must keep well back in future."

Duchess Andelin looked between them in surprise.

"But even if it had hit me, it wouldn't have done any real harm, it's just a practice sword," she protested, appealing once more to Davi. But even he shook his head.

"Can't take that chance, lady. His Grace would have our necks, if he saw that."

"It is a noblewoman's duty to keep herself safe," Mionet agreed, seizing the opportunity to drive the lesson home. "That is one of the reasons why nobles do not mix with commoners, and sit away from them when they are present. You cannot risk harm for *their* sake. What would happen to those boys if they accidentally hurt you? In the Empire, the penalty for drawing blood from a noble is a flogging."

This was a winning argument. It might even be sufficient to end this nonsense once and for all, and Mionet felt the momentum behind her as she went on, gently and regretfully explaining the necessary divisions between classes, not just for the lady's safety, but the safety of her people.

But she felt an unexpected twinge as she watched all the fun fade from the young woman's face.

Well, Duchess Andelin *was* young. Most women of her rank were comfortably middle-aged, and though Mionet knew the pleasures of noble society in the capital compensated for its restrictions, the duchess could not know that. This poor society in Tresingale was all she had.

It was the only society the Exile Princess had ever had.

"...your bloodline," Mionet went on, feeling a sudden, strange reluctance to employ the weapon in her hand. But no, such behavior had to be curbed now, before Duchess Andelin went to the capital. Nothing could be permitted to interfere with her social debut. "You are a child of the stars, and the blood in your veins is sacred. It is your responsibility to protect it, and join it to His Grace's ancient, noble heritage when you produce his heir. Would you risk jeopardizing all that for something so trivial?"

"No," Duchess Andelin replied, subdued. "I...I will be careful."

Mionet did not delude herself. She had won a battle, but not the war. The greater victory was the discovery of so potent a weapon. Duchess Andelin might be persuaded to do many things, if she was convinced it was for His Grace. It was a valuable thing to know, but...

As a victory, it felt strangely hollow.

* * *

To Her Grace Liliet, Duchess of Ereguil, at the estate of Mimosa in Segoile, from the Duchess Ophele of Andelin at Tresingale Manor in the duchy of Andelin:

Thank you so much for your last letter, and I hope this one meets you safely in the capital. What a long journey that is for you, and all by carriage! It makes my own seem like nothing at all. They are refurbishing some of the ships for passenger transport, so it will be quite comfortable, and Remin says we might make a hundred miles a day, if the wind is with us.

It has been one thing after another since my last letter; we hardly got through that bout of sickness when Sir Justenin fell and dislocated his shoulder, and I guess Remin will have told you and Duke Ereguil what happened to Sir Huber. He and I have spoken often enough that I feel I ought to do something for him, but I don't know what.

Remin said I ought not be afraid to ask you questions if I have them, and I do hope you won't mind, when everyone says that you are so very deadly in society and I have a few difficulties in that line. We have only a little society at present, but it is still enough to be troublesome, and I worry that perhaps I am not doing as I ought. Sir Justenin warned me many times to watch and be sure that the things people say to me match what they do when I am not there, and I have found that sometimes it does not. Only I don't know what to do about it.

The problem is, some of the ladies in town don't like the ladies from Benkki Desa, even though they are very nice and I have found their ways so interesting. And I will not have people being unkind to each other, but how do I make them stop? Lady Verr says it will do more harm than good to go at them directly, which is probably just as well because I don't see how I ever could. And I guess I can't force them to like each other, but they must at least be polite. Do you ever have such troubles among your own people?

Perhaps I will be lucky, and they will solve it for themselves while I am away.

But I do not wish to paint them in too unflattering a light, for they have all been so good to each other this winter, and Amise—that is my friend Mistress Conbour, she is Sir Auber's sister-in-law—says that almost every cottage by the North Gate has blankets and linens made by our sewing circle, or has inherited some of the ones Miche brought back from Aldeburke. I have quite forgiven him for his depredations, for I don't know what we would have done otherwise, with so many people coming to Tresingale unexpected. And of course, he pretends he planned it that way the whole time, so it is just impossible to scold him.

I will be so sorry to leave them all. I confess I am very worried about coming to the city, though it will be a great pleasure to meet you and Duke Ereguil, and see Mimosa. Remin says the house is beautiful, and I am excited to see the library and the gardens and mimosa trees.

I know that since this will be my debut in the city, I must have a grand ball, and I am sure it must be a great undertaking to hold such a thing, with all the food and music and everything. But Remin and I are hoping that we will only go and have our audience, and then come home straightaway. I hope you will not think me ungrateful when you have offered so much help, and inconvenienced yourself so much already, but I am afraid to stay in the city for long, in case something should happen to Remin.

And so, would it be possible to plan to hold the ball, with the understanding that it may not happen at all? Or would that be too rude. I shouldn't like to burn any of our bridges; I know that in time, we will come to the capital for a full season, and I wouldn't want to offend anyone. Maybe we could plan a debut ball if I must stay, and a farewell ball if we will be allowed to leave. That might answer, if you think it good.

I hope your journey is pleasant, and look forward to your next letter.

Yours,
Ophele

* * *

All at once, it seemed like Ophele knew everyone in town.

"That's Celande," she whispered to Remin as one of the Isigne survivors hurried off to fetch something from her cottage. "She embroiders the loveliest flowers, she said she would make a sampler for me..."

Remin drew Lancer up beside her indulgently, enjoying the wan sunshine. The roads had been cleared again by the long-suffering Third Company, and he seized the opportunity to go riding while the risk of frostbite was low. The snow had been relentless. As promised, the cottages were buried to their thatching, and some people had had to tunnel through the snow to reach their front doors. Celande was one of these, emerging from the snow in a waddling of many layers.

"Here 'tis, my lady," she said, presenting a folded bit of linen and bobbing a nervous curtsy at Remin. "I had a few moments to make it, it's lucky you happened by. I show each flower in stages, you see..."

The young widow was Valleth-pale, with fair skin and very light blue eyes. The ever-wary part of Remin watched her hands for the least threat, especially given the added provocation of her terrible losses from the devils, but Celande showed no sign of ill will as she chatted with Ophele.

"I mentioned her to Master Tiffen," Ophele explained when they moved on, tucking the sampler into her pocket. "Her husband died, so she must find work somehow, and he needs seamstresses and embroiderers. Perhaps she could even move into a house in town, in time. Or apartments, maybe? Master Forgess was telling me about the Tower, and it would be easier for some people to manage a few rooms than a whole house, wouldn't it?"

"It's a thought." Remin was reluctant to admit that the Masters of the Tower could have anything resembling a good idea, but might it be faster to build one apartment building than a dozen cottages? "I suppose they might all heat each other's rooms, with a dozen fireplaces going."

"We could ask Master Ffloce. He was talking about building more cottages anyway, by the river for the fishermen, and a few by the clay banks for Master Peltier's apprentices. That would free up cottages on this road for the people from Ferrede."

"Maybe on the road nearby, we're trying to keep the river itself clear." Remin glanced at her. "Master Peltier took on apprentices?"

"Yes, three: two boys and Placide Restruke, he's one of the men from Selgin. He lost his left foot," Ophele added delicately. "But the boys can do the hauling and Placide can sit while he's processing the clay, and Master Peltier says he doesn't mind."

"They won't get better training." Remin approved. Master Peltier was not just a potter. He was one of the Empire's Great Masters, a living treasure, and exacting in his expectations.

"Yes. And Mionet said it was all quite proper, my talking to them," Ophele added. "Master Didion mentioned we needed pots and crocks and bowls and everything for the kitchen, and I know you like things made in the valley, so I thought of Master Peltier..."

When she had first asked about inviting half the population of Tresingale to lunch, Remin had thought it was just an excuse to interrogate her victims for an hour uninterrupted. He had never in his life met anyone who was so curious about *everything*. It was a pity he couldn't present her properly to the Tower, when they went to Segoile; she *needed* a teacher, if only for the sake of everyone around her.

But Juste was right. This year, they must conceal her intelligence.

Listening to her now, though, he wondered if that was possible. Her ravenous intellect was obvious the moment she opened her mouth, and she was filled with excitement for her new society, from her fascination with Master Peltier's pottery to a recounting of her lunch with Azelma, Wen, and Noulen. Her snarling impression of Wen—in this case, belligerently defending his sourdough starter—made Remin laugh until he was breathless.

And those luncheons had proved fruitful in a dozen unlikely ways. In a matter of weeks, Ophele had her dainty fingers in a dozen pies all over town, listening to the gossip, learning the personalities, and then matching people together to help his folk help each other. Remin could not have been prouder. This was *exactly* what he wanted his duchess to do, though he could never have articulated it before. In his mind, his task was to build high walls and a sturdy roof for his people, while Ophele's was to welcome them in and make them feel at home.

This was all he wanted. This work, for the rest of his life. Remin could have spent days talking with her about his plans for Tresingale, debating the merits of row homes versus cottages, working together to find the best and happiest place for every one of their people. Yes, move the fishermen to cottages by the river, and let them teach others their craft. The first fishing boats would be done by spring, and the surviving fishermen of Isigne were slowly weaving nets as their wounded fingers healed. Remin looked forward to the day when he would see those boats on the river, hauling a bounty of fish to feed the town.

He wanted honest work for all of them. Let them rear their children. Let them flourish.

But for now, that was only a dream.

"I'll be late tonight," he told Ophele as they turned back to the manor. "We have some plans to finalize. If I'm not there for supper, go ahead and eat."

"Is there anything wrong?" she asked, her eyes flicking to his face.

"No. Just some business I'll be glad to have done." Sooner or later, he was going to have to tell her some of it. But not yet. Remin glanced at her, admiring her light seat on the Gevalle mare. "I hardly need to get you a horse now when you have such a fine one. Her feet barely touch the ground."

"Oh, but wasn't Huber counting on him?" she asked. "The Anglose? I thought Huber would help train him, once he's better. I want to call him Prancer."

"I forbid it," Remin said instantly, though the thought that she would want the horse for Huber's sake softened the rejection. But still, it was bad enough that she had named the mare Dancer. "Lancer can hardly hold up his head for shame as it is."

"He is very sensitive, for a warhorse."

"All he wants is a little peace and dignity," Remin said, suppressing a smile at the impish look she shot him. "What will you do with three horses? Surely you won't forsake Brambles."

"Miche said he'd teach me to drive Brambles in a sulky. He brought one back from Aldeburke. And I thought, when I go riding with you, then I could take the Anglose," she explained. "He would look fine beside Lancer, wouldn't he?"

"He would," Remin agreed. The battle-scarred Lancer would look very rugged beside an Anglose, but Ophele would make a pretty picture no matter what horse she was perched upon. It was Huber who had scoured the Empire for a likely beast, and the horse was already waiting for her in Segoile, a handsome stallion of perfect, unblemished black, gentle and intelligent.

Remin was not above using Ophele's scheme to draw Huber back out of himself.

He was not among Remin's knights when they gathered at the barracks later that afternoon, and Tounot shook his head when Remin caught his eyes. Well, Huber was still healing. Perhaps it was too soon for him to venture far from his bed.

That left Miche, Juste, Auber, Tounot, and Jinmin crowded into the cramped, windowless room that currently served as their council chamber, insulated by so many layers of plaster and stone that they could not possibly be overheard. Juste arrived last, pulling the door shut behind him and tossing a scrap of parchment on the table like a Noreveni glass grenade.

"That was found in one of the practice yards this afternoon," he said, as Remin unrolled the paper.

Miche frowned over Remin's shoulder. "An inventory? I don't recognize that shorthand."

"It may be," Juste said calmly, drawing up a chair. "There are men here from all over the Empire. We don't know every system of reckoning."

"I know that Edemir would have their balls for wasting paper." Tounot's eyes narrowed. "And I don't recognize that handwriting."

If anyone had been assigning men to do inventory about the barracks, it would be Tounot. Remin scowled.

"Who found it? And where?" he asked, passing the parchment to Tounot.

"A fellow from the night watch, Ferener Hoske, from Trecht," answered Juste. "He said it fell out of one of the fence posts in yard four."

"This isn't an Imperial cipher," remarked Tounot.

"That we know of."

"If you have a theory, Juste, I wish you'd share with the group," drawled Miche, and won a flash from Juste's pale eyes.

"Perhaps I am testing that theory on all of you," he said, with exaggerated patience.

"Like whetting a blade in a river," agreed Tounot, and made both of them snort.

It was possible the note was entirely innocent; a message between lovers, for all they knew. But Remin and his men had intercepted enough coded communications to recognize the warning signs in this one. Why would it refer to a *second* storehouse when the barracks barely had its first, and who was hiding inventories in fence posts?

Remin knew there were spies in his city. Even his allies would have agents in Tresingale. But the fact of the coded message, the concealment, the deception, the *betrayal* made him so angry, he only jerked his chin toward Juste when the paper made its way around the circle, refusing to touch it.

"Take what you need, Juste," he said. "Do what you do."

"Yes, my lord. I would like to show this to Her Grace, with your permission," Juste added, tucking the message into his breast pocket.

Remin blinked.

"Do you think she can decipher it?"

"No, my lord, there's not enough code for that. But it may be useful, nonetheless."

"Do not upset her." Really, it was a tossup which would distress her more: evidence that there were traitors in their midst or a puzzle she couldn't solve.

Unfortunately, there was a third option.

"We also have news from Edemir," Juste went on, flicking one-handed through his stack of reports. "House Hurrell is in the city."

"The Emperor...*pardoned* them?" Tounot asked skeptically.

"Edemir says they have a manse on Garderie Boulevard, which is in the Wold." Juste shrugged. "He is inquiring after their sponsor, but ultimately they would not be there without the approval of the Emperor."

"A strange chance, that they should be pardoned after eighteen years, and right before Ophele is due to visit the city," said Miche, his eyes hard.

It could mean nothing good. Remin had been moving heaven and earth to keep Ophele from being unduly stressed about what they might face in the capital, but he didn't see how he could possibly keep this from her.

"I want them watched," he grated. "Get someone into their household, Juste. Bribe, blackmail, I don't care."

"I will convey that to Edemir. But we are lacking eyes in this area," Juste warned. "I can make no promises about the state of this particular terrain."

It was their single greatest weakness. Before the Emperor had taken a hammer to Tounot's betrothal, Remin had hoped for help in this area; the society of the capital's women had always been closed to them, a place Ophele must go where Remin could not follow. Tounot's wife would have been a great help and comfort.

Instead, they must rely on Lady Verr. She hadn't done anything to deserve Remin's distrust, but something about that woman just put his back up.

"Huber's scouts report no sign of hostility in our neighboring duchies," said Tounot, evading the painful subject. "No mustering in Firkane, Leinbruke, or Norgrede, and no alterations to the patrols or fortifications at the estuary of the Emme. I have confirmed it with multiple persons."

"Well, we have made no overt threats ourselves," Juste noted, thoughtful. "There has been a great deal of movement around Starfall, but it is possible that the Emperor has not mustered troops because *we* have not."

"That he can see," Remin said with satisfaction. "Tounot?"

"We are building rally points and supply locations," answered Tounot, who had been busy with this project for months. "We have secured two-thirds of the route of our march so far. With supplies in place, I can put an army before the walls of Segoile in twenty-three days. Faster, if we move them to winter quarters downriver."

"That would be observed." Remin considered the map. Twenty-three days was a significant improvement. The Emperor would barely have time to summon support, much less march it to the city. But it wasn't enough.

"We must assume we are being watched, and particularly our shipyard," Juste agreed. "It was a good notion of Her Grace's, the fishermen and fishing boats, and that should conceal our intentions somewhat, if anyone is counting our ships. But it will be difficult to build a fleet large enough to move a significant force of men without raising suspicions."

"Have them begin building additional ports now," Miche suggested. "Everyone knows His Grace is impatient and unreasonable, and wants to begin the river trade straightaway. Have Master Gibel complain about it around camp."

"It is a plausible lie," Remin agreed dryly. "Do it. Pull the men off the Valleth border rather than from Tresingale. They'll be less noticeable."

"I'll see to it," Tounot offered. "I know a likely spot for a camp on the moors, and we'll need a waystation for the harbor anyway."

"I meant you to go with me to the capital, Tounot," Remin said slowly, recognizing this for the retreat it was.

"It's better this way," Tounot replied, and Remin could do nothing but accede.

Going through Darri's reports consumed many hours. Jinmin was handling the mobilization of supplies and troops on the Andelin side of the Brede, with additional men poised to cross at the Kiel Gorge Bridge. Remin expected the strongest defense from the Emperor at the bridges, and they knew that the Dukes of Firkane and Norgrede had been building defenses nearby, to intercept any forces that tried to go that way. Remin was prepared to give up a small force if it meant the bulk of his army passed unnoticed.

It was a vast improvement over the outlook of even a month ago. But at the end of that journey lay the city of Segoile, the heart of the Empire. With maps of the city laid alongside the map of Argence, Remin surveyed the familiar details of terrain, supply, and defense, a puzzle he had been contemplating for years.

"There is one advantage we did not expect," he noted with cold amusement, flicking over the painted lead markers that indicated the city gates. "How kind of the Emperor, to invite us in."

* * *

There would only ever be thirteen Knights of the Brede.

They won that name one chilly night in March of 819, when thirteen men mounted an insane, suicidal charge across the Gresein Bridge, gambling their lives on a plan that should never have worked, in a cause for which most of them felt ambiguous at best.

Some of them had gone for duty. Others had gone for vengeance. Many of them had gone for bonds of friendship and brotherhood. Bram of Lisle had no earthly reason to go at all.

Miche had gone for Remin.

The youngest of them at eighteen, Rem had already been a giant, still discovering his strategic genius. His was the vision that guided them, and his was the will that led them to the far side of the bridge, dwarfed by the fortress they proposed to conquer. And Remin was first into the charge, spurring his horse with a shout that called them all to follow, this boy who already knew how easy it was to die, and how hard it would be to force the world into a new shape.

Even then, there was something about the sight of Remin's back that inspired other men to follow.

The Charge of the Gresein made them instantly famous. Their battle in the gatehouse was the stuff of legend, the subject of poetry and song from one end of the Empire to the other. And though those stories always grew in the telling, it was incredible to have witnessed the truth of this one. Remin had gone through the doors of the gatehouse like a battering ram. Victorin with his lance, unstoppable and immortal. And Miche knew too the stories they told of him, the most beautiful of the Knights of the Brede, and the most infamous.

"Shhh, shhh...*ahh...*" He clenched his teeth to stifle his own groans as he pulled out of Masilie and came, spilling his seed on the laundress's belly. His orgasm was blinding, like the blazing of a sudden bonfire, but he kept enough of his wits about him to cover her mouth with one hand and finish her with the other, pinning her down and making her writhe through her climax with expert fingers.

It was dangerously close to dawn. They had only a few minutes to recover before he had to get her dressed and push her out the door, dispatched with the careful blend of appreciation and politeness that left no misunderstanding about what this was. Miche had been scrupulous about allowing the laundresses to decide amongst themselves whose turn it was to occupy his bed. He opened his door to all three of them, and did not seek out their company on his own.

The stories they told of Miche of Harnost were absolutely true.

Locking the door of his cottage, he hurried over to Juste's, his boots crunching in the snow. The stories they told about Juste were likewise true. The Siege of Iverlach, the Coldest Knight. They warned of the wrath of a patient man. Quiet, gentle Juste, slow to anger and difficult to discomfit.

Usually.

"You've got one more week in this thing, so quit complaining," Miche said as he arranged Juste's right arm in its sling. Every morning, he came over to help the other man dress and—on Gen's orders—to tie his arm to his side, since Juste could not be trusted to leave it alone and the men's fashions of the Empire really required two hands to secure adequately.

"I am not complaining," Juste said so flatly that it was a complaint all by itself. "Only observing that I never asked for your help. You have done enough, please leave. Now."

"Until Tiffen invents trousers that you can lace shut one-handed, you've got me," Miche replied, without offense. Juste was always surly in the mornings. "Unless you want to risk scandalizing the ladies."

"No, I believe I can leave that to you."

"Bold words from a bound man," Miche observed, tying the knots of Juste's sling carefully out of his reach. "Anything feel rumpled, other than your temper?"

Juste gave him a baleful stare, then sighed.

"The back of my jerkin," he admitted, shrugging his good shoulder to indicate the place, and Miche moved silently to adjust it. It would be aggravating, to have rumples and itches that he couldn't scratch.

It wasn't that he couldn't sympathize. Ordinarily, nothing could pierce Juste's thick hide, so it was fundamentally impossible for Miche not to poke at him a little. But Juste was an intensely private man. He *hated* having other people in his space and resented any disruption to his habits and routines. And no man could ever like having to rely on another to get his boots on.

Remin, who knew that Juste would've run off every squire in the valley inside an hour, had appointed Miche to be his keeper.

"I'll go fetch breakfast, try not to snarl at anyone while I'm gone," said Miche, once he had installed Juste in Ophele's solar, with stacks of paper to keep him company. So long as the roads were icy, Juste was restricted to his cottage and the manor house, lest he fall and break his other arm. In the morning, Miche made the rounds from kitchen to manor to barracks, fetching food, practicing with the other knights, and looking in on Huber, who was an even more difficult patient than Juste.

But then, *Juste's* arm was going to heal.

"At least light a few candles," Miche said as he barged into Huber's rooms, making a great deal more noise than necessary and setting down a stack of papers on his table. "I know you're a broody sort of fellow, but you don't need to actually sit in the dark."

Even as he was loudly lighting candles, opening the curtains, and tidying away the remains of Huber's breakfast, Miche looked the silent man over, lying in bed with his face averted. Much of the fine bronze glow was gone from his skin, but at least his clothes looked fresh. Tounot had taken charge of managing such things, and Genon came to the barracks every few days to examine the progress of the healing stump of his left arm. And though Miche could not imagine how he himself might cope with such a loss, he did hope someone would come stir him up, if he needed it.

"As it happens, I could use your help," Miche went on, setting quill and ink on a table. "You know, of course, that I am a man of many virtues. Thoughtful, kind-hearted, merciful—up you get, now—with a certain...generosity of spirit," he decided as he hauled Huber out of bed and shoved him toward the chair. "I have just never been able to tell people *no*."

"Is that what you tell yourself?" Huber asked flatly, a muscle clenching in his jaw. The jostling hurt, but he was too proud to let it show.

"It must be, it's the only possible explanation for why I find myself so consistently behind. Now, these are from Juste. He's been focused on matters in the capital just lately, so he hasn't had time to consider matters of the stables, but it seems a pity to miss a year's breeding when we've just had some likely horses come in..."

This would have rightfully been Huber's work anyway. Miche kept up a constant stream of conversation as he leafed through the papers, because when he had acquired Regal and Dancer—née Innuendo—from the Aldeburke stable, he had also seized their breeding papers, which were the equivalent of a patent of nobility for highbred horses. There were a dozen such beasts in Tresingale, with bloodlines more noble than most of Remin's knights, and come spring, the mares would be in season.

Miche had no idea what they might get, if they bred a Regal with a Dancer, but Huber had done as much lying in bed as was good for him. Soon he'd be able to wander all of Tresingale without worrying about running into Rem, if that was his trouble.

"You don't need to invent work for me." Huber looked down at the papers spread before him, unmoving.

"I didn't *invent* this work. I traveled halfway across the Empire and stole it for you," Miche retorted. "They looked like good horses to me, but what the fuck do I know? You have a look and tell me what the best crosses are."

"Did Rem put you up to this?" Huber asked, his copper eyes hardening, and Miche gave him a loving slap to the back of the head.

"No. I thought of it all by myself because it's time you stopped lying about, expecting people to come dress you and feed you. You've still got your writing hand. You can still work a bridle and bit. You've got two pages that you haven't looked at in a month and they need you. If you don't make yourself useful, I'll let Her Grace come and find occupation for you. She's already put all those footless fellows from Selgin and Isigne to work. Would you prefer making pots, or learning to weave?"

Miche leveled him with a remorseless stare and let the silence stretch. To him, Huber would always be a snot-nosed little brother, one of the Ereguil pageboys that Miche had bullied and brought up when he himself had just become a knight. And while Remin and Huber needed to sort out their problems themselves, Miche would only indulge them so long before he started knocking heads together.

Huber glared back. Three, two, one...

"...I'll go get her," Miche said, rising from his seat. "Her Grace has been so *worried,* you know? Only the other day—"

"Oh, fuck you, Miche," said Huber, with feeling. "I'll look at the honorable fucking beasts."

"Her Grace will be relieved." Miche clapped him on his good shoulder, rising. "And since you're up and dressed for the day, I have a couple more little beasts that need your attention."

He was pulling the door open before Huber could protest, revealing Lege and Nicco in the hall outside. Both pages looked as pale and wan as if they too had been missing the sunshine.

"Go gently, boys," Miche cautioned, and left them to look after each other.

* * *

By noon, Miche was back at the manor again, settled in the solar and helping Juste with all the work where penmanship mattered. Juste was enjoying *that* so much, he was teaching himself to write with his left hand.

Miche was beset by prickly people.

But he didn't mind. It was entertaining to watch the comings and goings from the Duchess of Andelin's eclectic salon, amusing to see her fussing over Juste, and Miche was quietly very proud of how far she had come. She was so like her mother.

It also gave him an excuse to overhear any amount of gossip, and unlike Juste—who would have been perfectly happy as a hermit—Miche was a nosy so-and-so.

They were just settling to the afternoon's work when there was a commotion in the hallway, and Juste turned with a definite snarl as the door opened to admit Ophele, Lady Verr, and a tall Benkki Desan woman, her ivory cheeks pink with cold.

"Your Grace. Ladies," Miche said, rising to offer his courtesies and nudging Juste to follow. "Here to escort Grandfather Tree upstairs at last?"

"Great-Grandfather, noble lord," Madam Sanai corrected, with a half-bow and quarter-smile for both men. She was tall for a woman, almost equal to Juste, willowy and long-limbed and dressed in a long-sleeved tunic that fit her very well. "Sir Justenin.

I hope I am not disturbing. Great-Grandfather needs a little more sun."

"All of us could use a little more sun," Miche agreed, ignoring Juste's warning glare. His smile widened, broad and charming. "Juste, where are your manners? If we cannot have the sun, we may at least be grateful for these other, lovelier lights that come to brighten our afternoon."

Lady Verr shot him a disgusted look.

"Good afternoon," Juste said stiffly. "Madam, any guest of Her Grace's is welcome. My secretary is regrettably easy to distract."

"It is a sad failing," Miche agreed, which made Madam Sanai smile, Ophele giggle, Lady Verr roll her eyes, and Juste stab him with a quill once no one was looking.

There was a great deal of work before them. Stacks of candidates for key positions in the manor, all of whose qualifications, connections, and convictions had to be investigated. But though Miche and Juste were accustomed to working in the chaos of a war camp, they both turned again as Sim and Jaose appeared, grunting with effort as they hauled Grandfather Tree through the door.

"Yes, by this window, please. Careful of your fingers!" Ophele said anxiously, dancing out of the way as the two footmen maneuvered the immense planter pot into place. The ancestor tree was taller than the diminutive Duchess of Andelin. "It really is lovely. Why is it called an ancestor tree?"

"It may only be a decorative tree, if you wish," Madam Sanai said carefully. "But for us, it is the memory of the Great Tree, that was once Mother to us all. And so we shape these trees with the growing of our own families, our *tali*—I think that is your word for House?"

A pair of pale blue eyes were pressing dagger-like into the back of his head. Miche bent obediently to his letters. They still needed a housekeeper and head laundress, and now that Tresingale had survived its first year with the devils, it seemed everyone had decided that Remin's generous terms of employment were worth the risk.

But the wider pool of candidates didn't make it any easier to *fill* these posts. They hardly needed more spies and assassins in Tresingale, and Remin and Ophele both had difficult temperaments. It would be a challenge to find a housekeeper with the spine to stand up to His Grace who wouldn't also trample all over the inexperienced duchess. Miche had written dozens of letters that were polite variations of, *thank you very much for inquiring, but...*

The musical chorus of female voices was far more interesting. Ophele, chirping questions. Madam Sanai's liquid accent rolled in answer, and every so often there was Lady Verr's aristocratic tones, carefully cultivated and perfectly shaped syllables that tolled like bells.

Glancing up, Miche was amused to find that Juste's head was subtly angled toward the conversation. Well, what might he be looking at?

It was Juste. It was possible he was admiring Grandfather Tree. But Lady Verr and Madam Sanai were both in that direction, like two wildly different species of flower, and much to appreciate in both. Lady Verr was a classic Imperial beauty, from the oval of her face to the perfect drape of her skirts, and Madam Sanai was an arresting sight for a man of the Empire, especially with those trousers clinging to her lean hips. There was a hunting grace about her as she crouched, her long hair falling loose past her thighs, explaining some point of lichen to a spellbound Ophele.

Women were so marvelous.

"Juste," Miche repeated, measuring the angle of Juste's pale blue eyes and tucking this delightful bit of gossip away. "This one. Look, I know she's from the capital, but she was in charge of the household livery—"

"We are hoping to avoid filling His Grace's household with people from Segoile." Juste took the page, inscrutable.

"It might be worth having Edemir interview her, if she knows what she's about."

"The matter of livery is pressing," Juste acknowledged. It wasn't just a question of aesthetics. The reason servants wore uniforms was to make it easier to tell if someone—an assassin, for example—was somewhere they ought not to be.

"If we're going to go to the trouble and expense, we ought to do it right," Miche shrugged. "Have Tiffen design something in the new Andelin style to please His Grace and a Mistress of Wardrobe to manage it properly."

"I'll speak to him about it." Painstakingly, Juste scrawled the addition on his to-do list with his left hand, waving Miche away. "I can do it. Request references and have Edemir speak to her."

Miche did not envy Edemir the task. Burrowing back into his papers, he made a fair bit of headway by the time the women were content with the placement of the ancestor tree, and Madam Sanai began making her farewells.

"Madam," said Juste, without looking up from his letter. "I have heard that Huvara Mahit was denied custom by the chandler. I hope you will be comfortable to inform us, if it happens again."

Madam Sanai turned back from the door in surprise, and behind her, Ophele instantly swelled with indignation.

"I hope it will not be necessary," Madam Sanai replied, her brows lifting. "Will the chandler expect us?"

"He has been informed of His Grace's expectations," Juste replied, glancing up at her. "While he is the only chandler in town, he will trade with everyone. Or he will leave."

"We have thanks for your aid. And—forgive me, if it is impolite to say, but your injury looks most uncomfortable, noble knight," she added, her dark violet eyes flicking to his sling. "There may be help for it, if you wish."

"That is kind of you."

"It is our task to mend the way, when it is fractured," she replied, and departed with Ophele at her side to see her to the door, filled with outrage over the chandler.

"She will insist on playing the servant," Lady Verr remarked, sitting down to take up her embroidery. This was not muttered. She meant for Miche and Juste to hear it.

"It is unlikely she will find anyone in Segoile that she likes well enough to walk out," Juste replied, practical and cutting. "But I have been hoping for an opportunity to seek your opinion, my lady, if you will indulge me."

"Oh?"

"You spent last season in the capital, did you not?" asked Juste. "After your absence."

Miche would never tire of listening to Juste remind people that he knew their secrets.

"Yes, I did," Lady Verr replied serenely.

"There must have been a great deal of gossip about Her Grace, after the Divinity's announcement."

"There...was." Lady Verr's brows lifted. "I am afraid...well, if I must tell the truth, I think she will surprise them. There was a great deal of speculation about the identity of her mother, and curiosity as to why a sacred Daughter of the Stars was such a great secret. Some suggested that Her Highness must be...lacking in some way."

She sounded apologetic, but that was only a coat of lacquer. That hateful society mask was one of the things Miche despised most about the capital, an affected blandness impervious to any amount of cruelty.

He always felt a mean compulsion to shatter it.

"It makes an entertaining story," he drawled, already contemplating how he might punish whoever was spreading the slander.

"It is also a strangely specific story to seize upon, in the absence of any evidence," Juste remarked. "Who would benefit from such a tale? That is the line to follow. Do you recall if anyone took particular pleasure in repeating it, my lady?"

"I would have to think." Her eyes went momentarily distant. "It was a great many people, I don't know if I could guess who was first. I wonder why that particular detail..."

"We heard it, too," Miche recalled, his gaze meeting Juste's. They had heard that lie in Aldeburke. Was that a coincidence? Or was someone in Aldeburke telling tales?

"I will be interested to hear what you discover, Lady Verr," said Juste, neatly shifting the discussion as Ophele returned, grumbling. "Your Grace. We were just discussing a new area of learning."

"Oh?" Ophele approached, her face guileless.

"Cryptography," Juste replied, so silkily that it made Lady Verr stiffen with alarm. "That is the decoding of ciphers. You have heard of the discipline?"

"I read about it," Ophele said, looking interested. "We have ciphers? Do I have to learn them?"

"You will learn many codes, in time," Juste replied, with a hint of wickedness. Reaching into the breast pocket of his doublet, he plucked out the slip of paper from the barracks. "This was discovered in one of the training yards, my lady. I have no expectation that you will decipher it, though we will discuss the methods for such work in time. But what could you tell me about this message now?"

Ophele took it, frowning.

"Second storehouse?" she read aloud. "In the barracks? I've never seen any writing like this. It's not any Imperial alphabet, is it? Do we have any foreign soldiers or mercenaries?"

"A few former mercenaries," Juste conceded. "But none in Tresingale."

Ophele leaned against the long table, thoughtful. Juste was content to let her contemplate it; indeed, there was a very small smile at the corner of his mouth, a satisfaction that only someone who knew him well would recognize. This interlude was not just about providing the Duchess of Andelin a new puzzle to play with.

"It makes it sound like an inventory, but it isn't one, is it?" she mused. "Unless it is a very short one."

"Why do you say that?"

"There aren't any numbers. Unless maybe these repeated symbols are numbers," she said, tapping the paper. "But those aren't whole words between them, are they ideograms? Look..."

Obliging, Juste bent with a solicitousness that made Miche want to smack him in the back of his diabolical head. No doubt Ophele would have some useful insights, but the parchment in her hands was not the message Juste was sending. *That* was directed at Lady Verr, who had not been invited to participate in unraveling this mystery.

And why was that?

Miche's quill scribbled on. There must be *some* reason that Duchess Ereguil had commended Lady Verr for Ophele's companion, but he was blasted if he could see it. There was something predatory in the way she watched Ophele, alert for the least crumb of information.

Perhaps it was too much to expect a Rose of Segoile to put the game aside long enough to be a *friend.* She ought to be alerting her lady to the real game afoot, not listening to gossip and pretending to be invisible.

Though perhaps that would be an awkward conversation in this case, Miche conceded, bending his head to conceal a grin. Juste hadn't offered Lady Verr the message for a reason. He suspected she knew something about it, and he was using Ophele to make the lady sweat.

Chapter 11 – An Experiment in Lace

It had been some time since Ophele had enjoyed the simple pleasure of a kitchen.

The scents of herbs and spices. The curious, almost magical transformation of batter and dough into cake and bread. Even Wen's puffing and blowing that duchesses had no business near an oven and the sacred white line on the floor had been *her* idea couldn't dent her enthusiasm.

Watching the familiar motions of Azelma's hands as she worked a mound of dough, Ophele thought that all she needed was an old wooden stool to sit upon and she would be perfectly content.

"What are you making?" she asked, squeezing out of the way of one of the kitchen boys. The long, narrow kitchen was delightfully warm, and she was pleased to have a few minutes to visit while Lady Verr was dropping off letters at the storehouse office. She had been dying to see how Azelma was getting on.

"Rye bread," Azelma replied, her hands scraping it rapidly over the counter, turning, kneading, a practiced rhythm she had been repeating for sixty years. "As if you didn't know."

"I was hoping for a fig roll," Ophele confessed. "Are there figs?"

"Rye will do better for your belly than sweetbread," Azelma replied. She had a white coif over her head and looked pleased to be lecturing Ophele about the health of her belly once more. "And there's a whole camp to feed besides, not one spoiled princess."

"Duchess. *Duchess,"* Wen barked. "A duchess standing in me kitchen, the stars only know why. Didn't I *say* it would come to rye?"

The question was addressed to the pot rack over his bald head.

"Speaking of spoiled," Azelma grumbled, and Ophele covered her mouth with her hand to hide her giggles.

"Do ye think I can't hear ye, ye old bat?" Wen demanded.

"No indeed, when I *meant* you to hear me, you great blowing ox," Azelma fired back, slapping the dough onto her counter as if it were his head. "Didn't we agree that this was my bit of counter? I can invite who I like to stand on the other side of it, thank you."

"I gave ye the counter, not the run of the whole bleeding—" Wen began, instantly igniting, and Ophele steeled herself and interceded.

"Please don't argue," she said, looking between them anxiously. "I don't mean to make trouble. Wen, am I really in the way?"

She gave him a dose of large, hopeful eyes, a sad and slightly wistful expression that Justenin had had her practicing for weeks. Granted, mediating a quarrel between Wen and Azelma was not one of the uses he had proposed, but if she didn't experiment, how would she know if it worked?

Gazing up at the massive Wen, Ophele believed with all her heart that she was grieved, and *sad,* and hearing them argue made her grieved and sad, and after a moment Wen's eyes shifted away.

"Well, it ain't for the likes of Wen the cook to say where a duchess goes, is it," he growled, and sank his knife into a carcass of something.

"Please tell me if I am any trouble," Ophele said earnestly, turning back to Azelma with her lashes lowered to hide the triumph in her eyes. "And I would like a fig roll when you have time, but I can wait..."

"Oh, get on with yourself!" The old lady laughed, and snapped her fingers under Ophele's nose with a puff of flour. "How worried I was about you all these months, and look how they've ruined you! Aye, I'll see about a fig roll."

"I told Remin about them," Ophele said, brightening instantly. "The one with the walnuts? He acts like he doesn't like sweets, but I only got three of those cookies that Wen made last time."

"And you're hoping to get around him with sweets from me," Azelma said knowingly. "You know I don't mind it, child. I can hardly blame him."

"I know." Ophele made a little ball of rye dough with a fingertip. "It's just, the kitchen in the house will be ready soon, and I hoped..."

"Give things time to rise," advised Azelma, who liked to couch her wisdom in baking metaphors. "It never does any good, trying to hurry a man along, child. He'll decide when he's good and ready."

Mionet frequently said much the same thing, in other circumstances. Like Justenin, her course of study was eclectic, and half the time Ophele wasn't sure what she was meant to be learning, or if the other woman was intentionally teaching at all. She was waiting outside by the sledge when Ophele exited the kitchen, and they climbed together into the rough but comfortable vehicle. It was well-padded with thick fur and drawn by Brambles, who was much happier pulling things than being sat upon.

"Who did you send letters to today?" Ophele asked as they settled in the back seat together, and Davi clicked his tongue to get Brambles moving.

"Lady Nicolet Firellion and Countess Laverey," Mionet replied. "Both their husbands are bannermen of Duke Ereguil, I'm afraid, but they both prefer to arrive early for the season and have sharp ears."

"Why is it bad that they belong to Duke Ereguil?" Ophele asked, tucking her hands under the fur robe. There were heated bricks at their feet, but it was still bitterly cold outside after the warm kitchen.

"There is some regionalism among the social sets in the capital," Mionet explained. "Most people are in their country homes over the winter, you see, for religious observances and so forth, and people know their neighbors best and then gravitate to them when they come to the city. People loyal to Duke Ereguil will be less likely to hear or repeat nasty things about you, when you are his foster son's wife."

"How will you find out, then?" Ophele asked, troubled.

"It is more difficult at a distance," Mionet admitted. "But we can at least hope to know the lay of the land before we arrive. There is nothing more unpleasant than being caught unawares. Half the trouble can be nipped in the bud if you are prepared. And then perhaps we might even catch *them* out, which is a great deal more fun."

"I wish we needn't at all," Ophele said glumly. She had been caught out too often to ever wish it on others. "I don't want to embarrass anyone else."

"Well, we certainly ought to shame them if they deserve it, but such things aren't always bad," Mionet replied, encouraging. "There is a reason people play such games, my lady. Why, there was one time I surprised Nicolet..."

She regaled Ophele with a number of pranks on the way into town, bending her head to whisper the more scandalous ones so Leonin would not overhear. Ophele thought sometimes Mionet shared such shocking things just to teach Ophele not to *look* shocked, but they were very funny, and nothing at all like Lady Hurrell's cruel tricks.

"Please warn me before you do such things," she said, hiding her smile as they went into Master Tiffen's shop. It had grown substantially since their first visit, and the nook by the hearth now contained two seamstresses, one of whom was Celande, who embroidered such lovely flowers. Ophele beamed.

"It is a matter of matching affinities, my lady," Mionet was saying. "Such pranks are no fun if your victim doesn't enjoy it. Sometimes they might even thank you for it," she added, suddenly filled with mischief. "I have just had the most marvelous idea. Shall I prove it to you?"

"Prove it how?" Ophele had learned to be wary when Mionet got that look in her eyes.

"A surprise," the other woman said cheerfully, turning to the counter to inspect a neatly folded stack of clothing from Master Tiffen. "I assure you, your victim will thank you for it, and perhaps you might get something that you want in the bargain."

"My...victim?" Ophele echoed. She had a sudden, dreadful suspicion.

"Well, who else?" Mionet asked wickedly. "He will thank you for it, see if he doesn't. Perhaps he will even be pleased enough to reconsider that other matter."

There was only one thing Ophele had asked that Remin had refused, and been disappointed enough to confide it to Mionet. Ophele hesitated.

"It does no harm to ask," Mionet reassured. "Now, listen, and do just as I say..."

Bending her head, she whispered her suggestion as Master Tiffen was gathering the remainder of their order, her red lips curving in a devilish smile. The bit of lace in her fingers stretched over the back of her hand in an explanatory sort of way.

Master Nore Ffloce, passing just outside the tailor shop, was very startled by the sudden squawk of alarm from within.

* * *

If anyone had asked Mionet's opinion, she would have said the chief trouble with the Duchess of Andelin's education was that too many people had their hands in it.

It was bad enough to have Leonin and Davi hanging about every moment of every day, privy to every discussion, no matter how sensitive the topic. But now that Sir Justenin had injured his shoulder, he was permanently occupying one end of the long table in the solar, leaving very few moments in the day for Mionet to impart the secret and perilous knowledge meant only for the ears of women.

She tried to make the best of it. The duchess changed her clothing at least three times a day, sometimes four if her dance lesson had been particularly vigorous, and today she had finally consented to allow Mionet to oversee her bath. With Leonin and Davi—and everything else—stripped away, it was the most opportune possible moment for sensitive conversation.

"My, we could spend *days* shopping for these things," she said, examining the toiletries near the tub. Not so bad as she expected, but certainly nothing like the luxuries of the Silver Avenue Market. On her own, Mionet wouldn't be let through the doors of those exclusive shops, but with Duchess Andelin...

She hummed.

"There is an alchemist I know that makes these lovely, scented crystals," she began, but when she glanced back at the tub, it was clear that the duchess wasn't listening. As a matter of fact, the lady was curled up so tightly, Emi and Peri were having difficulty finding anything to scrub.

"...big as apples," Mionet finished, without a flicker of reaction. Well, she had suspected something like this. It would be useful knowledge if she intended some harm, but Duchess Andelin could hardly visit the baths of Segoile if she was going to curl up like a snail.

The duchess flinched at Emi's hand, and Mionet's eyes went flinty.

"Emi. Peri. Please mind your hands," she said, as if *they* were at fault. "Her Grace is very fine boned. I assure you I will note the least scratch. My lady, I hope you will speak if there is any discomfort. Perhaps Emi and Peri are too used to scrubbing floors."

Emi stiffened with outrage, and Peri's mouth dropped open.

"Oh, no," Duchess Andelin said, sitting up at once. "They're not, it's not—it's fine."

Over her head, Peri met Mionet's gaze for a long moment, and then there was a flash of understanding. She had always been the more quick-witted of the two maids.

"It's all right, my lady, please say if you don't like it," she said, and the rest of the bath went much more smoothly.

How was Mionet ever going to sell Duchess Andelin on the delights and luxuries of Segoile when she knew less about these things than her servants? It was a tricky prospect already, managing access to Princess Ophele with only a few months' notice, but it would come to nothing if she spent all that time acquainting the lady with basic cosmetic alchemy.

And if that wasn't bad enough, *that man* was showing up in the solar even in the morning, and apparently not one other person in Tresingale had the sense to know that the absolute last thing the young Duchess of Andelin needed was a connection with *Sir Miche of Harnost*.

"You almost had it, Ophele, or would if Davi weren't such a clod," Miche said during one of her dance lessons, depositing his quill into an ink pot. "Here, Tounot, give us that bit again. My lady," he said to Ophele with a bow, and she laughed as he took her hands and led her through a difficult part of the dance, to demonstrate for Davi where he had gone wrong.

There was something there, but Mionet still couldn't put her finger on it. It did not seem anything as obvious and vulgar as an affair; the stars knew she had seen ample evidence that there was a great deal of love between the Duke and Duchess of Andelin. The duchess would no more betray him than she would fly.

But this was Miche of Harnost. He looked every inch the libertine with that long blond hair: dangerously beautiful, heartlessly charming, and absolutely nothing but trouble.

"Right foot, right foot," Miche was saying, and the duchess moved with more speed than grace to follow, her face glowing as she successfully executed the tricky maneuver.

"Oh, I did it!" she exclaimed, and then burst out laughing as he took her through it again. "No, you can't switch feet that fast, I can't keep up!"

"Sure you can, left foot, there you go," he encouraged. His dimples flashed as he smiled. "Ready to try it again?"

"Yes. No. Wait, I'm on the wrong foot!" she wailed, but they were all laughing now, and after a little skip, she was quick to catch up, sailing about in his arms with skirts fluttering and perfectly content.

She was far too familiar with him, and far too comfortable in his company. And Miche himself was worse, calling her by her first name and teasing her even with other people about. More than once, Mionet caught a flicker of trouble in Leonin's face that meant he had noticed it, too.

What *was* the relationship between them, exactly?

No one would *ask,* in Segoile. It was Sir Miche of Harnost. They would leap straight to one ruinous conclusion.

"And there!" Miche exclaimed as he landed her directly in front of Davi. Catching her hand, he bowed to press a kiss to the back of her knuckles, a gesture that would have been awkward from any man less infernally graceful. "You cannot complain of your pupil, Leonin. Light on her feet as anyone could ask."

It was just poor timing that he did this as Emi was ushering a batch of farmwives through the door.

"No, I have more often complained of her partner," Leonin replied dryly, but his eyes found Mionet's across the room.

For heaven's sake, they might just start assuming things in *Tresingale.*

"Sir Miche." With a smile fixed on her face, Mionet sidled across the room to stand beside him, speaking through her teeth. "I would like a private word with you. Tonight."

"Would you?" His face was pleasant, but his eyes chilled.

"Yes. Please see that you will not have other company," she said shortly, and went to wrangle the farmwives.

It was all she could do to keep from thundering warnings into the Duchess of Andelin's innocent ears.

But it was not fair to blame her. By now there was ample evidence that Duchess Andelin had been very, *very* poorly raised, without even the most rudimentary warnings a noblewoman heard from the moment she could toddle out of her mother's line of sight. But what was Miche's excuse? What was wrong with these idiot men? Did they really not understand how this could be perceived, or turned to the lady's detriment?

Of course not. Because it was never *men* that paid the price for these things.

It was wildly hypocritical and unfair, but it was innocents like Ophele that always suffered the most for these scandals. And to be just, it was not only men who were immune; there were Segoile matrons who entertained a new lover every Tuesday and managed to brazen it out, and certain debutantes could sail through four engagements in a single season and come out the other side without a scratch. The stars knew *Miche of Harnost* would hardly be affected by one more scandal.

But the Exile Princess, Duchess of Andelin, wife of Remin Grimjaw...

Once that wheel started turning, it would *never stop.*

Seething, Mionet made her way to Miche's cottage later that night, angry all over again that she must resort to subterfuge and resentful that His Grace, Remin of Andelin, had *no idea* the lengths she was going to, to look after his naïve wife.

Steeling herself, she knocked on the door.

They had parted after supper only minutes before; just long enough to ensure the servants were busy with clearing away. Firelight glowed on Miche's face as he opened the door and stood aside.

"I know *you* are accustomed to company at night," Mionet said scathingly, moving quickly through the door. "But *I* would like to be circumsp—what under the stars are you doing?

His fingers were working the laces of his jerkin free in a businesslike manner, baring an expanse of broad pectorals.

"You don't want to?" he asked, lifting one blond eyebrow.

"What—you—not every woman in the world wants to *sleep* with you!" Mionet spluttered, outraged.

"Oh. In my experience, they do," he said diffidently, and sat down on the end of his bed. "What do you want, then?"

"Ironically, to beg you to be a *trifle* less scandalous," she spat. "For your duchess's sake, if not your own."

"Since when have you cared about what's good for her?" he retorted. "Aren't you just trying to figure out how to use her once you get her to the capital?"

Miche was giving her too little credit. Mionet had decided long ago exactly how she could use the Exile Princess once she got her to the capital. But she was not about to tell him that.

"The trouble with men like you," she began, "is that you never consider the damage you do to others. To Her Grace, if you are as open with your affections in public as you are in private."

"This is not the capital, where servants so freely betray their mistresses," he said coldly, with a warning flash in his tawny eyes.

"It doesn't matter what's true, it matters what it *looks like,"* she snapped, exasperated. "Surely you are aware of your reputation?"

"It certainly seems you are."

"Well, I must ask. Ignorance is the only reason I can imagine why you would not already take steps to remedy it." She cast a contemptuous look at his open shirt, which he had still made no effort to close in the presence of a lady. "You may choose to bed half of Segoile and all the laundresses in Tresingale if you wish, but could you not at least be *discreet?* There is a reason no decent woman in the capital would allow herself to be seen with you."

He scoffed. "Fortunately, Tresingale has different standards of *decency.*"

"I daresay you would think so, for you would otherwise have been dismissed long ago," she shot back. "How are you not ashamed to so disgrace your lord? Even Duchess Ereguil has despaired of making a match for you. No lady could show her face in the capital, if every third woman there might tell her bed stories about her husband."

"How you presume, madam," he protested, his eyes glittering. "To think that I would ever choose *one,* and break so many hearts."

"Do you know what they say of you? Women talk, just as men do." Fury fizzed in her temples, but her face was cool and smiling. "Among themselves, they speak of Miche of Harnost like a new attendant at the Candle Street baths. Oh, my dear, you must try the blond one. So clever with his hands, and even better with his tongue."

"And yet here you are, with my scandalous self," he drawled, sprawling back on his bed with a provocative roll of his hips. "Sure you don't want to see what the fuss is about?"

She would sooner have set the bed aflame with him in it. How many women had accepted that invitation? How many women had been ruined by this man?

"Even if you care nothing for your own reputation, you might at least have a care for Ophele—"

He was on his feet and had her pinned to the wall in a sudden snap of fury, his beautiful face snarling an inch from hers.

"Do not trouble to speak her name," he hissed. "There are names for women like you, too, madam. Mercenaries in pretty gowns, padding their own purses, and nowhere to be found once the well runs dry. And the only reason you're here is because you're afraid I'll get in the way."

Mionet glared back, as if her heart wasn't hammering in her throat. But this time, she was the first to look away.

"You will ruin her," she said bitterly. "Scandal has a long tail. Thirty years from now, when you go to the capital, they will still whisper of your paramours. It doesn't just dangle after *you*, you fool. It dirties everyone you touch. *She* will pay for your reputation, just as your friends have. You make everyone around you filthy."

"Then you should leave quickly," he said, standing aside and waving his hand, as if she had bored him beyond bearing. "I should hate to sully anyone so *pure* as yourself."

Fuming, Mionet slipped past, drawing back her skirts so they would not touch him.

* * *

To Her Grace Ophele, the Duchess of Andelin, at Tresingale Manor in the Duchy of Andelin, from Duchess Liliet Ereguil:

I hope all proceeds well in Tresingale, and thank you for your good wishes. I swear, half the household falls ill every time we move to the capital, but it passed quickly, and Laud is quite himself again, may the stars have mercy on us all.

The compromise Lady Verr suggested is a good one. I think we must have <u>some</u> event for your debut, my dear, or we will leave too much space for rumor and speculation. But an outdoor ball will be the very thing, with room enough for half of society, and we might place you and Remin in one of the pavilions, where it will be easy enough to set up a guard. Do not apologize for needing one. I have told Remin all his life that I am a believer in placing the blame where it belongs, and it is not with him.

I was happy to hear that you resolved the trouble with your Benkki Desans. I quite agree with Justenin that it is one thing to let people freely associate, or not, and something altogether different when they begin barring one another from trade. We have experienced something like that in Ereguil, and more than once, I am afraid; we are rather pinned between Capricia and Noreven, and so there is frequent trouble between our merchants and theirs, and then they also have trouble with each other. It may seem a small thing, but people write home, and if you treat the people from other lands well in your country, then you may reasonably demand the same in theirs.

You have asked for my advice, so here it is: you must think further ahead, my dear. Do not consider only Tresingale today, but twenty or thirty or even a hundred years hence. Why, when I was first married, I recall I commissioned Caprician artists to paint a few frescoes, thinking only that they would look well behind the palmettoes.

Well, other ladies happened to admire them, and they hired more artists, and now we have a Caprician Frescoists Association in the city who argues constantly with the local Imperial Painters Guild and Laud has threatened more than once to kick them all out.

Those are the scales that a lady must balance. Do not play favorites with your own people, and still less between the merchants of other lands. Your people have a right to expect impartiality from their duchess, and I have found that becoming too friendly with the merchants of one nation may result in problems of state with another.

And this will be my final piece of advice for you: be careful in asking your elders for advice, for they might just indulge you. I really must fly. Take care of yourself and Remin and all those other dear boys, and kindly give the attached lists to Lady Verr. You may buy anything you like when you reach the city, but time will be short, and it will be a relief to your heart to have the things you need from home ready to hand.

Affectionately yours,
Liliet Ereguil

* * *

One month until they left for the capital.

How had winter flown by so quickly?

It seemed simultaneously fleeting and endless, for Ophele's days were busy ones, from the moment she opened her eyes. A deluge of information from a dozen sources and still there was always more, twelve years of Imperial education compressed into four months. And outside the windows the snow fell and drifted in great white walls, until she forgot there was any other color in the world.

The people of Ferrede arrived between storms and were welcomed, feted, and installed in the North Gate cottages, with very grudging gratitude. They were not happy to have been taken from their homes.

"Elder Brodrim." In the warm confines of the solar, Ophele greeted Ferrede's headman, a bearded old man who was a little hard of hearing. "Thank you for coming all this way. I am glad you arrived safely."

"Thank you, my lady," he said loudly. "I hoped to offer you the hospitality of Ferrede, rather than the other way around. I hope it will not be long before we can honor our lady in our home."

"We share that hope," Remin said beside her, with a rumble of warning in his voice. "Once it is safe."

"Yes, Your Grace." Elder Brodrim bowed. Rollon's quick wits had saved Ferrede from the horrors Remin's other villages had endured, but Remin was right; best to put them with the other refugees and let them hear the tales for themselves.

Jaose offered a hand to help the old man kneel, and twenty or so members of his villages knelt behind him to make their oaths.

"In the light of the stars and before all here assembled, I swear my fealty and homage to House Andelin, His Grace Duke Remin, and Her Sacred Grace the Duchess Ophele. If I should ever violate this oath, or fail in their trust, then may my life be forfeit..."

Ophele had heard these words many times by now, but she still felt a fraud, accepting them.

"I will come and see all of you soon," she promised when they were done, wishing there was time to ask their names and occupations. She liked placing everyone into her mental map of town, and often thought with secret delight of who she would introduce to each other, trying to match affinities, like Mionet said. "If you have any troubles, please ask after Sir Auber. Or the Mistresses Conbour. Amise and Lisset will be happy to help you."

Most duchesses must be very standoffish, if everyone was always so surprised when she said that. Ophele smiled, trying to look reassuring and harmless, and then puffed out a breath and slumped back in her chair, once the door closed behind them. It was always frightening to have so many people looking at her.

"Well, we didn't expect them to thank us," observed Davi, slouching against the wall with his lanky legs crossed.

"I will be just as pleased to send them back." Remin brushed a hand over Ophele's head and pushed out of his chair. "Wife, have you company for luncheon today?"

"No?" Ophele glanced at Lady Verr for confirmation.

"I am always the last to have the attention of the Duchess of Andelin," he complained. "It seems everyone else in the valley was invited to your salon first."

"Will I have you and your knights to tea?" Ophele asked, tickled by the idea. "It's been so long since we had supper together, hasn't it? Why don't we have everyone here?"

"I would like that," Remin agreed, nodding for Leonin to take the other end of the long table to drag it back to its usual place. "A farewell banquet, before we leave."

That departure seemed much closer on this side of winter.

Even as Ophele's days went by in a flurry, Remin was working late every day, and Ophele did not think it was Valleth or the devils that kept him at the Court of War so early, or making him jerk awake in the wee hours of the morning. Was it good that he was planning so carefully? Or worrying that he must?

Close as she was to the rhythms of the town, Ophele could not help noticing the alterations. She knew who came and went from her solar, and yet Tounot was no longer among them, and his lute was left behind in her keeping. It was hard to miss the massive form of Jinmin at the North Gate, but when was the last time she had seen him there? Two weeks? Three? Justenin said they were building ports further downriver, but would they really do that in *February?*

And despite all this activity, Davi and Leonin were both sporting black eyes again, and Remin was so bruised and welted, it hurt just to look at him. They were back at practice, even more ferociously than they had been before the fever.

"I will leave you with Lady Verr today," Justenin told her at breakfast the next morning, spooning up porridge with his left hand. His right was unbound now, used only with greatest care, and yet he had a brand new welt purpling on his cheek.

"Oh?" Ophele said politely. Remin had forbidden him to practice with his sword, so what had Juste been doing?

"Yes, I must speak to Guisse about the road down to the harbor. It's going to erode rapidly if we're not careful, between the wagon traffic and the spring rains..."

The harbor road was a matter dear to his heart. But it was interesting that they all seemed to go to the harbor so much when all the ferries were supposed to be docked for the winter...

Ophele glanced at Remin, who was halfway through his second platter of food and paying close attention to business. She could not bring herself to worry him with her suspicions, but the only other person who might have explained it was nowhere to be found. Sir Miche had all but vanished from the manor over the last week, and she found herself missing him dreadfully: that tilt of his head that encouraged her to try again, or the way he had of unraveling whole puzzles for her with a single word.

That left Mionet, and Ophele could hardly bring herself to look in that direction.

It was only that morning that she had finally presented Ophele with the forbidden article, a scandalous object that made Ophele's heart palpitate and her face flush hot and cold. It was currently buried in the back of her wardrobe, with all the guilt and suspense of a corpse they had murdered together.

And tonight, she was meant to bring it out.

"Nothing. I mean, it's good," she said, starting as Remin spoke to her. "Will you be very late tonight?"

"I hope not. I'll miss supper," he said, reaching for another platter of eggs as if to fortify himself. "There are a great many details to be seen to before we leave."

On the other side of the table, she saw the mischief in Mionet's gaze and looked hastily down at her plate.

It wasn't as if she was doing anything *wrong,* Ophele told herself. Remin would certainly have listened if she asked him to reconsider his decision, even without this little...surprise. What was wrong with making sure he was in a good mood when she asked? He would enjoy all of it very much, and tease her when it was all over.

Probably.

Maybe.

Oh, stars, what if he didn't?

* * *

"I don't know," she said later that night, wringing her hands as the hour of her doom approached. She was sitting at her dressing table with only Mionet and her guilty conscience for company. "He's going to be tired, and you know he doesn't like Segoile nonsense, and he already said no..."

"I think he has seen too much of the unpleasant parts of Segoile," Mionet told her, brushing Ophele's hair in long strokes. Ophele wore a new robe of shining blue satin, belted very securely about her trim waist. "I know you are both worried about going, my lady, and I will help as best I can, but that will include attempting to make the trip *enjoyable*. There is the possibility that you both might do more than grit your teeth and endure it."

She had been saying that for two months now. Painting pictures of the fascinating people Ophele would meet, the beautiful places they would go, the endless shopping excursions for objects Ophele had never heard of. It did sound very nice, a comforting counterpoint to Ophele's worries and Remin's abject loathing of the whole exercise. It would be good to distract him from all of it for a night, wouldn't it?

"It really looks all right?" she asked, looking at her reflection as Mionet clipped pearl earrings into place. "I've never..."

"It is lovely," Mionet promised her, rising with such assurance that Ophele felt a pang of envy. Of course, *she* would never be afraid to wear something like this. Mionet was perfect, tall and confident and beautiful. But Ophele had seen Lady Hurrell play tricks just like this, cruel pranks that her victims had *not* enjoyed, and what if there was something wrong with these clothes after all? What if it was like the prostitute thing again? She didn't know, and there was no one she could ask, and she folded her hands tightly together in her lap.

"You would not...let me look a fool in front of Remin?" she finally asked, forcing the words out with a wooden tongue. It was an unworthy thought, but Ophele knew what she looked like. She and Lisabe were of an age, and Ophele had always suffered in comparison to her foster sister, scrawny and ill-favored, barely a woman at all.

Mionet's hand paused in her brushing, her red eyebrows lifting.

"I don't know if I...look right," Ophele said, low. "In something like this..."

"You look perfectly lovely," Mionet replied, sounding surprised. "Whyever would you say that? There's nothing wrong with—ah. I see."

For a moment, her lips tightened.

"My lady, there will always be people who try to make you feel ugly. The charge comes first, and *then* they find the evidence. The greatest beauty in the capital could pass them in the street, and if she is tall, then she is too tall, and if slender, then she is bony, and if she is ravishing in every way, why then, she has the wits of a turnip. If someone wishes to be hateful, they will find an excuse."

Gently, Mionet nudged Ophele's chin upward, turning her face toward the mirror.

"Every woman has parts of herself that she loves, and parts of herself that she hides," she began, meeting Ophele's eyes. "Your beauty is a story you choose to tell the world. For you, it is this heart-shaped face, these splendid eyes, these darling little hands and feet. And perhaps it is not these lips, which are a little small. You must know where your own beauty lies. Do you see it?"

Ophele looked.

Mionet had not made her into a stranger. That was her, with a rosy pout to her small mouth that made it look lush. Her large eyes glowed in the candlelight, her lashes dark, thick, and mysterious. And around that heart-shaped face, her long hair curled in a glossy frame, maple-warm beside the cream of her skin.

Ophele met her own golden eyes, and color flushed her cheeks.

"When you feel beautiful, it shows in your face," said Mionet softly. "You should feel proud when you succeed. You are the best version of yourself. And you are making the whole world more beautiful for His Grace."

Oh, she hoped so. She hoped she would please him. He wouldn't admit it, but she knew he was very worried, and hardly sleeping at all, and even aside from all this business of surprises and strange costumes, she wanted him to forget his troubles. For one night, she hoped he would have sweet dreams.

Once Mionet bid her goodnight, Ophele was alone, seated by the fire and retaining absolutely nothing from the eighth volume of the Imperial Code in her lap. It was an age before she heard

Remin's heavy tread in the corridor, and she looked up as the lock clicked loudly.

"Wife," he said, locking it shut and stooping to kiss her hello. "You don't have to wait up for me."

"I wasn't tired," she answered. "Have you eaten?"

"I had a bit." He set a thick sheaf of paper on the table and began shedding his many layers of clothing on the way back to his dressing room. "But if you kept something back, I wouldn't say no. Stars, I thought we'd be there 'til morning."

"What were you talking about?" It seemed rude not to ask, but she didn't expect more than a vague answer. Ophele went to fetch a heavy earthenware crock from the hearth, where mutton and potatoes had been warming.

"Planning the spring planting," he answered. There were distant thumps as he shed his boots. "We've a great deal more people to feed than we anticipated. We can order additional supplies, but I'd like us to be self-sufficient as soon as possible..."

It was so comforting to hear his voice moving from dressing room to bath chamber and back again, washing up after the long day and hunting for his plainest and most comfortable robe. Ophele knew without looking that his dressing room would be a shambles by the time he was done, which was just the way Magne liked it. The valet enjoyed nothing more than wagging his head and clicking his tongue as he restored order to the world, and Remin was just the man to disarrange it for him.

"What did you do today?" Remin asked, sitting down to devour his snack in huge mouthfuls, washed down with warm wine.

"I had lessons with Master Forgess this afternoon. He said if I wanted more anatomy, then we would have to go to the To...Tower." Ophele could have bitten her tongue. She wasn't supposed to bring that up until *after*. "And we talked about the cataloguing of beasts, and how the connections between them are much clearer in the Empire than elsewhere..."

Fortunately, Remin was dividing his attention between her and his food, and his mouth was too full for any substantial response. Ophele babbled on, wondering when she ought to spring her surprise on him and feeling as if butterflies were battering wildly at her insides. Once he had settled in his chair by the fire, she took a sip of wine, made a face, and then went to confront him.

"I also...got new clothes from Master Tiffen today," she began, coming to a stop before him. Her fingers fiddled with the sash of her robe.

"I like them," Remin said immediately. "The robe?"

"Yes, and..." Ophele looked down, heat rising in her cheeks, and tugged her sash free.

The robe parted.

There was lace.

There was *only* lace.

She had hardly dared to look at herself in the scandalous thing, and she had certainly not allowed anyone else to see her. The lace nightgown ruffled apart over her thighs to expose her slender legs and wrapped tight around her middle, plunging between her breasts to reveal their inner curves. The darker pink of her nipples was clearly visible through the sheer lace. It was worse than being naked.

Remin's mouth fell open.

"Mionet said ladies in the capital wear such things," Ophele managed, feeling heat blaze to her forehead. "For their husbands, as a, a surprise..."

"Let me see," he said thickly. There was a strange, heated glow in his black eyes as he drew her between his knees.

"I thought you would like it," she breathed, flushing as she saw the evidence of exactly how *much* he liked it. His hands smoothed over her body, tracing the curves of her hips, watching the lace shift over her skin. The nightgown parted shamefully, long cuts over her thighs that slid open to expose smooth, silky skin.

"I do," Remin whispered. His palms slid up the backs of her thighs to squeeze her backside. "I do like it. Tiffen made this? He knew it was for you?"

"Yes? He took my measurem—mmph!" Ophele squealed as he snatched her up and headed for the bed, his hands wrapping her thighs tight around his hips, his mouth crushing hers in a hungry kiss. The quick, hard grind of his body against hers made her gasp as he flung her onto the bed.

"He shouldn't see you like this." Remin's tall shadow stretched over her, his breath harsh. He wasn't angry. That was something else entirely in his face. "You're *my* wife."

"Yes," Ophele agreed breathlessly. Her chin tipped back as he climbed above her with a muscular grace that made her heart stutter, sliding her arms over her head and pinning her wrists with one hand.

"Look at you," he rasped. "Don't move."

Just the weight of his eyes made her nipples tighten. Ophele's chest hitched as he cupped her breast, watching the lace move over her soft curves. And then he bent to close his mouth over one pink peak, his tongue moving in a lewd red roil that made her mind haze. She couldn't move, she couldn't breathe, she was so excited it was almost painful.

Lower. He kissed her navel. Traced the gentle swell of her hips. His hands stroked her curves, sliding her legs apart, his stubble rasping as he nipped the inside of her knees. And then they both went still as he slowly slid the lace upward, so it framed the naked space between her thighs.

Remin's eyes lifted to hers.

"Miche told me something once," he began. "I thought he was lying..."

He licked his lips, clearly uncertain at the prospect. But then he bent his head again, pressed her thighs apart, and *licked her between her legs.*

Ophele's eyes nearly rolled back in her head.

"B-but we can't," she gasped, feeling certain that somehow this must be against the law.

"Who says?" he asked, excitement purring through his voice. He licked again, his dark eyes riveted on her face. "Do you like it, wife?"

"I—I don't know...*ohhh, OH!*" She grabbed for his hair as his tongue stroked inside her, drawing the heat and wet in a sudden scorching surge, so very different from his fingers. Licking, lipping, thrusting with his tongue, his hands pinning her in place as she writhed.

"You *do* like it," he said, pleased, and when he flicked that sensitive nub between her legs, Ophele almost came off the mattress.

"Oh—oh, *stars!*" she gasped, her hips bucking, which only pressed her harder against his merciless mouth.

He wouldn't stop. He was always single-minded in his pursuit of her pleasure, but it had never been this maddening, this overwhelming, this thrilling helplessness, like her body wasn't her own. Even as her legs shook and her body arched taut, she could see Remin's eyes gleam, and his long fingers slipped inside her, curling up to rub mercilessly.

"Remin, *please—*" she began, maybe a protest, maybe a plea, but then his lips closed on that throbbing bud and sucked taut and the whole word detonated in an explosion of pleasure that blasted every word from her mind. Arching, straining, blown into some elsewhere of incredible sensation, a place where time stopped and there was only him, only this.

She was still tingling to her toes when she heard Remin's voice, as if it came from another world.

"Wife, I need you, I can't wait," he panted, sprawling beside her and yanking the sash of his robe loose. "Move down, get on me. I want to watch you."

His hard length jerked against his abdomen as he lifted her above him, clumsy with eagerness.

"All right—wait," she managed, her hands catching on his belly for balance. "Let me—"

Seizing her waist, he thrust upward, filling her in one deep stroke.

"Oh—*oh!*" she cried, as his hands closed tight and he thrust upward again, his teeth bared in savage pleasure.

There was not much to watch. All she could do was hold on as he pinned her on him, his hips spanking into her backside, jarring her to her teeth. Wailing as he surged upward, deep and hot and filling her behind bearing, her heated skin stretched with him. His hands were all over her, his mouth biting and ravenous, down her arms and up her neck and she didn't know where she was or what was happening because it was happening everywhere all at once and it was so, so *good*—

Dimly, she realized he was coming, too. His head thrown back against the edge of the bed, the cords on his neck like iron cables as he cried out, deep, wordless noises of pleasure. Inside her, he surged up, a boiling lash as he dragged her hips against his in grinding surges.

Ophele sprawled over his chest, boneless. Her ears were ringing.

"That...was good," he rasped finally. His fingers nudged her chin, turning her face up to his. His eyes were filled with wonder. "I never knew you could look so..."

His thumb traced the soft, swollen curve of her lower lip.

"Stars," he whispered, and kissed her again.

Ophele could not have moved if devils burst through the doors. She was utterly limp as he rolled her over again, murmuring and caressing, working his way up her lace-covered arms in sharp, scorching kisses. Only the jangling of a distant memory made her lift her head.

"Tower," she mumbled. "The Tower—Remin, about the Tower. When we go to the capital. We really can't see them?"

Remin sighed.

"I know it's important to you," he murmured. "But it will complicate things, if we let them test you and announce to everyone that you're a genius, wife. We don't want anyone thinking that you're dangerous."

"Couldn't I just be a mathematical genius?" Ophele gathered her wits and lifted her head. "We could say I didn't have anything to do but read books, and it's true..."

His hand ran lightly up and down her back, thinking.

"I'll talk to Juste," he said, bending his head to tease her lips with his own. "Maybe there's a way it could be done."

Ophele submitted to his kiss, feeling both pleased and guilty. It felt a little like tricking him, to ask him this way. Troubled, she wrapped her arms around his neck, and was surprised when he nudged her gently backward, his fingers trailing upward between her exposed breasts.

"My wife," he rumbled, like the warning tremors of an avalanche. That heated glow was back in his eyes, the one that made her blush and squirm and want to be touched.

"You're...you're not too tired?" she whispered.

"Oh, no," he assured her, his big hands cupping her backside and pushing her down so she could feel him stirring anew. "Not at all."

* * *

"Wife, do you want breakfast?" Remin asked the lump in the bed the next morning as he pulled on his robe. The lace nightgown lay halfway under the bed, in tatters.

The lump mumbled something that sounded like *yes, please.*

She sprawled on the mattress just as he had left her last night, too worn out even to turn on her side, and Remin felt a little guilty as he sat beside her. Her hair was an explosive tangle around her head and red and purple blotches marched the length of both arms. It made him feel foolish, in the light of day, but the way the lace had looked against her skin, he had just wanted to *bite* her...

"I'll bring it to you," he said, kissing the top of her head. He felt excellent, himself. A bit sore, but pleasantly satiated in the most wonderful way, and he couldn't help bending down to whisper, "do you think you would want to get another nightgown like that?"

One eye opened and rolled up to his face, round with alarm.

"Go back to sleep," he said, pulling the blankets over her shoulders, and went to see if there was any more of Genon's tonic about. Maybe he had overdone it a little.

Looking at her over breakfast, it was hard to imagine a more harmless creature in the world. Ophele looked absolutely tiny in their massive bed, a slender woman with love-bites marking her creamy skin. Even though he had let her sleep for another hour before he woke her for breakfast, she was nodding over her porridge, and at length Remin took the bowl away, poured some of Genon's tonic down her throat, and went to tell Lady Verr to let her sleep for a few more hours.

"Her Grace isn't ill, I hope?" Lady Verr asked, looking concerned.

"No. Just...tired," Remin replied vaguely, and departed with her gray eyes reproaching him for an utter beast.

Harmless. That was what Juste said Ophele must be. And if this was all they saw of her in Segoile, the vulnerable waif with eyes that wrung his heart, then Remin thought Juste was likely right; Ophele would be a powerful weapon. Even the cynical people of Segoile would never dream of the ferocious intellect working behind those eyes.

Half the time, he forgot it himself.

"Will Jinmin be back in time for our supper?" Ophele wanted to know that night, busy with the plans for the small banquet with his knights. It was the first formal occasion that he had left entirely in her hands.

"I shouldn't think so," Remin replied regretfully. And then something prodded him to ask, "What do you think Jinmin might be doing, wife?"

Even though they were alone in their bedchamber and the door was closed, she started and looked around reflexively, as if someone might be listening.

"I...well, you said he was working on building ports downriver," she said slowly. "I guess...it doesn't seem like work you would assign to him. I think he's working on defenses on the river. In case there's trouble?"

It was closer to the truth than he had expected. She would never dream that her husband was planning to make war on the Empire, and Remin hoped it would stay that way. He kissed her forehead.

"Why do you think that?" he asked tenderly, and listened as she laid out her observations for him, marveling at how much she saw and thought. He knew she needed a real teacher, but listening to her talk underscored exactly how much.

There would be other opportunities to visit the Tower. Both Master Forgess and Brother Oleare were willing to petition them on Ophele's behalf, to send for someone to evaluate her. But inwardly, Remin admitted he wanted to see her acknowledged for her own sake. He wanted the Tower to fawn over her. *He* didn't like the idea of presenting her to Segoile as the Exile Princess, an object of pity and curiosity. He wanted all of them to know how extraordinary she was.

And he wanted to rub her father's face in it.

"The trouble isn't what she knows or doesn't know," Juste said when Remin broached the subject in the stables the following evening. "The trouble is concealing it. Her Grace misses very little, when she is paying attention. But she is easily distracted and a very poor liar."

"Then we can do it last," Remin replied stubbornly. "Once our business in the capital is finished, they can make of her whatever they like."

"We won't be going back to the capital for a while anyway," Miche agreed, moving unobtrusively to support Juste as he dismounted. It was tricky with one arm.

The three men were accustomed to riding home together at the end of the day, and as warhorses would not accept handling from anyone but their masters, it gave them a few minutes for conversation while they were unsaddling and grooming the beasts. Fetching a hoof pick, Remin nudged Lancer's inquiring nose out of the way and bent to tend his hooves.

"I could go with her for the examination, I suppose," Juste said thoughtfully. "Normally it is a private interview, but they will make an exception for the Exile Princess. I will write a few letters tonight."

"You mean you will dictate them," Miche corrected, peering over his horse's shoulder. Blond, gallant Miche had a white horse, because of course he did. "I saw the stack of orders you sent off this morning. You need to save your arm for better things than correspondence, Juste."

"If I chose a secretary, it would not be you," Juste retorted.

"I would want me for a secretary," Miche replied seriously. "Perhaps that is my destiny. Somewhere in the capital is a rich widow crying out for a man of many talents."

"Just the one widow?" Remin asked dryly. "I'll take whatever orders you can send my way, Juste."

Miche already had too much to do. Because he never laid claim to any large patch of Tresingale's operations, he always ended up with dozens of little ones, and never uttered a word of complaint, even when he really ought to. Tounot and Auber had both reported finding him asleep in strange places, a warning sign that he was stretched too thin.

"I'll make sure he does." Miche waved a hand before Remin could argue. "I'm fine, Rem. Don't worry about me."

Remin shot Juste a look nonetheless as they parted, a silent command to see exactly how out of control Miche's workload had gotten. All of them were overburdened. With Edemir, Bram, and Jinmin away on their errands and over seven hundred extra people in town, there was enough work for a dozen Knights of the Brede. But there was no help for it.

Supplies were another problem. Grain cost the earth in February, but Remin seized the excuse of all those extra mouths to order it in vast quantities, to feed the refugees and his army, should they need to march. Juste had even suggested leaving early for the capital; the hundred or so people Remin brought with him would make a real difference to their storehouse. But Remin would not neglect Tresingale. The Duke of Andelin would be present for every one of the spring rituals, and the Emperor could go hang if he didn't like it.

This foolishness in Segoile was a distraction for a season. Tresingale would be the work of his life.

"Come and sit with me," he told Ophele one night after supper, taking his seat at the table in their bedchamber rather than his comfortable chair by the fire. "Juste isn't the only one with things to teach you."

"You're going to give me lessons too?" she asked, sitting on the other side of the table and scooting her chair forward.

Truthfully, he would rather not. At least not on this subject. Remin's mouth tightened as his quill slashed rapidly over a page, wondering for the hundredth time how to present this to her in a way that wouldn't frighten her or make her anxious. Miche had bluntly pointed out that keeping her ignorant was the opposite of protecting her.

"A few," he answered, frowning. "Leonin and Davi want you to come to our practices, so the three of you can get used to moving together. Practice swords only," he added grimly. He did not like this idea, but it was hard to argue that it was preferable to letting them figure it out while someone was trying to abduct Ophele.

"Oh, will you be trying to snatch me away from them?" she asked interestedly. "That could be fun. Am I allowed to climb?"

"It's not a game," he said, trying to sound stern, though the memory of their chase through the hazelnut grove made his lips twitch. He'd forgotten that; she was very quick on her feet. But the thought that she might *have* to be killed any real pleasure in the exercise. He was silent as he finished writing, and then pushed the paper to her.

"Usually, I'd have you copy this over a few times every night, and burn the copies," he said. "Let's see how well you can memorize it now."

She took it, rapidly skimming the page. It contained two columns of coded phrases and their translations.

I am well: I am writing this message voluntarily.

I am well enough: I am being forced to write this message.

They are looking after me well: Kill the bearer of this message.

Her eyes lifted to his.

"You think...I might need to know this, when we go to the capital?" she asked, and he saw the pulse beating faster in her slender throat.

"I hope you will not," he said levelly. "We are taking great pains to ensure it. But we always plan for the worst. That's all this is, wife."

"I know that," she said softly, looking again at the page. "You have to think of the worst thing..."

Her lips pressed together and she read it again. There were more than three dozen coded phrases, many of them repetitive and necessarily simple and vague, easy to embed in a longer letter. For ten minutes, she read and reread it in silence, and then handed the paper back to him.

"When you use these, you have to make it look natural," he told her. "If you think there's any risk that they might notice something odd, err on the side of caution. If they think there is code in your letter, they won't let you send it. A little information is better than none."

She nodded, filing this away in the vault of her memory.

"They are looking after me well," he prompted.

"Kill the bearer of this message," she said steadily.

"I have been sleeping well."

"They are keeping me in a place without windows."

Unsurprisingly, she had memorized all of them. Remin rose and thrust the paper into the fire. He would quiz her every night, from now until they went to Segoile.

"There are many things I haven't told you, and that I don't mean to tell you," he said, taking his seat. "You're not a good liar, and I don't expect you to become one in the space of a few months. But there are some things you have to know now. You remember I mentioned that I have guards of my own?"

She nodded solemnly.

"The old man got them for me when I was twelve," Remin explained. "I won't tell you who they are. They're not meant to be noticed. They are concealed somewhere nearby, and only a few men know who they are. It's harder to bribe or threaten them, if no one knows they're there."

That had happened to a few of his early guards. To their credit, none of them had betrayed him, but some of them had paid dearly for their loyalty.

"There will be many more of them, positioned about the city," he went on. "Even in Starfall. If they must, they will identify themselves to you by saying, *seven ravens roosting*. Don't think too much about it," he added, as the gears in her mind visibly whirred to life. "Don't try to figure this puzzle out. It's better if you don't know."

"All right," she agreed. "You really have guards all the time?"

"Yes."

"I'm glad," she said, and bent obediently over the next paper he presented to her.

There was so much to teach her. Maps of the capital, with safe houses and meeting places marked, though she had only seen one city in her whole life and the thought of her attempting to navigate Segoile by herself made his heart palpitate. It was his intention that she should never be separated from him, much less parted from Leonin and Davi, but he would prepare her as best he could. Lady Verr taught her about the finer parts of the city, the safe places with guards, frequented by nobles. Remin told her about the parts of the city she should avoid, and what to do if she ever found herself in them.

It infuriated him that she had to know this. That the bastard Emperor was forcing this upon them. Every night after these lessons, he looked into her eyes and worried that he might make her afraid, might make her anxious, might be teaching her that the world was an ugly place when he still believed it could be beautiful, if only they were let alone to make it so.

And finally, he told her about House Hurrell.

He did it while they were already at the table together and halfway through their study of the Wold, maybe in the hope that he could make it seem a part of the lesson. *On this street we have a safe house, and two blocks that way, House Hurrell has their new manse.*

"Edemir said they arrived a month ago," Remin said, covering both her hands with one of his own. "They must have received a pardon from the Emperor. Which means he has some use for them."

"They had to go somewhere." She tried to smile, but it wilted around the edges. "I did...wonder."

"Can you guess what they might know, or why he might have pardoned them?" Remin didn't have much hope for either.

"No. I did try to think of it, ever since you took me," she admitted, and looked up at him guiltily. "I didn't tell you. I should have told you. Lady Hurrell said...she said, if I didn't obey her, then she would tell everyone that I tried to run away from you. She said she would spread it all over the Empire. She said..."

Her slim shoulders hunched.

"She knew what my mother did," she whispered. "That day, when we left Aldeburke, she told me she would tell you if I didn't do what she said, and you would...kill me."

He was so appalled, for a moment he couldn't speak.

"No," he managed, and rose immediately, dismayed by the fear lurking in her eyes. "No, I would not. Ever. *Ever,"* he repeated, catching her shoulders in his hands and squeezing. “No matter what. You know that, don’t you?”

“Yes. I know,” she said, with a quivering sigh as he moved them both to his chair by the fire. “I should have told you, I’m sorry. I don’t know what she’ll do, but she’ll hurt us if she can. She wanted you to marry Lisabe.”

“Then I will continue to disappoint her,” Remin said firmly, and that was the end of lessons for that night.

These were not the things that he wanted to talk to her about. He *had* things he wanted to teach her, everything he had learned about how to lead and build and plan. He wanted to dream with her about their city. But now he had no choice but to let all the foulest things he knew pour out like poison.

He told her about poison. He taught her how to pretend to eat and drink–she was not very good at either–and explained how her food would be tested for poison and then tasted before her. As a daughter of the House of Agnephus, she had a right to demand proof that her food was clean.

He had an endless stream of cautions about how wine should taste, and how she should spit out anything if she felt the least bit suspicious, and also that she ought not linger near braziers, which might contain strange alchemical powders. If she ever saw or smelled smoke in a room, she was to instantly check the people around her to see if they were behaving strangely; incense might contain soporifics or intoxicants. And there were even worse things that he could not bring himself to tell her, powders with aphrodisiac properties, powders that...

Countless dangers, each one filthier than the last. Did he really have to tell her about *all* of them?

His lamb, whose innocence he wanted so badly to protect.

After these lessons, he took her to bed, where he tried to blot all these terrible thoughts from her mind, reassuring them both with the strength of his body. To prove that he could keep her safe. He *would*. No matter what it took.

Maybe he succeeded. After they made love, she curled up against him just as she always did and fell asleep, leaving him to look at her and wonder. Ophele always said she was fine. And he feared to even ask that question too often, lest simple, stupid repetition ruin all his efforts.

He wanted her to feel safe.

He never wanted her to feel the way he did.

He never wanted her to have nightmares like his.

At night, he lay awake in the dark and thought of all the worst things. Trying to tell himself that he was doing everything he could, and these dangers were in the future and might never materialize. It was necessary to think of them, and plan for them, but counterproductive to dwell on them.

The next morning, he woke to a knock on the door, and Auber's grim face on the other side.

"I'm sorry," Auber said without preamble. "I had to come get you. Someone tried to kill Wen."

Chapter 12 – A Taste of Poison

"I'm fine...I'm fine, didn't I tell ye I'm fine," mumbled Wen, one beefy arm flapping. "Just a...fucking scratch..."

It was not just a scratch.

Grimly, Remin watched as one of Genon's journeymen caught the waving arms and pinned them down, arms that were fishbelly white, hands that were still blue with cold. Wen had been lying in the snow for some time before they got him to the infirmary.

"If it's just a scratch, you can hold still while Gen closes it up." Remin stepped into the small room at the back of the infirmary, shutting the door behind him. Lying facedown on a narrow cot, Wen's tunic had been cut away over the massive expanse of his fat back, where blood pumped from multiple stab wounds.

It was anyone's guess how they had missed his heart, but Remin knew what Wen would say, with a mixture of pride and defiance: he was too fucking fat to stab.

"Hold him down, if you want to be useful," said Genon tersely, threading a fresh needle.

Obligingly, Remin nudged the journeyman aside and crouched down, whistling lightly through his teeth.

"Wen. Wen. Look at me," he said, and the cook's muddy eyes swam up to his. "You can sleep in a bit. Can you tell me what happened?"

"Dunno. Went for a piss," Wen said, the words emerging in staccato bursts. "After the bread...someone behind me. Hit me."

"Did you see them?" Remin squeezed his big, beefy hands. Wen had hands like a brawler.

"No. Fucker." His shoulders twitched, blood welling from the wounds on his back and streaming down his sides. "Didn't see...nothing."

"They didn't say anything?"

"No." He snarled through bloodless lips. "Tried to dr...dra—*agh,* fuck, stars and blazes, fuck! *Fuck you, Gen!*"

"Keep talking," Genon replied, tugging with thread and needle. "Finish your story and I'll give you some nice medicine."

"Tried to...drag me," Wen repeated, panting shallowly. His eyes rolled up. "Stupid...bastard..."

He wasn't going to make it to the nice medicine. Remin gripped those big hands as they went limp, and looked up to see that Genon had finally stopped the blood from pouring down his back. His breathing was shallow, but steady.

"He'll live," Genon said, answering the unspoken question. "So long as he doesn't suffocate himself, lying on his belly like this. One of the kitchen lads found him. Lucky it wasn't long before he went looking."

"That the boy with Auber?"

"Aye."

"Tell me if you need anything." Remin's voice was cold, but he was gentle as he arranged Wen's arms on the cot. He had known this would happen, sooner or later. It had happened before. It would happen again. And Wen was an obvious target.

Knowing that didn't make it any easier to control his own reaction. A spiral of useless thoughts and emotions, grief and fury and blackest hate for the fucking Emperor, who would *not leave him alone.* It made Remin want to push everyone away, send his guards off, make himself the bait and hope that the assassin would show himself. When he was younger, he had done exactly that, more than once.

It did no good. Assassins only came in their own time.

There was an order to these things. The note Juste had found in the barracks and the open window in the solar circled in the back of Remin's mind, but first he would eliminate the possibility that someone had tried to kill Wen for his own sake. It wasn't impossible; Wen was offensive all by himself.

But that theory was immediately obliterated by the boy who found the cook in the snow.

"Me and Jules got him, Your Grace," said the lad, a stocky boy of fifteen or so. "He didn't come back, so I went looking, and I saw the...the blood, and yelled for Jules..."

Perhaps that had saved the boy's life, if the killer was still close by. After that interview, Remin went to see the tracks in the snow himself, well-muddled with the high traffic between the kitchen and the storehouse. The essentials were clear. Around the corner of the woodpile, he could see the place where Wen had been stabbed, the sudden burst of red in the snow, the place in the snowbank where Wen had fallen, and the trail where someone had tried to drag him out of sight. This boy had interrupted them, and the murderer hadn't been willing to risk witnesses.

"Unlucky," said Juste, who had arrived quickly and begun investigating in his own way. "They should have cut his throat, if they wanted to be sure. Trying to drag a man Wen's size?"

"Did they mean to search him?" Remin wondered, his brow knotting. It was the only reason he could think why they would have tried to drag the vast cook out of sight.

"If they did, they didn't find what they wanted." Auber dangled Wen's heavy key ring from his fingers. "I checked."

That was the only good news of the morning. Whether they wanted the keys or Wen himself, they succeeded in their goal: removing a barrier between Remin and poison.

Leaving Auber to oversee the kitchen, Remin went to search for other witnesses with Juste and Miche. The odds of finding any weren't good. The secretaries who slept in cottages behind the storehouse had seen nothing, and neither had the Benkki Desans, whose *talimaru,* a small compound of houses and gardens, was only a short distance away.

"No, noble lord," said Master Balad. Though it was barely dawn, he was already up and on his way to the baths, with his head freshly shaved and his iron-shod staff in hand. "We heard something happened."

"News travels fast," Miche observed sourly.

"I think Imari heard it herself," Master Balad offered, apologetic. "I will get her."

Remin had almost forgotten Madam Sanai's first name until she appeared a moment later, her face flushed as if from exercise.

"I heard shouting," she said, her eyes widening. "I thought it was just Master Wen, we hear sometimes. Noble lord, please forgive, I never thought—"

"Nor should you," Remin replied gruffly. He didn't want his people to hear shouts and immediately assume someone was being murdered. But along with his guilt and fury was the familiar *embarrassment,* that he was the cause of this. The Emperor's loathing had been a plague on him all his life, striking down innocent people all around him.

"Please ask among the others," Juste told them, looking from Madam Sanai to Master Balad. "It would be a great help if you could remind them to watch carefully for anything strange."

"We will, noble knight," Madam Sanai promised, and both Benkki Desans bowed them out of the compound.

"If you don't mind, I'll go poke around myself," Miche said as they mounted their horses. "People might be nervous to speak with their lord asking them directly."

“Are you thinking of anyone in particular?” Remin asked, glancing at him sidelong.

“No. I wish.” Miche gave him a crooked smile. “The stars made me charming, Rem, let me see what I can make of it. Juste—”

“We will collect Auber on the way to the barracks,” Juste promised. Remin’s men would take no chances of his safety today, and Juste’s shoulder was not healed enough to make him a fit bodyguard.

Remin didn’t want bodyguards. As they rode around the bend of Eugene Street, his eyes went to the manor on its hilltop, the windows of his bedchamber visible even from the road. He had dragged Leonin and Davi out of bed and ordered them not to leave Ophele alone for even a moment, but he was sick at the thought that danger could come so close to her. That note. The open window. And now the man that cooked her food.

He knew, he had *known* that with so many people coming into Tresingale, it was inevitable that the Emperor’s servants would be among them. But it made him *furious* to think of the people he knew and wonder which of them might be a liar, a betrayer, a murderer. Was it one of the craftsmen? One of the refugees from his villages? One of the people he had allowed to come across the river, one of those people from the Empire who had come to the Andelin Valley against his wishes, who he had forgiven, and welcomed into his lands?

One person? More than one?

Someone Ophele had invited into his home?

“Your Grace,” Juste said gently. “Anger will not help.”

Both he and Auber were looking at Remin, their eyes filled with compassion. And he was right, but it was a long time before Remin could even bring himself to speak. There was nothing he could hit, no one he could shout at, no enemy he could fight.

“I am wondering if we ought to bother trying to stop the rumors,” he said, his voice crushed flat with the effort of controlling himself. “I expect it’s already too late to keep it quiet.”

"I think that ship has sailed," Auber agreed. "Too many people heard the racket by the cookhouse."

"I would discourage trying," Juste advised. "Whoever attacked Wen knows they failed. It might even be best to spread the word, to have as many eyes watching as possible. It will make further attempts more difficult."

"Do you think that's what Miche is doing?" Remin said a moment later, in tones of revelation, and Juste gave a rare bark of laughter.

"It would not surprise me."

That was one bright spot in a day that was otherwise infuriatingly like any other. Remin could hardly go about interrogating people himself; it would be counterproductive and dangerous, and not only to him. Too often, it was the people around him that suffered. Every one of his knights had scars from some attempt on his life, where they had given their bodies in place of his own.

Instead, Remin left the matter to Juste and went to the practice yards, burning off his fury so he could at least try to work. This was how it was, with assassins. The attempt on Wen's life didn't change anything. Perhaps they would get lucky and find witnesses, clues, but every single day of his life, Remin knew someone might come for him. And someone else might be hurt because of him.

And there was nothing he could do but wait for it to happen.

It was midafternoon when Juste appeared, bringing one small, anxious witness.

"Tell His Grace what you told me," Juste instructed, as Remin crouched down in front of the boy and reminded himself not to glare.

"I saw a man in the hideout once," said eight-year-old Valentin, looking from Juste to Remin, worried. "Was he a bad man? I didn't know."

"What's the hideout?" asked Remin.

"We have a fort, but we can't go there when it's cold, and a tree fell on it anyway," Valentin explained. "Back there, behind the big practice yard? We cut the bushes all up in summer, we used to hide from Barnabe there, he got so mad. But one day, I went there, and there was a man and he said wasn't I supposed to be with the other boys, and I said this was our secret fort and he said he wouldn't say anything if I didn't. And so I didn't," he confessed, with tears filling his big brown eyes. "Was he the bad man that hurt Mr. Wen?"

"We don't know, but it's good you're telling us now," Remin said, squeezing the boy's shoulder and giving him a little shake. "Do you remember what he looked like?"

It might be nothing. A soldier wandering into the trees for a break, playing hooky just as Valentin had. And the man Valentin described could have been one of hundreds in the valley: shorter than Juste but taller than Jacot, dark hair, plain clothes, and no visible scars or tattoos. The man had been in their fort back in autumn, before it got too cold for the boys to be sneaking off outside.

"He won't hurt Her Grace, will he?" Valentin asked miserably, after he had completed this description.

"No one will," Remin promised. "You did a good job, Valentin. Keep your eyes open and tell me if you see anything else."

"I will, Your Grace," he promised, his face filled with boyish determination.

Juste departed with the child in tow and a promise to see what the other boys might know. And while there was no reason for *Remin* to question Valentin—Juste could have done so easily, and he would be the one to investigate anyway—it was a little easier to concentrate, when he was gone.

There was still plenty of other work to do. Orders to be issued. Practice with Leonin and Davi, who left Tounot to guard Ophele for a few hours. The hunt for an assassin did not mean everything else stopped. It just added one more item to the list.

It was a very late night and Remin had nothing to show for the day but a headache when he finally came home, inspecting the faces of every guard on the way in and taking comfort in the massive Rendevan locks on his doors. No one could come in without his hearing it. He had guards inside and outside his home, and he knew every one of them personally. His windows were twenty-three feet off the ground.

They were safe. They were safe. They were safe.

His stomach was tied in knots.

"Wife," he said as he entered the bedchamber, looking automatically to Davi and Leonin, seated beside her by the fire.

"Remin." She rose at once to come to him, her eyes anxious. "Did you find anything? Is everyone all right? Tounot said Wen was hurt."

"Everyone's fine," Remin soothed, cupping her cheek gently. "Davi, Leonin, give me a few minutes to get settled and then we'll lock up."

"Of course, my lord," Leonin replied.

Remin would not leave Ophele alone even for the length of time it took him to wash up and change for bed. It was only when he was certain they would need nothing else for the night that he thanked the guards and locked the doors, then picked up his wife and buried his face in her hair.

"What happened?" she whispered, her hands stroking his back. "No one would tell me anything. Someone really tried to kill Wen?"

"Yes." Remin was trying to keep his outright lies to a minimum. "Someone stabbed him. But it will be all right," he added quickly. "Wen will be fine in a while, and no one else was hurt. These things...happen, sometimes."

"Because of my father," she said, pushing back against his chest to look at him. "He's trying to get to you, isn't he?"

"Maybe. It's fine." Remin set her down and sat in his chair, rubbing his head. "Well, not fine, but it's not the first time and it won't be the last. I don't blame you, little owl. It's nothing to do with you at all."

"Just my *father,*" she repeated savagely. "Whoever it was, they're here because he ordered it, aren't they?"

"Probably."

"Didn't anyone see anything?" She filled a kettle and set it over the fire with sharp, angry motions. "Did Wen hear anything?"

"No. No, it's all right, I don't want anything," Remin added, waving away the supper she had saved for him. He couldn't blame her for asking, but he did not want to talk about this. He should have thrown Juste in the door first to take the worst of the mauling.

"What if we tried to trap them somehow?" she wanted to know. "Could we lure them out? If we made it look like you were unguarded..."

She had read far too many books.

"It doesn't work that way," he answered, trying to be patient. "Don't worry. In some ways it's good to see where they struck, and who; it gives us a gauge of their capabilities. They've probably been watching us for a while, looking for an opportunity, and we're doing well if this is the best one they found. And it's not just because it's me, every duchy in the Empire probably has a few of his spies..."

But the harder he tried to reassure her, the angrier she became.

"So there's nothing we can do?" she demanded, furious. "They stabbed Wen! Because they want to kill you!"

Remin's jaw tightened. It was on the tip of his tongue to snap that Wen was not the first and would not be the last. And no, there was nothing to be done, there was nothing anyone *could* do but pray with all their might that the fucking bastard in Starfall dropped dead sooner rather than later, but he had promised himself he would not insult her parents before her. He didn't want her to be angry or frightened or anxious. Genon had said more than once that Remin should try to keep her calm and happy if they wanted to make a child together.

It took a massive effort to shut all of that down, to shove it all away somewhere to be dealt with later. But there had been days worse than this. For right now, this moment, she was with him and the doors were locked. They were safe.

"Ophele," he said gently. "Let's leave it alone. Come here and tell me about your day."

"I had lessons," she said, sulking. "Do you want tea?"

"I don't want anything but you," he replied, holding out a hand to her. "Come and warm me up."

This rarely failed to draw her out. And it was true, too; Ophele was always warm, a soft and wonderful little bundle of heat that Remin huddled around like a small flame. For a while it was good to wrap himself around her and listen to her talk about her day, and eventually she was calm enough to let him kiss her. Closing his eyes, Remin bent his head, trying to make himself feel it. Feel her, and nothing else.

"Remin," she whispered, turning her body into his. For the first time, her touch did not rouse him.

"Wife," he whispered back. Rising, he carried her to their bed, forcing himself to focus on the feel of her mouth, the soft and gliding caress of her tongue. Laying her on the bed, he moved over her, tugging her robe open.

He really did not want to do this. All he wanted to do was go to sleep and hope there were no dreams. But someone had come to Tresingale to kill him, and he had come too far to fail at the last moment. He must make an heir. He was the last of his blood, and he owed it to all his murdered family to ensure that their line did not die with him.

He must make a child.

Once he had done that, it wouldn't matter if an assassin finally got past his guards.

* * *

"My lady, I don't know if we ought to..." Davi began for at least the eighth time that morning as Ophele pulled up the hood of her cloak and stepped into the icy air.

"Did His Grace tell you to keep me locked in the solar forever?" Ophele was feeling a trifle belligerent.

"There is a difference between knowing an assassin *may* be there and knowing they are *certainly* there, my lady," Leonin pointed out as both men strode after her, their boots crunching through five fresh inches of snow.

"That is why you are with me. We will see them coming for a mile, with all this snow," she replied stubbornly. She had been pent up in the house for three days and had hardly seen Remin or any of his knights, and all anyone would say was that everything was fine and how could that *possibly* be true?

It took a great deal of bullying to get Leonin and Davi to saddle her horse, but soon enough they were on their way to the infirmary in a light snowfall, with flakes so small they seemed to hover in midair. They had dissuaded her from visiting twice already, but her worries for Remin aside, she wanted to see Wen for his own sake.

"Only for a little bit," Genon said grudgingly, when she presented herself in the infirmary and politely demanded to see the irascible cook. "I don't know that you'll get much sense from him..."

"That's all right," she said, trying to sound brave as she marched to the small room at the back of the long aisle of beds.

But it was something else when she reached the door, and Ophele had to nerve herself to knock and poke her head inside, half curious and half afraid of what she might see. Remin had told her Wen was stabbed more than once, and she could only hope it wouldn't be too horrid.

"Wen?" she asked hesitantly, entering on tiptoe. The huge cook was lying face down on a cot, his head angled to one side and his back swathed in bandages that only showed little bits of pink.

His big, rubbery mouth was partly open as he snored. Glancing at Davi, Ophele crouched down in front of the cot and prodded the cook experimentally. "Wen?"

He gave a snort.

"Master Wen?" Ophele gripped her knees nervously and scooted forward on her toes. He had freckles on his cheeks. She had never noticed that before. "Master Wen, could you—"

Looking at all those bandages, she felt guilty. He might have died, and here she was bothering him about supper. But just as she was about to retreat, he snorted, blinked, and glared at her.

She almost fell over on her backside.

"Your...Grace?" he slurred, and twitched as if he meant to rise.

"No, don't get up," she said quickly, patting his shoulders. "It's all right, Wen, I just—I just came to see you. Are you badly hurt?"

"Been stabbed a few times," he grumbled, licking his lips and turning his head to squint at Leonin and Davi. "Come to...visit me?"

"Yes. Oh, I am so sorry," she said, forgetting every word of the little speech she had planned. "I'm so sorry you were hurt. They told me you were all right, but I wanted to see...oh, and I brought you something," she added, fishing it out of a pocket. "I read that I ought to bring flowers to someone who's sick, but there aren't any, and Isilde showed me how to make sachets..."

She extended the little bundle of silk, a sachet inexpertly embroidered with lavender, calendula, and roses on the outside.

"For me?" Wen dangled the object between his fingers, scowling. "It smells."

"It's meant to smell nice," she explained. He didn't seem to like it very much. "It has lavender and ginger and other things. I thought...it all just smells like medicine here. But you don't have to keep it if you don't like it."

"It's fine. It's mine," he grunted, closing his fingers over it as she moved to take it back.

"You look terrible," she said sympathetically. "Does it hurt very much?"

"Bit." Even with his eyes half-closed, one corner of his mouth twitched. "You come about...His Grace?"

"Yes." Ophele was too worried to lie. "He keeps skipping breakfast and coming home after supper and he won't touch any of the food I save for him."

"Aye." Wen gave a huge sigh and winced. "Got my keys?"

"What keys?"

"Storehouse."

"Oh." Ophele glanced back at Leonin, who nodded.

"Auber has them."

"Good. Room inside the storehouse," he began, and explained his methods for protecting Remin's food in slow, slurred sentence fragments, sometimes falling silent for so long that Ophele wondered whether he had fallen asleep or just passed out. It was dauntingly complicated. Wen was meticulous about every single stage of food preparation, from cleaning and sterilizing every surface and implement to cleaning and sterilizing the cook.

"Hair tied up. In a cap," he said, with a snort that somehow indicated his own bald head. "Turn out all pockets, cuffs, sleeves. Make 'em wash their hands. And make 'em drink," he said, glowering with his one visible eye. "Case they spit."

"They...spit?" Ophele repeated, with dawning realization and then swift fury. "Spit...*poison?* Into Remin's food?"

"Aye. Don't take your eyes off 'em for one minute," he said, and had to suck in a pained breath. "Not for...one second."

"I won't." She had been angrier more often in the last few days than she had been the rest of her life, and she didn't really know how to handle it, but it wasn't Wen's fault. *He* had done everything he could, and more. "I didn't know how hard it was," she said, reaching to squeeze his fingers firmly, though he had already sunk back into unconsciousness. "Thank you."

Being angry didn't help. And the slap of cold air as they went outside again cooled her a little, but she was still so furious she could hear a high-pitched singing in her ears, like the distant whistle of a teakettle. Wen had done nothing to deserve this, and neither had Remin, and it was her rotten father who was doing this to them when all they wanted was to build Tresingale and take care of their people. How could she make him *stop?*

That problem was too big for her to tackle in an afternoon. Remin had been looking for silver linings for days, so she would try to make the best of this. If this *had* to happen, then at least it was a chance to get him to try Azelma's cooking.

On reaching the kitchen, however, Azelma was dubious about the prospect.

"I don't know, my lady," she said, as she chopped rapidly through a pile of carrots. "I expect His Grace will be even pickier now."

Azelma had neatly moved into Wen's position, but if the long-suffering kitchen boys had hoped for an improvement in their lot, they were swiftly disappointed. Azelma had been tyrannizing over kitchen staff for forty years. A snap of her fingers instantly produced one boy, who disappeared with the carrots.

"Well, I spoke with Wen," Ophele began, laying out Wen's measures for securing Remin's food. "Auber said he has kept Wen's keys all this time, so no one can have gotten into the storeroom. If we test all the food, and clean everything like he said..."

"I suppose it can't hurt to try," Azelma said doubtfully.

"When we bring it up to the house, we can test it with silver in front of him, and then everyone will taste it, that's what he said they do in Segoile." Ophele had memorized every word of the precautions. "Then he can be sure it's safe. He promised he would come home for supper tonight."

"Then we'll see there's a supper on the table," the old lady promised. "But it won't hurt my feelings if he doesn't touch it, child. I can hardly blame him."

"We will all watch, so we can be sure it's safe," Ophele replied, filled with determination as she headed to the storehouse, where every single ingredient would be tested before it went to the kitchen.

It was more nerve-wracking than she expected. Leonin and Davi insisted on doing the testing themselves, and even though she *knew* the room had been locked and they used the silver poison tester on the food, her stomach still gave an uncomfortable lurch as Davi dipped a finger into the flour, licked it, and made a face.

"Tastes like flour," he shrugged.

But he didn't drop dead over the course of the day, and three pairs of eyes watched Azelma through every moment of the preparations for a simple supper: mutton stew, parsnips, greens, and fresh white bread. Ophele even watched the sheep being slaughtered, which was just dreadful.

And even with all these precautions and assurances, it was still hard to face Remin that night.

"We watched Azelma make all of it," she explained, feeling inexplicably nervous as she looked up into Remin's opaque black eyes. "I thought, we could test it in front of you, and then taste it—"

"Not you," he said, looking over at Azelma. "You eat it."

"Of course, Your Grace," she replied, firming up her mouth. Azelma was a chef trained in the Imperial kitchens; she was accustomed to tasting her cooking. With four separate silver forks, she tasted each course, presenting them for his inspection with Leonin and Davi watching every move.

There were only five of them at supper. Ophele had apologetically asked Mionet not to come, judging that Remin would not appreciate company. Her guess was confirmed as he sat to the table in ominous silence, refusing Davi's offer to switch plates.

"I went to see Wen today," Ophele began, buttering a slice of bread and lifting it to her lips. "He was talk—"

"Wait." Remin spoke so sharply, it startled her, but his eyes were on the bread, not her. "We...haven't said the blessing."

It was an agonizing meal. No one else felt like talking, and Remin ate with a grim expression that was somehow different from his usual grim expression and responded to Ophele's attempts at conversation with monosyllables. His fork jabbed and lifted his food to his mouth as if every bite were a fresh-caught fish: raw, wriggling, and fighting to live.

Ophele couldn't help watching him from the corner of her eyes, and everyone else looked anywhere *but* in His Grace's direction.

"...and Master Forgess came at noon." Ophele soldiered on. She was learning the value of Mionet's lessons in making inoffensive and endless conversation. "He has been teaching me about taxonomy ..."

She very nearly resorted to listing off various classes of reptile before the interminable dinner was over. Everyone departed the instant they could and Ophele didn't even bother trying to keep any food back for later; it was enough that Remin had eaten *something,* without hiding it in the bread or stuffing it into the mashed parsnips. Surely it would get easier, once he got used to the idea of Azelma cooking his food.

"Do you want me to read to you?" she asked once the doors were shut and locked and the world shrank to the safe confines of the bedchamber, lit softly by candlelight. It was a relief to have him safe at home, where no one could hurt him.

He did. And a little while later, he took her to bed and moved in her with a different kind of hunger, taking her with hard, punishing strokes of his body. He had hardly finished filling her before he was rousing again, and took her with such passionate violence that Ophele dropped into sleep like she was falling into a pit.

And woke to an empty bed.

Still a little dazed, she sat up and pushed the heavy bed drapes out of the way. The fire had burned low, and the room was so cold, her breath puffed white as she slipped out of bed and fumbled about for slippers. It took a moment to realize that the hall door was open. It only led to their dressing rooms, privy, and bath chamber, but Remin never left *any* door open.

"Remin?" she called softly.

It was not a long search. The moment she stepped into the hallway, she heard a muffled noise that made her heart contract with terror.

"Remin!" she exclaimed, racing over to the privy and yanking on the door. "Remin, are you all right? Open the door!"

Again, the unmistakable sound of vomiting.

"Stay out," he said hoarsely. "Go back to bed."

"No! Are you sick? It can't be the food, I *checked!"* Her hands went to her mouth in horror as he threw up again. "Remin, let me in!"

"It's not poison," he rasped when he was done. "I'm...I'm just not feeling well, wife. It's fine. Go back to sleep, I'll be back soon."

"Stop telling me it's fine!" Tears filled her eyes. "Tell me the truth, oh, I'll go get Miche—"

"No." He sounded so miserable. "Don't bother him. It'll pass."

Ophele hesitated, torn.

"Then tell me what's wrong," she said. "You're not fine. This is not fine."

"I couldn't sleep," he finally admitted, low. "I had to...I know you were careful. I know it's not...poison."

But he didn't, really. He couldn't. She sank to the floor against the door, wrapping her arms around her knees as her tears silently overflowed.

"It really isn't," she said, scrubbing them away with the back of her hand. "I watched. We tasted every bit of it, and I'm not sick, and Davi tried it all hours and hours ago, he would..."

"I know," Remin said, and fell silent.

"Why did you eat it, then?"

"I didn't want to worry you." He paused, and she could hear him trying not to gag. "Go back to bed, wife. I don't want company for this."

If he didn't want to worry her, then he should stop trying to endure it all by himself. Ophele retreated to the door of the bedchamber and then hovered anxiously. From the sound of it, he was heaving up his toenails. She wouldn't want him to see her in such a state, either, but she couldn't just go back to bed.

Could she be *sure* it wasn't poison? Could someone have gotten to him after all? Ophele had imagined this, but in her daydreams it had always been distant and dramatic, a thing that could not *really* happen. She couldn't stop thinking of Davi offering to switch plates at supper, and remembering that moment when one of the kitchen boys had shouted and she had looked away from Azelma's busy hands.

At long last, the privy door creaked open. Ophele fled back to bed on silent feet and slipped between the covers, pulling them up to her ears. But it was a long time before she heard his heavy tread approaching and the loud *clunk* as he locked the door. On the other side of the bed drapes, she could hear him building up the fire, and then a chair creaked under his weight. A rustling of paper.

He did not come back to bed.

* * *

Someone had searched Mionet's cottage.

She had not been trained to notice such things, but there could be no other explanation. Shoe boxes slightly out of order. Ink bottles just a few inches from their usual position on her desk. The ribbon in her address book marking the wrong page. It was more alarming than an outright robbery.

It meant she was suspected.

By who?

Of what?

Had *everyone* been searched? It wouldn't have surprised her, if that were the case; the attack on the cook had shattered the peace of the manor, and Mionet could not blame Duke Andelin for almost any precaution. But though she watched the servants carefully, and listened to their gossip, there was no sign that they had endured the same indignity.

Ought she report it? Was it suspicious that she had not?

Standing in her violated cottage, Mionet's hands clenched at her sides and she lifted her chin, drawing three slow breaths. It was suspicious either way. Duke Andelin's threat rang in her memory, enough to send a prickling chill down her spine, but she knew there was nothing to be found.

It would be easy enough to claim ignorance, if anyone confronted her over her disarranged things.

There was nothing like a crisis to clarify one's position, and to Mionet's dismay, it was neither so high nor so intimate as she hoped. If she could have gotten her hands on the real culprit, she would have happily strangled him. In a single stroke, he had undone the patient work of months.

It wasn't just the rapport she had been building with the Duchess of Andelin. Ever since she arrived, Mionet had been molding the whole household in the appropriate direction. Just bringing its highest-ranking members—and Davi—to the table to share meals was a triumph. Eating together was not a trivial thing. Over time, even the most banal conversations built up into real intimacy, like flakes of snow in a blizzard.

She had been working assiduously to make sure those conversations were not banal. The Duchess of Andelin was her most important relationship, yes, but Mionet had been cultivating a rather intellectual understanding with Justenin, and fostering camaraderie with Leonin, a gentleman of the capital in every way. She had pushed the dangerous Miche of Harnost aside and—she thought—even made a little progress with Duke Andelin himself. He was not a friendly man, but he respected courage, and Mionet had chosen moments to distinguish herself carefully.

And then that botched assassination had blown everything to flinders.

"Why can't you just work here?" Duchess Andelin was entreating her husband as Mionet entered the solar one morning, a week after the attempt on Wen. This was an area where things were going askew.

"I can't hide away, wife." He darted a sharp glance at Mionet and moved them both away, but even from the other end of the room, Mionet's keen ears still caught the words. "I'll be fine. I'm guarded."

"Then at least come home for supper," she said, catching his sleeve. "Please."

"Ophele. You don't need to worry about this." His tone sharpened. "You don't need to do anything."

"I said I was sorry," she whispered. "Won't you just—"

"I said no."

The words were so harsh, Mionet stiffened. From the corner of her eye, she could see him looming over his wife, nudging her chin up with a finger to make her look at him.

"This is not a puzzle for you to solve," he told her, glowering. "Don't you ever do such a thing again. Promise me."

"Promise." It was not a request.

She must have said something satisfactory, but Mionet had to look away at that point, feeling the outrage rise clear from her toes to her ears. She couldn't imagine what the lady could have done that would merit the snarling correction of Remin Grimjaw.

"...stay here," he finished, his eyes flicking the command to Leonin and Davi, who were just coming in for breakfast. "Anyone who wants to see you can come here."

The duchess bit her lip and nodded, and Mionet couldn't tell whether it was because she feared to speak, or feared to speak in present company. In either case, her husband was not inclined to listen. He gave her one last black look and then ducked out the door, lumbering off to find some other tiny, harmless creature to brutalize.

It was not Mionet's place to comment. That was abundantly clear from all the *looking* that had just occurred: Duchess Andelin's appealing glance at Justenin, who had been standing just outside the door. His Grace's silent order to Leonin and Davi. The duchess's unhappy glance at those two men as she went to sit down to breakfast. It mattered, who sought whose eyes, and who participated in those silent communications.

And who did not.

Mionet was not being excluded. She was just not being *in*cluded. She had no place in the present crisis. And with no clear direction as to *why*, or whether she was accounted among the potential enemies, she could not even capitalize on His Grace's unpleasant behavior as a lever to move herself nearer the duchess.

But whatever their trouble was, it hung in the air like a stench, and through most of the morning's lessons, Mionet had the distinct impression she was talking to the air.

"...the horse races, in June," she went on, a recital of the highlights of the social season. "They are very popular, all the finest beasts in the Emp—"

"Mionet." Duchess Andelin lifted her head, which had been propped pensively on her hand. "Is there any way we could just not go to the capital? Surely if everyone knew that someone was trying to kill His Grace again, they would understand, wouldn't they?"

"I—I'm afraid it's not that simple, my lady," Mionet replied, concealing her surprise and alarm at this request. Well, she supposed it wasn't surprising. "The sacred Divinity has commanded it. He has the right to order his lords to come to court."

"So he can murder them more conveniently?"

That question was so shocking, even Leonin's mouth fell open. Mionet drew a sharp breath.

"That—that is...my lady, it is unwise..." she began, plunged abruptly into a sea of treason and searching desperately for land.

"I...understand that you may feel so. But those words might be considered treason for everyone that hears them."

"But it's true. Doesn't everyone already know it's true?" The duchess asked in confusion, looking from one face to the next. "Even in Aldeburke we heard about the assassins, and the only person who would—"

"Well, yes, yes, that is...something," Mionet intervened, before she could complete the dangerous sentence. "It has been very...unfortunate, for His Grace. But there are other considerations one must consider: the matter of his parents, his antagonism with the Divinity. You have not even heard of that first audience, everyone knows it went *so* poorly. And then the war, and the way he harrowed Valleth from the Andelin, and...other tales."

But even as she reeled off the charges, Mionet knew no one *really* believed them. They were common knowledge, easy lies everyone in the capital repeated without thinking, but now it felt as if they cut her tongue to repeat them. Oh yes, everyone knew Remin Grimjaw was the son of traitors, a violent and likely treacherous man who would sooner or later come to a bad end.

And everyone simultaneously knew that *someone* had been trying to kill him since he was a child. The Emperor always publicly and loudly denounced the attacks, of course.

"And so everyone thinks it's fine if the Emperor keeps trying to have him killed?" The duchess asked stubbornly.

"No. No, but it is...difficult," Mionet tried to explain. "It is not something that can really be discussed in society, my lady. Because the Emperor is Beloved of the Stars, and we must not...it touches a great many areas. The Temple, the House Melun, the Five Courts, all of them must weigh in, and...it is hardly the sort of thing one would discuss over a banquet. It is not the proper...*place.*"

Duchess Andelin looked at her for a long time.

"So they all know, in the capital," she said quietly. "I thought they just didn't understand, like they don't know about me. But they do, and no one will say anything because they are afraid it will happen to them."

And with those large, clear eyes fixed on her, Mionet could not think of a single thing to say.

It was true. No one wanted to think too much about Remin Grimjaw. He was such an unpleasant person, thoroughly unsociable, no sense of humor at all, a perfectly wretched guest at banquet. His rank and accomplishments made him impossible to ignore, but no one *really* wanted him around. His presence was a reminder of things no one wanted to think about. He spoiled everyone's fun.

"It's not...right." Mionet was shocked to realize she had said that aloud. But looking at this young woman, she found herself reaching out, unable to help herself. "I think most people know that. But—"

"No. I understand," Duchess Andelin replied, withdrawing. "I know. Thank you. Rem—His Grace said the same, that we have no choice but to go. And I knew...what they said, a little. Please excuse me."

Her voice was quivering, and she had gone off by herself to cry a few times, over the last few days. Watching her go, Mionet couldn't understand why she herself felt so disturbed. On a tactical level, this was good. His Grace was a dangerous subject; best not to say anything she might have to disavow. And it was hardly a subject that they could laugh away, or forget with a new gown.

But it was still a bit of a slap in the face when Mionet found out who the duchess had chosen as a confidante instead.

"You sent for me, my lady?"

Coming out of the dressing room later that day, Mionet heard the familiar voice and froze. *That man.*

"Yes," came the duchess's voice from the solar, with unmistakable relief. "Davi, Leonin, would you excuse us, please?"

Neither of those benighted men had the sense to protest leaving the duchess alone with an unmarried man, let alone with

Miche of Harnost. Mionet huffed out a breath and stole down the hallway on silent feet. Now she had no choice but to eavesdrop. Easing to the end of the corridor, she peered through the crack in the door.

"I'm sorry to bother you, I know all of you are working so hard," the duchess was saying as she allowed Miche to steer her to her armchair. "But I don't know what to do, I think I did something terrible..."

"Why don't you tell me first, and then we'll decide if it's terrible," Miche suggested, pulling up a chair opposite the lady.

"It's Remin," she said miserably. "He won't have meals here, since Wen got hurt. I even asked Wen how he makes Remin's food, and I had Azelma make it just like that, and I swear we tasted it and tested it and didn't take our eyes off it even once, but it still made him sick. And I don't think he's eating at all now. Not even tea. I can hear his stomach growling even when he's asleep, and it's been *five days,* and I don't know what to—"

"It's been that long?" Miche scrubbed a hand over his face, his palm rasping against blond stubble. "I didn't...I lost track. He's not eating at the barracks?"

"No! I asked Justenin and he said he wasn't, he's not even eating in town anymore, I asked Master Noulen and Mistress Tregue..." Tears filled her eyes. "S-so I tried to make him eat last night, it was just *bread,* but when I took a bite myself h-he...he knocked it out of my hand, and he was so *mad,* he yelled, and n-n-now..."

The words dissolved as she burst into tears, and as Miche scooted forward in his chair and pulled her face into his shoulder, Mionet had to bite her tongue to keep from instantly lodging a furious protest. It was the oldest trick in the book, the *scoundrel—*

"Now, now, it's not your fault," Miche murmured, in a very different tone than Mionet had ever heard him use before. His hand stroked over Duchess Andelin's hair, patting her gently. "I'm sorry, I should have been watching. He took it hard when Bon died. It would've scared the life out of him to see you testing his food for him. He told you about Bon, didn't he?"

She nodded, hiccupping.

"Well, it took him a long time to get over that. It was weeks before I could get him to properly eat again, even with Wen cooking. He'd sit to supper, but at night he'd lie there and fret until he went off and made himself throw u—"

She should not be hearing this.

Mionet recoiled, literally, physically retreating a silent pace from the door. She did not want to know this. She did not want to hear this, she did not want to listen to Miche explain that the Duke of Andelin sometimes starved himself because he was too afraid to eat. She wished she didn't know it. She wished she had never heard a word, and she wished even more that she could stop herself from thinking how priceless that knowledge would be in the capital.

How they would laugh, if they knew Remin Grimjaw had such a weakness.

"...can we do?" Duchess Andelin wept.

"It's not a...rational thing," Miche replied. "Duchess Ereguil thought the less attention we paid to it, the better. The second time he got poisoned, she would just give Victorin a pocket full of apples and tell him, *don't say anything, just eat one in front of Remin and then leave the rest*. And when he got hungry enough, he'd try one on his own. Raw things like fruit and nuts, where it's harder to hide a poison. Rospalme had a lot of orchards, he felt safe if he went out and picked something off a tree, and the old man taught him to fish. I'm sorry, my lady. I should've checked on him. I knew he'd have trouble, after this."

"It's not your fault." Duchess Andelin sniffled. "I should've asked. I thought I was so clever..."

"Even the smartest people make mistakes," he said, sitting her up straight and plucking a handkerchief from his pocket. "Look at me, I make them all the time."

"You have saved me from a few," she said with a watery smile. "Thank you."

"I'll have Azelma send up something simple from the kitchen," he promised. "Eat it tonight in front of him, but don't say anything about it. You just have to remind him that eating is normal and it's nothing to be afraid of or fussed over. All right?"

"I will. Maybe we ought to have breakfast in our room again, for a little while?" she said, brightening. "And if you brought it? He trusts you."

"I'll talk to him about it. He'll be all right, don't worry," Miche said, sounding more like himself. "We've all gone hungry for longer than this."

"I'll get Davi to bring up some apples right away," she added, much cheered. "Thank you so much, Miche. And the hazelnuts, we picked those ourselves, I could roast them—"

"Remember what I said about not making a fuss!" Miche called after her as she dashed away, shaking his head.

It would be best if Mionet pretended she hadn't heard any of this. She immediately moved back a plausible distance down the hallway, as if she had just come out of Duchess Andelin's dressing room. But whatever else she might say of the man, Miche was not easily deceived. Coming out of the solar, his eyes met hers and all that good-natured humor vanished.

"I suppose I should have checked *both* doors," he said coldly. "Did you hear anything to your profit, my lady?"

"I have no idea what you mean," she replied, sidestepping him, but he immediately moved right back in front of her, looming in the most unfriendly way imaginable.

"It might be too much to expect," he began, "but at least during the time when the duchess is useful to you, it would be good of you to remember that all *she* wants is to be left in peace. That's all either of them wants. You wouldn't think it would be that much to ask, would you?"

The look in his tawny eyes struck her like a slap. Not just anger and contempt, but something else, bent as furiously upon himself as her, and the last thing she would ever have expected to see from the scandalous Sir Miche of Harnost. It was a thing that she knew well. A thing she had sworn she would never let herself feel again.

Shame.

* * *

With a *crack* like lightning striking, Remin's practice sword struck Davi's and *shattered.*

Ophele only had a second to blink before Leonin whirled to shield her from the explosion of splinters, yanking her to one side and turning to absorb the stinging cloud with his armored back.

"You're all right, wife?" Remin asked.

"I'm fine," Ophele replied, peeking over Leonin's shoulder. "Do they normally do that?"

"His do," Davi groused, picking splinters from his cheek.

"My lord, perhaps we ought to try steel," Leonin suggested. "I don't believe this is appreciably safer—"

"No," Remin said immediately. His black brows lowered. "We'll try...something else. I would rather you kept Ophele away from swords altogether."

"That ain't quite what we practiced, Your Grace..." Davi pointed out as he trailed after Remin to dispose of his own damaged sword. Both of them had been made of solid oak.

The three men were lightly armored for this exercise, which had seemed very exciting when they first began and then became increasingly less so. The objective was simple: to allow Ophele to practice moving between her guards without tripping them. It didn't sound like a difficult thing to do, and Ophele had worn her most practical boots and presented herself at the mess hall of the barracks at the appointed time, secretly hoping to impress Remin.

Except Remin did not want to be impressed.

In fact, she got the distinct impression that he did not want any of this to be happening.

"Same objective," he said when he returned, plucking another practice sword from a nearby barrel and pointing to the end of the hall with it. "Try to make it to those doors. Go for speed this time."

"I'll defend first," said Leonin. "My lady, stay with Davi and just keep moving."

"All right." Ophele tried to sound enthusiastic, but she had a growing list of objections to this plan, the first of which was that Remin wouldn't let her do *anything*.

It was true that there wasn't much she could do against armored men, and a lady could hardly wander about Segoile in armor. She doubted she could even get her teeth through their gloves. Though if anyone *did* try to snatch her, she fully intended to bite whatever parts of their anatomy were available.

But surely she could try to dodge them on her own before then, couldn't she? All this time she had been privately planning to scramble up to some high place and wait for Leonin and Davi to dispatch them, or for rescuers to arrive, or for her abductors to get bored and go away. It used to work on Julot.

And that was another thing. What were the odds *really* of a three-hundred-pound juggernaut like Remin trying to abduct her? They must think of the worst thing, yes, and it was also possible that a Bhumi water bison might escape from the Imperial menagerie and try to run her down in the street, but it seemed to her that there were other, more likely scenarios they might have been practicing.

But Remin absolutely would not hear of anyone attempting to lay hands on her, so here they were.

"Go," he ordered.

Ophele went.

Stars, he was terrifying. She could hear armor rattling behind her as she bolted forward with Davi to her left, hauling her along by her elbow. He was a left-handed swordsman, an important advantage against most opponents, and a perfect complement to

Leonin. Backed into a corner, the two of them could defend for a very, very long time, even against the Duke of Andelin.

That was the last resort, though. They did not want to be backed into a corner.

"Don't look back," Davi warned as swords clacked together behind them, one-two-three, blows in such rapid succession that Ophele really would have liked to see it. But all too soon there was a curse, a thud, and then heavy, pounding boots, accelerating. Ophele knew that sound. It meant Remin was overtaking them. The double doors at the end of the hall were still fifty paces away when Davi suddenly swore and whirled about, flinging up his sword and thrusting Ophele behind him. She immediately stepped on the hem of her gown and sat down. Hard.

"I'm fine, I'm fine," she said immediately, scrambling back to her feet with a red face. Remin had already stopped and was shoving Davi aside. "It's this stupid skirt, I'm sorry."

"You could bundle it up while you're running," Remin said, coming to examine her hands. "Is women's clothing *meant* to hinder? Perhaps Tiffen could take off a couple inches..."

"Not in Segoile, Your Grace." Leonin shook his head, appearing with a fresh welt over his jaw. "We might as well announce that we're not able to defend her, quite aside from the scandal of fashion. If we really meant it, we'd have Her Grace practicing with a train and dancing shoes."

"This is sufficient for today," Remin said, looking grim.

"I can do it," Ophele said, trying to sound competent. "Shall we try again?"

The whole thing felt a little unreal. She knew that it was *possible* that someone would really try to kidnap her, but it felt about as likely as being run down by one of the Emperor's bison. It gave her an uncomfortable, queasy feeling to see them all so serious, when she was just a bastard, and no one could *really* want her for anything.

But this was a chance to prove to Remin that she could take care of herself, and maybe he didn't need to worry so much. She was fast on her feet. It was just trying to dodge about Leonin and Davi that was throwing her off.

So the next time Remin said *go,* she was off like a rabbit.

The familiar noises pursued her. Pounding footsteps. They turned as both Leonin and Davi pushed Remin back, and Davi even launched himself at Remin's legs, trying to knock him over while Leonin and Ophele raced for the doors. But Remin was so *quick,* all too soon she could hear him coming up from her left and even as Leonin was yanking her forward and out of the way, she snatched up her skirts and accelerated, bounding past him for the final twenty paces to slap her hands against the huge double doors.

"There!" she said triumphantly, turning. "Look, Remin, if they hold you ba—"

"Never leave your guards!" Remin exclaimed. "Why did you do that? Do you know who might be behind that door? I told you, always stay in arm's reach of your guards."

"But—but I thought we were close enough," she stammered, crushed. "I can run, too—"

"You're not supposed to run off by yourself. You're supposed to learn to run with *them,"* he said flatly. "This is not a game. There is no base."

"I know, but—"

Her nose was starting to sting and she looked quickly away, grateful that Leonin started talking. She didn't want to cry, that felt like it would only prove Remin's point, but she wasn't *useless.*

"Perhaps we ought to begin with that, then, my lord," Leonin was saying. "It's unrealistic to focus too much on stopping you. Our opponents in Segoile are likely to be less skilled and more numerous. We will not be attempting to hold off the Duke of Andelin."

"Thank the stars," muttered Davi.

"We'll try that, then," Remin agreed after a moment. "No weapons. Just keep me from laying a hand on her."

That was what he wanted anyway. The least possible danger. It felt like she had failed a test, and it felt like she hadn't even had a chance to *try*. Silently, Ophele moved behind Leonin and Davi, glancing resentfully up at the tall posts and beams lining the dining hall. She would have liked to climb up there and *then* see if Remin could lay a hand on her.

"Ready?" he asked, moving back a few paces to give them a sporting chance. "Mind that skirt, wife."

They lasted longer this way, at least. It was a child's game compared to the business of swords, but Davi and Leonin formed a shifting, flexible wall around Ophele, moving to deflect Remin away rather than confronting him directly. Ophele was quick to dance back whenever he lunged toward her, and after a little while she thought she even spotted a pattern in how Leonin and Davi were moving, the way their hands turned outward to push her back a split second before they stepped. It wasn't something she could reason through while she was trying to move, but once she had spotted it, it felt easier to focus on Leonin and Davi and stay with them, without being distracted by Remin.

Maybe that was the trouble? Maybe she was paying *too* much attention to him? It was hard not to, he made such a racket when he was pursuing, and sometimes he even randomly shouted as he charged and made her freeze, so she had to stumble backward.

Why, he was doing that on *purpose!*

Ophele had only an instant to appreciate his cunning before he did it again, lunging forward with a shout that made her backpedal automatically with fright, and then someone *else* stepped on her skirt and she tripped and the next thing she knew, she was ricocheting between all three of them like a small ball rattling between tenpins. For a minute, she didn't know which way was up.

"Stars, Ophele!" She heard behind her, and big hands dug her out of the pile of limbs and sat her up, Remin's horrified face swimming above her.

"Ouch," she said thickly, shaking her head. She had smacked her nose hard enough that her eyes were watering, and when Remin turned her hands over, both her palms were badly scraped by the flagstones. From the feel of it, her knees were in similar shape.

"I'll get some water." Davi shook his head and rose. "Bloody buggering hell, those skirts are a menace, I'm so sorry, my lady."

"It's all right," she said, touching her nose and wondering if it was bleeding.

"Let me see," said Remin, tilting her head back. "Anywhere else hurt? It's no small thing to get tackled by three men in armor."

"I'm all ri—" She let out a squawk of protest as Remin pushed her skirts up over her knees, ignoring their audience. Blood was trickling from long scrapes on both knees.

"This is why I didn't want to do this," he said savagely, producing a handkerchief and carefully wiping away the blood streaks. "Guard work isn't like soldiering, we're not used to maneuvering around someone to protect them, *look* at this—"

"They're just scratches," she protested, pinching her poor nose. "I can do it, next time I'll—"

"There won't be a next time," he retorted. "Davi and Leonin can borrow one of the pages until they learn not to fall on you."

"But there's only a few weeks left!" she exclaimed, trying not to yelp as he blotted at her bleeding knees. "I can *do* it! I have to learn not to trip them, don't I? I'll be careful, I prom—"

"I said no," he snapped. "Look at this! One fall! They're going to think I *beat* you! I won't have you getting knocked about—"

"It's not as if it's the first time!" she shouted back, and his mouth shut with a snap. All three men were staring at her with a strange, helplessly fury, and Ophele only belatedly realized what she had said and lifted her chin. "Well, it isn't. And if someone wants to kidnap me, I don't think they'll mind knocking me about. Remin, you can't—"

This was the last thing he wanted to hear, she knew it.

"You can't protect me from everything," she said. "I have to learn this by myself."

Remin's jaw tightened, his lips pressed flat as if he were suppressing a really crushing response. And then he sighed.

"I know that," he said, his wide shoulders sagging. He glanced back at Leonin and Davi. "Give us a few minutes."

"You can't," Ophele repeated as she let him steer her over to a bench to sit down. "Remin, I can *help*. At least let me *try.*"

"I don't want you getting hurt," he repeated, crouching in front of her and pushing her skirts back up over her knees. "Not even this much. Your knees are so...I *like* your knees, you have pretty knees, what if this scars? I'm supposed to protect you. I *hate* this, you're not supposed to get hurt, I hate watching—*wife!* What the blazes was that for?"

Ophele shook out her hand. She had slapped his head so hard, it felt like she might have broken it.

"You," she said, her voice quivering with fury. "You! How do you think *I* feel? I know you're not sleeping, you're not eating properly, do you think I like watching *that?* Do you think I don't worry? You won't even *tell* me, you won't *talk* to me, you don't even admit it when you're sick! How would you like it, if I just hid it and told you I was fine! *It's not fine!"*

He rocked back on his heels, his eyes widening.

"You won't even let me *help,"* she said, trying and failing to keep her voice steady. "I could get away from you, I know I could, but you won't even let me *show* you! I can climb, I could get into the rafters and you would never get me down and then Leonin and Davi could fight you or go for help but you won't even let me *try,* you won't even *listen—"*

"I don't want you climbing in the rafters," he began, faltering, and then rose up on his knees, pulling her into his arms as she started to cry. "Oh, wife, don't. I just don't want you to get hurt. If something happened to you—"

"Well that's how I feel, too!" she sobbed, slapping his chest. "All this time! All I could do is watch you hurt! Do you think I didn't know?"

"All right," he murmured. "All right. You're right, I'm sorry."

"You have to *talk* to me," she wept.

"I will."

"And you have to stop saying you're fine if you aren't."

"That's the pot calling out the kettle," he said, his fingers stroking the back of her neck.

"I don't care. I told you when I was hurting and it was embarrassing for me, too."

"You did."

For a little while, they were quiet, and she could feel his fingers moving through her hair, gentling.

"I want to help," she said, lifting her head to look up at him unhappily. "Am I that useless?"

"Of course not," he replied, low. "I just...I really was trying to keep you from worrying, wife. I want you to be happy. I want to keep you safe. I didn't want you to know..."

"That just means I have to figure it out by myself," she informed him, and made him give a short laugh.

"That's what Miche said." He bent his head, his lips brushing hers, and after a moment she decided to allow it. "I'm sorry."

"Then can we try again?" she asked, looking up to meet his eyes. Her mouth set in a stubborn line. "I can do it."

"Let's do something about your knees first..." He trailed off and sighed. "And then you can show me what you can do."

Chapter 13 – A Little Treason

Lord Edemir of Trecht was a steady sort of fellow.

In thirty years, he had yet to know a great love or great loss. When Valleth threatened the lands of Trecht, he had done his duty and gone to join Remin's army, expecting only another push to the banks of the Brede. Four months later, he found himself mounted at the far end of the Gresein Bridge, in a single explosion of recklessness that would change the course of his life.

Edemir was not the sort of man to charge. He was far more likely to be found at the rear of an army, making sure none of the supply wagons got left behind.

That was the skill that had brought him to Segoile, with mercantile negotiations to cover his real business. Edemir could never have been one of Juste's singers. The best he could do was endeavor to carry someone else's tune.

"Indeed not, when he ordered an entire bathhouse imported for her," Edemir told the knot of people gathered around him at

Count Heroulte's banquet. "I spent most of last summer acquiring gifts for His Grace's bride."

"The Duke of Andelin?" one of the women asked skeptically. Edemir had to admit he wouldn't have believed it, either.

"I swear it by my secretaries, madam," he assured her. "There were a number of late nights concerning such matters. I confess, we found it extraordinary, but His Grace will count no cost when it comes to her happiness..."

This was the best way that Edemir could think to sell this story: casting the tale of Remin's romance through the lens of complaints from a long-suffering subordinate. It was even true; Remin had just appeared in the office one day, announced Her Grace needed a proper bath, and did Edemir think a Benkki Desan or Empire-style bathhouse would be better. And that was followed by a flood of similarly unanswerable questions about everything from clothing to jewelry to furnishings, as if Remin's lady was far above ordinary chairs.

Remembering that, Edemir had to suppress a smirk. That *had* been entertaining, watching Rem flounder his way toward immense, if somewhat bewildered, bliss.

"She must be a remarkable lady, to overcome his...reservations," remarked another woman, testing the fabric of Edemir's story. If it were true, it would be the explosion of the social season.

"She is a child of the stars, and greatly worthy of his love," Edemir replied. "But I hope you gentle ladies will welcome her patiently, when she comes. She does not know her father's city."

Juste had threaded this needle delicately; that was the story he wanted Edemir to sell, without making presumptions about the Emperor's relationship with his daughter. It won exclamations of sympathy from some, and thoughtful frowns from others, who faded away, drifting to a cluster of listeners at the other end of the hall.

Edemir was not the only person in Segoile who could answer questions about Ophele.

Beside a wide bank of windows, he could see Lady Bette Hurrell, a tall and sophisticated blonde draped in the most popular fashion of the season, though it would be three months before anyone else knew that. The reappearance of House Hurrell had fueled a public frenzy and weeks of private speculation. They had been condemned with Remin's House in the Conspiracy, and now everyone was asking the questions Edemir must answer: how had they won a pardon? Who did they now serve?

The most popular theory was that it was an overture of peace between House Andelin and the House of Agnephus. It would be a significant first step, if it were true; pardoning a House that had suffered for its loyalty, and specifically the House that had stood guardian to the Emperor's beloved child.

Lady Hurrell had made no attempt to correct this impression.

Outside stories of Ophele's naïveté and timidity, Edemir played the game with a similarly delicate hand. Any discrepancies between his account and Lady Hurrell's would be instantly seized upon and torn to shreds.

"You make her sound quite an innocent, my lord," said a particularly feline lady, tapping her fan on her chin.

"If she had come to the capital this past season, she would have been one of the year's debutantes," Edemir said somberly. "His Grace sent me to ensure there should be nothing lacking in her debut. And to manage his business interests," he added, with a small salute of his cup. "I was instructed not to miss the spring livestock fairs on any account, the duke has great aspirations for his herds..."

It would not do to lay it on too thickly. And sure enough, as soon as he turned to talk cows with one of the men nearby, most of his audience drifted away toward the other end of the room.

Edemir had no one to send there. He could only wander that way himself a few times over the course of the night, blessing Countess Heroulte for distributing snack tables around the room.

"...and still no word of her, though she is like my own daughter," Lady Hurrell was saying the third time he passed, and something about the way she said that made his hackles rise.

This was the deficiency of Juste's network in the city. They had no contacts at all among the Roses of Segoile, saving the Duchess of Ereguil and her daughters-in-law, who had just arrived last week. It hadn't seemed a matter of great concern in Tresingale, but Edemir felt it keenly. Especially when Lady Hurrell glanced in his direction, smiled, and bent back to her cluster of admirers.

There were some places a man could not go.

Edemir talked livestock. He talked carpentry. He gossiped about Master Didion and Master Peltier, both men of renown in the capital. He hoped to parlay their support into better terms with the Court of Artisans, but there too, he had thus far been blocked.

"I have heard of the work in Tresingale," said Master Crochte, a master mason that Edemir had hoped might prove sympathetic. The man *looked* like a mason, gray and square and hard-handed, with a grand mustache that stretched across his cheeks from one ear to the other. "Very specialized materials there, aren't they? Andelin granite?"

"I have not heard that it's different from any other granite," Edemir replied, with no outward sign of offense. "I saw the work on the walls of House Sangevin's estate. It's quite similar to His Grace's manor in Tresingale, barring the height."

"Well, that may be, to a layman's eye." Master Crochte tapped the reddened tip of his nose wisely. "But we all know that the demands of the Andelin aren't like anywhere else."

"I have heard that said," Edemir agreed. "But you would be surprised, how well we have managed. I have letters from Master Guisse, Master Misler, and Master Didion..."

The master listened as Edemir explained that masonry in Tresingale was largely indistinguishable from masonry anywhere else, but it was clear that Edemir might as well have been talking to a block of Andelin granite.

"I would be pleased to present the letters for discussion at the guild hall," Edemir said, pressing onward nonetheless. "Particularly the recommendations from Master Didion. He has been quite adamant..."

"Oh, to be sure, we would be pleased to consider them," said Master Crochte, though his eyes had already drifted away. "Kindly send a note to the guild hall, and we shall see what we might do."

Two other guild masters had said as much, and done as little.

"I will do that," Edemir promised politely, and let Crochte excuse himself.

It was a problem close to his heart. The Court of Artisans dictated labor prices for all artisans accredited by their guild, and even before Remin won the war, the Andelin Valley had already been declared a *special case*. Edemir was inclined to Miche's point of view: there were many excellent masons in Daitia. But Juste had persuaded Remin to try working within the Empire for one more year, and Edemir was bound to obey his lord's command.

No progress with the Court of Artisans so far, he wrote to Juste later that night. *I am investigating ways we might acquire the influence we lack there, but I fear it will not be a simple prospect. Of greater concern is the social influence we lack. We need a few noblewomen to act as Rem's agents in Segoile. I can't swear to what Her Grace is going to find when she gets here.*

Though honestly, Edemir wasn't sure he could swear to what Remin might find, either.

Duke Ghislain Berebet had caused consternation last fall when he wrote to congratulate Remin on his marriage, offering to host the new Duke and Duchess for the social season months before they were summoned to go. His first contact with Edemir had lagged by comparison; he had been in the city for a full month before they finally met, at a different banquet a few nights later.

The fact that Edemir and the patriarch of a ducal House were at the same banquet was proof of exactly how curious the capital was about the Duke of Andelin.

"Lord Edemir of Trecht," said Duke Berebet, lifting a cup to Edemir as he approached. He was a lean man of medium height, with a neat mustache and salt-and-pepper hair. And Miche had bedded at least one of his daughters. "I am pleased to make your acquaintance."

"Your Grace." Edemir bowed his head. "You honor me."

"You will find yourself frequently honored, this year," Berebet replied cynically. "Everyone is mad for news of the Andelin. It was good of your lord to send someone to sate our curiosity."

"It would be hard to recognize the place, after the past year," Edemir agreed. "It is a proper town now, between Master Didion and Master Ffloce..."

That wasn't what the duke really wanted to talk about, but they were taking each other's measure. Berebet was the first nobleman of substance to make an overture to House Andelin. Why?

"I am glad to hear the land prospers," Berebet said approvingly. "It is hard work, building something from nothing. Do you know the origins of House Berebet?"

"Not much, I'm afraid," Edemir apologized. His own House Trecht was in the duchy of Leinbruke, and Edemir had been drilled on the glories of the House of Lein—which included wool, cheese, and many other sheep-related products—since he was five.

"We are not so ancient as some other houses," Berebet conceded. "We were not kings before the arrival of Ospret Far-Eyes. My ancestor, the first duke of Berebet, was fortunate enough to rule a bit of land in the back of beyond, and was content to keep it that way."

"I had not heard that," Edemir remarked.

"He was a clever man, Gllaomin of Berebet. In all those early wars of Ospret's ascendance, there were no battles over his bit of bog, and no notice of all the iron and copper in his hills. But when Gllaomin was called to the oathtaking in Starfall, he was the first to arrive, and bore the mightiest gift. For while all the other great lords had been making war, you see, he had been preparing for the peace."

"Great Houses are born of foresight," Edemir said carefully. Berebet was choosing some very alarming subjects.

"I thought you would understand," Berebet agreed. They had moved away from the press over the course of their conversation, and stood alone on a balcony now, out of earshot of anyone else. Berebet set his glass down on the railing and leaned back, exhaling a faint white puff into the chilly air. "It is telling, who a lord chooses to send as his emissary."

"Or if he sends no emissary, and comes himself," Edemir returned, and won a smile.

"Well, we have already endured the formalities." There was something about the cast of his face and the glint of his teeth that made Edemir think of a lynx. "Do you know what Gllaomin brought, as a gift to Ospret?"

"No."

"Copper and iron," said Duke Berebet. "Not treasures. Not heirlooms of his house. Copper and iron, because Ospret wanted to build."

Three days later, a message came from the masters of the Guild of Masons saying that they would be pleased to meet him at his convenience. Edemir hardly needed to see the Berebet insignia on the messenger.

It was a shrewdly selective use of Berebet's influence, all the more impressive for its subtlety, with the underlying message that House Berebet had determined it wise to offer the Duke of Andelin a gift.

The question was *why*.

* * *

Two weeks left.

Ophele was counting down the days, and there just weren't enough of them.

Every day she found another plan, another project, another corner of Tresingale that could do with a little tweak or two. In the middle of the night, she jerked awake thinking: *wait*. She had an entire library of books now, of all levels of difficulty, including some that Jacot could have been practicing on, and *why* hadn't she thought of that sooner?

She felt like a condemned prisoner, forced to spend her remaining days learning fan language and Articles forty-five through fifty of the Imperial Code. And even when she appealed to Remin, certain that he would agree that the welfare of Tresingale must come first, he had just told her to keep a list and give it to Lady Verr. That was a lady-in-waiting's job, after all.

Ophele made him pay for it by inviting company over.

"I got this tea from Master Guian today," she said as she lifted the kettle from the hearth and poured hot water into Remin's teacup, then Azelma's. She was careful to let him break the wax seal on the tin of tea himself. "It's from Bhumi, roasted with lotus fruits. Sugar?"

"I'm fine. Thank you," he added, in a touching and unsuccessful effort to look less forbidding. Ophele knew he wasn't actually glaring at Azelma, but an outside observer could only conclude the old lady had offered him some mortal insult.

"Azelma was the one who taught me to make tea," Ophele went on, pouring herself a cup and sitting in an armchair positioned diplomatically between the two of them. "I used to sneak into the kitchen at night when she was baking bread, and she always had me manage the kettle."

"It kept you out of other mischief," Azelma agreed, adding sugar and a dribble of milk to her own cup. "Can't go too wrong with a pot of tea."

"I just wanted to help," Ophele protested. The injustice still rankled. "It looked like fun, kneading dough and making buns."

"It's certainly a dangerous business when you liked to stuff dates and sultanas and cloves of garlic and the stars know what all else into it the minute my back was turned, mercy me," Azelma said tartly. "She did that with the apple bread once, my lord, studded it up with cloves like it was a haunch of ham. I've no idea how I missed it, but sure enough, up it went for breakfast the next morning."

"The Hurrells ate it?" Remin looked interested in spite of himself.

"They did indeed, sir, and all but seared the tongues right out of their heads," Azelma replied, to their mutual satisfaction.

For all that she had borne the brunt of Lady Hurrell's fury after that incident, Azelma often repeated the tale, especially when she wanted to forbid Ophele from doing anything interesting in the kitchen. And this really was working just as Mionet had said it would; Ophele knew the sorts of stories Remin liked to hear, and the sorts of stories that Azelma liked to tell, so all she had to do was give her an opening to do it.

It was also the *perfect* opportunity to show Remin how well Azelma ran a kitchen, though that was definitely secondary.

"And the cheese man, you remember him?" Ophele prompted. "Remin, there was this one cheese merchant that used to come to Aldeburke, but he could never fool Azelma..."

"Well, it was as plain as my nose that he wasn't selling *real* Norgrede cheddar," Azelma said, flicking her fingers. "You can smell it, Norgrede cheddar has a sharpness. He used to come every other month, peddling his fraudulent cheeses, and every time it was something new, red rinds on blue cheese or him trying to sell me on the new virgin Lein cheese. Virgin, says he, because the rennet came from unspoiled sheep. And here's this one next to me in the door," she said, nodding to Ophele, "wanting to know what's a virgin sheep."

"I trust you didn't explain it," Remin replied, with an amused flick of his black eyes to Ophele. He knew better than anyone how woefully ignorant she had been about all species of virgin.

"Indeed not, fouling a child's ears with that sort of talk," said Azelma indignantly. "She wouldn't stop asking for days, I had a little shadow pattering after me in the kitchen, wanting to know did we have virgin sheep, and were they different from regular sheep, and why couldn't we make virgin sheep cheese ourselves."

This was not *quite* the sort of story Ophele had meant for her to tell.

"But at least you never bought any of the nasty cheeses..." she interjected, trying to shift course back to the original subject, but Azelma was already off to the races.

"My stars, Your Grace, I think I spent half my life trying to guess what she might take into her head next," Azelma confided, as Remin scooted forward in his chair. "I think she was...twelve, maybe, when we had a sudden plague of squirrels in the kitchen garden, and no idea where they had come from or why. Into everything, making off with the tomatoes, I didn't know squirrels would even *eat* broccoli. Though they never did touch the peppers."

"They don't like spicy things," Ophele tried to explain. "The book just talked about them hoarding nuts for the winter, but I wanted to know what they ate for the rest of the year..."

And she had also been trying to train them to do her bidding, but she was hardly about to admit that now.

"Squirrels again?" Remin asked, and then of course he had to tell Azelma about the afternoon in the hazelnut grove, though he did omit certain key events. Azelma rocked with laughter.

"Oh! A legion of squirrels!" she chortled, wiping her eyes. "It was rabbits one year, as I recall, I found a nest of newborns in a basket under my bed one night, ugly as moles. But if you *do* roast hazelnuts yourself, Your Grace, mind you crack the shells first. That was one of the more spectacular of Her High—Her Grace's experiments."

"I saw you roasting peanuts and you didn't crack their shells," said Ophele, wounded.

"Peanut shells are porous. Hazelnut shells go off like they were fired from a crossbow," Azelma replied in tones of infinite patience. "And it was so hard to catch her, she was so *quiet!* I swear, half the time I never even saw her at her mischief. I would just wonder why all my measuring spoons had gone, or find a cat half-shaved in the pantry, or one fine day we'd have hazelnuts suddenly exploding in the fire. Kitchen boys scattering, scullery maids shrieking, you'd have thought there was a war on."

That actually made Remin laugh out loud.

"Shaved cat?" he repeated, looking expectantly at Ophele.

There was a breed of dog in Sachar Veche whose fur was often dyed and shaved in interesting ways. Resigned, Ophele confessed to the crime and then gave up trying to divert them, munching on a gingersnap and wondering idly how one *did* correct a conversation that had veered so wildly off course. It was worth it to hear Remin laugh.

This small dream was all Ophele wanted: that the two people she loved best in the world would get along. The evening flew by, and all too soon Azelma was glancing at the moon rising through the window and rising regretfully to her feet.

"It is a little late for a baker, my lord," she apologized, straightening cautiously. Azelma always said she stiffened up like lumber if she was still for too long. "I thank you for the invitation, and for indulging an old lady for an evening. Her Grace is very dear to me."

"It was a pleasure." Remin looked surprised to find he meant it. "I am glad to know that she had such a friend in that place."

"I am glad that she has come to this place," Azelma replied, unusually somber as she accepted her cloak from Ophele. "Good night, my lady."

"Good night." Ophele moved to embrace her, wrapped at once in the comforting smells of the kitchen.

"I'll see you to your cottage," Remin said when they parted. It was only courteous, given the hour and the cold, but Ophele thought it was a good sign that he had volunteered. And even better when she heard his voice in the hall, asking where the measuring spoons had gone.

This was something they could come home to.

Ophele recognized a pattern to their preparations, as the days dwindled: not just for their departure, but for the town that would go on in their absence. The size of both the house and household would *double* in their absence, and so she spent a few hours closeted away with Justenin and Adelan, making provisions for the staff, and then a further afternoon trailing after Sousten, reviewing plans for the library.

"It is inspired by the great libraries of Sachar Veche," Master Didion explained, as they craned their necks in the vast shell of the structure. "Imagine floors and floors of shelves, my lady, each built atop the other so the adjacent floors seem to *float,* with a lacework of railings and carved columns like trees..."

She could see it, looking from the sketches to the shell. The gaps for deep reading nooks under the windows, massive chandeliers, and immense fireplaces, yet all of it was...*natural,* as if it had grown together in those flowing shapes. Curving balconies, overlooking the floors below. Wide galleries, where she could just imagine the hushed murmurs of scholars, walking up and down in pensive conversation.

"That is where the murals will go, Your Grace," Sousten explained, flicking his fingers to make Matissen produce the next page. "There will be some in the manor, but *this* is where the history of your House will live. You can see I have broken them into sections, with each one punctuated by these immense vases and roses—"

"No roses," Ophele replied, leaning over to examine the sketch. Those vases would be taller than she was. "His Grace says they are capital nonsense."

Because of the Roses of Segoile, she assumed. Remin really did hate absolutely everything about the capital.

"His Grace is surprisingly sensitive to symbolism," Sousten observed. "But it is true, roses are the traditional symbol of the nobility. Every Great House has its own cultivar. Yet have I not often spoken of the Flower of the Andelin?"

He examined Ophele through narrowed eyes, as if she were a puzzle that wanted solving.

"They call the camellia the Rose of Winter," he said slowly. "For it blooms in unlikely places, when all other flowers have withered. That would be a fitting emblem for the Lady of House Andelin. Now, the murals, my lady. Have you any ideas for their subjects?"

Confronted with vast swaths of empty wall, Ophele's mind went blank. It was too strange to think of Remin or herself as subjects of a mural or inspiration for an emblem. And House Andelin was brand new, forged by Remin with blood and brute will. It hardly had any history, yet.

But...actually, that wasn't true, was it? Her brow furrowed as she thought of the painful history of the Andelin Valley, annexed to the Empire, ravaged by Valleth, and conquered again. It had a very long history, and a bloody one, and the people in the cottages by the North Gate were the last ones who had survived it.

"I don't know..." she said thoughtfully. "What do they have in other noble houses?"

"Usually, it is the story of their founding, my lady," offered Mionet, who had tagged along for the tour. "In Ereguil, every bannerman has at least one mural of Laisse Ereguil, who founded the House, and his son Valenot, who defended against invasion from Noreven."

"Just so," said Master Didion, nodding. "Duke Tries commissioned one like that for his new gallery, the largest in the Empire. Tries is very proud of their history."

"Perhaps a little too proud," Mionet said wryly. "You don't mean the one of Segeband? Rising from the waters like the Daitian Lord of Fishes, wearing nothing but some seafoam and his beard."

"Well, yes, I warned him about that," Sousten grumbled, with something perilously close to a pout. "If it is *too* grandiose, there is a point where it becomes counterproductive..."

"Let's not do that," Ophele agreed.

In the duchy of Andelin, *Remin* would be that founder. But what about *his* family? His ancestors were every bit as famous as Segeband, builders of a thousand-year dynasty whose name was synonymous with the lands they had ruled. That House had nearly been extinguished, save for Remin: their sole living legacy.

"His Grace's family had a great history, too," she said, watching the flicker of alarm in Sousten and Mionet's faces. She had tried to get both of them to talk about the Conspiracy, but so far they had skillfully evaded all attempts. And if it was treason to talk about his family, it was surely even worse to immortalize it in art.

As if his whole family had never existed.

"We can wait to decide," she said finally, sparing them both. "I don't want to just say something so the painters have something to do."

But the blank walls nagged her. It seemed everything she did was the shaping of House Andelin's story, from the livery she approved for its servants to the motif of camellias that would soon appear in her own clothing. Mionet's lessons in beauty murmured in her memory, and Ophele understood that this was her own contribution to history, superficial as it might seem: the unique form of the beauty of her home, as well as its mighty founder.

Which was how she came to supervise the fittings of the legend himself. A rainbow assortment of doublets, jerkins, coats, shirts, breeches, and other masculine accoutrements that Remin yanked at, complained about, and ripped off the instant he could.

"It's choking me," he growled under his breath as Master Tiffen and Magne consulted each other about various styles of collar. The high-necked collar was fashionable again, according to Lady Verr, and Remin claimed he would rather have worn a noose.

"Shhh, don't hurt Magne's feelings, he's been telling everyone all day how well His Grace looks in that lace thing," Ophele whispered, beckoning him down. "Let me see."

She had begun attending his fittings partly from a sense of duty: she was his wife; she ought to know what clothes he wore and how they all went together. But she had of necessity become the peacemaker. Master Tiffen repeatedly burst out in a passionate fury over the quantities of useless lace and braid and dangling chains, fashionable affectations of military honors that most wearers had not earned, which looked garish besides and served no useful purpose. And that was all the excuse Remin needed to agree, reject the whole project, and go back to the barracks.

Which left poor Magne as the lonely voice of reason. He had been valet to a capital gentleman for over thirty years, so he actually had the best judgment as to what those gentlemen were wearing and what would look best on Remin.

"A chain would be nice," he said now, as a frowning Remin bent to let Ophele adjust his collar, which was not actually choking him at all. "Pearl studs with those rubies, it is not nice if it's all black..."

"That will be your last chain, unless you mean to start laying rubies yourself, like a Yezi goose," said Tiffen around a mouthful of pins. "You ask me, you need it more on the black brocade."

"Yes, it's too dark, too dark..." Magne fretted, glancing from the offending garment to Remin's glowering face. The black brocade had no slashed sleeves or lace or silver braid to enliven it, which was exactly why Remin liked it.

Ophele thought him handsome no matter what he wore. The final reason she attended these fittings was because when he was dressed as the Duke of Andelin, she could hardly take her eyes off him and frequently trailed off midsentence. Dressed in a dark blue doublet with a stiff collar framing his strong throat, she could sympathize with Master Didion; Remin *looked* like he belonged in a painting. He looked like someone's ancestor that they would still be telling stories about, hundreds and hundreds of years from now.

"It itches," he complained.

"But there won't be anyone else in the whole capital who looks as nice," she whispered back, smoothing the lace so it was a little less scratchy, and colored like a strawberry when he stole a kiss.

"There will be at least one other person," he said with an approving glance at her ensemble, and unwittingly proved Mionet's contention that even the most unpleasant prospect was more tolerable when one was wearing a pretty gown.

* * *

"It's not possible for a live fish to carry poison, is it?"

Miche's question emerged in white puffs, floating over the dark water of the Brede.

"I beg you not to repeat that question in His Grace's presence," replied Juste. The Coldest Knight did not allow his teeth to chatter. He kept them clenched instead, the hard bone of his jaw jutting as he cautiously moved the oars of their rowboat, testing his healing shoulder.

There were a dozen fish traps in the small inlet of the river west of Tresingale, the same place where Remin had taught Ophele to do laundry. It took three or four pounds of fish *per meal* to sate His Grace's appetite, so twice a day Juste and Miche rowed out to haul in bass, trout, catfish, and walleye from the traps. There was one long, sharp-toothed specimen that kept getting into the traps and eating all the fish.

"I imagine if it can't kill the fish, it's not likely to hurt Rem," Miche said, tossing the empty trap back into the water and tucking his reddened hands into his armpits. "I'm half-tempted to let him try one of the biting ones."

"The last thing we need is for him to start thinking about where the fish are coming from," Juste admonished. He had even less sense of humor about Remin's food than Remin. And it wasn't that Miche didn't take the matter seriously, or he wouldn't have kicked a woman out of his bed before dawn to wade out into an icy river to catch his lord's breakfast.

Surely he was permitted to at least find it funny.

"If you were a fish, you'd be one of these," he informed Juste, wrestling one of the long toothy ones out of the trap.

"The fishermen from Isigne say those are good eating."

"Once you get past the fangs and armor plates," Miche retorted, and smacked the fish against the prow before it could whip around and bite him.

It was a decent haul for the morning. The sky was just lightening as they trudged up the hill to the manor house, Miche clutching the bucket of fish while Juste led the way with a lantern. It would be weeks before Wen was on his feet—a man his age didn't bounce back from eight stab wounds all at once—which meant the task of gutting and scaling the fish fell to them.

There were some downsides to being Knights of the Brede that no one ever talked about.

Sitting on a bench outside Juste's cottage, the two men pulled out their belt knives and set to their smelly work. Usually, it was Remin himself who came out to collect his breakfast, but that morning Ophele appeared around the corner of the house, picking her way lightly over the treacherous, icy ground.

"You're about early, my lady," Miche remarked, rising to steer her safely to the bench. "Mind that icy bit there."

"I woke up early," she said, surveying the steaming pile of fish guts with wrinkle-nosed fascination. "I've never seen fish being...prepared."

"I imagine most people would prefer to keep it that way," observed Miche as he beheaded one. "We're nearly done."

"It is a simple dissection, my lady, as we did with the devil's quill, and the goat," explained Juste, extending his knife for her inspection. "This one was female. See the eggs?"

"The little red things?"

"Those are a delicacy in Navatsvi," Miche remarked, watching with a strange and lonely contentment as Juste acquainted her with the anatomy of a trout. It reminded him of a similar lecture from his own father, when he was a boy. "You have to cut out the innards, or the fish will taste foul when you cook it."

"Like chicken and sheep," Ophele agreed. "I watched a sheep being butchered. Juomen at the cookhouse said it's easier once their heads are off and they can't look at you. Is that bit the heart?"

Miche had to look down to suppress a smile as she peppered Juste with questions, absorbing this new aquatic knowledge with the same earnestness she applied to all her other studies. Juste often bemoaned the deadly creature she might have been, if she had been properly raised, but Miche liked her just fine as she was.

And she was plenty hazardous already, in her own way.

"Thank you both for getting up so early, and in the cold," she said when they were done, rising with the basket of fish filets in her hands. Juste had gone to dispose of the inedible portions. "Would you like to come up for supper tonight? Remin is doing so much better, and it only seems fair, if it's the two of you having to go...col...lect...them..."

Miche turned to see what she was looking at.

"I'll talk to Juste," he said, quickly reaching to push the small sprig of purple flowers the rest of the way behind Juste's shutters. It was not the first such gift that Miche had spotted over the last month or so, and it amused him to play a small part in keeping Juste's secrets.

But there was no hiding it from Ophele. For a moment, she stared at the place where the flowers had been, the thoughts whirring away behind her large tawny eyes, and then she gasped and clapped a hand over her mouth, her eyes going instantly to Miche.

"Is that—"

"Juste has been very busy in the evenings, especially as we will soon be leaving," Miche said loudly, lifting a finger to his lips. "So I will ask him, my lady, but I would not count on his company."

“Oh—oh, of course.” Ophele hugged the basket of fish. “I am happy—that is, I am so happy if you want time to yourselves, or are busy with...other things. Both of you have done so much for us. I will just go te...thank you for the fish. Thank you.”

Stars, could she be more obvious? Miche watched with amusement as she retreated, and the instant she was around the corner of the house he heard her footsteps accelerate, bolting straight to Remin to tell him all about it. One day she would be dangerous, but first she was going to have to learn to keep a secret.

Why should he wish for that day to come faster?

But the day of their departure was certainly coming rapidly, and while Juste and Adelan made all the preparations for the household, Miche had been busy preparing for the journey itself. Nearly half of it would occur on the river, and the carpenters and shipwrights were hard at work converting one of the ferries into something a little more substantial, with cabins and charcoal stoves to keep the ladies warm. As Miche had good cause to know, it was bitterly cold on the water.

It would be a far more comfortable journey than the one they had made from Aldeburke almost a year ago, when Ophele had been sleeping in the supply wagon at night and Remin had watched her with the helpless resentment of a man fighting an enchantment.

There, at least, Miche thought he could be proud of his year's work.

“I have made a few provisions already,” he said as he sat down opposite Lady Verr in the solar, to discuss her portion of the preparations. She would be charged with Ophele's belongings and her comfort for the duration of the journey. “The carpenters are working on trunks and bandboxes for Their Grace's clothing and shoes and so on, and there will be enough room in the carriages for the entire contents of Master Tiffen's shop. But if there's aught that you need, or anything I have overlooked, you have only to say so.”

In this, at least, he was grateful for Lady Verr's presence. The job of a lady-in-waiting was often just to complain on behalf of the lady she served, and as Ophele would freeze to death before she thought to ask for a blanket, it was a relief to know that Lady Verr was both willing and able to take personal offense at the weather.

"I have already begun making a list," she agreed, which did not surprise Miche in the slightest. "Who will be managing His Grace's things?"

"Magne is going with us," Miche replied, accepting a sheaf of papers from her and skimming the first page. "You won't need to bring blankets; I have lap robes coming from the furrier. You and Ophele will have a carriage, not a sledge."

"That will make things easier," Lady Verr agreed, making notes of her own. "I hope it is one of the new carriages, perhaps with His Grace's heraldry. And matched horses. People will see them. It will not do to appear as if His Grace robbed a carriage house."

"All the insignia of Aldeburke has been painted over and we have a set of grays to draw Her Grace's carriage," Miche said, slanting a look at her. She missed absolutely nothing.

It was a fair starting point, and often after supper they would sit at the long table in the solar, comparing notes. It wasn't only questions of baggage and transport; every mile of their journey had to be planned with care, and all due courtesy extended to the lords of the lands they passed through. Most of them would have liked to either host or obstruct the Duke of Andelin, and the tricky task of avoiding them without giving offense had fallen to Miche.

"If we stay with them, then they'll ask to travel with us, and I won't have strangers near Rem or Ophele," Miche said when Lady Verr proposed staying with this or that acquaintance. No doubt she had many people she would like to introduce to Ophele. "There are plenty of good inns between Elantier and Segoile."

"You have warned them to expect us?" One perfect eyebrow lifted. "There will be many travelers on the road this time of year."

"They will have to seek rooms elsewhere, as we are renting the inn," Miche replied, jabbing his quill at his parchment in appreciation of his own cleverness. "It is much easier than attempting to secure it against other guests."

"Will Their Graces be dining at the inns?" Lady Verr met his gaze unblinking when Miche gave her a hard stare. Sometimes she was shockingly direct for a Rose of Segoile.

"His Grace is unpredictable," Miche replied repressively, which was all he was ever going to say to her on the subject of Remin's meals.

She was thorough, he would give her that. She had considered everything down to the herbs and tonics they might need on the road, and then went on to speculate how they might best use the journey itself to their advantage.

"There are a few places we might pause on the way," she said, examining their route on a map. "It would excite admiration and envy if Her Grace could speak of visiting the hot springs of Collume, or here, the alchemists of Metiche. It would be good if her anecdotes consisted of more than blizzards, plague, and stabbings. I suppose it is no accident we are passing through Lomonde?"

"They do remember His Grace fondly there," Miche said dryly.

"It will excite talk on the way to the capital, which is all to the good," she agreed, ignoring his tone. "It would be well if we carried silver sens for Her Grace to hand out. She is a child of the stars. The commonfolk will gather as she passes by, and cry for her blessing."

"I already have," Miche replied. "And we will not have much time to linger anywhere, but if you have orders you want sent ahead to the alchemists, I have a messenger leaving tomorrow."

"You have been quite meticulous," she admitted grudgingly, as if it pained her to approve him in any way.

"Well, I am not always a shame to my lord," Miche drawled. "It will do Ophele no harm to have a few of those things so coveted by the dear ladies of the capital."

"It should not surprise me that you know what those things might be," she said tartly. Lady Mionet Verr never backed away from a fight. "One wonders why you must ever be a shame to your lord at all, when you go to such lengths to serve him."

"Tragically, I have never been able to say no to a lady," Miche replied, scribbling busily and wondering if there was a polite way to tell a woman to shut her mouth.

"I suppose it is a question of *which* lady you are willing to disappoint," she observed. "I am quite sure the duchess will be disappointed, when rumor of your activities reaches her ears. Though you know, I have often wondered if it is a compulsion, in some men. Does it occur to you in the moment that you are disgracing yourself and the lady, as well as your lord? So many of your dalliances were married."

That was breathtakingly rude. The sort of remark that would get a man called out. But there was no particular venom in her voice, and when Miche lifted his eyes to hers, she met him straight on, with a challenging flash that dared him to answer. It made him want to tell her *exactly* what he had been doing. His beauty had always been a weapon and a weakness, and he had used it as best he could to protect Remin.

But it was also true that he had failed as often as he had succeeded, and too often, he had said *yes* when he should have said *no*.

"I suppose I must be grateful that such rumors have not already reached her ears," was all he said. He did not owe her any explanations. "Are you just waiting for an opportune moment?"

"If I thought she needed to know it, I would have told her already," she said, unruffled. "Whatever you might think, I am not seeking ways to wound her. His Grace ordered me to prepare her for the capital, and ensure that she suffers no scandal or undue anxiety while we are there. You *are* a scandal."

"It would surprise him to know how his orders were being interpreted." Miche had had enough. He scribbled a final few notes and rose, a little impressed with her sheer effrontery. "I will acquaint her with my scandals before we arrive in the capital," he said, bending to offer her a smile that made the dimples flash in his cheeks. "When will you tell her about yours?"

* * *

"The Second Company is on its way."

In the high, locked chamber of the Court of War, Remin moved the first of his markers onto the map at the center of the table, where his soldiers had begun their march to a new camp on the western moors.

"No scouts will observe them," he added, with grim satisfaction at the sight of that vast, uninhabited stretch of map, white as winter snow. "Auber, I will leave you most of the Third. You'll have to work fast to finish the wall reinforcements against the devils, but if it comes to it, the docks can be cut off from the rest of the port, and each one can hold fifty men. It'll be a long night, but you'll live."

The upper chamber was cramped tonight, and warm with close-packed bodies. In addition to the Knights of the Brede, Remin had expanded the circle to include a few of his other knights, as well as the commanders of the Third. Every one of them had sworn their loyalty to him. He sincerely believed that if the time came that they must choose between him or the Emperor, they would choose him.

But the time had come to test that belief.

"While Tounot and Jinmin are moving with the army, Auber will hold Tresingale," Remin went on. "Ortaire, you will remain to support him. Filipin, Rousse, Evgene, I rely on you to manage the Third. If you have doubts about any of your men, send them back to the border. Until the Empire actually marches on the Andelin, we will not require declarations from anyone."

He met their eyes as he issued this order, to make sure it was understood. He did not doubt these commanders. He would not like to doubt any of his soldiers. But it would fall to the commanders of the outer companies to make sure the Emperor found no allies inside Tresingale.

"The men are already talking about it, my lord," Rousse Voclait admitted. He was a battle-scarred veteran of fifty, who had spent almost thirty of those years at war with Valleth. "Not that they know any of this. But they don't think the Divinity summoned you to the capital to welcome you to the family."

"No one's said any treason," added Evgene. "But if you ask me, Your Grace...they're working themselves up to it."

"Then tell them to mind their tongues," Remin said sharply. "We don't need spies overhearing such talk."

"Though perhaps it ought not be squashed altogether, my lord," suggested Juste. "Loyal men will say such things. Angry men must have a vent. There are many productive ways they might work off their frustrations."

"Let them vent if they must, but give the Emperor no excuses to make trouble," Remin replied.

The commanders of the Third exchanged glances and nodded.

"I can keep them busy," Auber said mildly. "Between the devils and retaliation from the Empire, we need to prepare the commonfolk to either dig in or evacuate. At least the devils give us an excuse to drill them without realizing what they're being prepared for."

"Get them ready," Remin agreed. "But if it comes to it, give them a choice. You'll have warning, if things go badly. Anyone who wants to leave should be allowed to go in peace. If I die, make all efforts to bring the duchess back to the Andelin. If both of us die..."

This had been a difficult decision.

"Then Auber will inherit the valley."

This was news to all of them. Juste's face was empty, but Auber sat back in open-mouthed astonishment, and Miche caught Remin's eye and nodded in approval. Tounot just looked from Auber to Remin, as if searching for some connection he had missed.

"Rem, why," Auber managed. "I'm common-born, I'm not—"

"You will take care of my people," Remin said firmly. "And you have no scores to settle. Tounot, Juste...it might be that there will be no vengeance. There may be no justice to be had. Ever. I choose Auber as my successor."

"Heard and witnessed," said Miche.

"Heard and witnessed," echoed Filipin, Ortaire, and the rest. Remin had written this into the latest version of his will, with all proper ceremony and witnesses, but it was important for these men to hear it from him directly. And at length, Auber and Tounot lowered their heads and said the words. Juste only looked at Remin, cool and still.

"I will not agree," he said softly. "For as long as I live, I will have vengeance. But I will swear, if you fall, that I will not risk your lands or your people in its pursuit. And if I live, I will acknowledge Auber as your successor."

That was all Remin could ask. Juste had as much right as he did to pursue revenge, and Remin knew that a large part of himself that could die content if he knew that Juste would tear down the House of Agnephus, kill the Emperor, and ideally slay the Emperor's family before a screaming mob. *That* was justice. But he did not think it would make him as happy as knowing that Juste was alive somewhere, safe and happy, to die in his bed after a good, long life.

That was what he wanted for all of them.

They had so many plans to make. Contingencies upon contingencies. If House Andelin went to war, then Auber and Huber would be the last of Remin's knights left behind. Tounot was charged with moving men and supplies downriver and then marching with Jinmin to the capital, a lightning strike that—if things went well—would be too fast and overwhelming for anyone to oppose. The longer things dragged out, the worse it would be for all of them.

This was treason. A crime for which every man in the barracks could be executed, up to and including the pages. But it was a treason that had never been far from Remin's heart.

The question was, who else might suffer for it.

Every day the snow melted a little more. Drifts that had brushed the eaves of the cottages now only reached the windowsills. And after the long and biting cold of winter, even a cool day felt almost balmy when Remin stole Ophele from Juste one afternoon for a ride around town.

"I can't believe you still have them shoveling," Ophele said in an undertone as they rode down Eugene Street on Lancer, seated together as they had been the day they arrived in Tresingale. But she was far from the unhappy little waif she had been; dressed in a fawn-colored velvet gown with red and cream trim, she looked as soft and warm as a robin. She looked like a duchess.

His duchess.

"There will be four or five new roads for them to shovel, this time next year," he said wryly. Four or five new roads to name.

They passed Genon outside his infirmary, pulling a hood over his head as he bustled off on some errand. They saw the stableboys working in the yard, hauling in the day's allotment of hay. Ophele lifted a hand to greet one of the Mistresses Conbour—Remin still couldn't tell them apart—and leaned down from the saddle to exchange greetings.

"Of course I will come," she said, pleased, when Mistress Conbour invited her to tea in the cookhouse a few days hence. "Should I bring anything? Or would you like Azelma to make something?"

"Just yourself, m'lady," Mistress Conbour replied, offering a respectful nod to Remin. "Mistress Tregue says she's heard from a lady that might like to set up a teahouse in town, we're writing a letter..."

Ophele, of course, was delighted to add her signature in support, along with a postscript describing several lovely lots available in town to entice the new tea-mistress to emigrate.

Rumblings of this proposal had already reached Remin, and it pleased him beyond telling that the women of his town were taking part in its growth.

They rode on. There was Elder Brodrim, bearded and wizened, already a prominent man despite his deafness. He had forgotten more about running a town than Remin had ever learned, and Remin was not so grand that he would refuse to make use of his experience.

Turning before the North Gate, they ran into Siyoun Arpelle, the fisherman from Isigne, whose stutter had improved over the last couple months. Both he and his little girl looked much less emaciated as he lifted the child up to say hello to Their Graces.

"One of the ladies is minding her during the day while I work, in exchange for b-bass and trout," he explained to Remin, with only a little flinching and ducking. "We'll have boats on the water every day, come spring."

"That will be a sight," Remin said, wishing he would be there to see it. "Have you been making progress with Master Gibel on the fish market?"

"Aye, m'lord, and p-plans for eel ponds besides..." Warming to his subject, the fisherman was soon explaining their plans at length, as well as offering a recipe for fish fried with butter and peppers that made Remin's stomach growl.

Everyone was abroad, enjoying the sunshine. Remin even greeted Master Forgess when they spotted him in the market, trailed by his retinue of journeymen. The scholars had redeemed themselves somewhat, in his opinion; they might have been tardy in recognizing Ophele's brilliance, but they'd gotten there in the end. Their letters recommending Ophele to the Tower had been so effusive in their praise, Remin really had to *work* to glare at them.

But his glare appeared again as they passed Master Brestle's cottage just outside town, where a wagon was piled high with household goods.

"Your Grace," said the herbman, starting as he came out the front door. "I must...I must ask you to forgive me. My...wife is wanting to visit her family..."

"It is important to keep peace with your wife's family," Remin agreed flatly. "I wish you a safe journey."

"And you, my lord. We are all hoping that you will return safely," the man said, with a deep bow. "Genon says there are other healers on the way, so I believe I won't be leaving you short."

"Yes. From Lusse," Remin replied curtly, giving Lancer a nudge with his heels. Ophele turned to look over Remin's shoulder as they rode away, her eyes solemn.

"He's not coming back, is he?" she asked. "He wouldn't be taking furniture if he was coming back."

"No."

But Remin couldn't completely despise the man, now that he had a wife of his own. What would he have done in Brestle's place, with devils bearing down from one side and the possibility of war with the Empire from the other? The tales from Nandre, Meinhem, Isigne, and Selgin were all over town, and while Remin and his men had been focused on the Emperor, the people of Tresingale were worried about what might be coming out of the mountains when the snow melted.

Remin had been preparing for that, too.

"It looks like you're ready for a war," Ophele murmured, and Remin glanced down at her sharply. There was no insinuation in her guileless eyes, but it was truer than she knew. Beyond the high walls of the town, he and his men had dug lines of trenches all winter, deep enough that even wolf demons could not scramble out of the bottom. The base of the city walls was studded with immense pikes, long enough and strong enough to skewer even the Nandre devil.

"We're not coming home to another Meinhem." It was an oath. "When the devils come, we will be ready."

He had only meant to go a short distance beyond the gates; enough to see those defenses, to reassure himself and Ophele that he had done everything he could. But when Lancer snorted and sped up the slope of the perimeter road, Remin gave him his head, jogging lightly past the snowy pastures, the shadowed forest, the sweep of bare fields that would soon turn green with planting.

Their breaths puffed white as he turned at last, one arm wrapped tight around Ophele, turning to gaze upon their city.

Their home.

Their dream.

It was still so small. A cluster of cottages by the North Gate; the distant smoke of the market and craftsmen's quarter, barely visible above the treetops. One day, the spire of his cathedral would top those trees, magnificent against the wild blue sky. One day, the dome of the Court of War would shine white as alabaster, a beacon visible for miles upriver. And within those walls would swell the rumble and thud of people at work, the hew and cry of humanity, the great stir of life and love and growing.

"I don't want to go," Ophele burst out suddenly. "I don't. I don't want to leave."

"Neither do I." Remin's hands clenched on the reins. He had never in his life wanted to do anything less.

"It feels like we're running away," she said. "I know Huber and Auber will look after everyone, but we should be here. It feels like we're leaving them behind."

"I know."

It could not possibly feel any other way. Remin's jaw tightened as he looked at his town, his people, the small and vulnerable space of civilization in all the wide valley. They had bled to take it. Broken their backs to build it. And now they would have to bleed again to hold it.

"I...*hate* this," he said slowly. "I hate it so much."

Maybe it was because of where they were. Outside of Tresingale, away from their house, there was nothing around them but the cold, quiet hills and naked trees. Maybe it was that these words had been locked inside him for so long, a weight in his chest and a lump in his throat, and he was tired of fighting them down. They clawed their way out, raw and furious.

"I don't want to go," he said savagely. "I should be here to protect them. The stars only know what will be coming out of that mountain, and there is nowhere the devils will come but here, to beat on the walls. I should *be here* when they do. All these people have suffered so much already, I already failed them once, and now I'm supposed to tell them all will be well and go to the capital for the season? Knowing that any time—"

Ophele's eyes were on his face, quiet and watchful.

"It's fine. I just worry." He was trying to leash his tongue and finding it harder than he expected. "We'll be safe. I have planned everything, you can see the defenses, and if I really thought there was danger, I would leave more men behind. But we need—that is, I want to make sure you are protected. Not that it's dangerous," he added quickly. "I am taking no chances. They are good men, you haven't begun to see what they can do yet, so you needn't worry."

He couldn't keep the words back when she was looking at him like that.

"I don't want you to worry. But sometimes, I...we have so much, and it's safe, it is, but I...I have been so..."

"Afraid," Ophele said softly.

"Yes."

"I am afraid, too," she whispered, laying her hand on his. "I'm afraid all the time."

"Still?" he asked gratefully, running his other hand gently over her back.

"Yes. Well...of little things," she said. "Things you can't protect me from, I guess. I'm afraid of doing something wrong. Or saying something wrong. And of people I don't know, and leaving home, and all those people in the capital, and...Lady Hurrell. I think I'm...better, but sometimes I still get so nervous..."

"I'll be beside you," he promised.

"I know. I know, I'm just...saying. Lady Hurrell has been there all this time, and you don't know...well, you do, a little. But she knows things," she said grimly. "She knows them, and she holds onto them until just the right moment."

"But we have Lady Verr," Remin said very seriously, and made her burst into giggles. He kissed the top of her ear. "There are some good people going with us, wife."

"Yes," she agreed, giving him a smile. "I did think of that, we have Miche and Justenin, and Edemir will be there already...and we have good people staying here, Remin. Amise and all the other ladies promised me they would take care of things. It won't be just Auber and Tounot. The women know the devils are coming. They won't just sit about waiting for them."

"Really?" Remin felt his heart lift. "What did they say?"

"Well, they heard about the shell curtains your men made during the war," she began. "They're making those for the doors and windows, and Mistress Tregue wondered whether everyone ought to have a bell in the house, a great big loud one to warn everyone else if a strangler's spotted. Wouldn't that help?"

"Yes, it would." Remin's arms tightened around her. "That's a good idea, wife. I'll tell Auber to have it done."

"It's their home, too," she reminded him softly, and for a long time they sat together on Remin's big black horse, gazing down upon the dream they had so carefully nurtured, and hoping it was strong enough to survive without them.

Chapter 14 – Sacred Plantings

Year 800 of the Divine House of Agnephus

The sacred bulls of Sachar Veche were well-known throughout the world.

Admittedly, the connection between bulls and the Sachar Vechan sun deity eluded most outsiders, but it made sense enough to the people there. The sacred bulls lived lives of pampered luxury, fed only in the greenest pastures, the freshest hay, and—so it was said—water hauled from the spring of some associated demigod. Their horns and hooves were capped with gold and crusted with jewels, and multiple times per year, they were brought forth to breed before cheering crowds during the many fertility rituals.

When they were too old for breeding, they retired to a golden pen in a golden stable to live out the rest of their lives. When they were too old to stand, they were strapped upright in huge, jeweled harnesses, to dangle until they died. It was a terrible omen if a sacred bull fell over.

Emperor Bastin Agnephus had always felt a curious kinship with these revered beasts.

Five years after his forced marriage to Esmene of House Melun, he had found a little peace. It was the peace of work. The peace of having a plan, a goal, an objective toward which he was patiently plodding. He could not say he was *pleased* with his life, not as long as that Melun woman still dwelled in Starfall, but there was some consolation in knowing it would not be forever.

The greater part of his plans involved extracting her from him like a rotten tooth.

But that was not the extent of his ambitions. Esmene was a symptom of a far greater problem, and his divorce was only the first step in ensuring that the House of Agnephus would never again be forced to sell its children.

"Wealth, power, and influence," said Laud Ereguil, ticking them off on his fingers. With two young sons at home, Duke Ereguil would have preferred to stay in Rospalme, but had come to Segoile at his Emperor's request. "My father always said they are not the same thing. Overlapping, but distinct."

"All of the things that the House of Agnephus is lacking," Bastin said sourly, waving away a servant as he topped off his own wineglass. It took just as long to tell them to do it as to do it himself. "But the first is currently the most ruinous. It seems unreasonable that the Court of Nobility might vote us into wars which the House of Agnephus must pay for, and then the Five Courts can reject any efforts to refill the Imperial coffers."

"The Imperial Museum wasn't a bad idea," Laud offered. That had been the brainstorm of one of Bastin's secretaries, and they had been wrangling over the benefits of the proposal ever since. "Power and influence may spring from such unlikely places. Displaying the treasures of the Emperor makes you appear benevolent and powerful, and the common folk of the capital would enjoy it. Better than letting it all sit in a vault."

"Why not, when I am forbidden to sell it," Bastin replied ungraciously. It had been a frustrating week.

"You might even enlist the Temple to guard them," Laud added. "Theft from the Emperor is blasphemy."

"Oh, they're the worst thieves of all." Bastin waved a hand. "They've taken to leasing their lands to local lords, so they can avoid paying taxes on its produce. Had I sufficient power or influence, I would use it to charge my Temple with cheating me of my wealth."

"That's a problem," Laud acknowledged, with a glint of humor. No one lacked as much reverence for the Emperor as the Emperor himself. "But it might be you could use one problem to solve another. Even if the local lords are using the land, it's still consecrated to you, isn't it?"

"Yes..." Bastin brightened. "Making all its produce holy."

"Which means all those sheep grazing your sacred land make sacred wool, sacred yarn, sacred cloth, and sacred lambs." Laud slapped the arm of his chair, chortling. "All of which must be handled with due ritual and piety by everyone from the spinner to the dyer to the weaver, then sold at an inflated price to a merchant—"

"—who must warehouse it separately from his common merchandise," Bastin laughed. It would be ruinously expensive for *all* of them. "I don't suppose anyone wants to start unraveling *that* string, do they?"

"Your Temple least of all," agreed Laud, rubbing his hands together. These were a little different than the games they had played when they were boys, but they enjoyed them nonetheless, and the two men sat up late into the night untangling this one. Or more accurately, tying it into a more thorough knot to hang the lot of them.

There were so many ways in which his Agnephus ancestry was a double-edged sword. Everyone in the Empire knew that there must be an Agnephus in Starfall. Bastin's sanctity was the sanctity of the realm. In all the world, Ospret Far-Eyes had chosen *this* place to come and bestow his blessing and reveal his visions.

There was a strangely selective reverence for his descendants. Bastin was sacred in his body, in his blood, in his life. In many ways, he was like a chalice: an object of worship unmoored from the mundane world.

They were very careful of his safety. From the moment of his birth, he was protected. He had been assigned his first personal guard when he learned to walk; when he learned to run, he got two. Tasters sampled everything he ate. His chamberlain protected the sanctity of his personal chambers. He had three clerics that did nothing but cycle through his private chapel in eight-hour shifts, filling every moment of every day with prayers for the safety of the Sacred Radiance, the Divinity, Beloved of Stars.

His *person* was sacrosanct. His opinions and will, however, were decidedly not.

It was something Bastin struggled to reconcile. The history of the House of Agnephus was filled with many divine puppets and few assassinations. No one needed to harm him if he could be kept weak. It would be the work of his life to cut away those strings. He would see that the House of Agnephus collected its due, that it grew influence in all the Five Courts, and by...*himself,* he would bring *his* Temple to heel.

Otherwise, he might as well be one of those sacred bulls of Sachar Veche, groomed and grown to hump-backed glory, to breed and die in a golden pen.

But though Bastin had little reverence for his own divinity, he never dreamed that anyone else would dare to disregard it.

"Set it on the table," he said one night to a servant who brought in a tray of wine and pastries, an evening snack. Bastin did not entrust the running of his empire to secretaries. He had dozens of reports to read with due skepticism, and most nights he worked well past midnight. Pouring a glass of wine, he bit into one of the pastries, warm with apple and cinnamon.

Time passed. The level of wine in the bottle slowly fell, and after a little while, it seemed that he grew tired. Bastin blinked as the words on the page blurred and fumbled for his cup. His mouth was so dry.

"Husband."

The word seemed to come from very far away. Bastin started, staggering to his feet as the Empress slipped through the doors of his chamber. How had she gotten there? Who had let her in? He had given strict orders...

"What..." he tried to say, and she moved quickly to support him as he stumbled backward and nearly fell. His knees kept buckling under him. "How—*guards!*"

"Oh, dear, are you unwell?" Esmene's voice filled with concern as she helped him to his bed. Everything was wavering and rippling around him, and by the time he realized where he was, she was already pushing him down on the bed. Her hand caught his chin, forcing him to look up at her. "Are you dizzy?"

"...esss...poison..." he slurred. Colors streaked past his eyes, and he squeezed them shut, nauseated. "Call...my guards..."

"No. I don't think I will," she said serenely, and he felt her hands as if through a muffling layer of thick velvet, tugging him, touching him. Bewildered though he was, he still recognized Esmene Melun. She was not allowed to touch him. He did not want her to touch him. She should never touch him.

"St...stop." His tongue felt thick in his mouth, his arms wooden as he tried to shove her away. She batted his hands aside as if he were a child.

"My, it *does* work on you," she laughed, and he realized with horror that she had undone his belt and was unlacing his breeches. His eyes reeled up to her face, dizzy and disbelieving. The stars would see this. His eyes were the eyes of the stars.

"You...*drugged me?*" he whispered, trying to focus on her face. The motion of her silver hair blurred and streaked before his eyes, as if to conceal this terrible reality from him.

"Yes," she said, and, grasping his jaw, poured something into his mouth.

His memory of that night would always be confused. Whatever she had given him, it made it impossible to tell whether an hour had passed or a year, as if there had never been anything but this sickening whirl of fury and helplessness and unwanted pleasure. Again and again, she brought him to orgasm, and it seemed he had barely sunk into a drugged stupor before she was shaking him awake to pour more of that vile concoction down his throat. He choked. He tried to spit it out, but she fed it to him with her own lips, sealing his mouth so he had no choice but to swallow.

Was there an aphrodisiac? There must be, he had never wanted anything less. But he couldn't stop his body from rising, thrusting away like one of the sacred breeding bulls of Sachar Veche even as hot tears streaked down his cheeks. There was a roaring in his ears like the screaming of a crowd, cheering, cheering...

He could not even control his tears.

When she finally slipped out of his bed, it was morning. His head was light, so light it felt as if he might float away and never come back. His eyes rolled over and found her, the shape of her face wavering like a candle flame.

"Kill you..." he rasped. His hands fumbled for his trousers, a blanket, anything to cover his nakedness, but all he could feel was the mess she had left on his body. His voice sounded weak to his own ears, a sick mewling. It was just like his father had sounded in the last days before his death. "I will...kill you..."

"That would mean war," Esmene said, slipping a robe over her shoulders. "A war that you would lose. I hope we will not need to repeat this lesson, husband. You *will* give me a child."

Bastin rolled onto his side, turning his back to her.

She was right.

He was ill for days afterward. Oh, physically he had recovered by the next morning, but it took a further three days for him to come to grips with the fact that someone had done that to him. It was not...*possible*. He was a man. Men did not...

And it was blasphemy. Worse than blasphemy. She had...*polluted* him. He was sacred, he was supposed to be sacred. What she had done was so terrible, he would have been within his rights to demand her public and prolonged execution.

But first, he would have to tell the Temple what she had done.

Would they even believe him?

It was well known that he despised his wife. There was no physical evidence of the crime, except for the bites and scratches on his body; the bottle of wine and his cup had both vanished, and no one in his household had even known she was there. Or so they said. Had she bought them? Had she entered his palace some other way? Did he have sufficient power and influence to accuse the Empress, daughter of House Melun, and have her executed for her crime?

Could Emperor Bastin Agnephus, the sacred scion of Ospret Far-Eyes, Beloved of the Stars, even trust his Temple with the secret of his shame?

No. He could not.

Huddled in his chambers, he ordered all his servants and guards out and barred the doors. He could hear the bells of the Eternal Vigil ringing, the tones that signaled the change as one priest took over from the other. The prayer of the Eternal Vigil had continued uninterrupted for seven hundred and eighty-three years, continuously imploring the stars to look down upon their Beloved, to safeguard and protect the Emperor of Argence. Through all the hours that Esmene had been defiling him, he had heard the ringing of those bells.

The thought that she could do it again drove him nearly frantic.

What could he do? Where could he go? Who could he trust? To think he had been so proud, so confident that he was slowly but surely building his strength, increasing the wealth and power of the Emperor until one day he at least might have the right of self-determination. He had moved people into key positions. He had forced the Temple to pay what he was due, he was building a core guard that he had believed was loyal to him, and he had been patiently fostering alliances among the Houses and Courts of his Empire, right under the noses of House Melun.

But when it came to it, when it *mattered,* he did not even have the protection of the Temple that was built *on him.*

The only choice he had was whose mercy he would beg.

* * *

Year 827 of the Divine House of Agnephus

To Her Grace Liliet, Duchess of Ereguil, at the estate of Mimosa in Segoile, from Duchess Ophele Andelin at Tresingale Manor in the duchy of Andelin:

This must be the last letter before we depart for the city, so when next we speak, it will be in person. I cannot thank you enough for meeting us there, and please pass my gratitude to Duke Ereguil as well. You may say it is nothing, but as I watch all the preparations for our own journey, I can see very well how much work it must have been. You are both so good to come all that way, and offer us refuge.

Some of my gowns were sent ahead, so I have taken a page from your book and sent a few gifts with them, as thanks for the lovely presents you gave us when we moved into the house. We haven't many shops in Tresingale yet, but we do have skilled craftsmen. I am certain you will receive the box before this letter, so I am spoiling no surprises when I tell you the two vases were made by our own Master Peltier, who is apparently famous!

Now, let me tell you what Remin did to me. All these months I have been chattering away to Master Peltier like he was just anyone, and asking him questions, and no doubt making a nuisance of myself, and I even invited him to luncheon so he and the brick-makers could argue about kilns, never dreaming that he is one of the Empire's Great Masters!

I only found out because Master Didion—another Great Master—happened by when we were talking about dishes for the house and told me that Duke Berebet promised Master Peltier the moon, trying to get him to stay in Oleron. But Remin bribed him with exclusive rights to our Brede River pink clay, and so here he is, and I might have died right there when I realized we had someone so important in the valley. Why, I even shouted at him once, when he was ill and wouldn't take his medicine.

Isn't that just too mean, for Remin not to tell me?

But I see what you mean, about placating our artisans, for I would be ashamed to lose Master Peltier now that we have him, and I will be on the lookout for any other craftsmen we might acquire. I don't know how everyone can bear to do this every year, leaving their folk at home to go to the capital for months and months. I have so many lists, and yet I am sure to forget something.

Mionet says it will only make it sweeter when we come back, for then there will be birthday parties and festivals and blessings for the new babies to come, for there are a few ladies expecting. We will have a harvest festival this autumn, and then some other ritual before we depart to bless the fields for planting.

Do you have such rituals in Ereguil? Oh, I wish you and I might have some time to talk before we leave the capital! Everyone acts as if I should know what blessing the fields is, and I find such customs fascinating. And the stars know I could spend days and days while you told me all your stories about Remin.

I really do not know what is the matter with him; I cannot even scold him, because it isn't that he is intentionally keeping secrets as that it just doesn't occur to him that there are things I might like to know. There was the matter with Master Peltier, after which I made him tell me if he had any other great secrets, and he said not really, except that I should probably know that he has the crown jewels of the King of Valleth hidden away, in case we ever need to crack the whip over them.

Have you ever <u>heard</u> of such a man?

I heard about the Regalia of Valleth before. I thought it was a legend. But Remin says he acquired it at the end of the war and has been holding it over their heads ever since, and the Vallethi mind him now like lambs. As if the only possible and logical solution to any war is to steal his enemy's sacred bauble and bury it in the back garden.

Does he have a great many secrets like that? I will tell you all my secrets, but please, you must tell me all of his! For surely otherwise I will be old and gray and Remin will still be confessing that he also has the Seven Jewels of Thala hidden away somewhere, along with the Daitian Ark of Shadows. The stars only know what horrors our descendants may turn up, a hundred years hence.

Yours in great exasperation,
Ophele

* * *

"My lord? My lady?"

In the very early morning, Remin woke to the sound of Cruce Adelan's voice calling from the door, and a sense that there was something important he was supposed to do.

"Ophele," he mumbled, sitting up and raking his fingers through his hair. "Wife, wake up."

All the preparations had already been made. He steered his semiconscious wife to her dressing room, where Lady Verr and the maids waited to dress her in the ritual clothing: floating layers of unbleached linen, raw fabric sanctified by Brother Oleare. Magne waited with similar clothes for Remin, scratchy and thoroughly inadequate to the weather. In warmer parts of the Empire, they would have gone barefoot.

In March in Tresingale, they were lucky most of the snow had melted.

They emerged in the forecourt in the uncanny dark before dawn, a dreamy world of uncertain light and wavering silhouettes. A small crowd stood at the foot of the steps, all of the household's knights and servants gathered to partake in the blessing, yawning and solemn.

"I don't believe it's dangerously cold, my lord, but we will have bonfires awaiting your return at the gate," said Juste, who had horses saddled and waiting. He, Miche, Leonin, and Davi were armed and armored and hoping neither would be necessary.

"Any word from the night watch?" Remin asked, swinging atop Lancer and holding out a hand to Ophele. The cold had driven the fog from her eyes.

"Yes, my lord, Tounot sent a runner. No devils reported, and they've set up a perimeter with torches."

"Good."

It would have been very early for the devils to arrive in Tresingale, but Remin was taking no chances. Half the Third Company had spent the night combing the woods and fields north of the town to ensure nothing bigger than a mouse might threaten them. Remin wrapped his cloak around Ophele and clucked to Lancer, leading the way into town.

He suspected she was only pretending to be asleep, burrowed under both their cloaks and quietly mortified about what they were about to do. It wasn't easy for him, either; despite the earliness of the hour, people lined the sides of the road, lifting their hands in the gestures of revelation, calling the stars to witness. But he was the lord of this place, and this too was part of his work.

"Your Grace," said Brother Oleare as they reached the North Gate, flung open to the morning with bare fields rolling beyond. The holy man folded his hands and bowed low, his long beard nearly brushing the cobblestones. "I have everything in readiness. There are no clouds to obscure our view of the stars, and they promise to shine for a while yet."

"Thank you. Kneel here, wife," Remin added quickly, arranging his thick bearskin cloak to make a pad for her knees. Even through the black fur he could feel the cobblestones, like chunks of ice, and he hoped the earth of the fields would be a little more forgiving. Ophele arranged the layers of her linen skirt, glanced at his hands, and lifted her own in the same way.

"The stars witness this blessed union." Brother Oleare raised his voice for the benefit of the villagers clustered nearby. "Remin, His Grace the Duke of Andelin, lord of these lands. Yours is the hand on the plow, tilling the soil, sowing the field. You make an offering of yourself to the land, your flesh, your blood, your sweat, your seed, so that the time of reaping may come, to the nourishment of your people. Do you so offer?"

"I do."

"Blessed lady." Brother Oleare turned to Ophele, who looked up at him like a solemn little owl. "Ophele, Princess of the House of Agnephus, Duchess of Andelin. It is a rare blessing that a child of the stars comes to dwell so near the earth. The bond between a lord and his land is like a marriage, and every spring, that bond is renewed. You are the sacred land. You are the Andelin, the bounty of your people. Do not fear the earth. Do not disdain it. You make an offering of yourself as the land offers itself, with your blood, your sweat, your pain, your sacred flesh, to carry and bring forth life. Do you so offer?"

"I do," she said softly.

"Then on behalf of your people, I ask that you go, that the land will prosper. Go, sacred children, and bless the planting under the eyes of the stars."

Under the eyes of Tresingale, they rose to remove their cloaks and shoes, handing them off to Magne and Lady Verr. It was uncomfortably cold, their breaths faintly visible, and Remin stood rigidly to keep from shivering as Ophele straightened, her long hair flowing loose around her.

Taking her hand, they walked barefoot through the gates.

The fields stretched before them, dark and bare and still damp from melted snow. Torches shone along the treeline where his soldiers watched, alert for danger.

"I'll warm you soon enough," he promised as Ophele began to shiver, and won a small smile.

"You can tell they invented this custom somewhere warm," she observed, picking her way lightly on tiptoe.

"My parents always blessed the fields, though they don't keep the custom so much in the western Empire," Remin replied. "There was magic before Ospret, you know. They used to say that the life of the lord is the life of the land."

"That sounds like one of those things that seems more profound than it actually is." Ophele was difficult to impress before sunrise.

Just over the hill and out of sight of town, a tent awaited them, many layers of unbleached linen billowing in the breeze. Remin had checked to make sure it was opaque even with the light of multiple iron stoves glowing within, but the roof was gauzy and insubstantial, open to the stars. Six stoves had been burning constantly for several days to warm the soil in which they must lay. He meant to bless the fields properly, but it could not possibly be a good omen if he and Ophele froze to death.

"Oh, it's *warm.*" Ophele sighed with pleasure at the waft of hot air. Moving to the nearest stove, she held out her hands and then glanced up at Remin, a pink flush rising to her ears. "We really have to do this?"

"I hope it will not be too great a hardship to lie with me," he teased, though now that it had come to it, he wasn't sure himself. The earth had been turned several times over the last few days and all the stones raked out, but it hardly looked an inviting bed.

With a mental shrug, he crouched and pushed his palms into it, feeling the cold, damp earth. They had grown wheat here last year. Wheat they had milled and cleaned and made into flour, and the flour had become bread, warm and nourishing. Soon, they would sow again. This was a place of fertility. This was a ritual to encourage abundant life.

"Come here," he said, holding out his hand to Ophele. He hadn't the least idea what he was doing; there had been very little guidance beyond the act itself, but he meant to take it seriously. If they had to lie down in the dirt and make love, well, Remin would see that they did the thing thoroughly.

Together, they pressed their hands into the soil, a rich crumbling loam that left dark speckles on their skin. It was like swimming in the Brede, the sweeping motions of their hands through the dirt. His fingers brushed hers, and his big hands slid up her bare arms, painting streaks with the moist earth.

"I guess I am meant to be the garden," she said, examining the marks solemnly, and Remin bent his head to kiss her as he loosened the strings at the shoulders of her gown.

"I have always thought so," he murmured, laying warm kisses down the side of her neck as he brushed her hair out of the way. The light of the stoves glowed on her fair skin, and in a moment her gown slipped off, baring her beautiful breasts, her pink nipples stiff with cold.

They were going to get dirty. He laid her down on the ground on the cloak of her hair and pushed his own clothes off. Maybe that was even the *point,* to join the lord and lady to the earth of their domain, so they could never grow too far from this most elemental reality. He drew dark stripes over her sides with his hands, caressed the outer curves of her thighs, blending her into this patch of ground. But he left her breasts bare for his mouth, and she shifted beneath him as he bent his head, lapping.

"You too," she whispered. He felt the grit against his skin as her hands slid over his back, darkening his flesh with the earth. The fluid caress made him shiver. "I bet those people before Ospret did it just like this. Before they ever worried about being lords and ladies."

"None of that matters here," he said thickly. He could feel the heated wetness pressed against him between her thighs, and his hips moved automatically to stroke against her, making them both moan.

Even with dirt rasping his knees and blackening his fingernails, all he could think about was her. The earth was cool, even cold in some places, but her mouth was so hot and their tongues coiled together eagerly, breathing hotter, faster. *Ahhhh.* His hands clutched her, caressed her, feeling the response of her soft body as he roused her, his thighs moving against hers, belly to belly. Her hands plunged into the earth again, stroking his back, his shoulders, feeling the muscles that had worked this soil, to sow and reap in turn.

"Ahhh...Remin," she breathed as he bit down her throat, her ribs fluttering against him. His hips ground into hers and the feel of her wetness sent a blinding flash of pleasure down the length of his spine. Pressed against her, he could feel her throbbing in a deep, heavy pulse, an irresistible urge.

"Stars, let us make a child," he whispered, and drew back to put himself at her entrance.

"Yes," she breathed, her bright eyes glowing.

"Ah...haaaa..." A long groan escaped him as he pushed inside. Stars, let them make a child. His breath caught as he drew back and pushed deeper, a heavy thrust that sank him to the root.

"Oh, like that," she gasped, wrapping her arms about his neck. Her heels dug into the soil, lifting her hips to receive him, and Remin gave her a hard smack with his hips that made stars burst behind his eyes.

"Stars...stars, let us make a child," he said hoarsely, laying his hand on her abdomen and *willing* it to be so. Another bleeding had come and gone, dashing his hopes that she might already be carrying, and tomorrow they would be leaving the valley, and any moment his enemies might strike again.

"I want to, oh, there, *feel...*" Her hand covered his, guiding it, pressing it flat so that he could feel himself moving inside her, the deep stroking of his body.

"I feel it," he managed, but it was too much and he gripped her hips tight, leaving the dark marks of his hands as he rocked into the cradle of her thighs. Bending his head, he caught one of her nipples in his mouth, lapping at breasts that would one day be heavy with milk to nourish their children. Everything was bountiful. All of her was life. Stars, let them make a child!

Their voices rose together, and there were no more thoughts. Sweat burst on his skin and he groaned, the tent billowing around them as he mated with her, churning the earth into mud.

"Nngh...*nngh*...ah, ah, *ah!"* Ophele's voice leapt an octave, her body arching in a sinuous caress that made his hips buck helplessly. Bands of earth wrapped his legs, the fertile soil of his valley, and the greedy grasp of her body pulled him down, in, deep.

"Oh—oh there, oh there, oh...*good!"* she cried, and he felt her go, the rippling spasms of her climax that finished him instantly, deep, good, and endless.

He groaned, his head hanging. Inside her was fertile ground, a blessed place for planting, and he *willed* it to happen as he filled her, praying wordlessly that his essence would take root there, so part of him would grow and be with her always.

"Stay," he managed, catching her hips to keep his softening length inside her. His head was spinning and he couldn't make his eyes focus, but he found her lips and kissed her. "Brother Oleare said...we have until dawn."

"We're not done?"

"No." Holding her thighs to his hips, he let his forehead rest on hers, drawing long, deep breaths to get his strength back. "I will plant you as many times as I can. Does it hurt?"

"No. Just...muddy," she said, and kissed him reassuringly. "Is that what we're supposed to do?"

"I want to try." He grunted as she fluttered around him, slippery with his seed. She was so warm in his arms, always warm, his little flame. "Again," he made himself say, focusing on how she felt to him, all the things about her that made him hard and wanting for her. "And again, I will...you feel so good on me, my wife..."

Talk like this did not come naturally to him. Especially when her body was still wringing the last of his seed from him, and his muscles were twitching with the urge to move, and his own weight on his knees was making them ache. He didn't know if he even believed in the stars. He didn't know if they cared what he was doing, whether they would bless him with a child or let him die in his blood. All he could do was everything he could.

"So beautiful," he whispered, his sides belling in huge, deep breaths. Her small face was darkened with dirt and streaked with sweat, a jagged mask around her extraordinary eyes. Stars, she was lovely. His lips brushed hers, tingling. "Your face...your chin, I love your chin, this little point...it makes me want to catch you..."

"Kiss me," she breathed as he caught her chin in his fingers and tasted her tongue. Her skin, her body, the hot and slippery silk inside her, tangled around him and tugged tighter.

"You're...squeezing me," he said breathlessly, his big hands sinking into the dirt even as he sank into her, and felt like he was melting in the fire. "Oh, I do love you, Ophele, I do..."

And never more than when her arms wrapped around him and her body moved to meet him, receiving him like the earth opening to the plow.

He wanted to see it so badly. Small, lovely Ophele ripe with his child. He wanted to see the fields his people would sow, and the vision that flickered behind his eyes was like waves and waves of golden grain, alive with the breath of the wind.

Distantly, he heard her voice rising and falling, her high cries of pleasure. Felt her breasts against his chest and her legs wrapped around him, the heat and the wet and the grit and the hardness of his body, working furiously to completion.

"Rem—oh, *oh! Remin!*" She bucked beneath him, a seismic shock of joining that made him cry out hoarsely.

"No—don't, don't move!" Gripping her waist, he strained to keep himself inside her, when it felt so good he could hardly stand it. "I can...I can, one more time..."

He could, because he must. Through his closed eyelids he could see the growing light beyond the glow of the stoves, sense the approaching dawn in the noise of distant birdsong, the stirring of morning. But he could do it, he could do it once more. Plant, and bless the planting.

The back of his mind understood what he was doing, and why. He *must* make a child. He *must* give her a child. Beneath that heavy stone in his chest was the knowledge of his own weakness, the kernel of terror that fed him nightmares every night, that he would not be strong enough for this destiny, that he would fail and die and leave her all alone.

Remin was as mortal as anyone else. He could die. He could be afraid. He had been afraid, for so long.

Beneath him, Ophele's sides heaved. Her thighs flexed and her hands covered his and her eyes lifted to his face, willing to help even when she didn't understand why he was trying so hard. He loved her *so much*. He loved her, and he loved this valley, and it was his duty and his honor to bind himself to them for all of his life. He would give them everything he had.

One more time.

Pebbles chewed into his knees. Muscles burned. How long had they been doing this? How much time was left? Hurry, hurry, he had to go faster, dawn was coming and that would be the end of the spell, this blessed time when all the magic in the world was bent toward life.

"Stars..." Ophele gasped. Her legs tightened around him, her nails biting into his shoulders as she flung her head back. "Stars, let us—let us make a child!"

He felt her go. Felt the clutch of her body straining with his, sweat-slicked skin and so hot, so close, melding him and her and the earth and the air together at once. His hips plunged on as he gathered her up, holding her to him to shut out everything else. A thousand distractions clawing for his attention, aches and pains and itches and discomfort and that creeping knowledge of the dawn, but he pushed them all away. Behind his closed eyelids was something wide and dark and waiting, opening for him.

He fell into it.

Wordless noises punched from his chest. The climax burst through him, from him, flowing into her. He was spending himself like rain. Everything he had, everything he was, all of his love. His stubbornness. The powerful pounding of his heart and the huge breaths that filled his mighty lungs, all his strength and will and the relentless force of his life.

All of it. All for her. All for his land. He had come so far, he had fought so hard to live, he had brought so much death, and now his reward was to make life.

He was taken in, and accepted.

Far away, he heard the blast of a hunting horn. The last star had vanished from the sky.

"No...stay," he said fuzzily as he felt Ophele move under him. He felt very peculiar. He barely knew where he was, the words tumbling from his lips, disjointed and senseless. "Wife. Give it...time to root..."

And then he slumped forward, lost in the peace of the quiet earth.

* * *

Really, she ought to have known he would do this as thoroughly as he did everything else.

"Remin?"

Gently, she nudged him, turning his head to look at his face. His eyes were closed, long black lashes smudging his cheeks. Sprawled on top of her, he was limp and exceedingly heavy, and even though the feel of him inside her was uncomfortable and a spiky rock was jabbing her directly in the backside, Ophele exhaled and gave up. She guessed he had a right to be a bit tired, after that.

Lying on the cold, muddy ground, she was very much awake, which meant thinking. Justenin had a deeply unsentimental view of the Empire's holidays and festivals, and though Ophele had not dared to ask him directly about this one, she could just imagine what he would say. A pagan relic, when everyone knew there was no magic in the Empire, and impractical and dangerous besides. *And* it was mortifying; how was she ever going to walk back into town and face everyone, when they all knew what she and Remin had *just* been doing?

But Remin had delivered a surprisingly profound answer when she asked why they must do this: it was important because people *believed* it was important. And wasn't that a sort of magic in itself? A self-fulfilling prophecy. *Belief* was a curious thing, and her limited study of magic had made her quite sure that she didn't know enough to have an opinion.

It was some time before Remin finally stirred, a ripple of alertness through his body, and she smiled as his lips nuzzled her throat in a sleepy inhalation.

"We are not doing it again," she informed him, as his black eyes slitted open.

"Not here, anyway," he agreed, rumbling with amusement. Brushing a thumb over her cheek, he kissed her and sat up, wincing as he extracted his body from hers. "Did I hurt you?"

"I'm all right. I want a bath," she said with feeling, trying to sit up without touching anything.

"No, stay still," Remin objected, and it wasn't until he had dressed her, picked her up, and was halfway back to town that it dawned on her why he was keeping her more or less horizontal.

"You know you'll have to put me down when we get back," she said, laughing and crimson to her hair. Stars, he was the most determined man alive. But she saw the smile crease his cheek and wrapped her arms tighter around his neck, feeling that she could face even the mob at the North Gate so long as Remin was beside her.

It was embarrassing. It couldn't be anything else, dozens of people staring at her when she was wearing a wettish, muddy linen dress with the sticky feeling of Remin between her legs. This seemed one of the more unlikely ways to look after their people.

But the people themselves appreciated it. She could hear them cheering when Remin finally set her down, their hands raised in greeting and in blessing. The farmers were clustered to the front of the crowd, the Conbour clan as well as all the folk from Remin's villages, who would join them in the plowing as soon as the ground was dry enough.

This was even harder for Remin. The last part of the ritual was the sharing of the blessing, and while he wasn't easy to embarrass, he intensely disliked letting other people touch him. Half of Tresingale was reaching for him, hands out and sleeves rolled up, and Remin's knights were watching like hawks.

Remin squeezed Ophele's hand and held out his arms, rigidly enduring as the men approached to lay their hands on him, firmly enough to carry away a bit of dirt and mud. The virtue of the earth thus passed from person to person, blessing the work of the year, and they rubbed their hands together as they walked away, lifting their hands to their faces in the gestures of revelation. Miche and Juste hovered at Remin's side, watching this most dangerous portion of the ritual.

Bonfires blazed, heating the cobblestones, and Leonin and Davi took their places behind Ophele as Mionet appeared with her cloak and shoes.

"Oh, thank you," Ophele said, grimacing as she wiggled her dirty toes against the silk lining. "No, I'm warm enough," she added quickly, waving away her cloak. No point in ruining it.

"I will have it if you change your mind," Mionet replied, bundling it under one arm and extending her other hand. "Blessings, Your Grace."

"Blessings on you," Ophele replied, surprised and pleased. She would have expected Mionet to disdain so earthy a blessing.

"Blessings, my lady!" piped Elodie's voice, and Ophele turned to find her loyal pagegirl obediently waiting to be invited over, though a few bounces on her heels betrayed her excitement.

"I shall give you a good one," Ophele replied happily, holding out her arms in invitation and transferring a mighty benediction as Elodie flung her arms around her waist. The girl hardly needed help to grow; Elodie already bid fair to outstrip Ophele herself. "Will you be helping with the gardens?"

"Yes, I'll help Aunt Lisset, since Mama kills everything and Pirot's scared of slugs," Elodie answered as Ophele offered a blessing to her long-suffering little brother.

"I'm scared of slugs, too," Ophele whispered to the boy, and won a gap-toothed grin.

Gradually, she was parted from Remin, as the town's men gathered around him and the women clustered around her, hands pressing her hands, her arms, her shoulders, even sinking into her hair. If dirt was the blessing, that was surely where it lay most heavily.

The crowd only swelled as the sun rose, streaming down Eugene Street and the newly named North Gate Road, filling the wide, paved space before the gate. A few times Leonin ordered them back when too many people pressed close, but Ophele knew so many of them, she could not feel afraid. Mistress Tregue and Mistress Roscout came together to introduce the cobbler's wife, Mistress Hebbett, who had arrived with five children at the Gellege Bridge, presented her letter of invitation, and demanded that her husband come take charge of *his* children at once.

It took an impressive woman to bring five children halfway across the Empire by herself. And a special girl to bring a little boy all the way from Nandre, Ophele thought, as she spotted Amalie in the crowd. The two survivors of Nandre were hanging back, uncertain whether they were welcome.

"Oh, Amalie, come here," Ophele said, holding out her hands. The girl was nearly as scrawny as Ophele had been at her age, reared in the backslope, rocky soil of the mountains, and both she and her brother still hadn't recovered from their ordeal. Laying her hand on the girl's forehead, Ophele thought, *grow,* and wondered if it would do anything.

"Thank you, m'lady," the girl said shyly, ducking her head. "Could you—for my brother, too?"

"Of course I will. Iskerren?" Ophele bent her head to look at the boy, clinging to his sister's back with his face hidden in her shoulder. Roughly half the time, he refused to emerge, but this time he peeked up at Ophele and allowed her to pick him up. They were all so *small,* these children, she thought unhappily, hugging him hard to bless him thoroughly.

"He talked a bit yesterday," Amalie said, patting his foot. "Didn't you, Iske?"

"Sometimes you just don't feel like talking," Ophele replied sympathetically. "But you must be sure to eat and eat, so you can get strong like His—oh, I know. My lord!" she called, turning toward the crowd of men. "Your Grace!"

He was easy to spot; Remin towered head and shoulders over everyone else around him, and came promptly, bending down to have a look at Iskerren.

"Perhaps he might have a double blessing," Ophele said hopefully, tickling the little boy's side until he finally peeked up at Remin with solemn blue eyes. "Will you go to His Grace?" she asked.

"Yes," said Iskerren after a moment, perfectly clear, and Remin picked him up with an unusually soft expression, settling the boy into the crook of his arm.

"Well, you must be a grand big fellow," he said, patting the little back. "We'll give you a good coat of dirt, and mind that you tell the ladies it's sacred. The best boys are always a little grubby."

"'Mallie says knights have to wash their hands before supper," Iskerren objected, winning chuckles from the listening men.

"You can be as dirty as you like until then."

Amalie was almost beside herself as she listened, her hands clasped together.

"Thank you so much, m'lady," she said, hugging herself. "Oh, he hardly ever talks."

"No, it's nothing at all. Bless you," Ophele added to another of the village women, who solemnly ran her hands over Ophele's arms and then transferred her palms to her forehead, her lips moving in silent prayer. "Are you and Iskerren still staying with Mistress Gevenin?"

"Yes, m'lady, she was so good, taking us in," Amalie said earnestly. "Though...she says I'm old enough to earn my keep, and she can look after Iskerren. I don't like bothering, but if it isn't impertinent...do you suppose I might help at the big house? If there's work that needs doing? I don't mean to be rude," she added quickly, under the gimlet eyes of Mionet. "I'm not fussy, I can scrub and clean or anything."

"Well, I'm sure there is," Ophele replied, after a quick consultation of several mental lists. "I'll speak with Adelan. Maybe there will be room in the kitchen, can you cook?"

"A bit. Well, tea and toast," Amalie admitted. "But I can learn, m'lady."

"I'm sure there's something we can do," Ophele promised, though she did have a few qualms about handing the girl over to Azelma's tyranny. A Segoile-trained cook was particular and domineering, but as Azelma herself said, there was no easy life.

And wouldn't Azelma like to train up a few cooks to capital standards? They would need more cooks anyway, as well as pastry chefs and butchers and bakers and everything else, and one day Remin's knights would have their own households, too. One day, Tresingale might have its own cuisine, and its *own* school of cookery, and its own accreditations, and even *better* food than the Empire—

"Blessings, Your Grace," said Isilde, Auber's pretty sweetheart, and Ophele snapped back to the present, offering her hands.

"Bless you," she said, smiling. Ever since she had learned that Auber meant to propose, she had regarded Isilde as something like a prospective sister, or maybe cousin, but definitely a future fellow sufferer of noble etiquette. "How are you? Where is Vinzetin?"

Isilde's son was usually somewhere in line of sight; he was of that breed of boy that was simultaneously accident-prone and indestructible.

"Over being blessed by His Grace," Isilde said wryly, nodding to an area of the crowd where Remin was currently being swarmed with small boys, and Auber was presenting Vinzetin for the duke's approval. "Sometimes I think the stars brought me here just to unite them."

She said it with a smile, but there was a look in her eyes that smote Ophele with guilt. She had been the one to tell everyone that Auber had asked Remin's permission to propose, and they had all been so terribly happy and excited, but now it had been two months and Isilde must be so hurt.

"But of course, Auber is very fond of *you,*" Ophele said sympathetically. "There is nothing wrong, I hope?"

"How could I say so?" Isilde replied. "When he is so good to us both, and really he needn't trouble himself at all."

"He ought to at least trouble himself to make up his mind, the great lummox," said Amise Conbour, who had been standing nearby. She had no reverence at all for her brother-in-law.

"Please don't fuss at him for it, I am sure he has his reasons," Isilde replied, with a glance in Auber's direction that wounded Ophele's tender heart.

"Well, if he can't make up his mind, there's no reason you can't change yours," Lisset Conbour pointed out. "What about that nice young guardsman who came to call?"

"Oh, no, but you love Auber, don't you?" Ophele asked, dismayed as Isilde looked away. She had been looking forward to having another lady in the valley to invite to tea, and sewing, and shopping...

"Sometimes love is not the trouble," Mionet said wisely, which was probably true, but so very sad.

"Isn't Auber going to propose to Isilde?" Ophele demanded later, when she and Remin finally returned home. They had both had to stand in the courtyard and get doused with buckets of steaming water before they could go inside.

"I don't know," Remin replied, looking taken aback. "He didn't already?"

"No, and Isilde is unhappy, and there's a guardsman that's coming and bothering her, and Amise and Lisset are telling her to go ahead and invite him to supper if Auber can't make up his mind," Ophele replied severely. "What if he steals her away?"

"I would say it's her business if she goes, and it's not up to us either way, wife," Remin replied, seated opposite Ophele in their large bathtub and patiently washing her feet.

"But what could he be thinking, when they love each other? He was so upset when she and Vinzetin were sick. And Isilde would be a lady and everything," she said, disappointed.

"I am not going to encourage him to propose to her just because you want another friend to go about town with," Remin replied, amused. But his face quickly sobered. "And to be fair, he might have good reasons, for the present. It mightn't be about her."

"What do you mean?"

"I am not going to speak for him," Remin said firmly. "Nor should you. I would just guess—if it were me, perhaps I might wait a few months, before I tied her to me."

Ophele considered this, her brow furrowed. Then her eyes flew open.

"Because of the Emperor?" she asked. "Because of what might happen after we go to Segoile, if he wants to do something dreadful? And so there might be danger, because Auber is your friend? And if he had married Isilde, and he was punished—"

"Stars, I will never say another word in front of you." Remin pinched her toes and gave them a shake. "No. It's enough that he has his reasons, wife, and don't you go interfering. People have to sort these things out themselves."

"I wasn't going to. And we're leaving, anyway," Ophele replied, grieved. "But it seems a shame to let them flounder about and be unhappy when a few words might put things right. Won't you warn him, at least? Isilde thinks that maybe she isn't good enough for him after all. Wouldn't you want someone to tell you, if I was troubled and you didn't know?"

"I wonder that you can say that to my face, when you have Miche informing on me." Remin reached out a long arm to drag her into his lap, settling her comfortably against his chest. "We will see Auber for supper tomorrow. I'll see what I can do."

"We might have a new kitchen girl to help," Ophele remembered, and told him about Amalie as he gently washed the last of the Tresingale dirt from her body, their final scattering of seeds before they left home.

Chapter 15 – Last of His Blood

Year 800 of the Divine House of Agnephus

It was unpardonably late when Bastin arrived at Duke Ereguil's estate in Segoile.

If there was anyone in the world he could trust, it was Laud Ereguil. Bastin's father had chosen many blue-blooded sons to be his companion when he was a child, and over the last twenty years, every single one of those early friends had come to him for some favor, to capitalize on that relationship. To Bastin, it was inevitable.

If Laud was ever going to collect, it would be now.

The famous mimosa trees lined the long avenue to the manor, all pink flowers and lacy leaves, ending in a grand courtyard before the ancient house. It was one of the finest estates in the city.

"Divinity?" Duke Ereguil descended the steps in a hurry, looking as if he had dressed hastily in the dark. "Is something amiss?"

"Yes. I must speak with you now," said Bastin, with a pointed look at the servants. He had dismissed all his own servants and ordered his guards to remain outside. He could not trust them.

"Yes, Divinity. My office," Laud replied, recovering quickly. "Nencion, bring us a bite from the kitchen. See that we are not otherwise disturbed."

"Thank you." Bastin followed the other man down a long corridor with moonlight streaming through wide windows on either side. "I know it is very late."

That was as near as an Emperor could come to an apology.

"I heard you were unwell," Laud replied, glancing back at him. "I hope it was nothing serious."

"I am well enough." The doors of the office closed behind them and for a moment Bastin hesitated, the words hovering on the tip of his tongue as he looked at the other man. It was Laud. Bluff, brawling Laud was honest as few noblemen were, and shrewd enough to arrange matters so that he could be.

Was Laud truly his friend? Could he really confide in him, and trust that it would not be repeated?

"Divinity?"

"What I say must go no further than this room." Bastin selected a chair and sat in it.

"Of course," Laud said in surprise, sitting with obvious disquiet. "Do you require an oath of secrecy?"

He was joking. Bastin was not.

"Yes."

Laud gave it, with all the ceremony and careful phrasing that one might wish. But even as he spoke the ritual words, it just reminded Bastin of all the *other* oaths that had been sworn to him, even sworn *on* him. Bastin Agnephus, the Divinity, was an object upon which to hang an oath.

"...until death takes me, or the Divinity himself should free me to speak," Laud concluded, and looked at him expectantly.

"I hate my wife."

This was not a secret. Everyone in the Empire knew it.

"I want to divorce her," Bastin went on, gripping the arms of his chair. "I *will* divorce her, no matter what it takes."

"Radiance," Laud began sympathetically. "There is no such thing as divorce under heaven. You exchanged sacred, eternal oaths. The Temple sanctified your union. In the eyes of the stars—"

"I am their Beloved," Bastin snapped. "I am sacred. I am their son, the Divinity, if anyone may speak for them, it is I. The stars know that I was forced—forced to make those oaths. I was never joined to her willingly, *never,* not once. It cannot be this way. This cannot be acceptable, I cannot—"

His voice was rising, and he cut himself off.

"You have seen how my Temple regards me," he said, trying to be calm. "If I am sacred, how can it be the will of the stars for their son to be bound again and again against his will? How could it be the will of the stars for their scions, the rulers of the Empire, to be made slaves to the Temple and House Melun?"

"I cannot fathom the will of the stars," Laud said carefully, troubled. "I agree that it cannot be good for the Empire for our Emperor to be...treated that way. Whether by Melun or anyone else. I do believe that."

How pathetic, that Bastin must *argue* for that position. That so many of his lords would disagree.

His chest was tight.

"I have never truly...felt that I was sacred," Bastin replied, low. "I do not know what I am...*supposed* to feel. They said my father was sacred. The clerics prayed in his name and collected money in his name and trotted him out to the crowds and when they had squeezed all the blood from him, they sold what was left to Melun. How could they do that, if they really believed he was sacred?"

They had sold Bastin himself to House Melun, too. He had made it his business to discover what had happened to his father. Emperor Onsetin Agnephus's priests had taken money to leave him on his sickbed with Duke Dardot Melun. For three days, servants and priests had ignored the shouting from the Emperor's chambers, leaving the sick man trapped until he agreed to betroth his son to Esmene Melun. He had died shortly after.

Had he too heard the bells of the Eternal Vigil?

And had Bastin's own clerics sold him again? he wondered suddenly. Had Esmene paid them to allow her into his palace?

"Maybe that is the trouble," he whispered, more to himself than to Laud. "I have not believed myself sacred. Why should anyone else?"

"Radiance?"

"I will undo this marriage." Bastin drew himself up in his chair. "To do that, my Temple must be brought to heel. If I am sacred, I will *be* sacred. I will make them bow their necks to me. If I have the strength to do that, that will be enough. Will you help me?"

"Of course," Laud said slowly, and rose at a knock at the door without taking his eyes from Bastin. He had the Ereguil eyes, cinnamon-brown and sharp as a raptor's. "That will be the wine. I feel we will need it."

Bastin would never drink wine again without a moment's misgiving, but he sipped from his glass and felt it burn in his gut, a manifestation of the fury that would be with him for the rest of his life.

"Melun has the support of Pomeret, Sangevin, and Norgrede." Laud set a tray of fruit and cheese between them, beginning in the place where they were both most comfortable, like laying out game pieces. "They will not cross Melun's will in any matter. Firkane and Tries will support you, as always. Old Duke Lein is ineffectual, but you may have better luck with his son. Berebet never saw a fence they didn't want to sit on, though they would back you if you showed enough strength."

"If I could persuade House ________, that might be enough," Bastin said, seizing gratefully on the problem. "When was the last time Benetot was in the capital? I swear I have not seen him since I confirmed his title."

"The Eastern Empire suffered greatly in the war," Laud reminded him. The last war with Valleth had claimed many members of the high nobility, including both Benetot's and Laud's fathers, elevating young men who otherwise would have waited decades to inherit their Houses. It was one of the reasons why Bastin had had so much trouble building his power. Right now, the castles of the capital were slippery as sand.

"I need him here. They cling to the old ways in the East," Bastin remembered. "It may incline him to sympathy. Why has he been avoiding the capital?"

"It is more that a great deal of attention is needed at home," Laud replied diplomatically. "Benetot is just married, with a child on the way. That may make it difficult to persuade him in this matter. The people of the East revere the old ways, but that also means they take their oaths seriously."

"My marriage oath was not made in good faith," Bastin countered. "It cannot be good in the sight of the stars to compel someone to make an oath against their will. As a *principle.* I always said that Melun must have bribed the Temple—"

"Re-litigating your betrothal is unlikely to sway anyone to your side, Radiance," Laud pointed out. "That is settled business. There must be some other reason to justify such a measure."

That was an opportunity to tell him what the Empress had done, but even with wine bubbling faintly in his veins, Bastin could not make himself do it. The despised vision of his father was too present in his mind, that quavering, apologetic voice, praying to the stars to have mercy on his son. Weak. A man so weak *deserved* his fate. He could not call himself a man at all.

"She cannot give me an heir," he said instead.

"It helps that she has not," Laud agreed. "And that in all the years of the Agnephus dynasty, there has never been an infertile Emperor."

For a moment, Bastin imagined all of his predecessors, eight hundred years of Agnephus sons, and wondered if any others had been unwilling sires. Their beloved subjects would not *allow* them to be infertile.

"There will be no choice but to accept a divorce if the alternative is the extinction of the House of Agnephus," Laud was saying. "But Divinity, if the Empress were to conceive..."

"She will not," Bastin replied. He would die first.

"Is there really no way you can be reconciled?" Laud was watching him carefully. "We can work to separate the Empress from her House, and keep Melun in check. Even Pomeret and Sangevin might be persuaded to stay their hands, if we were merely seeking to restrain Melun. But if you could just accept the Empress—"

"No."

"I know how you feel," Laud said sympathetically, leaning nearer. "I do. My own wife was not to my liking, at first. But there are few noblemen who marry for love. If you viewed it as a partnership, an alliance—"

"No," Bastin repeated violently. Allow that bitch to go to banquet with him and smile at his side? *Dance* with her? The thought of her hand on him sickened him, let alone—but stars, that *was* going to happen again, wasn't it? It was going to be years before he could secure a divorce, and in the meantime...

He was going to have to go back to her bed. Not once. Many times. Regularly. To prove that she could not give him a child.

"I will not. *Ever*," he said, and was dismayed to find his eyes were hot. He gulped down his wine.

"As you command. I think it is too soon for any extreme measures." Laud popped a bit of cheese in his mouth and chewed. "I can begin planting concerns among the other Houses. It *is* a concern. The House of Agnephus must have an heir."

"The Duchess of _____ is of an age with your wife, I believe," Bastin said, groping for something resembling strategy. "Sidonie of House Roye? Perhaps she will persuade Benetot. Especially if they have a child on the way. It grieves me, to be denied the joy of a family."

"Liliet will be pleased to make her acquaintance, I am sure," Laud replied wryly. "Though I would almost pity the lady, Liliet is relentless. I tell you, we disregard our women at our peril..."

He did not sound angry. There was a grudging fondness in his voice, proof that he *had* truly reconciled himself to his marriage. In the space of five minutes, he was already boasting about his two sons, the most remarkable boys who ever lived, and there was a third baby already on the way. And Bastin was glad for his friend, he was, but it was the last thing he wanted to hear.

That had never been possible with the Empress. She wanted a sacred puppet, and her hands on the strings.

There was the possibility that she was already pregnant. He had to face that reality. If she was, then he would only have six or seven months to act before Esmene had a new and better puppet, and Bastin was likely to join the short list of the Empire's assassinated rulers. All this time he had been so careful about when he lay with her, to never seed her, to never finish the act. Most often, it had been too painful for that to even be a possibility. But now he did not even know how many times...

He could not think of it.

If she was with child, then he would find a way to deal with it. Accidents happened. And in the meantime, he would find a way to prevent conception between them, no matter what she did to him. It would have been a simple matter outside the Empire; all the mysterious and magical energies of the world would be at his disposal. But those powers did not hold sway in his lands, and they especially did not work on him. That was why his flesh was protected so vigorously. The sacred Emperors of Argence could only rely on their own mortal healing.

There must be a way. And until he found it, he could not let Esmene near him again.

"...Divinity. Radiance?"

Bastin started. The hour had grown very, very late.

"Yes. I am afraid I must trouble you a while longer," he said awkwardly. He could not quite make himself meet Laud's eyes. "I must ask you to play host for a time. I have reason to doubt the...loyalty of my household."

"It would be my honor." Laud's bushy brows lifted, and Bastin thought hopelessly that he might guess it all, just from that. "As long as you like."

"You have never asked me for anything." Bastin allowed Laud to haul him to his feet, catching the taller man by his jerkin to find his balance. They had both consumed a good quantity of wine. "No riches. No favors. Melun would reward you well if you handed me over to them. Why don't you?"

"Well...we are friends, aren't we?" Laud looked at him with some surprise. "I wouldn't do such a thing on principle, but I hope it is not a sacrilege to like you for your own person. We have been friends since we were boys."

"No, we are friends." Bastin felt a knot tighten in his throat and had to look away. "If there is ever anything I may give you," he said, meaning it with every drop of his own sacred blood, "you have only to ask."

* * *

A coded message on a folded scrap of parchment, concealed in the hollow of a tree:

Do what must be done. At all costs, they cannot be allowed to leave.

* * *

Their last supper in Tresingale was a grand affair.

Ophele had been planning it for weeks, with Mionet and Azelma's help. The dining table in the solar was almost unrecognizable with so much silver and crystal and fine-patterned china, groaning beneath platters of food and wine glowing like rubies. In the center of the table, a single arrangement of pine and red-berried holly had given Mionet an excuse to explain flower arranging.

It was like stepping into another world.

"Your Grace," they all said together when she and Remin appeared, bowing.

Oh, didn't they all look so fine! Ophele tried not to stare as Remin seated her at the table, marveling at all the silk and satin, gold and silver, the jade ornaments in Mionet's hair, and who knew Tounot had such a gorgeous silver chain? Miche was particularly eye-catching with his long blond hair gleaming over his shoulders and a crimson doublet studded with tiny golden suns. And when had she ever seen Justenin look so splendid?

At Remin's nod, they all drew out their seats to sit down, Tounot and Auber, Leonin and Davi, with Juste thoughtfully pulling out Mionet's chair and Huber at the end. Ophele was relieved that he had come, though she felt a pang at the sight of the sleeve pinned up over his missing arm.

"Wen was back in the kitchen today, my lord," said Miche, putting on his company manners as he and Justenin served the meal. "He said he's not too poorly to cook a cod."

So saying, he lifted the lid from the largest dish with a flourish, revealing an immense cod still dressed in its scales, bathed in a red sauce that promised to be spicy. It was arranged on a river of rice and greens shaped to look like rippling water weeds, and there was a murmur of appreciation up and down the table.

"Only Wen touched this?" Remin asked, and gestured for more at Miche's nod, filling his plate for the first time in weeks. Each dish was more beautiful and tempting than the last, and if Miche only offered Remin a selection of those dishes, and paused to murmur to him before each was served, at least Remin showed no sign of distress as everyone else devoured the rest.

Ophele had never had such a meal. Long before dessert, her sides were creaking, and she sat back to sip at a mixture of wine and honey mead, cultivating her palate to the taste of the grapes.

The table was a babble of conversation. Miche, Tounot, and Remin were filled with plans for a vineyard, with pleasant visions of trellises at the foot of Justenin's observatory. On Ophele's other side, Justenin had collared Auber and was issuing dire warnings about a bull with a penchant for escape. And across the table, Leonin and Mionet were teaching Davi how to discreetly dispose of fish bones.

But there was one person who was not participating in any of these conversations. Ophele had considered Huber carefully, when she was choosing the menu; a man with one arm could not cut his own meat, and she didn't want to embarrass him the first time he came to supper. But even though everything was tender and bite-sized, he still had to chase it about his plate with a fork.

Ophele watched through her eyelashes, her heart aching for him. She had never known anyone who had been hurt so terribly, or at least, anyone who had *just* been hurt so terribly. Davi had lost an eye, and it didn't seem to trouble him greatly, but after watching Justenin struggle with his dislocated shoulder, she could only imagine how hard it must be for Huber.

Ought she to say something? He was a proud man, perhaps he might not like to talk about his troubles.

"My lord," said Tounot as she was trying to decide, and rose from the table with a wave to include his brother knights. "As you have no minstrels yet for your hall, we will do our humble best to fill it with music. Lovely Lady of the Andelin, we hope to earn your favor."

In moments, they had produced instruments and moved the table out of the way, clearing a large space before the fire. But of course, they were knights; they would have learned how to play when they were boys. Ophele looked at Remin with delight as they strummed and piped, Tounot on his lute, Leonin picking nimbly at a mandolin, and Miche with a wood flute in his fingers, his dimples flickering as he smiled.

"A fisher that lived in a far country, On a low green hill, with a view of the sea..." sang Tounot, and Leonin joined in, the two men's voices blending pleasantly together as Miche tapped his toe to mark time. "Seven lovely daughters had he..."

Most songs were new to Ophele, who had always been denied such pleasures. It hadn't even occurred to her to arrange entertainment after supper; it had been enough to have food, to see Remin eat the food, and to have them all together one last time. But they must have discussed it amongst themselves, because Justenin borrowed Tounot's lute next and played a surprisingly moving song about a knight lost in battle, whose spirit came back as an owl to watch over his sweetheart.

Then Davi sang, and Leonin, and when it was Auber's turn, he glanced at his brother knights and clapped his hands in a rhythm that made every one of them instantly set aside their instruments.

Oh it's morning time, you sleeping lads,
and time to leave your beds

It's sunrise soon, take up your packs,
we've weary miles ahead

Oh it's morning time, green-handed boys,
let's be on our way

We'll break your boots and break your
backs before the break of day.

All of the men were singing, their voices loud and lusty, stomping their boots and clapping their hands in marching rhythm, clearly a song to pass long and weary hours. And Ophele could see the memories that bound them together, the endless miles they had traveled, especially as Tounot picked up the next verse as if he had done it a hundred times before.

Oh the noon has come, brave soldiers all,
and the day's half-gone behind

A bite, a sip, a little breath, that's all the
rest we'll find

Oh, the sun's well up, you marching men,
but smoke's rolling in the sky

So check your armor, check your steel, for
we'll get there, by and by.

To her delight, Remin took the third verse himself, his deep voice strong and true, thumping into the notes along with the stomping steps, his big hands clapping.

Oh the evening's come, you men of war,
and a red sky lies behind

We broke the wall and burned them all,
but there's more hell yet to find

Oh the evening's here, you iron sods, you
proved the mettle of your soul

So pick it up and march along, for we've
a long way yet to go.

"Been a while since I heard that one," Davi said appreciatively, as the floorboards gave a final shiver beneath their feet.

"We used to sing it on the march," Remin explained to Ophele. "It makes the time go faster, if you've got something else to think about besides marching."

"I liked it," she said sincerely, though it almost felt as if she were trespassing to listen. It was something she would never understand because she had not been there, something that was both mundane and sacred to them all.

Of course, Miche could not long abide the sacred. He picked up his flute to pipe a short and oddly familiar tune, and shot Ophele a wicked glance.

Oh you can search the Empire wide

And never find a better guide

To the precious things you unfortunately let fall...

"Oh, not again!" Ophele wailed as Remin burst out laughing, and Miche went merrily into the song of the Lady of the Wall, who this time sat atop it, peering into the distance in search of the home of the devils, and demanding whole libraries as compensation for her efforts.

It might be devils, plague, or plunder

That makes our blessed lady wonder

And there's only one place that she'd think to look

Whether it's a blacksmith's iron bars

Or the sacred mysteries of the stars

Can you tell me, might I find it in a book?

Even Mionet laughed as Miche repeated the final chorus.

"Impertinent! You are impertinent, sir!" she cried, clapping her hands. "My lady, that is what is called a *chancun glore,* a praising song, though many of them are affectionately satirical. And if it does not please you, it is acceptable to pelt him with sweetmeats."

"It's the only way a hardworking musician can get a little dessert," Miche said mournfully.

"No, no, you are all ridiculous," Ophele said, covering her mouth with her hand to hide her uncontrollable giggles. Stars, she had never expected to hear that again. And she wished even more that she knew a song herself, right up until the moment that Mionet volunteered her to demonstrate a different skill.

"Perhaps you would like to show His Grace what you have learned, my lady," Mionet suggested. "If I might find a knight who will help me keep you company?"

Her gaze landed on Justenin, who rose so promptly that Ophele could not find a polite way to refuse. Amidst a sudden and extreme attack of stage fright, she forced herself to her feet, her tongue rooted firmly to the roof of her mouth. Everyone was looking at her.

"Well, haven't we been learning not to trip over each other?" Remin asked lightly, taking her hands and drawing her into the open space before the fire.

"I can't promise I won't," she replied, assuming the proper position for an Imperial Tournel, her right hand clasped in his and her left on his bicep, which was as high as she could comfortably reach.

It was a bit of a stumbling start; Remin was five inches taller than even the lanky Davi, and his feet were very big. But after a few missteps, they found a pace that suited them both, a gliding, graceful step, *one* two three, *one* two three. She had done this every day for almost four months, and beside her, she could hear the familiar accompanying steps of Mionet and Justenin, keeping the time. Remin's hand pressed gently at her back.

"Look at me, wife," he whispered, and she lifted her eyes to find that he was smiling, watching her dance, and her feet moved even better when she stopped looking down at them.

"You did say you knew how to dance," she said bashfully, feeling a wide, foolish smile spread across her face.

This was what Mionet had been trying to describe, when she sighed after the balls of the capital. The flourishes of the Imperial Tournel were meant to allow a man to display his partner: the flare of her skirts, the grace of her limbs, the glitter of her jewels and all of her beauty. Remin's hand squeezed a gentle warning and then he spun her outward in a whirl of pink and cream satin, and it was like *being* a flower as it unfurled, contained safe in the frame of his arms and for a single, exquisite moment: perfect.

The watching knights applauded.

Ophele only just remembered that she was meant to backstep so Remin could draw her back in, but she did it, and moved straight into the next figure, *one* two three, *one* two three. She looked up at him, as surprised as anyone to find herself exactly where she was supposed to be, and found his dark eyes were *glowing*.

He was proud of her.

She had promised she would learn how to dance.

It was just one thing, the tiniest subset of all the *other* things she had to learn, but she had done it. Maybe she wouldn't disgrace them in the capital after all. She could learn. She could make him proud. She would make them all proud.

Miche set aside his flute to claim the next dance, and then Tounot bowed and took her hand, and one after another, she danced with them all. It was like a dream, the glow of the fire and the whirl of the music and the dancing, some timeless magic, as if the vision of this night and these fine knights and lords would linger here forever.

But there was one man that could not dance.

When she finally sat down to catch her breath, her eyes sought him out unthinking, sitting in the shadows with his chair angled to conceal his missing arm. Was there a way she might invite Huber to dance? He probably would not like to all at once, without even a chance to practice. And then she wondered with a sudden pang whether he had learned how to play an instrument too, when he was a boy.

He would never play one again.

As if he could hear her thoughts, his head turned, and copper flashed as his eyes met hers.

Instantly, her gaze dropped to the floor, embarrassed. But no, it would be even worse to avoid him. They had only spoken a few times over supper, and he had been so often away that she had not had much chance to know him, but somehow she had always felt a kinship with Huber. Ophele looked at him with mute inquiry, filled with her concern for him, her goodwill for this good man. Four times, he had risked himself, trying to help Remin's villagers.

In the end, it had cost him his arm.

Maybe it was the gift of two people who did not find it easy to speak to find other ways to communicate. For a long moment, their eyes met in eloquent silence, and when Tounot plucked the first few chords of the next song, and all the other knights lifted their voices in a familiar ballad, Huber turned his head in the shadows, and softly sang along.

* * *

Why did every important occasion require her to be hauled out of bed before dawn?

"Here is your traveling gown, my lady," said Mionet, far too cheerfully when it was still dark outside the windows. Ophele mumbled and put her arms out so Emi and Peri could slip a soft wool gown over her head. She had finally learned what a *houppelande* was, a full-skirted gown with a high, frilled collar, after the style of the Western Empire. Amber and jasper glinted on her sash, and Mionet chose matching ribbons to weave through her hair.

This was the last time Emi and Peri would dress her. The last time she would sit to breakfast in the solar with the household, half of them still tousled and sleepy. Justenin had brought a stack of papers to the table, his pale eyes skimming over their contents.

"At least our new chambers will await us when we come back," said Miche, leaning back in his chair with the satisfaction of one man watching another work. "I've ordered woodwork enough to deplete a forest, Rem. Hope you don't mind."

"It's furnishings for the household, you're part of the household," Remin replied between large bites of egg and sausage.

Most of their trunks and baggage had been carted down to the harbor the day before, but it was still a rush to collect the last few objects. Remin had a steel casket of papers that he refused to let out of his sight, lined with oilskin and surrounded on the outside with leather-wrapped hollow logs, to ensure it could survive both fire and shipwreck. He checked so many times to make sure it hadn't been forgotten that Miche offered to tie it to his wrist.

The sun was rising behind the Berlawes when the household gathered in the courtyard, with a line of carriages and horses and all the servants clustered to bid their lord and lady farewell. The house and all the incoming servants would be under Adelan's care, along with oversight of the construction, with firm orders to restrain Sousten's more flamboyant impulses.

"Tell Auber if you need any help," Remin said, offering a hand to the butler. It was not the way of the Empire, but Adelan only hesitated a moment before he reached to firmly clasp it.

"You'll find a place for Amalie?" Ophele reminded him as he turned to her. She had been very surprised when Adelan expressed reservations over employing an undersized thirteen-year-old girl.

"I have already spoken to Mistress Bessin," he assured her, glancing at that lady. "She says she knows how to find occupation for small hands."

"She does," Ophele agreed, with a wave of nostalgia. "And her pay—"

"I know she has a brother, my lady, but it will cause disruption among the other servants if a kitchen maid is paid more than a footman."

There wasn't enough time to have this discussion. Ophele had had no counter for the contention that Sim and Jaose, trained footmen of three and four years' experience, should not be paid the same as a girl who knew how to make toast. The obvious solution to Ophele was to pay everyone more, which provoked a discussion on the scarcity of goods and the stability of the valley's economy and three additional books on economic philosophy had been added to her satchel.

"Just—look after her, please," she said, looking from Adelan to Azelma.

"We will," Azelma promised, stepping forward to gently pinch Ophele's cheeks in both hands. "And you look after yourself, and His Grace. Keep your eyes open, child. Think before you speak. And be brave."

"I will," Ophele promised, bending to accept an embrace.

"Now, here, I've made you both a lunch," Azelma said briskly when they parted, producing a bundle wrapped in cheesecloth. "You can tell His Grace that no hands touched it but my own and Wen's. And I will come, my lord, if you need me," she added, looking over Ophele's shoulder. "I can be packed and on my way in a trice."

"Thank you," Remin replied, plucking the bundle from Ophele's hands. "I think your testimony will suffice, but I will send for you, if it is needful."

"Testimony?" Ophele echoed, but he only kissed her cheek and handed her up into the carriage. And then all the servants were waving as they moved off, and Samin the bootboy ran behind them to the top of the hill, calling *good-bye, good-bye!*

It reminded her of the day she left Aldeburke, seated before Remin on Lancer with lunch in her lap and knots in her stomach, the first time she had ever left the estate.

"It is always so exciting, beginning a new journey," Mionet said, looking out the windows of the carriage with satisfaction. "And much more comfortable than the one either of us undertook to come here, I daresay. I have examined the cabins on the ferry myself. They are small but very comfortable, perfectly acceptable for the third woman in the Empire. I am told they consulted Sousten..."

She filled the silence with agreeable chatter as the carriages rolled smoothly over the cobblestones. The descent to the harbor was a rougher ride; the hill by the barracks was deeply rutted and cut with stones to keep the soil from eroding further, and Ophele turned around in her seat to look back at the hillside, wondering how to solve the problem. They could not add more soil to the hill, or build it out into the river, and the stones were already getting bounced off the side by the traffic, so how...

"I hope they will have this fixed before we return," Mionet said, clinging to the strap behind the carriage door to keep from being tossed onto the floor.

Five ferries bobbed at the docks as Ophele stepped from the carriage, square-sailed caravels with smoke puffing from internal stoves. They were not quite ready to make sail; porters scurried up and down the gangplanks, making their way through a mountain of baggage. Remin's soldiers had lined up with their gear in neat rows, each man's personal belongings stowed in one line and their horses' gear in another, and Ophele's eyes widened as she watched Lancer go up the plank onto one ship, followed by Justenin's horse and Miche's, and the four grays that would draw her own carriage. But of course, how else would they have horses when they got where they were going?

It did make her request for a satchel of books feel much more reasonable.

Several colorful trunks and boxes appeared amidst the generally drab baggage and Mionet's head snapped up, her eyes narrowing, like Remin about to plunge into a melee.

"Mind your hands, if you please," she called, clear and commanding, moving to intercept an unfortunate pair of porters and demanding to know what they meant by handling a lady's shoebox like it was filled with soldiers' moldy old boots.

"Oh, she is right, she is right," Magne said anxiously behind Ophele, dancing in place. "Fine clothes can be damaged, they must be caref—oh, dear, dear, dear! That's the hats! No, they must go on top, *on top!*"

And he was off, to join his handwringing to Mionet's imperious commands. Ophele was tempted to join the fray herself when she saw her books going up, flung in a bag over someone's shoulder with no care at all for the leather bindings.

"My lady! Your Grace!" she heard behind her, and Ophele turned to see a cascade of boys tumbling down the hillside, all the pages descending from the barracks and waving wildly.

"Oh, be careful!" she called, going to meet them. "Be careful! Haven't you got lessons right now?"

"We wanted to say good-bye," Denin said breathlessly, and several boys thrust out small, scrubby bundles of spring's earliest flowers. "For you, my lady."

"Master Epagne gave us leave, my lord," Gavrel added, as Remin loomed into view with Miche one step behind him. "He said it was just down the hill, after all."

"Then say it, and get back to your studies," said Remin, looking harassed. "It is crowded on the quay already."

"Actually—my lady," said Jacot, approaching with one of Ophele's books in his hand. "I'm glad we got to come and say good-bye; I wanted to s-see you and say—"

Everything happened at once.

Ophele squealed in surprise as she was suddenly flung down onto the dock with Leonin on top of her and Davi's sword ringing free of its sheath, his voice roaring for the boys to get back. Boots thudded. Remin shouted. Someone was swearing, everyone was scrambling, there were splashes and chaos and something heavy thumped onto the dock.

There was a moment of silence, and then all the pageboys started screaming.

"What—what," Ophele kept saying, trying to shove Leonin off her and feeling as if she couldn't breathe. "Leonin, what—Remin! Remin!"

"Get her back," Davi snapped, and suddenly Ophele was hauled to her feet as if she were weightless, batting at Leonin's hands as she sought wildly for Remin. No—that wasn't Remin on the dock, that was Jacot, only something was wrong with his head, and she turned to find Miche beside her, standing with his arms flung out before a stricken Remin.

"No," Remin said into sudden, complete silence. "No, no, no, *no...*"

There was a blade sticking out of Miche's chest.

"Oh, fuck," said Miche, looking down at it, and then plucked it out of himself with a strange, detached curiosity. The three slim steel prongs of the weapon were red with his blood, and smeared with something darker.

"I told you I didn't want this. I *told* you." Remin's voice was shaking. "Miche—"

"I said, *move!* Lie him down, don't touch that blade!" came Mionet's voice, and yes, that was Mionet shouting, Mionet *running,* shoving her way through the crowd even as Remin wheeled to face this new threat, one huge fist raised.

"N-no...no, Remin, she knows healing!" Ophele lunged for his arm even as Mionet jerked to a halt. "Remember, Duke Ereguil said!"

Mionet lifted her chin.

"I can save him," she said.

A violent shudder wracked Remin's body, his black eyes blazing down at her, his arm straining in Ophele's grip before he bowed his head and stepped aside.

"Do it," he said hoarsely.

"Thank you, my lord. Sir Miche, be so good as to lie down," Mionet ordered. "Davi, for heaven's sake, cover that up."

Davi cursed under his breath and threw his cloak over the remains of Jacot's head. It was as if Ophele had blinked, and lost a few seconds. It was confusing. Somehow she was with Remin, kneeling on the dock and shaking so badly she had to lean against him to stay upright, her chest quivering and hitching in silent, sobbing gasps. Her fingers clutched his shirtfront and his arm was clasped around her like iron.

"You can just unbutton it," Miche was saying helpfully. "It seems a shame to tear Tiffen's finest—"

"Do shut up, and try not to breathe," Mionet snapped, cutting away his shirt and assessing the three puncture wounds in his chest. "Let me see that knife. Someone fetch me a bucket of water."

"I don't understand," Ophele said, her voice high and thin. She was still trying to construct these events into some coherent narrative, and she started wildly as Justenin thudded by her with a grim expression, off on who knew what errand.

Examining the bloody weapon, Mionet sniffed it and flicked away a miniscule amount of the black substance on a fingernail, then set it aside. This couldn't be real. This was a dream, a terrible dream, where beautiful, perfect Mionet bent to cover Miche's wounds with her mouth, sucked, and then came up with red lips to spit blood on the dock. Rinsing her mouth, she bent and did it again.

"Why, why did you do this?" Tears streamed down Remin's face as he gripped Miche's hand. "I told you, I didn't want anyone else to die for me, *why...*"

"You're the last of your blood," Miche said. His voice caught in his throat, a sudden wet wheeze. "If you die...that's the end...of your House..."

His face was ghastly pale. Pink froth bubbled to his lips.

"And what about you? What about your blood?" Remin asked hoarsely. "Miche—"

"The last of my blood is right here." It seemed horribly literal. Blood trickled from the corners of his mouth, dark red, but for some reason he was looking at Ophele, his hazel eyes made golden in the sunrise, the same unforgettable honey of her mother's eyes, the same tawny hue she saw in the mirror every morning. Even before her mind grasped the unthinkable truth, her heart had frozen in her chest.

No one knew what had become of Rache Pavot's brother.

Miche smiled the smile that could charm birds from the trees.

"Take care of her, Rem..."

Epilogue

The message arrived in Starfall five days later.

Bastin was breakfasting on the balcony behind his office at the time, watching gardeners trim the winter from the hedges and prepare the grounds for the year's planting. The rhythm of spring in the palace was a familiar one: the windows flung open to air rooms long closed against the cold, with miles of rugs and draperies to be taken up and beaten out.

He had given Selenne charge of his private gardens this year, and watched the new patterns emerge with interest. There were traditional forms in the outer hedges bounding the garden, with a fillip of rose trees at the ends, and an impressive tapestry of flowers within, in scrolling, ornate beds that reminded him of Dulcian carpet gardens.

The use of so many bulbs—tulips, daffodils, and dahlias that promised blooms as large as dinner plates—required careful planning and forethought, but Selenne was patient for such a young woman.

She took after her father, in that way.

It should not be wondered that she had ordered the central fountain to be cleared; long dry and overgrown with vines, the first jets were now rushing free to dislodge the debris of long disuse, filling the gardens with an unaccustomed splash and patter. Three unfortunate apprentice gardeners were barefoot in the chilly water, scrubbing the granite clean.

Along the furthest hedgerows, a white animal appeared and whisked away, the morning sun glimmering off long whiskers.

"Beg pardon, Divinity," said his door warden, and Bastin turned to accept a sealed parchment from a messenger whose dusty clothes and red eyes spoke of many hours in the saddle.

"Thank you. You may go." Bastin waved him away. Inside, his heart was thumping as he broke the seal of the message.

"Will your beloved child be joining us for the season?" the Empress asked from the door of his office, and he crumpled the page in his fist. He had not invited her into his office, much less to breakfast, but he had learned long ago that it was safer to allow her a little proximity than none.

"It appears so."

This is not the end.

There's a lot of pain in the *Empire of the Stars,* but it will always be a story of healing and rebuilding. Thank you for joining me on this journey. I hope you'll keep going.

And if this story affected you as much as it did me—because believe me, I shed a few tears writing it—I hope you'll consider writing a few words to share the experience. I love every review I get, but this book will always have a special place in my heart.

Want to stay a little longer in the *Empire of the Stars?*

Sign up at melissajcave.com to receive *House of the Broken Tower,* a subscriber-exclusive short story. Journey to Starfall with the Knights of the Brede as they reap the rewards of their victory...and uncover the Emperor's deepest secret. And if you've already read it, you might want to read it again, in light of this book's revelations...

Read on for an excerpt from *A Congress of Roses,* Book 4 of the *Empire of the Stars.*

A Congress of Roses Preview

On Crown Princess Selenne Agnephus's sixteenth birthday, her father gave her a palace.

It was a very beautiful palace, roughly equidistant between her father's private residence and her mother's Palace of the Distant Star. Selenne's palace was called the Palace of Mirrors, a fanciful construct of high towers and terraced gardens, taller than it was wide and illuminated with lamps of crystal, the firelight refracted through their many prisms.

It might be another species of cage, but at least it was a cage whose doors she controlled.

She was nine years old when her father taught her how important that was.

"You cannot assume that because a person serves you, or has even sworn oaths to you, that they are loyal to you," he had said over luncheon one day, when they were sitting alone in his private dining room. "Do you see that fellow over there? The one with the beard?"

Their guards were standing on either side of the door, far enough away that their conversation might go unheard. She nodded.

"That man is my creature," her father said, with a flourish of his butter knife. Bastin Agnephus had been forty-three then and already completely gray, with a luxuriant and perfectly groomed beard. "The other one belongs to your mother. Anything you say, anything you do, whether you tell lies to your nanny or sit up late reading when you ought to be asleep, we will know."

Selenne did not like this.

"But they're *my* guards, they're supposed to do what I say," she protested.

"They are sworn to keep you safe," Bastin corrected. "And so they will, or their lives are forfeit. But their loyalty is another matter. Do you understand what that means, to be loyal?"

"Master Campion says it cannot be bought," Selenne remembered, frowning. "Or it isn't loyalty."

"That is very good," her father agreed. "It is also one of the rarest qualities you will encounter, when you become Empress. You must watch for it and test it, like alchemists test the purity of gold."

He had taught her, in ways a nine-year-old would understand, the methods he had devised to test the loyalty of his servants. Both her parents were full of such lessons, arming her against each other. And in the eight years since, Selenne had dutifully applied this learning. She watched which of her servants stood together, and which ones whispered to each other. She watched which servants exchanged glances with her mother, and which ones looked to her father.

Thus far, the only guard that kept his eyes on her was Lucan.

Lucan was the second son of a family of no particular note, sworn into the Guard of Ange at eighteen on the strength of his sword. And so it was he that stood watch outside one of the six pavilions of her palace, dressed in blue-and-silver livery with a silver star emblazoned on his chest and an unadorned sword belted at his side, no doubt eavesdropping as her parents came to tea.

Not together, of course. The Emperor and Empress only occupied the same space when there was absolutely no other choice, and even then they stood as far apart as possible, like two generals facing each other across the battlefield. Master Campion would have called that a structural defect of the Empire, if he had dared, and Selenne knew it was ripe for exploitation.

"Daughter," Bastin Agnephus said, drawing up his chair on the other side of her tea table. "You look well."

"Thank you, Father. I hope you have not been working too hard," Selenne said, noting the shadows beneath her father's famous starry blue eyes.

"No more than usual. Your tutors tell me that you continue excellently," he said, arranging his scones and tea sandwiches neatly on his plate. After a quarter hour of small talk, he came to his point. He set down his teacup and said, in the abrupt way that meant he was probably about to tell the truth, "I have not spoken to you much of your sister."

"You have not," Selenne agreed, perking up. She usually had to feign disinterest when Princess Ophele was mentioned, and it was *never* safe to introduce the subject herself.

"I hope you will not consider her presence a slight upon yourself," her father told her, touching her hand with one fingertip. "You are my true heir."

"Thank you, Father." Selenne glanced at his hand, mystified. Her father never touched her except in greatest need. The Divine Emperor did not like to be touched.

"But I hope you will make her welcome, when she comes to the city."

"Of course, I will." That set off any number of alarm bells. Selenne signaled a maid to fill their teacups. "I have been very curious about her."

"I am not the one to enlighten you," said Ophele's father, though if he had any regrets, they did not show. "You will hear much gossip in the city, but you know what I have taught you."

"Listen, and note who speaks. Then form my own impressions."

He nodded.

"I will endeavor to keep her away from the Empress," he said. "You are the peacemaker, Selenne. Do you understand?"

"Yes, Father." She was fairly certain that in this area at least, he was sincere. Since the Empire had discovered the existence of Princess Ophele, the Empress had never once been heard to speak her name. It was *your father's bastard* when she was among allies, or *that poor child* when she must appear charitable. Though truthfully, even if Empress Esmene had said *Princess Ophele* in tones wafting sunshine and music, Selenne would never have believed it.

"Have her to tea," suggested her father. "Show her something of the city. She must be sanctified and named before the stars, and you might set her at ease about it. She is no threat to you, but she will rattle the game board of the capital. We must have her in *our* pocket. Make her feel that she is your sister."

"Yes, Father," Selenne said again, and a little while later, she watched him go with an inward frown, though only a pleasant smile showed on her young, pretty face. On the other side of a curtain of purple wisteria, Lucan's face appeared, his green eyes skeptical.

Not a threat? Selenne had understood that Ophele was a threat the day she learned she had a sister. For though Selenne thought she had a goodly number of proofs of her father's love, the question remained whether that love was greater than his hate for her mother. Would the Emperor sacrifice Selenne if it meant the defeat of House Melun, once and for all? Especially if he had another heir already standing by?

Selenne was not the only person asking this question. Her networks in the capital were juvenile, but she knew people whispered that Ophele was the older sister, and the stars could not bless a marriage that their Beloved so reviled. The matter of the Emperor's marriage had become an increasing scandal over the years, to the point that even members of the Temple openly raised their voices, asking how it could have ever been sanctioned. It could only be blasphemous to bind the sacred flesh of the Emperor of Argence against his will.

Selenne had known since she was seven that her father had not wanted to marry her mother.

She received Empress Esmene Melun in another pavilion several days later, a marvel shaped of iron lace from Rendeva and fine Noreveni glass, a tropical garden that might have been plucked straight from the Silver Shore. The Empress swept across the intricate tile floor with four guards behind her, eyed Lucan coldly, and then turned her attention to her daughter.

"My child, you grow more beautiful every time I see you," she said, kissing Selenne's forehead and running appreciative fingers through her long, silver-blonde hair. "I must have a glasshouse like this, it is just the thing at the tail of winter. How are you?"

"I am well, mother," Selenne said dutifully, without rising from her crouch by the pond, where she was feeding bread pellets to her pet fish. The presence of guards rather than her mother's ladies-in-waiting was significant; this was sensitive business, not merely a social call. "You look well. I had heard you were ill."

"Just a chill," Esmene assured her, sitting on a nearby bench. Her mother had the look of brittle crystal, her collarbones a little too protruding, the elegant bones of her face too sharp. But even in her mid-fifties, she was beautiful, her skin and hair tended with the finest alchemical substances. "I knew I should not go home with snow in the air, but Ereseide is so beautiful this time of year. You ought to visit your grandfather, daughter. He will not be with us forever."

Even after thirty-one years in Starfall, the Empress still called the Melun estate at Ereseide *home*.

"I have missed him too," Selenne said, tossing some bread pellets into the water. Most of the lacefin carp only approached if there was food, but the small plum-colored fellow liked to have his head rubbed. "Will he be coming to the city for the season?"

"Oh, of course, there will be quite the stampede this year." Esmene flicked out an embroidered blue fan and wafted it. "No one would dream of missing the spectacle, if the Duke of Andelin is to come. They are already selling access to the Greater Court, hoping to witness another standoff between the Duke and your father. It was quite exciting, last time. At least at first. Then it was so tedious."

There was an undercurrent of mockery in her tone. Her mother had always considered the Emperor's feud with Remin Grimjaw to be faintly ridiculous.

"Do you think it will be exciting?" Selenne asked, glancing back at her mother. "I thought he was only coming to present his wife."

"That is a convenient pretext, my dear, but no one cares a fig for that baseborn creature. The Court of Nobility will not be making a habit of legitimizing bastards."

That loss clearly still rankled. The Emperor's announcement that he had a bastard daughter had been such a bombshell, no one had had time to marshal their forces before the Court of Nobility had made their ruling, and named her a true child of the Emperor, with all the protections and legal responsibilities pertaining thereto. It had been a powerful blow against both the Empress and House Melun, but Selenne thought it was inevitable. Mathematically speaking, Princess Ophele was as much a child of the stars as she was herself.

Though the Court had been careful to specify that a baseborn princess could not inherit.

"After all, *you* are the Crown Princess," Esmene said, reaching again to pat Selenne's silver hair. "But even if she is your father's disgrace, I would like it if you welcomed the poor child."

"You would?" Selenne could not quite hide her surprise.

"It is not her fault your father dishonored our marriage," Esmene said firmly. "And one cannot blame that poor creature for the crimes of her mother. And I cannot welcome her myself, or lower myself to acknowledge her; she is an insult to me, and I must defend the dignity of Empress. But you are in a position to be generous, and it will be good to show that *you* will not blame the innocent for the crimes of their parents. But it is your choice, dearest. I will never force you, if you would prefer not to recognize her yourself. She is an insult to you, too."

"Do you think she will be received?" Selenne asked, partly as a stalling tactic while she tried to decipher what her mother *actually* wanted, and partly to see how far the Empress had already gone. If Esmene had arranged matters in the city so that no reputable noblewoman would associate with the bastard Princess Ophele, then the game was already over. But it would have surprised Selenne to learn that her mother wielded *that* much influence.

"Well, they are all curious about her," Esmene said, a little playfully. "I would never deny the Roses their pleasures."

"You make me curious too, mother." Selenne offered a mischievous smile. "I think I will meet her. I have heard that she is a little...backward."

"Bastards are crooked in the sight of the stars," her mother agreed, shaking her head. "They are often afflicted. You must be very kind to her, Selenne."

Selenne promised that she would, of course. And when her mother finally took her leave, Selenne waited for the noise of her and her guards to fade away and then stroked the plum-colored fish's head, sighing.

"So you'll be having tea with Princess Ophele, then?" Lucan inquired respectfully, from just outside the door.

"Guards are meant to have neither eyes nor ears, save in defense of their charge," Selenne quoted.

"I think we have established that I am the worst guard. Thanks," Lucan added, snatching one of the bread pellets from the air as she flung it at his head and popping it in his mouth.

"Whereas I will of course obey the wishes of my honored parents," she said, rising with resignation to pull the stout corded rope beside her chair to set off a distant chiming of bells. "You may call Francot back, Lucan. I must speak to my ladies."

***A Congress of Roses*, Book 4 of the *Empire of the Stars*, is available for preorder!**

Coming May 2026

Glossary

The Nobility of the Empire, in Order by Faction

Imperial Loyalists

1. **House Agnephus**
    a. **Bastin Agnephus:** *(BAH-stinn ahn-YEH-fuss)* The Divine Emperor, Beloved of Stars. The ruler of the Empire.
    b. **Selenne Agnephus:** *(sel-LENN ahn-YEH-fuss)* Crown Princess of the Empire and Ophele's younger half-sister.
        i. **Sir Lucan of Versigne:** *(loo-KAN of ver-SEEN)* Guard of Ange sworn to Crown Princess Selenne and loyal only to her.
2. **House Firkane:** *(fur-KANE)* A northern duchy located due south of Tresingale, on the south side of the Brede.

3. **House Leinbruke:** *(LINE-brook)* A northern duchy bordering the Brede and Rendeva, which includes House Trecht and Aldeburke in its territory.
4. **House Tries:** *(TREES)* A large duchy south of Norgrede on the Sea of Eskai. Frequently serves as governors to the Four Isles.
5. **House Hurrell** *(restored)*
    a. **Lord Meverot Hurrell:** *(MEH-veh-roh HUR-rell)* Former lord of Hurrell lands in the eastern Empire, lost and exiled after the Conspiracy.
    b. **Lady Bette Hurrell:** *(BET HUR-rell)* Matriarch of House Hurrell and foster mother to Ophele.
    c. **Julot Hurrell:** *(ZHOO-loh HUR-rell)* Son of the lord and lady and notionally foster brother to Ophele.
    d. **Lisabe Hurrell:** *(LISS-uh-beh HUR-rell)* Daughter of the lord and lady and foster sister to Ophele.

Melun Loyalists

1. **House Melun**
    a. **Esmene of Melun:** *(ESS-men-nay MEH-luhn)* The Empress of Argence and eldest daughter of the powerful House Melun.
    b. **Duke Dardot Melun:** *(DAR-doh MEH-luhn)* Patriarch of House Melun and the oldest and longest-serving member of both the Court of Nobility and the Court of War.
2. **House Norgrede:** *(NOR-gredd)* Remin's last southern neighbor, bordering both the Brede and the Sea of Eskai.
3. **House Pomeret:**
    a. **Wandrille:** *(wahn-DREE poh-meh-RET)* Duke of Pomeret, an inland duchy long loyal to Melun.
    b. **Edelene:** *(eh-deh-LENN poh-meh-RET)* Duchess of Pomeret, a pious woman with many children and great influence in the Temple.

4. **House Sangevin:** *(SAN-jeh-vinn)* A saddle-shaped duchy between Leinkbruke and Remin's former lands, wealthy and unscrupulous.

Unaffiliated Houses

1. **House Andelin**
    a. **Duchess Ophele of Andelin:** *(oh-FELL ANN-deh-linn)* Her Grace, the Duchess of Andelin, and Princess of Argence. Daughter of the Divine Emperor and colloquially known as the Exile Princess.
        i. **Lady Mionet Verr:** *(mee-oh-NET VURR)* Widow and former lady-in-waiting to Duchess Ereguil's daughter-in-law, Lady Carolen. Ophele's cunning new lady-in-waiting.
    b. **Duke Remin of Andelin:** *(REH-minn of ANN-deh-linn)* His Grace, the Duke of Andelin. The son of traitors and despised enemy of the Divine Emperor, he is sometimes called Remin Grimjaw.
        i. **Lord Edemir of Trecht:** *(EDD-eh-meer of TREKT)* Second son of the Count of Trecht, whose lands are close to the Brede. Master of Treasury, Exchequer, and Supply.
2. **House Berebet**
    a. **Duke Ghislain Berebet:** *(ZHEE-slane BEH-reh-bett)* Head of House Berebet and a tricky fellow, who made offers of friendship to both Remin and Crown Princess Selenne.
3. **House Ereguil**
    a. **Laud Ereguil:** *(LAWD err-GEEL)* Duke of Ereguil and foster father to Remin after the execution of his parents. He frequently sends good advice.

b. **Liliet Ereguil:** *(LILL-ee-ett err-GEEL)* Duchess of Ereguil and foster mother to Remin. She frequently sends gifts.

4. **House Pavot *(destroyed)***

   a. **Michinot Pavot:** *(MEE-chin-noh pah-VOH)* Earl of Murewood and father of Rache and Consotin.

   b. **Dorame Pavot:** *(DOH-rahm-eh pah-VOH)* Lady of Murewood, mother of Rache and Consotin.

   c. **Rache Pavot:** *(RAYCHE pah-VOH)* Ophele's mother and mistress to the Emperor. Coerced into accusing Remin's father of killing the Empress's unborn child.

   d. **Consotin Pavot:** *(CONN-soh-teen pah-VOH)* Younger brother to Rache.

Consecrated Knights of the Empire, in Order by Name

1. **Sir Auber Conbour:** *(AW-bur CONN-boor)* A farmer's son that joined Remin's army at its mustering by the Gresein. Volunteered for the charge over the bridge and was subsequently knighted. Has charge of Remin's farmlands.
2. **Sir Bertin of Loure:** *(bur-TAN of LOOR)* One of the young knights who came of age after the war's end, he competed in the joust at the tourney.
3. **Sir Bram of Lisle:** *(BRAHM of LILE)* Former mercenary who served Duke Ereguil for various activities before the war, and volunteered for the Charge of the Gresein. Assists Tounot with the Tresingale garrison, as well as other sensitive activities.

4. **Sir Darrigault of Ghis:** *(DARE-reh-goht of GHEES)* The Subtle Blade. One of Remin's knights who is frequently trusted with tricky or clandestine work.
5. **Sir Huber Adaman:** *(HUE-bur ADD-uh-man)* A knight from a long line of knights in Ereguil and childhood friend of Remin. Master of Remin's scouts.
6. **Sir Jinmin of Oskerre:** *(JIN-minn of oh-SCARE)* Originally from Norgrede, he switched loyalties to Remin during the war. The only knight capable of posing a physical challenge to Remin.
7. **Sir Justenin of Tresingale:** *(JUST-enn-inn of TRESS-in-gale)* The son of one of Remin's father's retainers, unnamed for his own safety. Master of Beasts and counselor for Remin and his men.
8. **Sir Miche of Harnost:** *(MEESH of HAR-nohst)* Longtime bodyguard and friend of Remin. Master of Snow.
9. **Sir Ortaire Berange:** *(orr-TARE beh-RAHNJ)* One of the young knights who came of age after the war's end, he went with Huber to Ferrede and then to Meinhem to retrieve any surviving villagers.
10. **Squire Rollon of Hollisey:** *(ROH-lone of HALL-iss-see)* Huber's first squire, knighted for his defense of Ferrede. He sacrificed himself rescuing Amalie and Iskerren from Nandre.
11. **Sir Tounot of Belleme:** *(TOO-noh of bell-EMME)* First son of the Earl of Irenvale, disinherited by his father. Commands the Tresingale garrison as well as the unauthorized visitors camped on the south side of the Brede.

The Page Boys, in Order by Name

1. **Denin:** *(denn-NEEN)* Edemir's page, just turning twelve.
2. **Gavrel:** *(GAV-rell)* Tounot's page, ten years old.

3. **Jacot of Caillmar:** *(JACK-uht of KALE-marr)* Page boy who won his position by swimming the Brede.
4. **Legeriot:** *(leh-JHARE-ree-oh)* Huber's page; an eleven-year-old from Ereguil.
5. **Niccoliot:** *(nih-KOH-lee-oh)* Huber's page; a seven year-old from Ereguil.
6. **Valentin:** *(VAHL-lenn-tinn)* One of Edemir's pages and the pet of the barracks.

Recognized Masters, in Order by Name

1. **Sousten Didion:** *(SOH-stenn DIH-dee-ohn)* Master architect, chief designer of Tresingale Manor, as well as the future Court of War, Academy, Temple Tower, harbor, and similar projects.
2. **Nore Ffloce:** *(NORR FLOCE)* Master architect, chief planner of the city of Tresingale.
3. **Hayas Forgess:** *(HAI-yass for-GESS)* Master of the Library of Beasts.
4. **Bellchior Gibel:** *(bell-KEE-orr gih-BEL)* Master of Tresingale harbor.
5. **Odan Guisse:** *(oh-DAN GISSE)* Master engineer, chief engineer of the walls, harbor, Temple tower, and similarly massive projects.
6. **Ammon Misler:** *(AM-monn MISE-ler)* Master mason, has charge of all stonework along the wall.
7. **Erthu Peltier:** *(ER-thoo PEL-tee-eh)* Master potter, and one of the Great Masters of the Empire.
8. **Faviet Roscout:** *(fah-vee-ETT rohs-KOOT)* Master weaver, relation of Ortaire, and very savvy negotiator.
9. **Cam Sharrenot:** *(KAM SHARE-ran-noh)* Master carpenter, specializing in ironheart oak.
10. **Marin Tiffen:** *(mah-RIHN TIFF-en)* Tresingale's new tailor, arrived from Belleme.

Tresingale Manor, in Order by Name

1. **Azelma Bessin:** *(uh-ZEL-mah BESS-sin)* Cook at Aldeburke and friend to Ophele.
2. **Cruce Adelan:** *(CROOS ADD-eh-lann)* The new butler at Tresingale manor, formerly a footman at Rospalme in Ereguil. Uncle to Samin.
3. **Emiset of Giry:** *(EMM-ih-set JEER-ee)* Called Emi for short. One of the maids at Tresingale manor.
4. **Frechard Dubosc:** *(FREH-shard doo-BOHSK)* One of the stable boys at Tresingale manor.
5. **Jaose Thiraman:** *(JOWSE THEER-ah-man)* One of the footmen at Tresingale manor.
6. **Lousiton Magne:** *(loos-ih-TONE MINE)* Remin's elderly valet.
7. **Masilie:** *(MAH-sil-lee)* One of three newly arrived laundresses.
8. **Peritenn Emberoy:** *(PAIR-ih-tenn EMM-bur-roi)* Called Peri for short. One of the maids at Tresingale manor.
9. **Samin Adelan:** *(SAH-minn ADD-eh-lann)* The seven-year-old boot boy at Tresingale manor and nephew to Cruce Adelan.
10. **Sim Gedot:** *(SIMM geh-DOH)* One of the footmen at Tresingale manor.

Commonfolk, in Order by Name

1. **Conbour Family**
    a. **Amise:** *(ah-MEES)* Wife of Thiry, mother of many children, including Elodie and Pirot.
    b. **Elodie:** *(EH-loh-dee)* Daughter of Thiry and Amise, nine-year-old pagegirl to Ophele.
    c. **Lisset:** *(lih-SETT)* Auber's other sister-in-law.
    d. **Pirot:** *(peer-ROH)* Youngest son of Amise and Thiry, little brother to Elodie.
    e. **Thiry:** *(TEER-ree)* Farmer from Engleberg and brother to Auber, he risked his family for a better life in Tresingale. Husband of Amise, father of Elodie, Pirot, and several other unnamed children.
2. **Dresten Family**
    a. **Isilde:** *(iss-SILD-eh DREH-stehn)* Daughter of a Vallethi warlord, mother of Vinzetin. A survivor from Meinhem and Auber's sweetheart.
    b. **Vinzetin:** *(VIN-zeh-tin DREH-stehn)* Seven year-old son of Isilde and a passing Eagle Knight.
3. **Istaire Guian:** *(ISS-stare GEE-ahn)* First merchant to arrive in Tresingale; provider of tea.
4. **Genon Hengest:** *(GEH-non HEN-ghest)* Herbman and surgeon for Remin and his army.
5. **Maugher Family**
    a. **Amalie Maugher:** *(AM-uh-lee MAW-her)* Thirteen-year-old sister to Iskerren, one of two survivors from Nandre.
    b. **Iskerren Maugher:** *(iss-KARE-renn MAW-her)* Four-year-old brother to Amalie, one of two survivors from Nandre.
6. **Hemelot Oleare:** *(HEM-eh-loh oh-LARE)* Brother of the Path who disobeyed his own order to come to the service of Tresingale.
7. **Wen of Tallford:** Camp cook and guardian of Remin's food.

8. **Tregue Family**
    a. **Attenait Tregue:** *(ATT-ten-nay TREEG)* Mistress of the tavern, mother of many children, official town gossip.
    b. **Ros Tregue:** *(ROHS TREEG)* Baker and tapman, father of many children, not so much a gossip.

From Benkki Desa, in Order by Name

1. **Chagada Balad:** *(CHA-gah-dah BAH-lad)* Master of the Tresingale men's bathhouse.
2. **Bilaki:** *(BIH-lah-kee)* One of the attendants of the Tresingale women's bathhouse.
3. **Huvara:** *(hoo-VAH-rah)* One of the attendants of the Tresingale women's bathhouse.
4. **Imari Sanai:** *(ihm-MAH-ree sah-NAI)* Mistress of the Tresingale women's bathhouse.
5. **Pili:** *(PIH-lee)* One of the attendants of the Tresingale women's bathhouse.

The Author, picking off your favorites, shattering your dreams

About the Author

Melissa J. Cave writes emotionally charged romantic fantasy set in the aftermath of war. Her *Empire of the Stars* series explores arranged marriages, forgotten ruins, and the slow rebuilding of broken worlds. A military brat and a veteran, Melissa has always been fascinated by new places, languages, and cultures. She lives in Virginia, where her strawberry beds are currently under siege by raccoons.

Keep up with Melissa on your favorite platform:

Instagram | X | Amazon | Goodreads

Questions for Readers and Book Clubs

If you're reading this with a book club or just love to talk books with friends, here are a few questions to spark conversation:

1. Both Remin and the Emperor are shaped by the belief that their lives belong to others. Remin offers himself freely, while the Emperor was claimed from his birth. What does it mean to choose to sacrifice? Where would you draw the line?
2. As Tresingale grows, Ophele and Remin take different but complementary roles in leading its people. How do their forms of leadership interact? What does each offer that the other cannot?
3. When Ophele learns the truth of her mother's coerced confession, she must reckon with the devastating consequences it caused. How much guilt does her mother deserve? How would you feel if you inherited the consequences of such a choice?
4. Both Ophele and Remin entered adulthood with deep gaps in their knowledge, shaped by isolation and trauma. While Ophele's are acknowledged and addressed, Remin's are often masked by confidence and authority. What blind spots does he still carry? How do they shape his decisions and his relationships?
5. If you were in Ophele's place on Solstice Night, as Remin confronts the full weight of all his choices from the war to the present, what would you tell him?
6. Tresingale is filled with long relationships and deep bonds. Which relationship—romantic, familial, or platonic—did you enjoy most? Why?

7. Which character's choices frustrated you the most, and why? What was the moment when you just wanted to *shake* someone?

8. Bastin and Esmene's marriage is not built on love, but on duty, meant to protect and perpetuate the state. Where is the line between individual welfare and the welfare of a nation? What are the costs of expecting people to sacrifice one for the other?

9. The revelation that Miche is Ophele's uncle, Consotin Pavot, echoes through both past and future. Why do you think he kept the secret for so long? How might this change the course of the story to come?

10. Miche or Juste?

Want to share your thoughts? Tag Melissa on X or join the discussion on Instagram!